The Sea Leopard

A Pirates of the Narrow Seas Adventure

M. Kei

KEIBOOKS
PERRYVILLE, MARYLAND, USA
2014

ISBN 978-0692228074 (print)
Also available for Kindle.

Printed in the United States of America, 2014.

KEIBOOKS
P O Box 516
Perryville, MD 21903
Email: Keibooks@gmail.com

Table of Contents

1. Night Chase 5
2. A Persistent Enemy 10
3. Dawn Attack..16
4. The Fog of War 21
5. Cat's Paws 26
6. Rising Wind 31
7. Sardinian Valor..37
8. The Captive 42
9. The Butcher's Daughter 47
10. The Marriage Proposal 53
11. Captain's Quarrel 59
12. Negotiations 65
13. Female Sailors 71
14. The Captain's Harem 77
15. The Dabchick Pirate 82
16. The Pirate Bay 87
17. Biya's Booty 92
18. A Rising Storm 99
19. Ambush 104
20. Mutiny 109
21. Captain Down...115
22. Houri in Paradise 119
23. The Reluctant Patient 125
24. The Price of Freedom 131
25. A Not So Happy Reunion 139
26. On Patrol 144
27. Letters from Home 150
28. The Dey's Revenge 157
29. Dispatches 163
30. Enemy Sighted 168
31. The Failed Trap 172
32. The Thunder of Distant Gunnery 177
33. Skulking in the Dark 183
34. Repel Boarders!..189
35. A Running Fight 194
36. A Desperate Battle 199
37. A Welcome Friend 204
38. Wedding Feast..210
39. The Reluctant Bridegroom 216

CHAPTER 1 : NIGHT CHASE

The *Sea Leopard* ambled along with her great lateen sails spread to the light and variable breezes. Normally she slid through the water with the speed and predatory grace of the leopard for which she was named, but in the faint air a man could have kept up with her by walking, had he been able to walk on water. Her desultory crew rested in the shade of the sails, black or bronze arms bared to the shoulders, turbans or fezzes protecting their heads from the glare of sunlight. Loaded guns poked out from her sides in the hopes that they would be needed.

After supper, Isam Rais turned her around and sent her back the way she had come; he was stalking the southern coast of Sardinia. The evening breeze failed entirely, so he put them through an hour of rowing practice as the light faded and the night came on. He maneuvered the vessel forward and backward, held water, made turns, spun in place, and other such evolutions as a rowed warship might be obliged to execute. They rarely practiced at night, but Isam Rais felt it was important for them to be able to carry out maneuvers in the dark as well as the light. He set an easy pace for the rowing so the men were pleasantly tired when they turned into their hammocks. He made notes in his journal, washed up, and turned in himself.

The breeze rose during the night but remained mild. The captain woke when he felt the shift in his vessel's behavior. She was new, so he didn't know her every mood and quirk yet, but he was learning rapidly. The silvery sheen of moonlight through the quarterlight cloaked him as he lay in his hanging bed. He looked up at the compass mounted to the deckhead above his bed, then at the clock mounted on the wall where the moonlight fell on it. Then he took in the thunder glass. The blue water was black in the darkness. For a moment moonlight limned his features: a short black beard, a long nose with a hump at the bridge where it had been broken, and dark eyes.

"What is it?" the bass voice beside him rumbled.

"The wind died. I'm going on deck to have a look. Don't get up. There's no need for the men-at-arms."

The big black man propped on his elbow and yawned. "Don't you ever sleep?"

The tall captain rolled out of bed, put his feet into navy blue slippers, put his navy blue jacket on over his shirt and pantaloons, and plopped a black fez on his head. He grinned, "When I get the chance, yes, but somebody named Kateb keeps me up at night."

The black man grinned. "And you sleep like a baby afterwards."

The captain bent and kissed his bedmate on the lips. "I'll be back. Keep the bed warm for me."

Arriving on the quarterdeck, the captain nodded to the men who touched their turbans respectfully. Stepping up to a lean, white-clad figure, he quietly said, "Report."

Second Lieutenant Yafi, whose watch it was, replied in an equally low voice. "Course due east, three knots. There's nothing to see and all's well." The faint sound of snores drifted up through the hatches from the hammocks below.

Isam Rais looked up at the stars, looked all around the misty horizon with the night spyglass, saw nothing, and nodded. "We'll find something tomorrow when we're off Cagliari."

The lieutenant nodded.

The captain went back to bed. He didn't sleep immediately, but when he did, it was as Kateb had said: he slept very well indeed.

Several hours later Ensign Taslim woke him urgently. "Rais, there's a ship in the darkness! Square-rigged!"

Isam snapped awake in a moment. A square-rigged ship could not be an ally. A neutral vessel perhaps, but given that they had been hunting the Sardinian coast for several days, more likely an enemy. "Where away?"

"Two points off the starboard bow, about seven miles distant. We are beating to quarters quietly."

"Very good. Carry on. I'll be on deck shortly."

Kateb jerked awake and sat up. If the ensign was surprised to find the agha of the marines in bed with the captain, he didn't show it. Instead he bowed, said, "Yes, rais," and departed with only a fleeting look at the naked black man climbing out of the bed.

This time Isam Rais dressed properly. Battle required him to look like the captain he was and to be properly armed and equipped. He appeared on deck with his scimitar on his right hip—the captain was a left-handed man. A clean white turban wrapped around his fez and tall black boots were on his feet. In between he wore striped pantaloons and a navy blue wool jacket with little embroidery. The night was hazy and mist coalesced on his pewter buttons. Below him, the weather deck was a buzz of quiet, purposeful activity as the men stowed their hammocks and went to the guns. Any noise would carry in the still night. So would any light.

"Douse lights," he said as he set foot on the quarterdeck. Kateb followed two steps behind him and took his own look around.

"Aye aye, sir." First Lieutenant Khadim turned to greet him with a respectful dip of his head and a flourish of fingertips against his chest, lips, and the air. In the darkness, his African complexion was nearly invisible. The ghostly whiteness of his garments moved like a specter. In obedience to the order, the midshipman on the quarterdeck opened the great stern lanthorn and blew out the light. A messenger carried the order quietly to all the lamps on the weather deck. Only the faint glow of the binnacle light remained; the helmsman had to see the compass to steer. He pulled the hood up over the binnacle to shield the light.

"Report," Isam Rais said in a low voice.

Khadim answered softly, "A fully-rigged ship, rais. She just put her stuns'ls out."

Isam put the night spyglass to his eye. The vessel was upside down in the glass; two lenses were required to turn the image right side up, but each lens dimmed the light. For daytime use that was fine, but for nighttime use, it darkened the image too much. Isam was used to looking at ships upside down; it was part of his job and he was good at his job. At this distance, he couldn't discern much about it, although he could tell she carried studding sails.

"She's coming for us," the captain remarked.

"She knows what we are," the lieutenant replied.

Isam thoughtfully stroked his short black beard. "She kept a good watch. Her crew is alert." Low slung and with little rigging aloft, the xebec would have been hard to spot in the misty dark. Isam meditated. Any square-rigged vessel that went charging after a lateen-rigged vessel was obviously an enemy warship. At the moment it didn't matter which enemy. The question was, what kind of ship were they up against?

"She's probably a frigate. Very well, shake out all reefs, then prepare to wear ship. No need to keep quiet; they're on to us."

Khadim bawled out, "All hands on deck! Out reefs! Prepare to wear!"

Many hands hauled lines and brought the toes of the great antennas low enough for men to swarm aloft by grabbing the wooldings and shinning up the trebled timber. Working swiftly, they untied the reef knittles. The folds of canvas that had been held against the spars dropped loose, increasing the size of the already immense sails. On deck, they adjusted the sheets and the big sails filled full of air. She ghosted along at a cat's pace in the evening calm. The enemy frigate was in the same situation; with every scrap of canvas set she moved only at a walking pace among the tendrils of mist.

Kateb Agha shouted his own orders. "Sharpshooters aloft!" A team of six men came running with muskets on their backs. They mounted to the quarterdeck, swung out onto the ratlines, and scrambled up to the mizzen top. It was the only top on the vessel because the mizzen was the only mast with a square topsail. They loaded their muskets and surveyed the dark.

"Helm, hard over," the master told the helmsman. It was his job to translate the captain's orders into the specific commands to carry out each step. The tiller cranked as far as it would go and the vessel curved around.

"That's well. Steady up," Isam Rais said as the vessel came onto the new heading. She was now running northwest towards the coast of Sardinia on her best point of sail. "Keep her as close to the eye of the wind as you can." The square-rigger could not point as sharp; the captain expected to lose the enemy via geometry.

A single gun barked and spit a flame. At this distance, it was little more than the flaring of a candle. The roar came to them faintly several seconds later.

"She wants us to stop," Lieutenant Khadim remarked.

"Ignore it. There's no point in wasting powder," Isam replied. He studied the traverse board. It was used by the generally illiterate helmsmen to note the speed and direction they'd been traveling by placing pegs in a compass face. They'd been off the southwest corner of Sardinia when they had turned back; by noting the speed and direction on the traverse board he was able to work out where they were now.

"Cape Spartivento should be due north of us. I want to be sure and clear Cape Teulada, but I'm not positive we will on this course."

Lieutenant Khadim looked back at the strange ship chasing after them. "Do you think she'll overtake us? Cape Spartivento must be at least twenty miles north."

"I don't want to get into trouble on an unfriendly shore. There's no point in courting unnecessary danger. Prepare to tack."

"All hands, prepare to tack!" Khadim sang out.

Isam went and stood at the rail looking down at his crew and vessel. With no lanterns lit, the xebec was ghostly silver in the light of the moon, except for the shadow of the sails where it was absolute black. It was a chiaroscuro of a half-seen world. He savored the beauty for a moment, then said, "Ready about!"

"Ready about!" Khadim bawled into the night.

"Ease down the helm," the master ordered the helmsman.

The helmsman slowly eased the tiller over. The hands on the quarterdeck hauled in the mizzen sail gradually to keep her full as long as possible.

"Helm's alee!" the master reported.

"Haul down your jib," Isam said. The stentorian voice of the first lieutenant carried the order. In battle Isam Rais would take direct command, but there was no point using up his voice before then.

The *Sea Leopard* had good way on her; she was making the most of the light breeze. That pleased her captain. Still, he was taking no chances on stalling her as she swung her bow through the eye of the wind. Regaining headway and having to make a second try at the tack would waste time and allow the square-rigger to gain on them.

Step by step, the massive lateen sails were brought around: the foresail and mizzen sail first. That required shifting the tack on each sail. To do that, they had to ease halyards, and that required the sweat of a large team of men. When that was done, the bowlines were unhooked, the toes of the antennas dipped and brought around the rear of the masts, then rehooked on the other side. The halyards were hauled to bring the sail back up, and then the bowlines hauled taut.

"Mainsail haul," Isam said.

"Mains'l ha'l!" Khadim sang out.

Now they had to do the same with the big lateen main and her seven thousand square feet of canvas. That required the crew to move with authority. If they didn't, the big sail would take charge of them. Fouling the mainsail with an enemy in pursuit was an error they couldn't afford. Fortunately, with the airs so light, it was easy to muscle the gigantic sail around. The lines drew taut and the mainsail bellied out full of air.

Isam nodded and raised his voice. "Well done! Less than five minutes! My compliments to the crew!" The captain rarely addressed them directly; when he did, they paid sharp attention. They grinned and some of them bowed to him or touched their brows in respect. His constant training paid off. They were proud of their skill.

Isam consulted the wind and the binnacle. "Keep her southwest by west."

"Southwest by west, aye," the master replied.

The bearded master watched over the lazyboard. "She's coming onto our new heading."

The square-rigger was altering her course to chase after them. She had been on a starboard tack to begin with, so she continued that way. Even so, she could not overtake them, even though she was on a better point of sail than before.

Isam watched her until he decided the *Sea Leopard* was headreaching on her and the distance was widening. He checked the wind and weather again, but the night was fair and calm. To Kateb he said, "Stand down the marines. Watch below, go below. Nothing will happen for a while. I'm going back to bed. Call me if anything changes."

"Aye aye, captain," Khadim and Kateb replied.

Isam descended the ladder to the weather deck, went into his cabin, removed his weapons, boots, and turban, and crawled into bed fully dressed. Just in case. A few minutes later Kateb joined him. Being a sailor, Isam was used to waking and sleeping whenever required and instantly dropped off. Kateb, being a marine, was able to keep more regular hours. He found it harder to adjust to the sudden interruptions at night, but wrapping his arm around his lover's waist, he settled down. Eventually, lulled by the vessel's gentle motions, he too slept.

CHAPTER 2 : A PERSISTENT ENEMY

A few hours later, Hamza, the black ensign, woke him. "Good morning, sir. It's your watch. The weather is calm and foggy. We are becalmed."

"Thank you, ensign. I'll be up presently." He rolled out of his hammock. He poked Kateb's muscular shoulder. "Rise and shine." With a groan the big black man pried his eyes open, then lumbered out of bed.

Isam's servant arrived a few minutes later with water for washing and a hooded lantern that gave a dim light in the predawn darkness. The captain stripped in the chill morning air, felt the humidity clammy on his skin, and shivered. He washed up quickly with the cold salt water, then dressed. Kateb did the same after him; the captain had precedence in everything.

When Isam was done, his servant was there with coffee and oranges. Breakfast would come after the morning chores were done. He gulped hot coffee with plenty of honey in it, felt warmer, and put the orange in his pocket. Feeling sufficiently awake to begin his day, he gave Kateb a swift kiss on the cheek, then went on deck. Kateb, who had fewer responsibilities at the moment than the captain, took advantage of the stillness of the sea to shave his head and jaw.

"Captain on deck!" the cry rang out as Isam Rais appeared.

He nodded in acknowledgement. "As you were."

He climbed the ladder to the quarterdeck and received the salutes of his officers. The night's mist had thickened into a murky fog. The stars were only visible at the top of the masts. The sea was as still as glass.

"How long have we been becalmed?" Isam asked.

"A couple of hours, rais," Third Lieutenant Urve replied. He was a yellow-skinned man with almond eyes that bespoke his Turkish ancestry.

"Why wasn't I called?" Isam asked curtly.

"Begging your pardon, rais, but nothing was happening."

Isam fixed his eye on the man, but before he could say anything, the masthead lookout cried, "Deck ho! A sail! Fine on the port quarter! About a mile distant!"

Isam swore. "That is why I want to know when we're becalmed!" Then he tilted his head back and called up, "What kind of sail?"

"Square! I caught a glimpse of her t'gallant above the fog!"

"How many masts?"

"I don't know! I can't see her anymore!"

"Battle stations and quietly! We don't want them to know we know where they are. They may not have seen us," Isam snapped. "Muffle the oarlocks. Hands to the sweeps, silently! Sharpshooters to the top!"

An orderly scramble ensued. The watch lights were doused and the galley fire too. Breakfast would wait. Kateb scraped away the last of his stubble as quick as he could, giving himself a razor burn in the process, then stuffed his scimitar into his red sash and ran to quarterdeck. He was right behind First Lieutenant Khadim who came to the quarterdeck to relieve Third Lieutenant Urve. Urve went to the weather deck to supervise the larboard guns. Every man had his station in battle and they knew them by heart. Even the servants had their duty: Isam's servants hauled his personal items to the hold while the master's mates cleared the chartroom and master's cabin. Crews entered the cabin to work the stern chasers housed there.

"Deck ho! Sail! I saw her! A three-master for sure!"

"Oars, out oars," Isam said quietly. The long sweeps threaded through the oar ports with a quiet rumble. "Starboard, oars, give way together. Port oars, back water."

Slowly the sweeps creaked and gently splashed in the still waters. The *Sea Leopard* rotated in place, bringing her port side to bear.

"Oars, boat oars and stand by. Gunners make ready."

The powder monkeys had already run for their cartridges. When the powder arrived, the guns were quickly and quietly loaded. Isam cocked his head and listened to the fog.

"Pass the word: If their boats are in the water, aim for the boats." To Khadim he said, "They are either using their boats to tow and don't know we're here, or they have seen us and are trying to sneak up on us. Pass the word to all the lookouts: Keep a sharp eye in case they're trying to board under cover of fog."

More minutes ticked by. Every eye strained to pierce the foggy darkness. Isam cocked his head and listened to the night. Someone coughed. The acrid scent of slow match drifted up from the linstocks. The gunners blew on them periodically to keep them burning, but they held the matches below the railing to make certain the glow could not be spotted by the enemy. The indifferent fog drifted aimlessly above the water. Kateb paced the weather deck. The men-at-arms had to do the rowing while the sailors handled the sails and guns. There were no slaves on the *Sea Leopard*; every man aboard her was a fighter.

Isam suddenly said, "That was an oar splash. Pass the word quietly: Boats coming. Prepare to repel boarders."

Ensign Hamza was the designated messenger. He slipped down the ladder to the weather deck. The oars were stowed to make room to work the guns. The gun captains hunched over their weapons and peered at the fog and adjusted their quoins. Then they waited for something to appear.

The air remained absolutely still. The temperature and humidity were right at the point where Isam felt suffocated by the moist air, but when he took off his jacket, the damp chill soaked through his linen shirt and made him hunch his shoulders. He put the jacket back on. Everyone kept staring into the fog.

Another soft splash. "Oar!" somebody hissed.

Sharpshooters in the bowl of the mizzen top put their muskets to their shoulders and pointed into the darkness.

Something moved in the wisps of fog. A flicker of phosphorescence showed where the oars stirred the water even though the boats themselves were still invisible.

"Fire!" Isam shouted.

The *Sea Leopard's* broadside roared. The crackle of small arms erupted overhead. Tongues of flame licked the night and the cannonade rumbled through the fog. A man screamed. Wood cracked. A hit! No need for silence now, the attackers set up a wild battle cry and rowed like madmen as the *Sea Leopard* reloaded.

"Oars, out oars! Starboard, give way together! Port, back water!" Isam was giving the orders directly now so there would be no delay. The xebec's sweeps shot out, splashed into the water, and eighty backs bent. The *Sea Leopard* rotated with slow majesty. "Fire as she bears!"

The *Sea Leopard's* bow came around and the first bow chaser banged out her shot with no result. The *Sea Leopard* kept turning. The attackers could be seen now looming out of the grey mist. They were pulling their oars as fast as they could, desperately trying to reach the xebec before she brought her second broadside around. They had no breath for battle cries and charged in silence. It was a race: Who would get into position first? The boarders or the broadside?

"Put your backs into it! Row, you scabrous whoresons! Row!" Kateb roared at his crew.

A crackle of small arms answered him and balls whistled about his head as marines in the enemy boats opened fire with their muskets. Lieutenant Khadim grunted and blood began to ooze from his thigh. He pulled off his turban and tore a piece to bind up his leg. Isam was untouched. He only glanced at Khadim, saw that he had the matter in hand, and carried on.

The *Sea Leopard's* second bow chaser barked. No scream or crack of wood answered. The attackers were only fifty yards off. The *Sea Leopard's* sharpshooters in the mizzen top snapped off shots as fast as they could load. An enemy sailor jerked and threw up his hands. He fell backward into his boat and his oar dragged alongside. Wood clattered as the other oarsmen accidentally struck the trailing oar.

The *Sea Leopard's* starboard battery came around. The gunners depressed the barrels as far as they would go. Fortunately, the *Sea Leopard* had a low freeboard, or the approaching boats would have been able to slip under her guns. Blood spouted and men died as the cannonballs tore up the attackers.

"Oars, all together, pull!" Isam roared at them. Men working the oars had to stand between the barrels of the bronze guns as they reloaded. The cannons were only warm now, but they would heat up quickly. He had to repulse the attack quickly or lose his edge.

Just as the battered attackers reached the *Sea Leopard's* side, she slipped away from them. A gentle bow wave spread out and rocked the attackers. They bent their backs to the oars and pursued her.

Isam shouted, "Port oars, back water!" She rotated in place, and the attacking boats chased her stern. He saw that they would catch it too. The stern chasers in his cabin didn't wait for his order; when the enemy swung into view, they fired. A cloud of acrid smoke drifted up through the grated lazyboard to the quarterdeck.

He waved it away, but he couldn't tell what damage, if any, had been done. "Oars, all together, back water!" He would run them over if he could. He darted a glance to the weather deck, but Kateb's black clad figure was still erect among the bent backs of the rowers. He smiled and returned his attention to the battle.

The smaller, more nimble boats managed to dart to either side, and the *Sea Leopard* slid backwards between them. Their marines stood up in the boats and fired at him, but he dropped below the rail and the hail of lead passed a few feet over him. He looked up; his own marines were still in place peppering the attackers. He leaped to his feet before his men could worry he'd been shot.

"Fire as they bear!"

Grapeshot shattered the enemy. The survivors threw the dead and dying overboard and tore off their shirts to stuff the holes in the gunwale. On the starboard side, the *Sea Leopard's* guns weren't loaded yet and the other boat was trying to get at her. The attackers had to push through her oars, but the rowers swung the long wooden shafts to try and sweep them away.

"Oars, in oars! Repel boarders!" Isam roared. He needed his gun crews to be able to reload more than he needed his oars to row. The enemy had caught up to him. It was a boarding action now.

The oars jerked inside and were thrown onto the deck with a clatter as the rowers seized boarding pikes to meet the enemy swarming up her larboard side. The low freeboard made it easy for their assailants to grab onto her chains and gun ports and haul themselves over the rail. The marines ran them through and threw them into the sea.

Isam spotted the third boat rowing up on his bow. "Bow chasers, ware the enemy!" His baritone carried loud and clear the length of the vessel. He had a powerful set of lungs when he cared to use them.

The gun crew slewed the starboard bow chaser as far as it would go and fired on the approaching boat. A lead ball nipped at Isam's jacket in retaliation, but he felt no sting. He slapped his hand against the spot, but it came away dry. He was unhurt. On the main deck, Kateb's warriors thrust viciously at the boarders, cut them down, and left them dying on the deck. Blood slicked the pale deck with dark smears and splatters. The *Sea Leopard* was assailed from three directions. He looked over his tafferel to make certain they had not gotten under his stern. Close at hand, the quarterdeck crew opened fire with the swivel guns mounted on the rails. Powder monkeys no more than twelve years old ran past him in bare feet, delivering shot and cartridges for the small iron guns.

The bark of the swivels added to the din. At point blank range, they couldn't miss. They aimed for the enemy officers and wrought a fearful carnage in the attacking boats. Isam strode first to the larboard and then the starboard rails to look down at the boarding action on either side. None of the starboard boarders had managed to get aboard; they were too badly shot up. Their boat was sinking and water was already within inches of their gunwales. Desperate sailors struggled to pull themselves up the xebec's side, only to be driven back by the pikes.

A whistle sounded the recall. The attackers scrambled into their boats, except for those on the starboard side. They had no boat left. As the other two boats pulled away, those hapless sailors had no choice but to surrender. Isam's crew pulled them aboard and put them on their knees on the deck while the port guns finished loading and fired on the retreating boats. When they passed the *Sea Leopard's* stern, thunder and gunsmoke erupted beneath his feet as the crew in his cabin fired. The lurid flash of the muzzles was broken up by the latticework of the lazyboard, but Isam's eyes were dazzled all the same. He rubbed them swiftly. He needed to see. Marines in the retreating boats kept firing, and Lieutenant Khadim spun around and dropped at his feet. The master shouted, "Stretcher!"

Isam shouted, "Out oars!"

The retreating boats had an evil gauntlet to run. Freed of the need to fend off boarders, the *Sea Leopard* could once again maneuver in place to bring her broadsides to bear. Majestically she rotated until the starboard battery lined up and fired. Then she yawed to bring her larboard battery around. Meanwhile, the enemy boats rowed as hard as they could to escape into the darkness of the fog. They split up and took weaving paths to confound the gunners' aim.

The frigate had kept out of the fight as long as her boats were attacking, but now that they were clear of the *Sea Leopard*, she opened up. The first broadside whistled over the bulwarks and sizzled through the open air between the masts. Her muzzle flash glimmered like orange heat lightning in the fog, then she was invisible again. She must have aimed for the *Sea Leopard's* muzzle flash, for surely the xebec was as invisible to them as they were to her.

"Eighteen pounders," Isam said, observing the size of the hole made in the bulwark.

Lieutenant Khadim didn't answer; loblollies were loading him on a stretcher to take him to the cockpit.

They'd shot the hell out of the boarding crew. More than a hundred men had tried to take the *Sea Leopard* and been cut to pieces. At least thirty were dead, wounded, or prisoner aboard the xebec. That didn't even the odds. The *Sea Leopard* was as big as a small frigate, but a small frigate would be armed with twelve-pounders like the corsair. Eighteen-pounders said she was a good deal bigger.

"Damage report! What's the butcher's bill?"

Ensign Hamza found himself filling in for Lieutenant Khadim. "I don't know, sir."

"Get me a messenger." Hamza knew who his replacement was, and he passed the word for the master's mate. Meanwhile, Isam went to the rail and shouted, "Damage report! Casualty report! Report to acting-Lieutenant Hamza!"

They all knew what that meant even if they hadn't seen Khadim being carried below.

The two lieutenants on the main deck did swift head counts and sent their messengers to the quarterdeck. Hamza turned ashen in spite of his dark skin as he received the reports. Isam heard them too, but he waited for his acting lieutenant to collate the information and present it. "Three dead and seventeen wounded, sir. Minor damage to the vessel, no damage below the waterline."

"Excellent. My compliments to the crew. We're going to take the frigate."

CHAPTER 3 : DAWN ATTACK

The xebec searched through the fog. Out there was a ship, an enemy ship, a more powerful ship. The enemy guns were heavier and more numerous, and the enemy crew—in spite of their casualties—as large as their own. It was a daring pursuit and not one Isam intended to leave to chance. "I'm going up."

Since they were becalmed, the main antenna was bound with its peak as high as possible to provide the most vantage for the lookout. That brought the toe of the spar down close to the deck. Isam grabbed the wooldings and swung himself up. He shinnied up the long spar—seventeen stories high—by use of his arms and legs.

The lookout greeted him as he reached the peak. "Still there, rais. We're slowly closing."

This high up, the man at the peak of the antenna was above the fluffy grey fleece of fog. The sky was much lighter from this view; the eastern stars were fading into the silver gloaming and the golden hoops gleamed in the captain's ears. Isam made note of the imminent dawn, then turned his eyes northeast where the frigate lay becalmed.

"She gave us her broadside," the captain remarked. "She must have had her boats tow her around before she dispatched them on the raid." The lookout nodded. "I want you to call down any changes in her position. I can't see anything from the deck. My goal is to cross her stern and rake her repeatedly. If she can maneuver, she'll catch us with her broadsides and we can't stand that. Her guns are too heavy."

"Aye aye, sir." The lookout understood his plan; the stern was the weakest part of the ship.

"On deck!" Isam Rais roared. Below all hands looked up from what they were doing. "Hamza! The enemy has presented her port broadside! Helm, right five points! We'll rake her stern as we cross it. Small arms, continue firing on her boats at will!"

"Aye aye, sir!" Hamza cupped his mouth and shouted the orders. "Small arms to fire on the boats at will. Guns, make ready to fire when crossing her stern!" To the helm he said, "Right five points." Only then did the men obey; they'd all heard the captain shouting, but they waited for the orders to come through their chain of command before they executed them. It prevented confusion, especially in the heat of battle.

Isam watched as the xebec came around on her new heading. He checked positions again, and satisfied that he would cross the frigate's wake (not that she had a wake in the calm), he slithered down the long antenna and finally dropped on the deck. He returned to his post on the quarterdeck. His stomach growled. No time for breakfast; a quarter of an hour would bring them to the enemy's tail. He took out his orange and began to peel it.

Before five minutes had passed, the lookout shouted, "Deck ho! She's turning!"

Isam swore in Turkish. After a pause he said, "Her masthead lookout must be able to see our spars now that it's getting light. Pull all the antenna peaks down so they're within the fog."

Word was passed, and slowly the angle of the main antenna was lowered, the lookout clinging tight with his legs and balancing as he rode it. When he was doused in fog, Isam called out, "That's well!" The other antennas were lowered to the same positions. The *Sea Leopard* disappeared into the fog. The square-rigger could not do the same, not unless she struck her topmasts. Which she probably wouldn't—the wind could reasonably be expected to rise with the sun and she'd need her topgallants in the light airs.

"Masthead, can you see anything?" he shouted up at the man.

"Yes, I can! Her masts are almost lined up!"

That meant she had turned her bow to point at where she thought they were. If they moved on where her stern had been, they would be confronting her broadside instead.

Isam swore again. "She must have sweeps of her own."

Some frigates did: a dozen long oars to maneuver themselves in harbor, or in and out of tight places. Smaller and more nimble than battleships, frigates could work in closer to shore and wend through tight channels where bigger ships couldn't go. A xebec was even faster and nimbler in a wider range of conditions, an advantage Isam had counted on to stalk a blind and becalmed foe. Alas, she was not as laggard as he supposed. Yet having made the decision to attack, he was loath to break off. He consulted the binnacle.

"Helm, right three points."

"Right three points, aye," he replied. The *Sea Leopard* curved through the fog.

"Guns, hold fire. New target, the frigate's quarterdeck. Wait for my command. Double shot. Small arms, wait for my command!"

Word was passed and the xebec's guns fell silent. With the frigate's bow pointed at them, it would be impossible to reach her quarterdeck. The *Sea Leopard* rowed away. It was a risk because he was exposing his own stern to her, but he was counting on the fog to cloak him. Even if the frigate could detect his movements, her gunners couldn't see the *Sea Leopard* any better than she could see them.

The frigate's guns thundered. The orange flash lit up the fog in a fuzzy and diffused glow but revealed her position to them. She had grown suspicious when the *Sea Leopard's* guns stopped. The enemy's cannonballs went whistling into the sea where she would have been had she kept her previous course.

Isam smiled. He let the xebec run further, then, "Helm, left eight points. Silent running."

"Left eight points, aye." The tiller swung back the other direction. The *Sea Leopard* now followed a course perpendicular to her last maneuver. She was paralleling the frigate, but neither vessel could see the other. Commands were passed in whispers. The rowers stuffed more cloth into the oarlocks to muffle them.

Isam checked his watch. Doing the math in his head, he decided he needed to hold this course for fifteen minutes to pass the frigate and reach her stern. Few mariners had as good a command of geometry as the corsair did; that they might navigate around an unseen object by knowing nothing but right angles and relative speed would have struck them as sorcery. Even fewer men had the nerve necessary to implement it. Most men itched to take action and could not muster the patience to wait with nothing but the bending backs of the rowers and the muffled creak of the oars to tell them anything.

Once again the guns of the frigate roared out, but since they were rowing well away from where they had been, the broadside was a waste of ammunition. Isam could imagine the desperation aboard the frigate. Where was the corsair? Had she broken off? Was she using the cover of fog to escape a superior enemy? Was she stalking them? What sort of corsair would be crazy enough to take on a frigate by herself? Did she have a consort they didn't know about? Was it even a corsair? Had they run into a warship in the night? A corsair would not be bold enough to attack them, would it? Corsairs preferred to pick on merchantmen and fishboats that offered no resistance.

Members of Isam Rais' own crew squirmed with impatience. They all knew they needed to rake the frigate's stern to have a chance at victory, but that didn't make the wait any easier. The only sounds were the breathing of the rowers and the soft whoosh of water along the hull. The fog continued to lighten as the pink arms of rosy Eos reached above the horizon to open the gate of heaven.

"Ahoy the masthead! Where's the frigate?"

"Broad on the port beam, about a cable's length away."

"What's her position?"

"Larboard to us."

They all sucked in their breaths. They were close enough for the frigate to pummel them, if she knew where they were. Isam kept watching his watch, but he didn't neglect to look around. The same fears that the frigate must entertain were the same concerns he must consider. Was another ship lurking in the fog, rowing as hard as she could to answer the sound of gunnery? He couldn't allow himself to be surprised as he intended to surprise the frigate.

Nerves frayed. Still he waited. Gunners blew on their matches to keep them burning. The rowers kept their cadence with sinews bulging beneath their swarthy skins.

Two minutes later, Isam called up, "Ahoy the masthead! Where's the frigate?"

"Broad on our port quarter," the lookout replied.

"Range?"

"About two and a half cables."

Isam did the geometry in his head. "Helm, left eight points."

"Eight points left, aye," the helm replied.

The *Sea Leopard* swept into her turn. As she came around on the new heading, Isam said, "Charge as quietly as you can! Guns, wait for my command."

The tempo of the muffled drum suddenly increased and the rowers threw themselves bodily against the sweeps to make them fly. The frigate came into view off their port side as a grey ghost in the fog. A moment later and the frigate could see the low slung xebec too. Her drums rattled and the boatswain's whistle pierced the fog; orders were shouted in Italian, *"Sparare i cannoni!"*

There was no further need for silence. Isam shouted, *"Allahu Akbar!"*

The ululating cry rose from hundreds of throats as the corsairs shouted, *"Allahu Akbar! Allahu Akbar! Allahu Akbar! Allahu Akbar!"*

The Italian guns roared, drowning out their cries. Shot splashed all around them, flew over them, and one crashed into them. The Italians had traversed their guns as fast as they could, and their aim was bad.

"Remi!" came the shout.

Too late. The *Sea Leopard* crossed their stern as the Italians fumbled their sweeps into the water. The *Sea Leopard's* double shotted guns roared and leaped against their tackle. Balls smashed through the frigate's transom and into the quarterdeck and great cabin. The pair of stern chasers in the great cabin roared back, flinging gouts of fire and iron at the impudent corsair. At such a close range they couldn't miss. Wood shattered and splinters flew. A man screamed. Yet it was nowhere near the carnage the *Sea Leopard* was inflicting on the Italians. Her twelve double-shotted larboard guns fired and twenty-four cannonballs found their target in the frigate's stern. Screams and prayers came to them, *"Madre Maria, difendici!"*

The Italians labored desperately at their sweeps and the frigate slowly turned. It was enough. Now it was the *Sea Leopard's* turn to receive a fiery broadside as she let loose her starboard guns. Even though they were hastily pointed, they still scored.

A ball struck the main antenna low down, shattered one of the two spars that made up the lower limb, and caused the other spar to bow badly. The rigging held and didn't drop the massive timbers onto the deck. Nearby, a gun leaped from its shattered carriage and a headless corpse lay bloody on the deck. A match tub was smashed, but the force of the impact blew out the matches. Balls tore through the port quarter and shredded the chartroom, but all the precious charts had been safely stowed in the hold before the action. Another ball tore through captain's cabin and ripped out the other side. Both of the *Sea Leopard's* stern chasers barked defiance in spite of the damage.

"Row, you bastards, row!" Kateb bellowed at his crew. The *Sea Leopard* darted away and disappeared into the fog.

When the grey curtain closed over them, Isam ordered, "Cruising speed," then, "Damage report. Casualty report."

"One dead, one gun dismounted," acting Lieutenant Hamza reported.

"Ahoy the deck! Frigate's turning to starboard!"

Isam swore. If they returned along the course they had taken, they'd be pounded by the frigate's broadside and not be able to rake her stern. He plotted the frigate's position and their course in his head. "Helm, right eight points."

At first the men thought the captain was breaking off the fight, but he wasn't. He was boxing the compass in the fog beyond the frigate's sight. He ordered, "Cold breakfast to the men. Keep them standing by the guns. I want them all double shotted." He checked his watch. The silver circle lay on his swarthy palm as he watched the minute hand inching around the dial.

CHAPTER 4 : THE FOG OF WAR

Silver mist lay in heavy banks upon the sea. No wind stirred at all. The men of the *Sea Leopard* ate brown bread and olive oil for breakfast and washed it down with mint water sweetened with sugar. It was not a substantive breakfast, but it calmed the growling in their stomachs. The dawn prayer was not called. Isam was not a pious man and didn't observe the five daily prayers, but it was his custom to at least offer the dawn prayer. Given the situation, he was pretty sure the men were praying all right, even as they worked the guns and the boys threw sand on the bloodstains on the deck.

"Ware the frigate!" the bow watch suddenly sang out.

The fog between the two ships thinned enough that they could see her bulk looming in the gloom about a cable and a half away. Her sweeps were not as numerous as the corsair's, but she had guessed their general location and rowed up on them. Her guns thundered their outrage. Double shot clawed them from stem to stern. A pair of balls smashed through the quarterdeck bulkhead, passed to either side of Isam, shattered the binnacle, and took off the helmsman's leg. Ensign Hamza stood paralyzed with shock at the near miss and his black skin turned grey. Bullets whipped about them as the quarterdeck came under heavy fire from marines in the frigate's tops. Hamza crumpled.

Isam shouted at his crew, "Fire! Hit them back! Oars, charge! Break your backs! Row, damn you! Row!" The *Sea Leopard* had to disappear into thicker fog before the Italians could reload.

Matches touched primer, and *Sea Leopard* roared in retaliation. Her shot peppered the frigate. Isam Rais was a devotee of the Devil's art; his gun crews were well-trained and every shot told. The frigate sported new holes in her side. Alas, but the parting fog had allowed them to see that she was a two-decker, and with the calm seas, she had both gun decks open. They had caught a Tartar.

The *Sea Leopard* pulled into the protective cocoon of the fog. Isam bellowed, "Damage report!"

Casualties were mounting and morale was dropping. Isam was angry about the damage he'd taken, but he wasn't willing to give up. "That was a bit of bad luck, but the plan is sound." He checked his watch. "Triple shot the guns."

Considering how hot things had been on the last pass, he said, "Master Imrich, if I am disabled or killed, take command and withdraw the *Sea*

Leopard from battle. Get us safely into Tunis." Tunis was the nearest Muslim port and only a hundred and fifty miles away.

The Dutch renegade was a good sailor; it should be no trouble for him. "Aye aye, Captain. Pardon me for saying it, but I think you've bitten off more than you can chew."

"That may be, but I don't want her to think so. We're going to cross her stern one more time. She thinks we've run away."

"She'll reload anyhow," the shaggy Dutchman replied with a sailor's fatalism.

Isam checked his watch. "Helm, right eight points."

The *Sea Leopard* swung around again and began her approach. Isam let her cruise for five minutes, then the lookout sang out, "The frigate's turning to starboard."

Isam swore again. "Of course she expects us to box her, just as we are doing. She has a clever captain. Helm, hard left. Bring her around."

The *Sea Leopard* broke off her approach and ran away. Once again Isam ordered, "Helm, left eight points." That would bring her across the Italian's stern again if the frigate was trying to track the corsair on her old course. "Masthead! How's the frigate?"

"Holding position. We're approaching her stern!"

"Let me know the instant she changes!" Then, "Pass the word: aim low on the transom. Sink her."

The men were grimly quiet. No one spoke except to acknowledge orders. The *Sea Leopard* was fighting above her class and everyone knew it.

"Charge silently."

The muffled drums beat out the pace and again the rowers threw themselves into their exertions. Stertorous breath and groans came from the men as they plied the oars with all their strength.

The ghostly frigate came into view again. "Fire as she bears."

But if they could see the frigate, the frigate could see them. Heavy guns were slewed around as fast as the Italians could manage. Shots peppered the water around them, smashed into the hull, and skimmed across the deck. More splinters flew and more blood spilled. Another ball went careening into the great cabin and a cry of anguish told him another casualty. Their aim was bad, but at this range, some were certain hit anyhow.

The frigate's stern came into few. Holes gaped in the stern lights, shattered the gallery, and busted up the transom and quarterdeck. The first of the corsair's bronze guns roared and belched out three iron balls each to smash into the stern, down low, around the rudder. The gun hurled itself against its tackle and thumped back onto the deck. The second triple-shotted gun roared and more carnage ensued. Gun by gun they smashed the rudder and stern, opened many holes at and above the waterline, and sent massive splinters flying like spears. The stern chasers in the great cabin spouted at them and two balls smashed along their deck. One thudded into the mainmast with a blow that made the xebec shiver in all her timbers.

"Damage report!" Isam shouted. He wanted to know the condition of his mainmast. If he lost it, he would be crippled and in range for a dangerous foe.

The *Sea Leopard* came out the other side and had to run the gauntlet of the other broadside. She dashed as fast as she could, and the balls splashed into the sea behind her, thumped her port quarterdeck, and sent more men screaming to oblivion.

"Helm, hard right! Double back!"

He was counting on the *Sea Leopard's* greater agility. She came back, crossed the stern again, and this time, neither Italian battery was able to answer the attack. The Italian crews were sponging and ramming as fast as they could go, but the *Sea Leopard* dashed past their stern and unloaded her other triple shotted battery. A cloud of gunsmoke hung in the unmoving air, tainting the fog with brimstone and death. The frigate's badly mauled stern could not hold the weight above it; the great cabin groaned and dropped to hang aslant at the rear of the frigate. Her ensign had hung closed and limp, but swayed open enough to show a glimpse of red, black, and white. She was Sardinian.

A wild cheer went up from the corsairs as they saw how much damage they had inflicted on the frigate. The frigate's rudder was useless and her stern chasers were now pointing into the sea. Their crews scrambled up the buckling deck to the safety of the weather deck. The eerie battle cry of the Barbary warriors trilled high pitched and loud, penetrated the fog, and chilled the nerves of the Christians who heard it.

The *Sea Leopard* darted into the fog as three or four of the frigate's guns loaded fast enough to throw their sting into her tail. Isam let the *Sea Leopard* run out to long range. She was cloaked in fog and only her lookout could see any trace of the frigate, and that was only the very top of her spars. Isam received his damage and casualty reports, then went down to the weather deck and belowdecks to make his own inspection. She was shot up to the point that were he to meet a vessel his own size, he would have to run for his life. He needed to make repairs. At the same time, his blood was up and he was loath to give up his wounded prey. On the other hand, she'd be making repairs too, and he had not done any significant damage to her guns.

He let her run further away into the fog, then, "Heave to. Make repairs."

A collective sigh of relief went through the crew. They began to chatter.

"Quiet! The Italian is only a mile away. Don't give away our presence with your noise. They may come after us. Keep a sharp lookout. Relieve the masthead lookout."

The crew quieted. A new man was sent aloft and the previous lookout came down. The cook wasn't allowed to light the galley fires, so he served a vegetable salad in lieu of couscous and gave them an orange each. The men downed their food in a few gulping swallows and went back to work.

A watery sun rose on their efforts. The carpenter and his mates started by plugging holes. The boatswain brought the mainsail on deck and the huge lateen sail was unbent. The wooldings were undone so that the three great spars that made up the antenna came apart. The broken one was removed and a spare spar laid in place. This took time, and during that time, the fog thinned under the power of the sun.

"Ahoy the deck! Frigate's on the move!"

Isam swore. He had his big antenna on the deck in pieces and was nowhere near done replacing the wooldings. His carpenters were well along in their repairs and were even now using the fore antenna as a winch to lift a heavy bronze gun to put it into the spare carriage brought up from the hold, but the starboard guns were all curtailed by the main antenna running fore and aft on deck as it was repaired.

"What course?" he shouted back.

"Southeast. Coming our way."

Isam swore in Turkish, Arabic, and lingua franca. Then he announced, "I'm going aloft."

He swung over the quarterdeck railing and up the ratlines to the mizzen top. His xebec had a square topsail above her small mizzen lateen and a small top where his marksmen were still on duty. As he clambered around the futtock shrouds and into the bowl of the top, the marines saluted him by pressing their hands to their foreheads. They were a motley crew, some with bare arms, some with jackets, some with turbans, or fezzes, or a topknot, and they wore whatever color they pleased, although white was very popular on account of the Mediterranean sun. Isam's dark clothes were a strong contrast.

The mizzen top was not clear of the fog, but he could make out the frigate's topgallant masts moving like a ghost in the hazy dawn. The three masts were not in a line, so she was not coming straight at him, but all the same, she was coming. In a half an hour she would arrive in his general vicinity. The noise of hammering would guide her to him.

He swore softly and at great length. The *Sea Leopard* was in no shape to meet a refitted frigate. "Damn them for being good at what they do."

He clambered down the ratlines to the quarterdeck with a grim face. "Out oars. Silent running. Get that antenna fixed! Carpenter, no more pounding!"

The men moved hastily to their posts. They put out the sweeps, and two to an oar, stood ready for command. The sailmaker and the mainmast crew continued their labors while the white canvas lapped against the starboard rowers' legs.

Isam leaned over the quarterdeck rail. "Boatswain! Make haste, but take all care. The antenna *must* hold if we use it."

No breeze stirred the wisps of fog. As long as the air remained calm, his superior number of sweeps would allow him to escape the frigate. Once the wind began to blow, he needed his mainsail. Without it, the enemy would easily run him down. His stomach tightened.

"Oars, out oars." The sweeps shot out through the cloth-muffled ports. It sounded like thunder in his ears. "Oars, give way together."

With a soft splash, they dipped and began to pull in cadence. Isam checked the binnacle. "Helm, left three points." Tunis was only a hundred and fifty miles away. They could row there in three days if they had to. If they repaired the antenna and a wind came, they could sail there in one. More than that, the closer he came to Tunis, the more likely he was to encounter corsairs going in or coming out. Right now what mattered was staying hidden in the fog so the frigate couldn't find him.

CHAPTER 5 : CAT'S PAWS

The *Sea Leopard* crept southward over the next hour. The frigate's course was eastward of their own, so gradually the distance between them opened. That relieved Isam. Every mile was a half of hour safety. He reckoned the frigate with her sweeps could not sustain a pace of more than two knots, and he expected she would not be able to charge. Fewer oars and a deeper, rounder hull meant more drag and less speed. By contrast, the xebec was a descendant of the galley, and could, if necessary, put on a burst of speed that reached eight or nine knots. That speed wasn't sustainable, but it was enough to get her out from under the frigate's guns, should it be necessary. Isam fervently hoped it wouldn't. He bent all his considerable mental faculties to observing, analyzing, predicting, planning, and preparing. Most of all, he had to get the broken antenna repaired. The sailmaker and his mates were tightening the wooldings as fast as they could while being certain the work was well done.

Isam paced his quarterdeck. He kept looking over the rail at the thinning fog. The xebec was cruising along at three knots and the rowing gang was getting tired. Every half hour the boatswain swapped in fresh men, but with eighty men needed to row, the supply of fresh men was rapidly depleted. A faint flicker of breeze ruffled the fog, then settled again.

"Ahoy the deck! Frigate changing course! South southwest!"

Isam swore again. "She's seen us. Oars, charge!"

The muffled drum beat out the dash speed, and the rowers' brawny bodies bulged with effort. Isam ran up the mizzen ratlines and hauled himself into the top. The fog was veil-like and fine now; he could see the frigate's topgallant masts in their entirety as they poked above the mist. They were in a line pointed directly at him. He swore some more. As he watched, the xebec drew ahead. The enemy spars grew vague as the increasing distance put more fog between them. At this level, a bit of breeze fluttered the tail of the turban hanging beside his left ear. That was all it did, one flutter, then nothing. Soon the sun would burn away what was left of the mist and a breeze as soft as a cat's paw would rise. If he had his mainsail, he would make his escape. If. As he watched, the frigate's hands shook out her topgallant sails and clewed down.

Isam bellowed, "On the fore, make sail, high points!"

The fore chief repeated the orders and the second biggest sail on the boat dropped like a curtain, hung listlessly, then filled once as the breeze caught it, then went limp again. Sailors hauled the lines to lift the peak of the foresail as high as it would go. It caught the faint of air aloft, but only the peak filled. Isam wetted his finger and held it aloft to determine the wind direction and speed, but there was hardly any. At the moment he could row faster than he could sail. For that matter, he could have walked faster than he sailed.

Isam Rais ran down the ratlines to the quarterdeck, said, "Set the tops'l!" The small square sail opened and the sharpshooters aloft helped by kicking the bunt out of the top.

The captain descended to the weather deck to inspect the work on his biggest and most important sail. The great spars that made up the antenna were lashed together with temporary ropes as the teams of men woolded them together with lengths of stout rope and Spanish windlasses. Half the wooldings were in place. He put his hands on the finished wooldings to tug at them and make certain they were sound; if they came loose or pulled apart when the antenna was under stress, it would be a disaster. He checked each of them, nodded, and said, "Carry on." Long legs carried him back to the quarterdeck. There he paced and paced like a leopard in a cage.

He checked his watch. After ten minutes, he called, "Oars! Cruising speed. Three knots." He must not use them up. He must husband his strength so that he would have something left when he needed it most. The sweating rowers happily slowed their pace.

He paced some more. The minute hand swept around the watch's impassive face. The sun shone more hotly and the fog continued to thin. He pulled the spyglass out of his pocket, stretched it open, and adjusted it. The frigate came into view as a dark bulk in the glass. Sometimes a splash of white showed where her sweeps dipped into the glassy waters as she came after them. Her topgallants hung limp. Each vessel was poised to catch any breeze, but the dawn stillness taunted them.

Isam studied her for a long time. "She's about three miles behind." The news gave him great satisfaction. He was outrowing her. He had known he would, but it pleased him to see the evidence manifested in his glass.

Strand by strand, thick ropes wrapped around the spars. At last all the wooldings were done. The sailmaker and his crew then bent the big sail to the spar. They had kept the sail neatly bound with gaskets so it didn't flop open in a mess, but now it was time to do it properly. Meanwhile, the boatswain changed out men from the rowing gang. The weary men stepped over the sail and went to drink water and wipe their faces with their turban tails. New men took their places. While this happened, the *Sea Leopard* lost headway and the frigate gained. Once the replacement crew was at work, the *Sea Leopard* drew away again. The new men were not fresh; all of them had already rowed during the morning. They kept the pace, but the strain on their faces and the grim determination with which they bent their backs showed the effort it required.

The boatswain and his mates re-rigged the halyards and jeers, brayles, sheets, vangs, topping lift, and bowlines. If they fouled a line the sail wouldn't rise to the masthead, or wouldn't open correctly if it did. The riggers worked as quickly as they could. Isam descended the ladder to the weather deck once again and inspected their work. He knew more about rigging his vessel than anyone, so he went to work. Straddling the big spar, he and the boatswain worked together to secure the halyard.

At last the great sail was ready. The halyards and jeers were extended down the middle of the deck between the banks of oars. The men who weren't rowing tailed on. Isam took his place at the head of the jeers. A tall, muscular man, he was stronger than most of his sailors.

"You give the orders. I'm hauling line," Isam told the boatswain. He was one of the few fresh men aboard.

The boatswain sang out, "Main mast, take a strain!"

The crew planted their feet and drew on the line until it came taut. The sailor at the tail took a turn around a horn kevel.

"Haul away!"

The men heaved and a cheer went up as the big antenna lifted off the deck. Isam bent his back and hauled. Hand over hand, dragging the thick line through the sheave in the knighthead, forty backs bulged and strained in unison. Suddenly he began to sing.

"Allah helper, Allah helper, give strength to my arms and all of me. Allah helper, Allah helper, breathe thy winds bravely to speed my sail!"

A chorus of male voices joined in, "Allah helper, Allah helper!" Inch by inch the great spar rose, the men pulling in unison to the beat of the Arabic chantey. The drummer for the rowing gang shifted the tempo to match the rising spar. It allowed the rowers to pull more slowly, which was a great relief to them. They sang along with the chantey. The song heartened them, even if their breath was ragged from exertion.

The great antenna reached the masthead. The brayles and sheets and bowlines and vangs were belayed to their proper places. A great cheer went up then. A faint breath of wind tickled Isam's beard. "Make sail, high points. Oars, boat oars."

The rowers hauled the oars in but left the blades outside; they had not been given the order to stand down yet. They rested and tested the wind to see if it would hold. It didn't. The great sails hung limp. The frigate gained on them. There was not even half a knot of wind, just the occasional flutter of a breeze. The great curtains of canvas swayed a little, but the wind didn't blow enough to press the wrinkles out and fill their bellies with speed.

"Oars, out oars." Once again the blades shot out to splash into the sea. The fog thinned. All that remained was a sultry dampness in the air. They could see the frigate clearly now—and the frigate could see them. The morning sun glared down on the pair of foes as they toiled in the waveless sea. "Oars, give way together."

The sea was brilliant white, a glaring brightness that gave back exactly what it received. Sun diamonds shimmered on the surface. The *Sea Leopard* was like a toy on a glass table, and still the frigate came after them.

Isam swore again. That morning he had sworn almost as much as he had spoken. "Damn him for stubborn infidel."

Imrich spoke. "He has a bigger crew. He can keep them working longer than we can. If he's patient, he may catch us yet. Our men are tired."

"That will take hours."

"It's already taken hours, but he hasn't given up yet. As long as he can see us, he will chase us."

Isam rubbed the wool sleeve of his jacket against his brow to soak up the sweat. He watched the frigate; she was falling behind. On this glassy sea, she could see for miles. She would not lose sight of *Sea Leopard* until the xebec's top hamper disappeared below the curvature of the Earth. At this rate, he would reach Tunis before he shook her. "Ensign Taslim, you have the deck. I'm going below for a few minutes. I'll be back."

Taslim stood up straight and his brown eyes widened as the weight of authority settled on his shoulders. He was being left in charge of the quarterdeck with the enemy in sight. That had never happened before. "I have the deck, sir," he acknowledged.

"Send word if any thing changes, and I do mean anything, no matter how small. Master Imrich will advise you."

"Aye aye, sir." He was glad the captain would only be gone a short while. He was also glad that the chase had settled into dullness. There was nothing for him to do except stay out of the way of the carpenter and his mates who came to mend the bulwarks and replace the shattered binnacle case.

The stern chasers' gun crews were sitting idly when Isam entered the great cabin, but leaped to their feet when they saw their captain. He said, "As you were," and they relaxed again.

"How's the frigate?" one dared to ask.

"Falling behind," Isam replied.

The cabin was completely different. All of his personal possessions had been stowed in the hold. All that remained were the two guns, their bronze garlands with cannonballs in them, the stench of gunsmoke, and the men themselves. Several holes punched through the cabin walls had not yet been mended, but that didn't matter. Those holes were nowhere near the waterline and didn't lead to anything important. They would be among the last patched. A red stain on the deck was covered in sand. He avoided stepping on it.

He removed his jacket and hung it on a peg in his sleeping quarters. Even his bed was gone. All that remained was the compass in the ceiling. He checked it automatically, then his thunder glass and thermometer. The blue water in the pitcher-shaped glass was rising up the spout, indicating dropping air pressure. He set his jaw. Rain, perhaps bad weather, was coming. He was sufficiently repaired not to worry about a gale, but he wondered how well the frigate's damaged stern would hold up to a smashing sea. He began to hope for a storm.

He kept looking at the thunder glass as a pretense while he breathed away some of his tension. Chases wracked the nerves and the men hated them. They hated them even when they were the pursuer and likely to take a prize at the end, but now they were the prey and would be the prize—if their foe could overtake them. Surely a wind would rise before the rowers' strength gave out. It must. He tapped the thunder glass to make certain it was telling him the truth. The blue water kept its level.

Isam Rais squared his shoulders, took a deep breath, then went on deck in his shirt sleeves. He rolled them up above his elbows and let the sun bake his hairy forearms. The watch changed, and he checked his watch. A breath of fresh air stirred the sails, getting his hopes up, but it fell again. He put away his watch and hung over the rail, watching the cat's paws of wind walking across the surface of the sea from the southeast.

"Qibli winds, and the thunder glass is rising," he commented to the master.

"We'll have a simoon before this is over," Imrich agreed.

"Allah willing, we'll be safe in Tunis harbor before that happens."

"Allah willing," the heavyset Dutchman agreed.

"Still, I wouldn't mind if it caught the infidel."

Imrich smiled crookedly at that. "I wouldn't mind either."

There was nothing to do but wait.

CHAPTER 6 : RISING WIND

An unexpected gust whipped the tail of Isam's turban around his face. He pulled it away and tucked it back into his turban. The sails swelled out for just a moment and the *Sea Leopard* lurched. Then the wind left them. He was debating the sail trim when Ensign Hamza called out, "Isam Rais! The frigate has made all canvas and is heading our way!"

All heads snapped aft. Isam pulled his spyglass out of the pocket of his pantaloons and opened it. Sure enough, square sails full of wind were driving straight at him. As they watched, studding sails broke out on the larboard side. The surface of the sea rippled and small waves began to lift. The wind caught the *Sea Leopard* then. Isam bellowed, "Oars, in oars! Stow oars!"

Kateb flew down the ladder to oversee his men. The rowing gang pulled in the long sweeps and were lashing them to the bulwarks when the wind caught them. The *Sea Leopard* heeled over and her sails bellied out. A cheer went up as the xebec began to cruise under her own power. Every man who'd taken a turn at the oars had blisters and was glad to be quit of them.

"I have steerage," the helm reported. "What course?"

"Due west," Isam replied. He went forward to the rail of the quarterdeck and stared up at the main antenna. He put his spyglass to his eye, adjusted it, and studied each and every woolding, but they all seemed to be holding. He ordered, "Toss the log."

The master and his mate tossed the triangle-shaped board over the stern and watched the sandglass. At twenty-eight seconds, Imrich announced, "Time!" The log was hauled in and his mate wound it on the spindle.

"Four knots, rais," Imrich reported to the captain.

Isam grunted an acknowledgment. The breeze gusted fitfully, then fell back. He stared at the frigate through his glass. "Helm, keep her full and by."

"Full and by, aye," the helm replied and moved the tiller a few inches. He looked up, watched the sails, and moved the tiller a bit more.

Isam turned to watch the sails as well. "That's well," he told the helm. "Master Imrich, trim the sails. I want maximum speed."

"Aye aye, sir." Imrich gave orders for the fine adjustments that would improve the shape of the sails and harvest the most speed from the wind.

Isam watched the frigate through his glass. He spoke in satisfaction, "Just like I thought. She can't keep as close to the wind as we can. We'll lose her for sure."

The wind increased and sea continued to get up. White crests broke and long plumes of lace spread over the brazen sea. To the south, brown murk climbed into the skies until the sun itself was enveloped in the dust flying up from the distant Sahara. Still the wind rose. Hail peppered them with little speckles of ice that had formed around dust and stung like bees where it struck exposed skin. The hail lasted a few minutes, then stopped as abruptly as it started.

The frigate threw up plumes of white spray as she charged after the escaping xebec. "By Allah, I think she means to chase us all the way to Africa!" Isam exclaimed. Then he asked Imrich, "What speed?"

Again the log was tossed. "Six knots," Imrich replied. "Rais, we must think about putting reefs in. The time is now, not when the simoon hits."

Isam eyed the sky, looked back at the frigate. He mused, "He'll have to pull in his stuns'ls soon."

"And put reefs in too." Imrich had served as mate aboard a square-rigger before taking the turban.

"Very well. Put in all three reefs. We'll need to keep a sharp lookout. She might be foolish enough to risk carrying away her top hamper when she sees us reducing sail."

"Good for us if she does."

"True enough."

The sailors clambered up the great yards, and holding on by their legs, bent down to grasp the sails and pull them up. They tied the first set of reef knittles, then bent again to haul up more sail and tie the second. As they were putting in the third, the lookout sang out, "Deck ho! A sail! Fine on the starboard bow!"

Isam peered forward, but couldn't see it. He fished his spyglass out of his pocket and searched again. He found a vague white spot on the horizon. He couldn't make out any details, so he said, "I'm going aloft." He climbed up to the mizzen top and had another look.

"Lookout! What do you see?"

"Can't tell," came the reply from the lookout on the main.

Isam held up his thumb to judge the size of what he saw, then waited. A while later, he held up his thumb again. The blur was a tiny bit larger compared to his thumb. The stranger was driving straight at them. Unfortunately, all he could make out, even with the spyglass, was a white smudge.

Isam descended to the quarterdeck and took another look over his tafferel. The Italian frigate had disappeared in the haze beyond their wake.

He knew he hadn't truly lost her; it was the increasingly dirty weather that hid her. The air was thick with humidity and had a yellowish tint.

"Helm, left eight points."

"Left eight points, aye." The tiller moved and the xebec heeled to the wind. She slashed across the sea, luffed with a thunder of shaking canvas, and corrected. "I can't keep her due south, rais," the helm reported.

"Very well. Keep her as close to the wind as she will bear. Notify me if she changes more than a point."

"Aye aye, rais." He made the adjustment. The master's mate moved the peg in the traverse board.

Master Imrich made a note about it in the log. He checked his watch for the time, noted the speed and relative positions and courses of the other vessels, and wrote about the wind and weather. He and the captain would need the details to reckon their location later.

"I'll have the iron tiller, Master Imrich."

"Iron tiller, aye."

The word was passed. In a few minutes, the boatswain and his mates arrived with the replacement. Iron was sturdier and would bear the strain of bad weather better than wood. Imrich supervised the replacement, then made a note of it in the log. "Iron tiller in place, rais."

"Thank you. Carry on."

The new arrival turned south to parallel them off their starboard. She could not approach them directly because no vessel could sail dead into the wind, but it was obvious she did not intend to let them escape. Leeway from the qibli wind would push the *Sea Leopard* closer to her.

Isam muttered a Turkish imprecation, then, "Beat to quarters."

The rattle of the drum stirred the torpid crew. They had not stood down from their previous alarm, so it was the simplest thing to extinguish the galley fire and put away the remains of the noon meal. In less than five minutes everything was shipshape. After that there was nothing to do but wait and watch.

An hour later and the lateen-rigged stranger was coursing along a mile off their starboard quarter. That she was lateen-rigged meant either friend or foe; the Italian states had lateen-rigged coastguards. The only thing she could not be was Spanish because a rare peace prevailed between the Sallee Republic and Spain. Which explained why the *Sea Leopard* was hunting far east of her usual ground. Then again, the peace between the Iberians and the Africans was so brittle, it could have easily been broken while the *Sea Leopard* was at sea and didn't know about it. A cunning Spaniard might think to take advantage of their ignorance to get close. There was nothing he could do about it. He was caught on the horns of wind and frigate.

Wind whipped about them and rain spit down in earnest. Isam's servant brought his tarpaulin djellaba and he wrapped it about him. The big hood and long sleeves of tarred canvas protected him from the increasingly bad weather. The sea heaved up and the *Sea Leopard* rocked like a camel as she bucked over the waves. The wind shifted more to the south, and the helm had to shift too. The same applied to the mystery vessel. As the waves accosted them, the port bow raised a shoulder and the vessel heeled aft and to the starboard. As the wave passed under them, they tilted down the far side and the starboard quarter kicked up, pitching the vessel's head down and rolling them to the port. It was a motion weak stomachs could not withstand, and the first of the seasick marines puked in the waterway to the amusement of his hardier comrades.

"Hoist Spanish colors," Isam Rais ordered.

His ensign obeyed. The red and gold flag of Spain streamed in the wind. Those Italian states who were allies of Spain wouldn't fire on them, and those that weren't wouldn't dare offend the much more powerful Spanish. The western Mediterranean was *Nuestra mar*, "our sea" to the Spanish. "Fire a shot."

As the larger vessel, the *Sea Leopard* had the privilege of challenging the smaller one. By the ruse of the Spanish flag he hoped to get close enough to identify and take the lateen stranger without having to chase her down. She was the weak side of the triangle that hemmed him in; he must take her or be taken by the frigate or the storm.

The smaller vessel also ran up a Spanish flag. Isam hmmed thoughtfully. The other xebec might well be Spanish; Spain had dozens of xebecs in service. It was a little odd to see such a small vessel so far from home, but not implausible, either. She could be running dispatches between the Spanish mainland and the Kingdom of the Two Sicilies. The stranger could be alone, or she could be a scout for a larger force. That she had run so boldly toward them suggested she was not alone. If he fired on her, the sound of guns could draw a vessel hidden in the rain. For that matter, there was still the remorseless Sardinian somewhere behind them that would certainly answer the sound of guns. Isam decided his best choice was to take the smaller vessel without firing a shot. He kept the Spanish flag flying.

In less than half an hour the two xebecs had closed the gap. That brought them close enough together to note one another's manner of dress. Isam laughed at the sight of the turbans. "She's no Spaniard, anymore than we are. Strike the Spanish colors. Hoist the Man in the Moon."

The ensign and master's mate brought the soggy flag on board and replaced it with the red and gold "Man in the Crescent Moon" flag of the Sallee rovers. The other vessel lowered her false flag to be replaced by the purple flag of the Sallee Republic with its white crescent moon and star. She was sailing under patronage of the Sallee Republic while the *Sea Leopard* was an independent privateer.

"What ship?" Isam hailed the other in Arabic.

"The *Renegade*, Murad Rais!" was the answer he received. "What ship?" they queried in reply.

"The *Sea Leopard*, Isam Rais!" Isam bellowed back. "I'm being chased by a Sardinian frigate!"

Murad Rais was a handsome figure in his white turban and red fez. His oiled burnoose covered up whatever else he was wearing, but Isam knew the man. A few years older than Isam, he was a successful corsair. Murad shouted back, "Let's go get her!"

Isam was pleased with this proposal. He shared what he knew about the infidel, "She's a two-decker, but her stern is damaged! She has casualties!"

"Why didn't you take her?" Murad asked.

Isam smote his thigh in frustration. "She's a two-decker! With eighteen pound guns! The infidel captain is stubborn!"

"We'll double her and board!" Murad Rais shouted back.

"Agreed!" Isam replied. Together their firepower was about equal to the frigate, but their combined crews would outnumber the frigate by a large margin.

"Where is she?"

"We were heading due west when we lost her. She's probably still heading that way!"

Murad nodded and did the calculations in his head. "She's probably about six or eight miles north of us!"

"If she kept her course, yes!" Isam replied.

"Set course northwest to overtake her then!"

That would put the wind over their port quarters. They would make excellent time.

"Agreed!"

"Shake out a reef! You won't catch her if you sail small!" Murad had only one reef in his own sails.

"Shake out a reef," Isam ordered his crew. He would do it while they were hove to and chatting.

"Rais, I don't think that's wise. The weather will only worsen," Imrich replied.

With Murad to goad him, Isam was no mood to care. He pulled out his watch and checked the time. "At this rate we have an hour or two before that happens. It's still daylight. I'll take my chances. I want that frigate. With Murad Rais' help, we can take her."

"Daredevil," muttered Imrich. Then he cupped his hands to his mouth and bellowed, "Shake out a reef!"

Hands swarmed aloft. Seeing his crew at work, Murad Rais shouted, "Catch up to me!" The *Renegade* wore ship and swept northwest.

Isam clenched his hands as the man gave him orders, then acted on the assumption that he would obey. The *Sea Leopard* was the bigger, newer vessel and ought to have pride of place, even if Murad was his senior and therefore his superior. In a fit of spite he thought about letting Murad get beat up by the frigate so he could rescue him, but let it pass. The frigate was a good prize. They'd split the prize money, but it was better than not capturing the frigate at all. They were *al-ghazut*, warriors for Allah. They must work together against a common foe.

"Helm, follow the *Renegade*!" he barked once the reefs had fallen. The temperature plunged and the rain came down in sheets.

Imrich shook his head. "It'll be the Devil to pay to put that reef back when we really need it."

"Enough. I have decided."

The *Sea Leopard* and the *Renegade* surged northwest, chasing their fates in the Sea of Sardinia. Imrich's jaw set. So far Isam had been a daring but skillful captain, but he was a proud man and he didn't like to lose. Two light lateeners against a sturdy frigate with a skilled crew and a doughty captain would be a hard fight. If the guns didn't get them, the weather would.

But Isam was rais, and he owned the *Sea Leopard*. He was not beholden to any investors who might urge caution. If he went down, he would lose both his ship and his life, so there was no reason to be cautious with either. He would win all, or lose all. Imrich didn't like the gamble.

CHAPTER 7 : SARDINIAN VALOR

The two xebecs surged north at ten knots. Spray constantly broke over the bow of the *Sea Leopard* and the rain drenched them. Isam ordered lifelines strung. Those members of the crew who were not immediately necessary huddled in the coach. The doors between the watertight compartments belowdecks were dogged shut and the hatches battened down. More than once the xebecs plowed the sea with their prows and shipped water over their bows. The foaming burden drained swiftly through the numerous grates on deck, into the scuppers beneath the deck, and out the sides in white cascades.

The lookout shouted, "Deck ho! Signal from the *Renegade!*"

"What is it?"

"Green!"

"She's spotted the enemy."

The frigate had wested them while they were on their southern leg. As a consequence, when they found her, they were behind her. Or more precisely, broad on her port quarter. She was a brave sight as she bowled along under doubled-reefed topsails and topgallants. The waves were heaping up three feet high and the watch had to tie themselves to keep themselves in place on the pitching foredeck. Water sluiced constantly along the deck, even to the point of flooding the coach. It was cold, too. The oppressive heat had given away to a raw chill. The corsairs were overheated in their foul weather gear, but if they opened it, the wind sucked all the heat from their bodies.

The frigate swept around to meet them. She was keeping good watch and they did not surprise her. With the wind coming out of the south, she could not drive directly at them, but she braced her yards around as sharp as she could and closed the distance. Murad Rais looked over his rail to check the *Sea Leopard's* position, and Isam pointed. By gestures they agreed to cross her fore and aft.

The *Sea Leopard* altered her course to cross her hawse while the *Renegade* would cross her wake. As they approached, the *Renegade* fired a single shot in challenge. Isam glared at him; it was the bigger ship's prerogative to make the challenge. That made it the frigate's privilege. Or, if disinclined to await the infidel's pleasure, the *Sea Leopard's*.

The frigate hoisted her colors and her bow gun barked defiance. The wind caught the ancient crusader flag and it streamed out: a red cross on a white background, and in each quarter, a black, blindfolded, decapitated

Moor's head. A hiss went through the crew. Isam's temper instantly reared up, and he shouted, *"Allahu Akbar!"*

His crew took up the cry. It rose from hundreds of throats, and the crew of the *Renegade* joined them. *"Allahu Akbar! Allahu Akbar! Allahu Akbar! Allahu Akbar!"*

The wild cry pierced the storm and carried across the sea. The Sardinians raised their own battle cry in response, *"Arborea! Arborea!"*

Isam gave Imrich a puzzled look, "What's 'arborea'?"

Imrich spread his hands in ignorance. "Something to do with trees?"

"That's not very intimidating."

"It doesn't matter. These Sardinians are good fighters."

"True."

The frigate fired her bow guns at them as they swept across, but her broadside she gave to the *Renegade*. She was more afraid for her damaged stern than her still intact bow. The *Sea Leopard* let loose a thundering barrage that smashed her fo'c'sle head. A stay parted and her inner jib went flying. The falcon figurehead was clearly seen as the xebec cut across in front of her. Meanwhile, the *Renegade* swept aft, coming under heavy fire from the lower gundeck as she did so. The upper gun deck could not depress the guns enough to counteract the frigate's heeling; those shots went whistling among the spars and sails of the *Renegade*. Damage was done, but not enough to prevent the *Renegade* from pouring a broadside into the already battered stern. White wood from the repairs gleamed in the rain. The great cabin still sagged; sea repairs could not raise it. All that could be done had been done; the deck was propped with timbers beneath it and new wood filled the shattered stern. The rudder had been repaired by fishing new timber to it, but it was an ugly job. The *Renegade's* nine pound balls broke open some of the repair work.

"Double shot!" Isam roared. The gun crews stuffed more wad and balls into the bronze barrels in response to his order.

The two xebecs ran past their prey, met, and the *Sea Leopard* crossed the *Renegade's* wake. They turned to make another pass. This time the *Sea Leopard* took the stern while the *Renegade* took her bow. They were sailing circles around the less nimble frigate and it exhilarated every red-blooded man of the crews.

The bronze guns roared in unison and every shot found the frigate's stern. New and old wood shattered and debris flew into the sea. For a moment a wave lifted the Sardinian's stern, then she sagged into the trough and water poured through the fractured wood. The *Sea Leopard* bobbed upon the wave as lightly as a cork while the frigate struggled to rise. Isam grinned, but the Sardinian captain shook his fist in defiance. The frigate turned to starboard, which gave her stern more directly to the waves, but eased her heel and brought both gun decks to bear on her tormenter. The

Sardinian fired triple shot. She was determined to pulverize the saucy Salletine.

Screams erupted from the *Sea Leopard's* deck. The bulwark was torn to pieces so that as the ship rolled, one of her bronze guns raced forward and out the side. Half the tackle held, the gun carriage twisted around, then the tackle parted. The gun disappeared below the surface of the sea. Other guns thumped against the side as they ran loose—their crews too shot up to haul the tackle tight.

"Secure those guns!" Isam roared.

The stunned men shook themselves awake and leaped to service the guns, but a good many of them lay bloody on the deck. No one could spare any attention for the wounded; there were too many. They were shoved out of the way and nothing more.

On the quarterdeck, damage was equally great. The mizzen antenna was shattered and the pieces hung from its topping lift and brayles. The bulwark was torn out again, and in the same place that had been repaired earlier. Imrich was sitting on the deck with a twelve inch long splinter protruding from his thigh. His mate knelt by him, drew out the splinter, and used his turban to make a bandage for him. Then he helped the master to his feet. By a miracle, Isam was unwounded.

He ran the *Sea Leopard* out to long range as he tended his wounded ship and crew. Meanwhile the *Renegade* continued the attack, passing the frigate's stern and pummeling it again. The Sardinian vessel was settling by the stern.

"He must strike or sink!" Isam exclaimed.

Aboard the *Renegade,* Murad Rais was swearing and shouting at Isam, although the other couldn't hear him. "God burn your father and grandfather! Coward! Why aren't you supporting me? We have her! God damn it, we must board her before she sinks!"

When the *Renegade* turned to attack again, the *Sea Leopard* came flying in to assist. Isam had needed time to clear his wreckage. Now he brought his less damaged starboard battery into play. "Double shot! Aim for the quarterdeck! Muskets! A reward to the man who brings down that stalwart captain!"

Once again the *Sea Leopard* poured iron and fire into the stern of the Sardinian frigate. His gunners aimed true; they thirsted for revenge. At the same time his marksmen in the mizzen top poured lead onto the quarterdeck. The *Sea Leopard* was too lowslung for Isam to be able to see what was happening on the frigate's high quarterdeck, but what he could see told him that it had been badly shot up. The hated Moor's head flag fluttered down.

A fierce exulting cry went up on both of the xebecs. The smaller, more agile *Renegade* immediately lay alongside and threw her grapples. The waves made it a dangerous business and the two hulls clashed violently as they came together, but the grapples held. The *Sea Leopard* approached the other side and as she did, the Sardinian blew up.

At first there was a strange buckling of the fabric of the Sardinian hull, but that was instantly obliterated in an orange fireball that was all motion and heat. The *Sea Leopard* was less than twenty-five yards away; the intense roar instantly dried the rain on their faces. They were showered with burning debris and leaped to bat out the embers that lodged in their clothes.

"Fire stations!" Isam shouted.

Embers had caught in the debris of the mizzen sail and spars, and no one on the quarterdeck could reach it. The marksmen in the top looked down in horror as they realized they were caught above the fire.

"On deck!" one of them shouted. He climbed around the futtock shrouds, and clinging to the black tarred lines, lashed out with his knife.

Isam dove aside as the halyard parted and the mizzen debris came crashing down. The fire was now on deck where they could fight it. Isam whipped off his djellaba and beat the flames with it. The marksmen came skipping down from the top as fast as they could. Fire buckets were snatched from their habitual place on the forward railing and the brayles were put to duty to haul water. The buckets went over the side and rose to douse the fire.

The immediate danger to the quarterdeck extinguished, Isam surveyed the weather deck. Fiery brands that had fallen to the deck were quenched by the quick acting-crew. The sails were peppered with rips and holes; he had lace for sails.

"Damage report!" he bellowed.

"Fire out, two dead, eleven wounded on the foredeck!"

"Fire out, five dead, twenty-one wounded on the main deck!"

The mizzen chief said, "Fire out, one dead, three wounded on the quarterdeck."

Isam could spare a glance for the *Renegade* at last. She was still afloat, but listing badly to port. Her sails were scorched and shredded, but she had hove to, and her crew was fighting the fire in the collapsed heap of her foresail and antenna.

"Master Imrich, lay us alongside the *Renegade*. We will render aid."

Twenty or so Sardinians were swimming or clinging to debris. They were all that remained of the frigate's crew.

"Pick up survivors," Isam ordered.

Lines were thrown over the side for the able-bodied to pull themselves aboard. The soggy infidels were reluctant to accept the corsairs' help; but it was better to be enslaved than to drown in the cold sea, so they came aboard. The *Sea Leopard* was now close enough to the *Renegade* to shout a conversation through the pouring rain.

Isam leaned over the larboard rail and shouted, "Can we help?"

"Go to Hell!" Murad Rais performed a gesture that demonstrated exactly what sort of punitive sexual act he would like to perform on the object of his fury.

Isam swore in Turkish at him. "Go fuck yourself!"

Murad was as much a Turk as Isam and replied in the same language. "You coward! You didn't back us up!"

"You fool! I was shot to pieces!"

"We could have had her!"

"We would have blown up with her!"

"You held back on purpose!"

"You're a fucking moron!"

"You're a fucking sodomite!"

The conversation degenerated from there.

CHAPTER 8 : THE CAPTIVE

"There's someone you should see, rais," Lieutenant Yafi said. 'Someone,' not 'something.' Isam's ear detected the difference. Giving the Moor a quizzical look, he descended to the main deck. There, among the huddled Sardinian survivors, was a man in a white coat and breeches. The bloodstains on his arms and legs were brilliant against the smoke-stained and water-drenched white. Both arms were shot through and both legs were broken. He was hatless, wigless, balding, and shoeless. He had one red stocking, but the other was gone.

"Who is this?" Isam asked in the lingua franca.

"Matteo Vargiu, captain of His Sardinian Majesty's frigate *Eleanora d'Arborea,*" the man replied in a bass voice clenched by pain.

"You survived?" Isam replied in astonishment.

"I didn't intend to. I expected to die when the magazine blew up, but fate threw me clear and broke both my legs. Why God wishes me to be a slave rather than a martyr, I don't know."

Isam pressed his hand to his sodden turban as he bowed deeply from the waist. "You're a valiant warrior. I salute you, sir. I'm Isam Rais al-Tangueli and this is the *Sea Leopard*. You'll be well treated while you're aboard."

Vargiu's Roman nose flared and his lips turned down in disdain. "The compliments of a heretic mean nothing to me."

Isam's temper—which had already been tried several times that day—flared again. "Maybe you ought to thank God for putting you in my hands. You could have done worse. If you persist in insulting the man who has saved you from the sea, God will smite you for ingratitude."

Vargiu's mouth turned down even further. "You know nothing of God."

Isam raised his hand and Vargiu's eye darted to it. Isam restrained his temper with an effort. "I will not strike a wounded man." Rising, he said, "Take him to my cabin. After our men are tended, the surgeon can tend to him. Pass the word for my servant. Tell him to bring up my furniture and to make Captain Vargiu comfortable. Kateb, when you're done on deck, will you personally watch over our guest?"

Kateb gave him a look that said he'd rather stick toothpicks under his fingernails, but replied, "If you command it, rais."

Lowering his voice, Isam said in Arabic, "Judging by what we've seen so far, he'll get up to mischief even with two broken legs. He's not going to surrender quietly."

Kateb grunted noncommittally. "When I'm through with my work, I'll attend him." He turned away and assigned a pair of marines to go stand watch in the great cabin.

The two damaged xebecs stayed together through the storm. Neither liked it, and each was inclined to leave the other to his just deserts, but as damaged as they were, they might need each other. Had the weather been fair, they would have taken their chances and gone their separate ways. Moreover, there was something eating at Murad: Isam had picked up all the Sardinians. Small though the prize was, he felt entitled to half. Murad's resentment simmered through the storm.

It was not until the evening meal that Isam went below to his cabin. He removed the tarpaulin djellaba and hung it on a hook to add its drips to the runnel of water running across the deck. The gun ports were dogged shut, but the rest of the cabin was not so tight. A stream of water ran through the cat flap in the cabin door. A few drips came through the deckhead, and another stream ran down the wall where damage to the quarterdeck was letting water leak into the great cabin. The cat had taken refuge on the divan and hooked his claws into the cushions to resist the rolling of the vessel. Kateb sat next to the cat with a stoic face. One hand petted the animal's grey head.

Captain Vargiu had refused to lie on the Muslim captain's bed or divan, so a canvas cradle had been hung for him. The surgeon had come to attend him, and he was now splinted and bandaged into near immobility in the swaying hammock.

Kateb sat up, disturbing the cat, and his expression lightened. Isam smiled, and glancing over at the hammock to determine the prisoner was asleep, leaned forward and kissed him. "Thank you."

"The doctor gave him laudanum. He'll sleep a while. Forever would be good, if you ask me."

"He'll bring a good ransom," Isam replied. He scooped the cat into his arms and settled cross-legged on the divan. He flexed his back to remain upright through the rolling. He murmured Turkish to the small beast, *"Ah, Gümüsh, zavallı kedicik."* His voice was a baritone purr. Gümüsh purred back as Isam stroked his head and back. It seemed master and cat spoke the same language. The cat soothed Isam who was tired after a long day with little profit to show for it.

"I don't care. Put him in the hold with the rest of the prisoners."

"I can't put a wounded man in the hold."

"I don't see why not. He called me a 'black devil' and made the sign against the evil eye at me."

Isam sighed, rubbed the cat under his furry chin, and asked the animal, "Why are infidels so obnoxious? All you do is walk on me with cold wet feet in the middle of the night."

43

Such questions were irrelevant to a cat. Gümüsh ignored him and turned his head to transfer the rubbing to the back of his ear.

Only then did Isam deign to examine the prisoner. Still holding the cat in his arms, he rose to stand over the hammock. He was cold, wet, tired, hungry, and out of patience. Vargiu was sound asleep and wrapped in warm blankets. As much as he respected the Sardinian's skill and courage, he was still the man who had shot up Isam's brand new xebec. Even observing the man asleep made his temper twitch.

When he stopped petting the cat and scowled, Gümüsh put a paw on his beard to reprimand him for his dereliction of duty. Isam quirked a smile, removed the paw, and resumed petting the animal. The fluffy purring soothed him. He had no doubt the surgeon had done as well as could be done and didn't feel too solicitous about his prisoner's welfare. Isam owed him humane treatment and nothing further. He braced his legs as the vessel rolled through a particularly strong wave. The cat braced too, prepared to leap out of the corsair's arms should he topple. Both corsair and cat remained upright. When it was safe to move again, Isam crossed and resettled on the divan next to Kateb.

"Help me with my boots, please. I don't want to put the cat down."

Kateb cocked an eye at the corsair and thought about it for a moment. "Do you want me to call your servant?" he asked politely.

"I'm weary, Kateb. I'd rather be alone with you. Alone as we can be."

Kateb grunted and slid off the divan to kneel on the floor at the captain's feet. Breathing deeply, he took one of the tall black boots in his hands and pulled firmly. The wet boot and sock stuck. The agha's muscles flexed, and the boot came off with a sudden pop. The wet sock came halfway off the captain's foot. With studied motions, the black man pulled off the other boot and both socks.

Isam sighed in relief. "Thank you." He leaned back against the sloping wall of the transom.

Kateb was a soldier who had been a slave. He'd smelled things far worse than Isam's feet. In fact, Isam's feet didn't smell bad at all. The smell of saltwater, sweat and gunsmoke clung to the corsair, but it was an appealingly masculine scent. It was the menial nature of the task that bothered him.

"For you only," he said. He went to the round house, unhooked the basin from the wall, poured water into it from the ewer hanging on its rope, and brought the basin to bathe the corsair's feet.

Isam tensed and peered over the cat to see what the agha was doing. Then he put the cat down, propped some pillows behind his back, and lay back. The tension of the last four and twenty hours drained out of him. Gümüsh curled up next to his thigh where it was warm.

When a knock sounded on the cabin door, Kateb swiftly picked up the basin and carried it to the roundhouse to dump it. Isam waited until the black man was out of sight before calling, "Enter!"

Abdul brought a four-legged tray and put it on the divan next to the captain. With water sloshing across the floor, rugs had not been put down. Abdul tried to step over the runnels to keep his feet dry, but to no avail. Kateb stepped out of the roundhouse with a nonchalant air as if he had been making use of the necessary. He didn't want the actual servant to know he had done a servant's duty.

"Come eat," Isam said to him.

The galley fires could not be lit in bad weather, so the meal consisted of black bread, slices of hard yellow cheese, raisins, and almonds. His drink was water with a dose of vinegar. Kateb sat down on the opposite side of the tray. They flexed as the ship rolled, automatically adjusting their position to the vessel's perambulations. The water sloshed in their tankards, but the rest of the food obediently stayed put. They ate without conversation. The gloom steadily increased. The single lit lamp cast writhing shadows as it swayed.

Abdul returned and put a bowl of raw fish down on the floor for the cat. The big grey hesitated at the edge of the divan even as his whiskers twitched. The leaks were still leaking, and the water on the floor was still swishing. He gave the steward an expectant look.

Isam noticed. "He doesn't want to jump on the wet floor. Here, give it to me."

The steward passed him the dish. Isam put it beside his left thigh. Much happier with that position, the big grey hunkered down next to the corsair and began eating. Isam stroked his back, and the cat grumbled a protest at having his dinner interrupted. Isam smiled in the fading light and kept rubbing the cat's ears and head. The cat shook his head violently and twitched his ears. Isam shook off the fur clinging to his hand and continued eating.

"Lucky kitty. Your meal isn't upset by the weather."

Kateb didn't speak Turkish. "What does 'Gümüsh' mean?"

"Silver."

"A fitting name," Kateb replied.

"So in spite of everything, I have silver in my cabin," Isam jested.

Kateb cracked a smile and the tension went out of him. He was jealous of his freedom, but he liked the corsair. "Is the damage to the ship very great?"

Isam grimaced and his eyes darkened. "Bad enough. I'm going back to Zokhara to refit. I caught a Tartar by the tail this day."

"By the tail, ha! You certainly did," Kateb said.

Isam gave him a lopsided smile. "I spanked his posterior, that's for sure. I never thought he would blow himself up." They both turned to look at the sleeping man in the hammock.

Kateb lowered his voice. "What will you do with him?"

"Hold him for ransom. Somebody will want him back. Assuming he lives."

"I don't fancy sharing a cabin with him."

Isam sighed. "You have a cabin of your own. We could sleep there."

"You do him too much honor."

Isam didn't answer. They ate in silence. When he was finished, Kateb wiped his hands with the napkin and said, "I'm going to bed." He rose and left the cabin.

CHAPTER 9 : THE BUTCHER'S DAUGHTER

Zokhara was the crown jewel of the Sallee Republic and Isam was never gladder to see it. A fortress occupied the island just outside the harbor and was even now undergoing expansion to catch up to improvements in European armaments. The purple and white flag of the Sallee Republic flew bravely from the flagstaff, and he ordered the requisite number of guns to fire off a salute. The fortress replied, saluting the red and gold Man in the Crescent Moon that fluttered from the xebec's stern.

Coming from the city of Tanguel on the Atlantic coast, Isam could never quite embrace the capital, in spite of the city's temptations. With a population two hundred thousand, its shipyards, arsenals, fortresses, mosques, fountains, inns, cabarets, and markets were equipped with all the goods that could be brought from the land and sea, whether it be ivory, black slaves, gold, and ostrich feathers from the interior of Africa, or coffee, spices, jewels, rugs, and porcelain from the Middle East, or manufactured goods, white slaves, and cash from the Europeans. Zokhara had everything. A man only had to be bold enough to seize it and strong enough to fight off his rivals.

He hated it. The fleshpots of Zokhara, male or female, did not interest him because he didn't want to catch the clap. The politics were savage with brawls in the street, poison in the coffee, daggers in the palace, and intrigue in every alley. He was a sailor and a soldier. He hated how he had to haggle for everything and always keep a sharp eye out lest he be cheated. Stubbornly, he flew the same flag his father had flown, and they all called him 'al-Tangueli', the "man from Tanguel."

On top of everything else, his last supplier had cheated him by putting rocks in the bottom of the barrels of mutton. As a consequence, he had only half the meat he'd paid for. He had petitioned the caid of Zokhara to investigate, but that had required a bribe. It would be more expensive to sue than accept being cheated, but he was positive that if he let himself be cheated like this, the deceit would never end. Everyone would cheat him if they saw they could get away with it. Such were the thoughts occupying his mind as he made his way through the dusty streets without really seeing where he was going.

Meanwhile, Jamila bint Nakih was supposed to be sweeping the street in front of her father's butcher shop, but she had to pause to let a herd of sheep pass. She glanced over the men and a couple of women with burdens on their heads following behind the sheep. The scene was nothing new;

animals were slaughtered every day in the meat market. What was not normal was that a man so much taller and more handsome than all the others should be walking down the street with them. The stranger was not an ordinary person, not with his swaggering walk, striped pantaloons with muscular thighs, a short navy blue jacket, and a white turban around a black fez. A small gold hoop in each ear added color to his well-tanned countenance. The beard was short, black, straight, and neat, but the nose had a hump at the bridge. He wore his scimitar on his right hip. That by itself made him stick in her memory—there weren't many left-handed swordsmen in Zokhara. Not that Jamila could be sure of that, but she had never seen a left-handed swordsman before, so they must be rare. One look at him and she fell in love with all the passion of her seventeen-year-old heart.

As the tall stranger came abreast of her, she dared to step forward and ask, "Pardon me, effendi, are you looking for a butcher shop? I know a good one."

Had she been a lady of rank, she never would have been so brazen as to speak to a strange man, but she was a butcher's daughter. Like other women of the working class, she didn't wear a veil as she went about her chores. As for the cloth over her hair—she had such a vast amount of auburn curls they could not be contained. She braided her hair into a plait as thick as a man's wrist, but even then it hung down to her thighs. She wore an embroidered red vest that fit snug under her breasts in the Moorish fashion, but the white tunic under it showed no cleavage.

Isam didn't realize at first that she was speaking to him. The female half of the human race held no interest for him and were never employed in any profession for which he had use; they were effectively invisible to him. It took a moment for the message to register. He paused.

"Yes, I am. I suppose you represent the finest butcher shop in all of Zokhara." His voice was skeptical, but there was a touch of humor.

Jamila was tall for a girl, but she was a head shorter than the corsair. She had to tilt her head back to look up at him. "I don't know if it's the best butcher shop in all of Zokhara, but it's an honest one."

Isam actually looked at her then. "Very well. I'll try it. Who runs this shop?"

"My father, Nakih bin Nasir. My brothers, Shakil and Kasim, work with him."

Isam nodded. "Please let them know that Isam Rais al-Tangueli is here to talk business with them."

Jamila almost swooned. "Isam Rais al-Tangueli," she replied, committing the name to memory. "Are you a corsair?"

A ghost of a smile hovered on his lips as he noticed her awestruck expression. "I am." She was only a girl, but she was giving him the respect he felt he deserved.

Jamila's infatuation became adoration. That was more than her maiden heart could withstand, so she ran into the interior of the shop shouting, "Baba! Baba! A man is here to see you! A corsair captain!"

Isam stepped through the open front of the shop. Spicy merguez sausages hung in strands while the counter displayed various cuts of mutton, lamb, and goat. The hard packed dirt floor was strewn with clean straw. The meat smelled fresh.

In a minute a short man with a broad belly came out from the back room. A white cloth cap on his head barely contained the mop of short black and grey curls. Nakih bin Nasir was not a tall man, but he was a strong one. His shoulders and arms were burly, and his legs were thick enough to hold up the weight of his belly. In spite of his bloodstained leather apron, he was a jovial man.

"Peace be upon you, rais, and good fortune to your ship!" He had a booming bass voice.

"And also upon you, effendi. I need meat to supply my ship. The last rascal cheated me with rocks. I pay a fair price and I pay on time."

The butcher broke out in smiles. "We can supply you, noble captain. We are honest men and we give good measure for our fee. I am sorry to hear you were cheated; who was the rogue that did it? May Allah roast his father."

"It doesn't matter. Can you supply me with three tons of meat, cut into pieces of five to ten pounds each, well salted in good barrels that won't leak?"

"I can! What kind of meat?"

"Any kind. I need it in less than two weeks. I need to make repairs, then will set sail in a fortnight. I'll give you a bonus if the meat is delivered on time."

"I can get my hands on plenty of mutton, if that will suit you."

"It will. How much?"

They settled down to haggle the price. Nakih knew his business, but he was not inclined to gouge. He wanted a fair profit and was satisfied with that. By going straight to the butcher and skipping his agent, Isam was making more work for himself but paying a cheaper price for the meat. They were both satisfied with the bargain.

All through it, Jamila hid in the back room and peeped at the captain. Meanwhile Shakil and Kasim were cutting meat.

"Jamila, what are you doing?" the older of her two brothers called to her.

Guiltily, she left off spying and came up to Shakil. "Isam Rais is buying three tons of meat from Baba!" she told them excitedly.

The two men looked at her in astonishment. "Three tons! He must be equipping his ship," Shakil said. He was of average height, slim, with a fine fringe of beard along his jaw. His hands were delicate when they held still, but they wielded his butcher's knife adeptly. He had short brown hair and hazel eyes.

By contrast, Kasim was taller than average, not fat, but muscular and fleshy. He had close curls like his father. In fact he looked so much like Nakih that there was no denying the relationship. He scowled at his little sister. "You shouldn't be spying on them. It's rude."

Jamila was abashed. "They didn't see me."

Shakil smiled at that. "So. You defend yourself by saying that you're a successful spy!"

Jamila blushed and gave him a pleading look that involved batting her eyes, a sheepish smile, and a shoulder shrug. "But he's so handsome! There's nothing wrong with looking, is there? Besides, he's a dashing corsair and will be good for the business."

Shakil said gently, "You shouldn't stare at men. It's immodest. He'll think you weren't raised properly."

She grew glum. "I don't think he even noticed me." Then she tackled Shakil's arm. "Baba should invite him to dinner. We want to cultivate a relationship with him. Maybe he will bring other ships to us, if he is pleased with us."

Kasim's ears pricked up. "She's right. We could use the business."

Shakil was silent for a moment. His sister's real motive was obvious to him, but there was sense in the suggestion all the same. "All right. I'll suggest it to father. Maybe he'll be able to hire another apprentice to help us." He wiped his hands and went to the front of the shop.

Jamila could barely contain herself. Her brothers were going along with her plan! She clasped her hands gleefully, then prayed, "Please, Allah, let him come to dinner so I can see him again!"

In the front room, Shakil spoke softly in his father's ear. Nakih cocked his head to listen, then beamed. "By Allah, you're right! That is an excellent suggestion." Turning to Isam, he boomed, "My son suggests we invite you to dinner. Come, you must dine with us. We'll feed you the same meat we are providing to your ship, so you can see the quality for yourself."

Isam rarely received social invitations. He demurred, "I don't want to impose."

"You're not imposing! I insist. We will be happy to have such a distinguished guest."

Isam Rais was a man of the world; he understood why they would be happy to entertain him. He gave a lopsided smile, then his eyes roamed over the butcher's son. He liked what he saw, so he let himself be persuaded. "All right then. When shall I come?"

The matter was settled and he left. Of course Jamila the spy knew all the details. As soon as Isam was out the door, Jamila was besieging her father.

"May I have some money to make a new outfit? I want to look my best when he comes to dinner!"

Nakih snorted. "You? You're not coming to dinner. This is men's business!"

Jamila pleaded, "I want to marry him. He's a good catch. I'm seventeen and I don't want to be an old maid!"

Nakih laughed heartily at that. "You're a crone! I don't know who I'll find to marry an old spinster like you!" Then he sobered. "Didn't you tell me just last month that you were too young to get married? And now you're telling me who your husband should be?" He shook his head, but his voice was affectionate.

"He's the one, Baba. I know he is. I can feel it." She pressed her hands dramatically to her heart. "Please ask him for me? Please?"

Nakih rubbed his chin and thought about it. "A corsair captain would be a good catch. Still, I don't want to marry my only daughter off to a man unless I'm certain he'll treat her decently. And you, you're a silly girl! It's asking a lot for a grown man to put up with your whims! If only your mother were still alive, she would have raised you right. Widower that I am, I did the best I could. All right, I'll ask about him. If he has a good character, I'll make the proposal. But you must be prepared for him to say no. We are far beneath him and you're too skinny. If you were plump, we'd have a better chance. You must eat sweets so you get nice and curvy. If you do that, we'll have no problem finding you a husband."

Jamila's face underwent several changes of color and expression as she listened to the paternal harangue. Elation, frustration, hope, despair, and stubbornness all danced across her face. "I don't want to get fat! But I promise I won't climb trees anymore and I will work on my trousseau." That seemed a fair compromise to her.

Nakih wrapped his arms around her and hugged her close. She was an inch taller than him, but she was still his little girl. "My baby. You're going to be married." Not necessarily to the corsair, he added silently. "Now if only we could find a wife for Shakil."

Shakil had heard that before and said nothing in response.

Jamila smiled very sweetly at her father. "Then you'll give me the money for the new outfit?"

Nakih smiled crookedly at her. "My little shyster. Yes, you may have the money. Ask Shadha to help you. She'll know the proper thing for a girl about to be married."

Jamila kissed her father on the forehead, then scampered off to find her sister-in-law. "Thank you, Baba!" trailed after her.

Shakil asked, "Do you really think the corsair will consider it?"

Nakih shrugged fatalistically. "All I can do is ask. Perhaps one of his lieutenants needs a wife. If we can get the corsairs' business, we'll never want for money."

Shakil's eyes darkened. "I want her to be happy. Or, if not happy, at least safe. If he's a drinker or gambler, promise me you won't ask."

Nakih patted his son's shoulder. "I promise." A heavy silence fell. "How are Kasim and Shadha getting along?"

"All right for the present. She's a good woman. Kasim should treat her better. He doesn't know how lucky he is."

"Let's invite Shadha and the children to spend a few days at the farm with Jamila. They can sew and gossip. It's time for her to learn things that a married woman ought know. Shadha will teach her. I'm sorry I can't give you or Kasim any time off, though. I need your help. Three tons of meat!"

"It's all right, Father. We are butchers. It's an honest trade." Shakil bent and kissed his father's brow.

"I wish I could afford to send you to the mosque school. You could be a great scholar! But I need you here."

"I know, Father. I'll keep reading on my own."

"All right then. We have a lot of meat to cut and salt. We'd better get busy."

CHAPTER 10 : THE MARRIAGE PROPOSAL

Nakih bin Nasir lived in a house over his shop. To reach it, Isam Rais had to let himself into a gated alley that ran between the butcher shop and the next business. Curious about the place—he was not usually on personal terms with tradesmen—he followed it to the back. There was an open courtyard shared with other butcher shops. Piles of manure told him that this was where the livestock were held before they were slaughtered. He supposed slaves must shovel it out periodically. He held his nose and returned to the steps that led up to the second floor. On the upper level, he was surprised to find a pleasant gallery: a wooden deck connected one side of the alley to the other. No windows from either side looked into it, and the front, rear, and roof of the space were covered in lattice. Planters filled with mint and other herbs, vegetables, and strawberries lined the space. A flowering vine climbed the fretwork to add its scent to the pungent aroma. A barrel in the rear corner caught rainwater on the rare occasions when it rained.

A large wicker cage held a pair of ring-necked parakeets. Isam paused in front of the cage and poked his finger between the wicker bars. One of the birds promptly bit him while the other said, "Peace be upon you!"

He jerked his finger back and shook his hand. The bite really smarted; the bird had cracked his nail and bruised his finger. "Let that be a lesson to me. Even a birdcage is a palace to the one who lives there, and his guards will defend it."

Unbeknownst to him, the entire encounter had been witnessed. Jamila bint Nakih was peeping through the door's curtain in a state of constant excitement in anticipation of the corsair's arrival. She wanted to run to him and doctor his finger, but that would have been highly improper. Instead she ran deeper into the house and rousted out her father.

Nakih came to the door and drew the curtain aside. "Peace be upon you," the older man greeted him.

Isam replied, "Peace be upon you and all within this house."

Nakih smiled and held the curtain aside. "Please come in."

Isam ducked under the curtain and stepped into the dim interior. The front part of the reception room was lit by light streaming in from a *mashrabiyah*, an oriel window completely encased by carved wooden fretwork. Potted plants and clay basins filled with water occupied the window sill.

Two divans with bases made of dark-colored wood faced each other on either side of the window. They differed from one another in design and color and so did the coffee table between them. The formal part of the reception room was not elevated, but it did have a kilim rug beneath the furniture to separate it from the rest of the room. The rug was done in shades of brown, brick, and cream. The upholstery was brick red with earth-colored pillows in various sizes and trim. The result was darkly masculine but faded by age.

Isam toed off his boots and stepped into the slippers placed at the edge of the rug for his convenience. They were brand-new and a little loose; Nakih had taken his best guess at what size such a tall man would need. The two settled cross-legged on the divans facing each other and Shakil glided forward. He was dressed all in white, like a scholar or sage, with a white cotton cap on his head. He bowed deeply as he knelt and set the wooden tray on the table and transferred a copper tea pot shaped like a camel to the table.

"You remember Shakil, my oldest son. He's a pious and learned man. He knows the Qu'ran by heart. It is his misfortune to be the son of a butcher. If he wasn't, he'd be a teacher in a mosque." His voice was fond. Shakil kept his eyes modestly down and continued setting up the tea.

"Peace be upon you," Isam replied in his rolling baritone. He let his eyes linger on the younger man.

Nakih continued, "Shakil, this is Isam Rais al-Tangueli, captain of the *Sea Leopard*. It is for him that we are gathering so much mutton. He and Murad Rais sank the *Eleanora d'Arborea*." Unlike Isam, Nakih was a son of Zokhara and knew who to ask to get the gossip.

"Peace be upon you. I hope Allah grants you all success," Shakil replied with a graceful bow.

"I remember you. We met briefly at the shop," Isam replied with a smile.

Shakil was in his early twenties, and he must resemble his mother because he didn't look like Nakih. His nose was long and straight, but his mouth was firm with a sensuous curve to the upper lip. He was the sort of man who could be called 'beautiful' rather than 'handsome' without diminishing his masculinity. A slight fringe of beard ran along his jaw, perhaps in an attempt to snuff out the prettiness, but it did not reduce his attractiveness to a man like Isam Rais.

"I'm gratified," Shakil replied.

Isam's baritone was warm when he replied, "On the contrary, it is I who am fortunate to make your acquaintance."

Shakil felt the weight of the corsair's eyes and busied himself in pouring tea into aqua-colored ceramic cups.

Isam realized he had been too frank in his gaze and said, "I'm a sailor. I'm used to the blunt manners of seamen. I hope I haven't offended you."

"No, of course not," Shakil replied, but there was a pink tinge on his cheeks. He wouldn't meet Isam's eyes.

Nakih noticed the exchange, but he kept his thoughts to himself. He was all joviality when he picked up his tea cup and said, "Let us hope this is the beginning of a long and prosperous relationship."

Isam took up his cup, but his eyes strayed back to Shakil as he said, "I hope so too."

Shakil froze for as long as those coffee-colored eyes were upon him. When Isam bent his head to drink the tea, he felt as if he has been freed from manacles. He rose smoothly to his feet. "I'll fetch the fruit." He disappeared quickly through the door to the back of the apartment.

Isam watched him go, entranced by the graceful flowing of the long robe around his lithe form.

"He's a good boy, pious and hard-working. He hasn't taken a wife yet. He says we can't afford the burden. Perhaps he's right, but that didn't stop Kasim. He's married and has a child already. I'm a widower, so it's good to have a woman in the house. Although Jamila is now of age, so all's well."

"You have a happy household. Two fine sons and a grandchild already. You're a fortunate man. I'm an orphan. I was raised by my uncle. He had nineteen daughters and not a single son."

Nakih lit up. "So it's true! I've heard stories about Halim of the Many Daughters, but I thought it must be a fairytale."

Isam smiled. "Some of the stories are true, but not all of them."

"Did you marry one of your cousins? I would think your uncle would be desperate for an heir."

Unaware of the butcher's motive, the corsair captain shook his head. "It wasn't easy growing up in a house with so many women. I had to sleep on the divan in the reception room. All the other rooms were stuffed with girls and their frippery. I ran away to sea and have been avoiding women ever since."

Nakih inspected Isam. For all his amiability, he was a good judge of character. The man he saw before him was about thirty, tall and lanky with the poise of a man accustomed to an athletic and successful life. Tonight he had adopted a long blue coat with short sleeves. The long gauzy sleeves of the shirt underneath barely concealed the muscular well-tanned arms within. The white pantaloons were of equally light linen. They were visible from the knee down. A black fez and white turban topped his short hair and his beard was as black as a moonless night. He had dressed as lightly as formality would permit, and wisely so. The apartment was stuffy in spite of the fretwork window.

"You should get married. You're a successful man and a handsome one, too. It's time you took a wife. Children are a blessing in your old age. They can carry on your work and allow you to retire. You can dandle your grandchildren on your knee and live a life of comfort."

Nakih's home and family gave every indication of fulfilling that dream for him, even if he still had to work.

"I expect to die on the deck of my ship, like my father before me," Isam replied shortly. The topic was not a welcome one with him.

"You can't sail forever. Where do you stay while the ship is in harbor?"

"At the ship, unless she goes into dry dock. Then I get a room at an inn."

"Wouldn't you rather come home to a comfortable house with a wife and servants to attend you?"

Isam fixed Nakih with a glare like the muzzle of one of his bronze cannons. "No."

Shakil returned with a tray. He knelt and put the platter of fruits on the table between them with a dish of pistachios to the side. He refilled their cups of tea. Isam tried to keep his attention on his host and pretend he didn't notice. The younger man hovered in his peripheral vision like a cupbearer attending the heroes in Paradise.

Nakih stared at his guest in astonishment. "Why not?" He was not normally so blunt, but Isam's manner seemed to require it.

A vein in Isam's temple twitched. This was one of the moments he hated, moments that happened oftener than he liked when he was ashore. At sea, he was the master of his vessel and no man dared question or rebuke him. "Because I prefer the company of men in all things."

Nakih pretended bewilderment. "But of course. We all do."

"You don't understand me. When I say I prefer the company of men in all things, that includes my bed." His jaw set as he stared down their reactions.

Shakil was shocked and it showed. "You don't mean . . ." He couldn't say the word.

Isam turned a hard gaze on him. "Sodomy. Buggery. Pederasty. Whatever word you want to give it. I would rather lie with a man than a woman. I have a man waiting for me in my cabin right now."

Whatever Nakih and Shakil thought was unknown because a female shriek erupted from the kitchen. Jamila had been spying. A sudden thunder of feet on stairs told of her flight into the upper reaches of the house. The disconsolate sobs of a heartbroken seventeen year old girl drifted down from above.

"You've upset my sister. You shouldn't say such things," Shakil rebuked him. He rose and stalked to the stairs. A minute later the sobs were interrupted. A low murmur of voices ensued, punctuated by occasional wails from Jamila.

Nakih picked up his tea. "You must forgive them. They're young and not so worldly."

Isam was astounded. "Why would the sins of a man she doesn't even know upset her?"

Nakih gave him a crooked smile. "Isn't it obvious? She's in love with you. She asked me to arrange the marriage."

Isam nearly fell over. His eyes popped out of his head and his jaw hung slack. His astonishment made Nakih laugh.

"Marriage. You've heard of it, I'm sure. The delight of women, the source of children, the fountain of happiness."

Isam found his voice. "I don't want children."

"Don't you want a son to follow you to sea and inherit your ship?"

For a moment Isam flashed back to his childhood. Hamet Rais Fawad had died with his guts beside him on the deck. The boy Isam had been twelve; his father had been forty-three. Nakih had already lived longer than Captain Hamet. Nakih had three handsome, healthy, intelligent children, and a grandchild who must be beautiful because all grandchildren were. Hamet had left behind an orphan boy and little more.

Isam had loved his father and thought him the greatest corsair in the world. Hamet had loved him too. He had taken his son to sea at the age of seven when his mother had died. Always Isam remembered with pleasure his father teaching him to tie knots, to identify the birds of the sea, to swim, and to read and to write. He remembered how sometimes his father would tuck him into his hammock, wrap his arm around him, and sing him a song of the sea.

Nakih's questions made him wonder: did his father enjoy these things as much as his son? Looking across at Nakih, then around the modest but comfortable home, he thought he might have. Not until now had he attempted to put himself in his father's shoes and see himself as his father had seen him. His father had loved him. Of that he was sure. If Isam had a son, would he love him? He didn't know.

"Do you enjoy your family?" the corsair asked the butcher.

Nakih's eyes crinkled up at the corner. "By Allah, yes! Even when they drive me to distraction!"

"I have never considered an heir," Isam replied. It put him in a brown mood to think of it. He picked up a candied orange slice and put it in his mouth. A suspicion grew in him. "Is that why you invited me to dinner? To propose marriage?"

Nakih shook his head. "Not yet. I intended to talk business while I learned what kind of man you are. I want my daughter to be happy." The flatness with which he spoke suggested that he did not think Isam qualified on that account.

"Then let us stick to business. My current agent is angry that I've gone around him in the matter of the meat. We've argued, and I've given him an ultimatum. He is to deliver me proper quantity and quality of couscous and other foodstuffs to prove himself, otherwise I will dump him and choose another agent."

Nakih's eyes lit up. "I see. I believe you would find Shakil to be the man of probity you require. He handles purchases for the shop. He goes around to the farms to buy up sheep and lambs and whatever else we need. He's honest and accurate. If you left a thousand sequins and your virgin sister with him and came back ten years later, you would find them both still intact!"

"I haven't any use for sisters, virgin or otherwise, but an honest bookkeeper is a man I could love." He glanced at the stairs, but Shakil had not returned.

"I'll see what's keeping dinner," Nakih said. He rose and disappeared for a few minutes. When he returned, Shakil accompanied him with a platter of food. They settled down to eat. There was no more talk of business; that would have been impolite. They drank sweet black coffee and spoke of poetry and pomegranates and other pleasant things. Everyone except Jamila was pleased with how the dinner turned out.

CHAPTER 11 : CAPTAIN'S QUARREL

Kateb and a bodyguard accompanied Isam to the old bathhouse that was now a prison. The stucco on the bagnio's outside was cracked and had fallen away from the brick in places. Weeds grew around it and vines climbed on a surface whose whitewash had long ago washed away, leaving a dull tan color. Inside it was cool and dim. Several armed guards stood or sat idly in the lobby. At the counter where guests had once paid their fee for the bath, Isam stopped to check in with the sergeant of the guard.

The sergeant was dressed in the white uniform of the army. He wore yellow boots and had a white turban wrapped around a red fez. He recognized Isam, but Kateb was unknown to him.

"Peace be upon you, rais," he greeted the corsair in bored Arabic.

"And also upon you," Isam replied perfunctorily.

"Put your basket on the counter," the guard told Kateb. Kateb lifted it up. Inside were cabbages, onions, and turnips, along with two bottles of olive oil.

The guard removed the olive oil from the basket. "No glass to the prisoners." He put the oil behind the desk.

"Will you give it back to us when we leave?" Kateb asked suspiciously.

The sergeant stared him down with dark and cynical eyes. "No. You were caught red-handed attempting to smuggle contraband. You're lucky I'm not throwing you in prison with the rest of them."

"I'm not smuggling!" Kateb retorted. He would have said more, but Isam put a hand on his arm.

The corsair said, "These are for my captives. If I wish to allow them a little olive oil, what does it matter to you?"

"They might use the broken bottles as weapons, that's what it matters," the sergeant replied. Isam was a captain and a corsair, but that was nothing to him. He was a soldier and answered to different masters.

"When I was a soldier-slave, we were allowed to have olive oil," Kateb replied. His shoulders flexed.

"If you continue to annoy me, I'll turn you over for punishment. You're defying the law." The sergeant's eyes glittered dangerously.

Isam pulled Kateb's arm. "Leave the olive oil. They'll do without."

The iron gate creaked open, and the three men stepped through. Kateb clutched the handle of the basket and flinched when the iron gate slammed shut behind them. The guard who was their escort locked the gate behind them before opening to the gate to the interior. Once again they stepped forward, and another iron grille slammed behind them. Having passed through the doubled doors, they were now in the first room of what had been the bath house. The privacy of the place had once been protected by a screen before the door, but that had been torn down to let the guards look into the room. The tile was cracked and had been badly patched with mismatched tile that had in its turn been broken. When it had been a bath, it had been a handsome place. Neglect and the rage of its captives had shattered it.

"I don't see our captives," he said. He had never been in the bagnio before.

Isam explained, "These slaves are owned by the government. The ones you see here are too feeble or ill to work right now. The rest of the gang is out working on road repair or some other service."

He led Kateb and the guard deeper into the bagnio. Around the sides were basins, but the spigots had been broken off and nothing remained but holes where no water flowed. In the center of the room was the remnant of a stove that had heated the room. It was covered in white and turquoise tile, much chipped, and the top broken in a futile escape attempt. The stove led nowhere. Above that, a piece of the dome had fallen years ago and left behind a large, jagged opening too high up to reach. Today the hole let in sun and air and made the room below fresher than the others, but when it rained, or a sandstorm blew, or the winter came, the room below was miserable.

The recently captured Sardinians were huddled on the shady side of the room along with other recent captures. They were still fleshy, but the way in which their eyes darted to the basket told their hunger. Some of them got to their feet and advanced, but the guard with the cudgel swatted the nearest and sent him reeling.

"Captain Vargiu?" Isam asked.

The Sardinians pushed away the other captives and came forward. "He's over here." They gave Isam resentful glares.

Isam walked forward and Kateb followed reluctantly. He scowled fiercely and the hovering captives retreated.

Vargiu was lying on the floor. His men had contributed some of their clothes to make a humble bed for him on top of the bit of straw that was supplied for sleeping. He was pale and haggard; infection had set in. Vargiu raised a hand to shade his eyes. "You," he said to Isam.

The captain took the basket from Kateb and knelt on one knee to show the man what was in it. The Sardinians leaned in to look. The vegetables would not go far in serving twenty men, but they were a welcome supplement to their bread and vinegar.

Vargiu gave Isam a dark look. "We need more to eat than this."

Isam shrugged. "That's up to your consul to arrange. It's a prison. We provide enough food to keep body and soul together. There's no reason to provide more. Once you're sold, your masters will feed you. Until then, you're the consul's responsibility."

A voice in the next room boomed out, "Blerim Shala! Where's Blerim Shala?"

Isam stiffened. He knew that voice.

A man in Albanian garb recoiled when he heard the name, then stepped forward. He squared his shoulders and stiffened his spine. He was a handsome man in white pantaloons and a red velvet jacket heavily embroidered in thread of gold. A red and gold scarf wrapped around his head in the manner of a turban. The tail hung over his shoulder. Although he was dirty, the quality of his clothing was much better than the other captives.

A moment later Murad Rais came striding into the room accompanied by several bodyguards. He stopped when he saw the man. "You've been ransomed. Five thousand sequins," he informed the man.

Shala's face lit up. "And my companions?" They spoke the lingua franca of the Mediterranean.

"Not yet. They'll be sold in the market." Murad pointed to the door.

The Albanians embraced the young lord and spoke in their own language. They kissed him on the cheeks and he patted them on the back and spoke earnestly to them. Shala was apparently reassuring them that he would not forget them because they all nodded and looked hopeful.

"Very touching. Now move." Murad jerked his thumb to the door and two of his guards took hold of Shala's arms and pulled him away from his companions. The Albanians watched him go with expressions of mixed grief and happiness. They were glad that one of them was getting ransomed and it gave them all hope, but all the same, he was a chieftain and had rich relatives. The rest of them did not.

Isam and Kateb watched the little vignette unfold without comment. It heartened the Sardinians; maybe their ransom would come soon! They kissed their thumbs and sent their prayers towards the ransomed captive, as if he could carry them to someone who would answer.

Murad had been too busy with his own business to notice the others, but as he turned around to leave, he stopped abruptly. "Isam Rais!" he exclaimed.

"Murad Rais. Peace be upon you," Isam said coolly.

Murad glared at him. "No thanks to you! You didn't support us in the attack!" His eyes went past Isam to the Sardinians. "What's this? Captives? Captives you didn't share with us?"

"I plucked them from the sea. You could have done the same."

"I was busy making repairs! My ship was damaged by the explosion!"

Isam shrugged. "Mine was damaged in the battle, too, but I was still able to pick up captives."

The captives looked back and forth between the two. None of the Sardinians could understand Arabic, but they understood hostility.

Murad stepped up until he was about six feet away from Isam. He had on red pantaloons and a short blue jacket with his scimitar through his sash. A big white turban went around a red fez. He was taller than average, but not as tall as Isam. His beard curled around his chin and bristled as he shouted, "You cheated me! I demand half the captives!"

"I took them through my own efforts, and I won't share. I battled that frigate before you ever arrived. They're mine!" Isam's baritone was growing louder, but his expression remained cold.

"You were running away!" Murad sneered.

The Sardinians watched with interest. Although they couldn't understand the words, they knew that whatever the angry man was shouting about boded ill for them. Therefore, although they held considerable opprobrium against Isam, they were persuaded to prefer his side to Murad's. Isam had made captives of them, it was true, but he had not been brutal to them and had even brought them extra food. That was about as generous as they could expect from a corsair. Murad had not done the same for the Albanians. Three days in the bagnio had showed them the differences among their masters.

Murad crooked his finger at Kateb. "You. Bugger-boy. Come here."

Kateb glared at him and wouldn't move. His hand went to his hilt. "Take back your words, or I'll cut out your tongue."

Isam's teeth ground together. "He's the agha of the men-at-arms. Not a slave!"

Murad's eyes narrowed. "I don't believe you. We all know what you are." To Kateb he barked, "Where are you from, boy?"

"Nowhere. I was a soldier in the army, and I'm not your boy!"

Murad sneered at Kateb. "A soldier-slave. I'll take you as surety for Isam Rais making good on sharing the loot. You'll fetch a good price in the market."

Isam thrust between them before Kateb could answer. "Your quarrel is with me. If you want to pick a fight, say it to my face."

"You're a god damned sodomite, a coward, and a cheat!" Murad snarled.

Isam lunged for his throat with his bare hands. Murad threw up his arms to fend off the other captain's longer reach. His bodyguards rushed forward to defend him. They grabbed Isam and pulled him off. Kateb waded in to defend Isam.

"Grab the black!" Murad shouted. With his half dozen men, they outnumbered the rais and his agha. They tried to pull Kateb off their captain.

The Sardinians leaped into action. They rushed Murad's men and the battle dissolved into a general melee. The prison guard that had accompanied Isam and Kateb flailed with his cudgel, attacking all present. He smashed his club into the back of Kateb's head, and would have smacked Murad too if he could have reached him. A Sardinian leaped on him and he howled, "Mutiny! Riot! Guards!" in Arabic.

At the same time, Isam found himself assailed by Murad's guards. Although he had the greater reach, there were more of them and they landed several painful blows. He gave as good as he got. Not to be left behind, the Albanians leaped into the fray. They were glad for a chance to assault their captors. The men of the *Renegade* fell back.

Murad wrapped his arm around Kateb's neck, and although the black punched him, the loss of air was a power no man could resist. Darkness gathered at the edge of Kateb's vision and crowded ever closer. He attempted to pull Murad's arm from his throat, but Murad knew what he was doing. The blackamoor passed out. Isam pursued Murad, but the other captain's guards covered his retreat. The doorway was a bottleneck easily defended. Isam couldn't break through, even with the help of the prisoners.

Meanwhile, the bagnio's guards rushed into the warming room. Murad's message was simple, "Mutiny. The prisoners are revolting." The guards swore. They relieved Murad's men at the doorway, and armed with cudgels, bashed their way into the room.

"Stop him! He stole my agha!" Isam shouted.

The guards didn't care who stole what; they wanted to squelch the riot. They'd sort out the details later. Two men guarded the door while the others waded into the prisoners. The inspiration for the riot waunderls gone. The captives melted away from Isam and retreated to the far side of the room. The guards pursued them and continued beating them. They covered their heads with their arms but didn't resist. They knew worse punishment would fall on them if they did.

"That's enough!" Isam roared. "They were defending me!"

The guards delivered a few more blows to make certain the prisoners were properly cowed, then their corporal turned to Isam. "What happened here?" he demanded.

"Murad Rais has stolen my agha!" he fumed. "Let me through!"

"Why did he do that?"

"He claims part of my captives are his and stole my agha as compensation!"

"Oh, well, if he's stolen your slave, you'll need to file a report. There's nothing we can do about."

Isam smote his thigh in frustration. "Kateb isn't a slave!"

"You'll need to talk to the sergeant."

While the Sardinians and Albanians nursed their wounds, Isam filed the report with the sergeant. He had seen Murad and his men carry off the unconscious Kateb, but he didn't feel inclined to do anything about it. "It's not my job to settle quarrels between captains." He referred the matter to his supervisor. The lieutenant came, pronounced that inciting a riot was a very serious business, and referred the matter to his supervisor. The captain came and fined Isam for fighting in the prison.

Isam was livid and it was all he could do not to lay hands on the captain. "If that's so, then you must fine Murad Rais as well!"

"He's not here. You are."

"He started it!"

"I don't care. I caught you."

"Nobody 'caught' anyone! I went to the sergeant to file a report!" Isam fumed.

The commander held out his hand. "The fine."

Isam pulled his purse out of his pocket and counted out the silver coins. Coins that the commander put into his own pocket. He didn't even pretend to put it in the prison's coffers.

A blue hatred for Murad Rais and his cronies filled Isam's heart. He stormed out.

CHAPTER 12 : NEGOTIATIONS

"Come!" barked the voice from within the cabin of the *Sea Leopard*.

Shakil bin Nakih hesitated at the angry sound, but the guard on the captain's door opened it. Reluctantly he stepped in. He paused just over the threshold to let his eyes adjust to the dimmer interior. He was dressed in his usual white and carried a string bag in either hand. One supported a watermelon, the other a yam three feet long and several smaller vegetables. Inside the cabin Isam was pacing angrily back and forth. He was dressed in his usual blue and black striped pantaloons, a navy blue short-sleeved shirt that showed off his biceps, and black doeskin slippers. His head was bare but for the short-cropped hair.

He stopped pacing and gave Shakil a curt greeting, "Peace be upon you!"

Shakil bowed very deeply. "And also upon you, rais. If I have come at a bad time, I apologize. I can come back later."

Isam threw himself onto the divan. "No. Tell me your business. Is there a problem with the mutton?"

Shakil toed off his sandals and stepped onto the rug. He bowed deeply, hands weighed down by the bags of heavy produce, then knelt on the rug. "No, rais. The mutton will be delivered as ordered. I have brought you a gift." He opened the bags and turned out the watermelon, yam, and several smaller potato-like vegetables.

Isam allowed the younger man's calmness to rub off on him. Less grumpy, he said, "Thank you very much. I shall enjoy the watermelon." It was true, he did like watermelon. He shifted his gaze to the yam. "What is that?"

The yam was about six inches thick and three feet long. It looked like a log. Half a dozen smaller things he recognized as greenish potatoes lay beside it.

Shakil said, "This is a yam. The blacks grow them as a staple crop. We have been experimenting with them at the farm. They keep a long time, months and months if they are kept cool and dry. I thought yams might interest you, since they keep longer than any other vegetable."

"I am interested," Isam agreed. "I have sometimes eaten yam, but I had no idea this it what it looked like before it was cooked."

"The drawback to yams as compared to other vegetables is that it must be cooked before it is eaten, otherwise it will make you ill. However, once cooked, it's a remedy for dysentery and other stomach ailments. Even if you do not use it as a staple, I thought you might want to have it for the feeding of sick and wounded men. It is very filling and cheap."

Isam was nodding his head. "Yes, I am interested. I would like to know more about yams. Can you prepare some for me, and teach my cook how to prepare them?"

Shakil bowed. "Of course, rais. If you and your cook are willing to come to the farmhouse, we will show you. My mother's farm is on the other side of Mosque Point. It isn't far from the city. Also, if I may, these are 'air potatoes.' They too must be cooked before eaten, but they keep well and are nutritious. They are much smaller as you can see, so they can be soaked, peeled, and baked whole. The two plants are both yams, but grow differently. New plants sprout from them if they are not harvested, so they are greener and softer than the yams."

Isam took a deep breath and let the anger go out of him. The butcher's demeanor calmed him and the bucolic gifts were practical. He was pleased that Shakil was looking for ways to be useful. At a profit for his own family, of course, but a man had to make a living. An honest agent would be better than the old, corrupt one. And he was much better looking. He would enjoy his business meetings more. His mood improved, so he smiled and said, "You are very handsome. I hope you don't mind me saying so."

Shakil ducked his head and put his hand to his face. "Surely that has nothing to do with yams," he murmured.

"No, it doesn't. But you're an intelligent man. Surely you must know that your looks capture more attention than your yams."

Shakil raised his head, squared his shoulders, and looked Isam in the eye. He said quietly, "My yams are for sale. My body is not."

Isam was amused rather than offended. "I didn't mean to imply that it was. Even if it were, I have someone else on my mind."

"Jamila."

Isam laughed out loud. "No, not your sister. I'm not the marrying kind. No, my thoughts are for my agha, and Murad Rais, who has kidnapped him. May Allah burn his father. I have to wait for the Kapitan Pasha to return to make my complaint in person. His secretary has accepted my written complaint, but won't take any action until Karliss Rais returns. Further, Murad Rais has made a complaint against me regarding the Sardinian captives. The Sardinian consul has made an offer for Captain Vargiu, but I can't accept until the case is settled." He smote his palm against his thigh and fumed.

Shakil bin Nakih had never been close to a corsair captain before and had certainly never heard any details of their bickering, although he was aware that politics must move the *taifa* the same as any other collection of men. Cautiously he asked, "What is Murad Rais' complaint, if I may ask?"

Isam realized that he had let his temper provoke him to words, but all the same, he found Shakil easy to talk to. He tugged the center of his beard and considered the matter. "Are you a man of discretion?"

Shakil folded his hands in his lap as he settled into a more comfortable cross-legged position on the rug. He considered the question carefully. "I believe that I am, but I must encourage you not to answer my question if it is indelicate. I asked out of curiosity, but upon reflection, it is obvious that your business is your business and not mine. Forgive me for having asked an inappropriate question." He bowed slightly.

Isam smiled crookedly. "It was inappropriate, but I'm not offended. I like you."

Shakil didn't show any visible reaction to that remark. He remained grave, still, and quiet. Isam watched him, but Shakil was starting to get used to the corsair's frank stares and didn't move. He remained seated with his back straight and his hands folded in his lap.

"You look like a student," Isam commented.

Shakil thawed a bit. "Do you think so? I wish I was." Then he regretted speaking and schooled himself to blandness.

"Can you read and write?"

"Yes, rais."

"Do arithmetic?"

"Yes, rais. I attended the mosque school until I was twelve."

"You probably got good marks. You know how to sit still. I'm the restless sort. I learned my lessons, but I admit I had trouble paying attention. I got my knuckles rapped on a regular basis."

"Reading the Qu'ran is wonderfully soothing, rais. I recommend it. Once you have learned to enjoy our Prophet's words, everything else becomes easy."

"You're a pious man. I respect that. I'm sure it's a great comfort for your family too. However, I love tobacco, sodomy, and the sea. The Qu'ran would deprive me of two of the three."

"The Qu'ran doesn't mention sodomy. I have been looking. I was startled by your announcement at dinner." A slight blush colored Shakil's cheek.

"It doesn't? I haven't read the whole thing. I only know the parts about ships and Paradise and defeating our enemies. That's all that really seems necessary."

Shakil warmed to the topic. Speaking earnestly, he said, "There are several schools of thought regarding the Qu'ran. Some say that only those things mentioned in the Qu'ran are permitted. Anything not mentioned is therefore forbidden. That rules out tobacco, hashish, and sodomy. Others are of the opinion that if it was important for us to know about, the Prophet would have surely mentioned it. Since tobacco, hashish, and sodomy are not mentioned, they are not important and are permitted. A third school of thought is that we must use the intelligence Allah gave us to understand the principles that underlie the Qu'ran. Thus, by consulting parallels, we can draw conclusions. Since hashish intoxicates, it is like wine, and since wine is forbidden because it intoxicates, hashish is also forbidden. About tobacco and sodomy I cannot find any consensus. What I have found is that love between two men is acceptable. They may embrace and kiss one another. What is not clear is whether they may caress one another, and if so, how intimately."

A knowing smile grew on Isam's lips. "You didn't look that up solely on my account, did you?"

"It is a topic of religious curiosity. I ascribe to the notion that Creation is so very large that not all topics can be addressed in a single book, therefore we must use the intelligence our Creator gave us to draw conclusions about matters not mentioned." He sat very stiffly even as his face reddened.

"Have you ever embraced a man?"

"That is an impertinent question and I won't answer it."

Isam laughed. "You have. If you hadn't, you would have indignantly told me so."

Shakil gave him a shocked look.

"Tell me, have you sinned according to your interpretation of the Qu'ran?"

Shakil reddened. "That is none of your business!"

"I suppose it's not, but the man who warms my bed is not your business either, yet I'm willing to discuss it with you. Men like us are not so rare, but we're not common either. Haven't you ever wished there was someone you could talk to about it without fearing condemnation?"

Shakil didn't answer for a long time. The breeze gave a slight tug to the spars and *Sea Leopard* rocked as gently as a baby's cradle. Sun dogs spangled the interior of the cabin.

After a while, Shakil said, "I have sometimes wondered . . ."

"Go ahead. Ask me. Once I was your age and I wanted to ask the same questions. I was lucky when an older man answered them for me."

"I'm twenty-one. That's not so young," Shakil replied.

"I was nineteen when I lost my virginity. I thought I was a full grown man!" he laughed. "Well, I was. But a young one, eh?"

Shakil couldn't help smiling. "I'm not sure if I'm a virgin. When I was young, I had a friend. We kissed and hugged and enjoyed it greatly. We touched each other, but that was all."

"Did you come?"

Shakil was red again. "Does it matter?"

"You're not being very explicit, so you leave me to guess. I can't tell you if you're still a virgin if I don't know exactly what you did."

Shakil swallowed hard. "We touched each other down there. And we came. But I have never committed sodomy." He had never told anyone, either.

"It requires an act of penetration to lose your virginity. If there was no penetration, then you're still a virgin and on the right side of the Qu'ran. However, my opinion is that once you have learned to enjoy the pleasures of another's man body, you can't put the genie back in the bottle. You have eaten the forbidden fruit and are no longer innocent. Inexperienced and naive perhaps, but not innocent. You know lust."

Shakil was pink, but he listened carefully. He weighed it against his own thoughts and tested it against what he had read in books, then nodded slowly.

Isam slid off the divan, knelt on one knee before him, and took his chin in hand. He pressed his lips firmly against Shakil's. The younger man's eyes flew open wide, then closed. It had been a long time since he had kissed anyone, and he liked it. Yes, he knew what lust was.

So did Isam. When Shakil did not resist him, he reached out to wrap an arm around him. Shakil suddenly pushed him away. "You have a lover," he accused.

"Yes. Although he is not exactly a lover. I like him, and he respects me, but we are comrades, not lovers."

Shakil couldn't see the difference. "I'm not loose like that." He stiffened his spine.

Isam's brown eyes sparkled with mischief. "Would it be so bad to have a bold corsair to teach you the pleasures of your body?" Isam leaned forward to capture his mouth again, but Shakil shoved him away.

"You're very certain of yourself, Captain Corsair! Maybe other men fall to your charms, but I won't. I know you only want sex."

"Well, yes, but you want it too. There's no reason why we shouldn't enjoy it together."

Shakil got to his feet. Coldly he said, "Do you want the yams and watermelon? I came to talk business and nothing else."

Isam let him escape, then rose to his feet. "I don't know. I am vexing my mind over Murad Rais." The aggravation returned and he paced a few steps from cannon to cannon.

Shakil watched warily, but he seemed to have successfully deflected the corsair's amorous advances. "How much is he asking?"

"Half the loot from the *Eleanora d'Arborea*, little as it is. He's trying to force me into sharing the ransoms with him." He explained the matter.

Shakil listened carefully. "I am no expert on the law of prizes, but while you might be legally entitled to what you plucked from the sea, I don't think you're morally right. Murad Rais accepted your invitation to do battle with a dangerous enemy and was hurt in doing so. You invited him to the danger, so you must share what little reward there is."

Isam shook his head. "He was right there. He could have plucked them from the water, but he didn't. He shouldn't complain when another man takes the prize he didn't want."

"You're taking advantage of the situation to chisel Murad Rais. Just like you complained that your agent is taking advantage of the situation to chisel you. You can't have it both ways and always to your advantage. If you want men to deal fairly with you, you must deal fairly with them." Shakil was nowhere near as big as the corsair, but he had the strength of his moral conviction. He was as slim and strong as a sword. Hazel eyes met brown without flinching.

It was the corsair who blinked first. "Damn you for a righteous man, Shakil bin Nakih." He resumed pacing. "I can't afford it. It was a terrible cruise. I need money to repair and resupply, but I'm already in debt for the guns. The moneylenders won't loan me more money, and I don't want to borrow. Debt is too expensive! Praise Allah, I own the ship myself, so there are no investors howling about my ears."

"Even so, you must split the ransom like an honest man."

"I concede your point, but I can't afford it. If I let him get away with kidnapping my agha, no one will respect me."

"Surely Karliss Rais will order his release."

Isam grew glum. "Maybe not, since he's being held hostage for a debt."

"If I can obtain credit for you, you can resupply. Then you can afford to be magnanimous about the loot, and Murad Rais will have to release Kateb."

"Do you think you can?"

"Yes, I think so. I know some people I'll ask. I'll be discreet, so don't worry about that. No one will know. If your other creditors think you are in funds, they will give you credit again."

"If the Kapitan Pasha decides for me, I'll keep the loot and Murad will have to return Kateb. But if he decides against me, then I want to concede graciously. I won't give Murad the satisfaction of seeing me sweat."

Shakil gave a curt nod. "Very well. I can make the arrangement on those terms."

CHAPTER 13 : FEMALE SAILORS

The *Sea Leopard* clipped along at eight knots with a southwest wind over her quarter and dry dusty air flying all around her as she coasted eastward. The dun line of the Rif was on the starboard as they left Modiq Bay behind. The officers were all gathered on the quarterdeck to enjoy the wind, watch their captain, and sulk. The crew was not large; after the problems of the previous cruise, Isam Rais had had trouble recruiting for the mission. On the weather deck below, several women followed the gunner as he explained their duties.

One of the mizzen crew made the sign against the evil eye. Isam saw it and snarled, "They aren't devils; they're women. You will treat them with the respect to which Muslim women are entitled!"

"It's bad luck to have women on board, rais," murmured Lieutenant Yafi.

"Being short-handed is worse luck!" Isam rounded on him. The rest of crew shrank away. The captain had been in a foul humor for a week. Getting to sea had only marginally improved his temper. "We will carry out the gun drill as planned. The women and boys must learn their duties."

"Aye aye, sir," Yafi replied. His jaw set beneath the short beard.

"I'm going to inspect the women. You have the conn."

"Aye aye, captain. I have the conn." He stepped away stiffly.

Isam stomped down the ladder to the deck. "Gunner!" he called.

The gunner stopped and turned around. "Aye, sir?" He was a French renegade with auburn hair that curled around his neck and face. He was a handsome man, aside from the scar that marred his right cheek. He had regular features and sensuous lips. A red fez topped his curls, and a white shirt, grey vest with red embroidery, and loose-fitting grey pantaloons suited his physique.

"We're going to start the gun drill, but I want to inspect the women first." He turned to the gaggle of females and roared, "Women, line up!"

Five of the six were afraid of him and skittered in panic. The tallest one lined up and used gestures to get the others to line up with her. She was dressed all in blue and kept her face veiled and every inch of her body covered except for her hands. She even had shoes. She looked quite respectable and Isam briefly wondered what desperation had driven her to take a job as a sailor. It didn't matter. They were hands, and he needed them to know their work. The other women were ragged. Faded henna marked the hands and feet of some. They had their hair and breasts covered as stipulated, but a couple of them wore short sleeves. They had probably made a choice between prostitution and sailing. Sailing was only marginally better for their reputations.

Isam glared at the women with bared arms. "This is not acceptable dress. I hired you as sailors, not whores. The next time any of you is caught showing skin, you'll be caned six stripes on your bare hands." He couldn't very well cane them on their posteriors or even their feet. To cane the bottoms of their feet would require them lie down and lift their legs.

He continued. "You will not speak to men except as necessary to carry out your duties. You may speak the boys under the age of twelve and to each other. You will not take lovers, flirt, or let the men kiss, fondle, or ogle you. If any man takes liberties with you, you will report him immediately and he'll be caned. This is a ship of war, not a brothel! I did not hire you to warm beds. You will serve the guns the same as the boys. I expect you to do your duty. If you show signs of cowardice, you will be flogged, same as any other sailor. You must do your work, no matter what. You will see terrible things. Ignore it and keep working. The guns are your life. If you falter, you will die. The guns are what keep us alive."

He paused to look over the women. The tall one stood stiffly, but her eyes were riveted on him. He could see no sign of emotion beneath her veil, but her hands clenched. The other women gazed at him in wide-eyed fear. He was grimly pleased by their reaction. If they were more afraid of him more than the enemy, they would work.

"We are going to have a gun drill. No shoes, no sandals, and not a bit of jewelry on you! No metal. The slightest thing could strike a spark, and with the dusting of gunpowder that always escapes the cartridges, you could set us on fire. I warned you when I hired you what kind of conditions you would be working in. Off with your shoes."

Nobody dared say anything. Nobody did anything. They were all having second thoughts about joining, but it was too late now. They were as desperate for money as Isam was for crew, but maybe not as desperate as they'd thought.

Isam roared again, "I said 'Off with your shoes!' I will not repeat myself. If you do not obey the first time you are ordered, you will be caned, same as the men!"

Those with footwear scrambled to remove it. The tall girl with the face veil bent gracefully to remove her shoes. That done, they all stood with their footgear in their hands, careful to keep the soles turned towards themselves. They didn't want to offend the volatile captain.

Isam sighed in frustration. He was unfairly taking his bad temper out on them, but it was important to instill a backbone in them. Still, having terrorized them, he must now hearten them. He pointed at the girl in blue.

"Stand up like her. Pretend you are brave, then everyone will think you are brave. After a while, even you will start believing it. You must understand the importance of your job. You are powder monkeys. You will bring gunpowder to the guns. Without gunpowder, we can't shoot. Without guns, we can't fight. If we can't fight, we lose. If we lose, whatever thing you dread will happen to you. You *must* carry the powder."

Tears started running down the face of one of the women. She made no sound and rubbed her hand across her face. The blue veiled girl remained absolutely still. The oldest of the women, a short, skinny woman about forty, set her jaw and sulked. Nobody dared to do or say anything.

Isam said to the gunner, "Get rotten tomatoes or something else red from the cook. Throw it down on the deck during the drill to simulate blood. Teach them how to throw sand on it and how to clean it up. If any of them faints at the sight of blood, cane them. Do whatever it takes to keep them on their feet and working."

The oldest woman said, "We're women. We see more blood every month than most men see in a lifetime."

Isam stared blankly at her. He had no idea what she was talking about.

"The monthly flux. Not to mention, childbirth. We know what pain and danger is," she retorted. "We're not as weak and fragile as you think we are!"

The rest of the women looked at her sideways.

Isam's face fell. Nobody had ever mentioned menstruation in his presence before; it simply wasn't done. Bachelors had no need to know such things. He sputtered, then said, "I'm putting you in charge of the women. What's your name?"

"Nusrat. It means 'victory,'" she replied.

The corsair captain smiled at her. "That's a good name. A propitious name. We have victory on board already." Relief flooded through them that his wrath had been assuaged. He decided he ought to meet them all, so starting with the tall girl, he asked, "What's your name?"

The voice under the veil was so faint, he couldn't hear her answer.

"Speak up!"

A cough sounded and a faint raspy voice answered, "Ami."

He nodded. "Ami," he said, with the air of a man memorizing it. He went along the rest of the line and got their names.

That done, he came abreast of the gunner. "Zosime. You keep your hands off of them. I know you. They're not here to entertain you."

The gunner knew better than to argue with the captain. "Aye aye, rais."

"Stand by to beat to quarters. We will have a gun drill. Allah knows we need the practice."

"We do, rais, but I'll whip them into shape."

"Carry on." The captain returned to the quarterdeck.

Zosime told the women, "Stow your shoes and jewelry. We're going to beat to quarters very shortly. By Allah, I hope you remember your positions!"

The women milled around. Ami said softly, "Everyone give me your shoes. I'll put them away. We don't all have to go."

They piled her with footwear and a few cheap necklaces and rings. Not one of them wanted to face another dressing down by the fierce captain. Ami took them to their cabin. While she was in the room stowing personal items, the drums broke out with their wild tattoo. Her heart leapt into her mouth. She slammed the sea chest shut and came running. The rest of the crew was scrambling into position. The marines broke out their weapons, and the servants packed all the captain's personal effects down into the hold. The cook extinguished the galley fire. In two minutes, the gun crews were in place. Ami ran swiftly up the quarterdeck and arrived in time. She stood between the two stern chasers with her heart hammering in her chest.

Isam whirled on her. "Take the windward ladder! If you take the lee in a heavy sea, you'll fall overboard. Always take the windward ladder. Make a habit of it! That way you won't have to think about it during battle or storm. You'll do the right thing by instinct."

She nodded in acknowledgment. It made sense. The windward side was the high side. If she fell, she would fall to the low side, which would be the deck. If she was on the low side, and she fell to the still lower side . . . that would be the sea.

Isam forgot her immediately. "Serve the guns!"

Commands echoed along the decks. Zosime had already explained what they would be doing, so she knew what to do. Careful to take the windward ladder, she hurried into the bowels of the ship. When she returned, she had a pair of leather cartridge cases hanging from her shoulders. She was the biggest of the women and presumably the strongest; therefore she was assigned to the two stern guns. Short-handed as they were, she must do double duty. The stern guns and bow guns were undermanned to keep up the strength of the broadsides.

A cask was heaved overboard and left in their wake. The *Sea Leopard* skimmed away, then swept around. The gun captains called their orders and readied their guns. Isam took out his pocket watch. "There's watermelon for every gun crew that can hit the target! Wait for my command!"

They approached the cask at a range of about half a cable's length. "Bow guns, fire!"

The two smaller guns in the bow cracked out. The new recruits jumped and flinched. The acrid smell of gunsmoke drifted back over the weather deck in tendrils of grey smoke.

Master Imrich gave his own orders, and the *Sea Leopard* turned and brought her broadside to bear.

"Larboard battery, fire!" Isam roared.

Eleven brazen monsters roared and belched smoke. The xebec heeled in reaction as the guns shot across the deck and flung themselves against their tackle. A cloud of smoke gathered just outside the hull, then drifted over the weather deck all the way to the quarterdeck. Those who weren't used to it coughed and sneezed. They wiped runny eyes and noses. Isam checked his watch.

The *Sea Leopard* yawed again, and this time it was the stern guns that roared. Ami covered her ears and cringed at the noise. She was deaf afterwards, but her gun captain gave her a shove. "More powder!" he roared into her veiled face. She ran for the ladder. She was a blue streak passing the officers, and then she was gone.

The *Sea Leopard* swept around to charge the cask again. "Fire at will!" Isam roared.

The starboard guns thundered out. Ami was running back with two cartridges. Her gun captain roared, "Faster, damn you!"

They loaded the guns as quick as they could, but they had missed their chance. The *Sea Leopard* swept past the cask.

"Don't just stand there! RUN!" the gun captain bellowed at her.

It dawned on Ami that as soon as she delivered one set of cartridges, she'd better go back for the next. Sometimes there was a traffic jam in the companion way while at other times she had to wait while the powder monkeys ahead of her received their cartridges. Having to run from the highest point on the vessel to the lowest, it took her longer to serve her guns than the other powder monkeys. She noticed the sailors skimming down the ladders by the rails and imitated them. She landed with a thump and kept going. This time she got the powder up in time. As the drill progressed, her thigh muscles and calves ached and her shoulders grew sore from the weight of the powder cartridges hanging from their straps. She forgot that she was carrying explosives that a stray spark could ignite and concentrated all her attention on forcing her weary legs up the ladders yet again.

At first nobody could hit the cask. It floated unharmed in spite of all their exertions, but after several passes, Number Four gun shattered it. Loud cries of delight went up.

"God they're bad," Isam told Khadim.

The first lieutenant was still recovering from his wounds and used a cane. "They have good speed, though."

"Doesn't mean anything if we can't hit what we aim at." They drilled for an hour. By the end, most of them were able to put the shot into the general vicinity of the broken cask. Satisfied with their progress, Isam said, "That's well. Stand down the guns."

Gratefully the crews relaxed as they ran their guns in again so that they could be swabbed out and snugged down. The bronze barrels sizzled loudly as the wet swabs were thrust down their throats.

Isam turned to watch the quarterdeck gun crew. "You did well," he told them. "Even you," he told the girl. "What's your name?" He had forgotten.

"Ami," came the exhausted reply. She was bending over with her hands braced upon her knees as she tried to catch her breath and not fall over.

"Get yourself a drink, then serve water to your crews."

Ami had to go down the ladder again. This time she returned lugging a bucket with a ladle. She set the bucket on the deck, and turning her back to the men, lifted her veil so she could drink a ladle full of cool water. That done, she brought the bucket to the men. They were just as thirsty and drained the ladle again and again.

Isam drank last. She had to tip up the bucket to fill the ladle as he held it in his hand. She kept her head bowed. Isam put a hand on the bucket to steady it as the ship rolled lazily. She dared to glance up, but the corsair paid her no attention. All he cared about was the water. She hastily ducked her head again. He was not used to women, especially not young women. Her peeking and ducking annoyed him. He straightened up, took the ladle from her, and drank deep. He tilted his head back to get every single drop of water in the ladle, and she gazed up at him again, mesmerized by the sight of his adam's apple bobbing beneath the beard. As he lowered the ladle and put it in the bucket, she ducked her head again.

The gun captain told her, "Take the cartridge satchels below and stow them."

Ami nodded and slipped away.

CHAPTER 14 : THE CAPTAIN'S HAREM

The female crew could not be housed with the male crew. Isam Rais didn't trust his men not to take advantage of them, and given what he suspected regarding the prior employment of some of the women, he felt it was just as important to protect the men from the women. The only location that was both secure and private was the great cabin. His servant had erected a canvas curtain to wall off the portion of the great cabin formerly used as his office. That meant the women had to pass through his space to go in and out the cabin door, a door that was guarded by a marine. That kept them safe from the men, but he resented it all the same. The captain's cabin was his private domain and he didn't intend to change his habits.

After the evening gun drill, his servants restored his furniture. Rugs of dark blue painted canvas covered the floor, but he had one good Turkish rug in geometric pattern of black and blue. His desk was a low table that also served as a coffee table. The air was warm and smelled of gunsmoke. The steward had replaced the glass windows, but they were swung up on their hinges and secured to the wall above to let the sea breeze into the room. A lantern made of bronze and glass hung in the center of the room and illuminated the desk below. Isam sat cross-legged on a cushion as he wrote with a reed pen in his left hand. His head was bare and so were his arms as he wore his dark blue shirt, pantaloons, and black slippers. Unbeknownst to him, he was being spied upon.

Ami had laid herself down flat on the floor of the women's quarters so that she could peer under the edge of the canvas. The bottom edge had been secured with twine to eyebolts in the floor in several locations, but the canvas didn't come all the way to the floor and there were several inches open beneath it.

"What are you doing?" one of the female sailors asked her.

Another one cackled and said, "She's spying on the captain! What a naughty girl!"

"Sh! He'll hear you!" somebody else whispered.

Red faced, Ami swiftly retreated and sat up. There was no excuse; she had been caught. Rather feebly she said, "I just wanted to see what he looked like when he wasn't angry."

"Has he taken off his shirt?"

Ami turned bright red. "No, he hasn't. He's properly dressed." For a man in the privacy of his own home, if he thought he was alone.

One of the women got down on the floor and took her place. "Oh, he's got nice arms!" she cooed. She was less discreet than Ami, and the captain noticed her.

Isam's brow clouded up and he leaped to his feet. He strode across the confines of the cabin and flung open the canvas flap door. The woman who had been peeking scrambled up and away. All of the women retreated as he barged in.

"You!" he pointed at the woman caught spying. "Come here! I'm going to cane your hands myself!"

"It was Ami who started it!"

Ami had hidden behind the other women and grabbed her veil when the captain stormed in. She had not had time to pin it in place, so she held it up over her face as the women parted.

"Were you spying on me?" the captain demanded.

Frightened, she nodded her head.

"Both of you, in my cabin for punishment." Realizing he couldn't have women alone in his cabin, either, he said, "Nusrat come with them. You will supervise them." He wished he had a eunuch to supervise the women, but he didn't, so Nusrat would have to do.

"She's a good girl, not like the others. I'll punish her and see that she doesn't do it again," Nusrat replied. "They were just curious. Forgive them this once, rais."

Isam glared at them in irritation. But he had assigned Nusrat as chief woman, so he must let her exercise her authority. "Very well. See to it that they don't annoy me. They must keep quiet when they are in quarters. I have a great deal of work to do. When I sleep, I need my rest. You must prevent them from disturbing me."

Nusrat bowed deeply to him. "It shall be as you command, rais."

Isam let his temper settle. "You'll need a cane. Come borrow mine." He hadn't personally caned anybody in a long time. Generally speaking, his crews were well-disciplined. This time was different. He had to take what he could get and not be choosy. He was glad to delegate this particular duty to the chief of the women.

Nusrat wrapped her hijab around her head and followed the captain into his dayroom. She stood waiting while Isam hunted for his cane. The rearrangement of the great cabin to accommodate the women meant that things were not where they used to be. That irritated him, but it was his own decision to hire women, and his decision again to house them where they were. He had no one to blame but himself. Slowly he settled into what would become the new routine. Finding the cane, he gave it to her.

"Sit down. I am making a petty officer of you with a commensurate increase in pay. I am going to explain your duties to you." He settled on his cushion and pulled the desk back into position. She knelt on the other side with the cane across her lap. She was pleased by the promotion.

"You are the chief of the women. You will supervise them to make certain they dress properly and behave properly. You will see that their needs are taken care of. When on duty, they are subject to the authority of their lieutenants and midshipmen and you won't interfere. They must all do their duty. The officers have a duty to inspect their divisions to make certain they are clean and don't have any contraband, like alcohol or hashish. Obviously, men can't inspect women, so you will do it. You have permission to move through the ship to do your duty. You have permission to use the cane to strike the hand of any man that gropes you or leers at you. I will let my officers know that you are be allowed to move unmolested through the ship and to have the same privileges as the other petty officers."

Nusrat was no sailor. "What's a 'petty officer'?"

"A crewman with extra responsibilities. They are different from the commissioned officers and warrant officers. The regular officers have great responsibility and great authority. They can order punishment. The petty officers cannot. If captured, the petty officers are put in with the regular crew while the officers are separated out. That should be a relief to you; the Spanish frequently execute the regular officers."

Nusrat was paying close attention. "What do they do with women?"

Isam was silent. "There are rarely women aboard corsair ships. I expect they will consider female sailors to be whores and treat them as such."

Nusrat's mouth twisted. "I have been a whore," she said matter-of-factly. "I expect Spanish men are much like Muslims: unkind to those they don't respect."

"I suppose they are."

Nusrat tested the limits of her new authority by asking her captain a question. "I know you need crew, but women? Why not slaves?"

"I don't trust slaves. Women might panic, but they won't stab me in the back."

"I suppose so. We are Muslims. We won't help the infidels."

Isam suddenly rose and went to his sleeping quarters. He returned in a with his tobacco pouch and pipe. He busied himself with filling the bowl. Nusrat took a stick from the tinderbox, rose, and opened the lamp and lit it. She knelt down and lighted Isam's pipe. He puffed until the tobacco was well alight. Smoke wreathed his head and wafted through the cabin.

"We're not chasing infidels this time."

"Where are we going?" Nusrat asked as he settled down.

Isam lowered his voice. "We're looking for pirates. Muslim pirates," he said with distaste.

Nusrat looked at him in surprise. "Why?"

Isam missed having Kateb to talk to. Nusrat seemed reliable. He liked her matter-of-fact attitude. "You must swear to keep it secret. I will tell the men when I decide. If there's any gossip, I'll know where it came from."

Nusrat's eyes gleamed. "You have my word. I know how to keep secrets."

"Politics. We have a treaty with Spain that requires us to suppress piracy on our coast. We lost a lot of corsairs in the last war, so we need time to rebuild our fleet. Therefore the Dey has agreed to appease the Spanish by making an effort to apprehend some pirates. Actual pirates, not corsairs. They don't have letters of marque and they don't share their profits with the government. They are the ones that give the rest of us a bad name. I am ordered to sink or capture them. If I can capture them, the Dey will buy the captives from me. He paid for the repairs and resupply of the *Sea Leopard*. Profit, however, will depend on capturing them and selling them to the Dey. He's expanding the fortress again and needs the labor." He looked morose.

Nusrat needed time to absorb that. "I thought you were all pirates," she said apologetically.

He gave her a crooked smile and puffed his pipe. "So the infidels say. The corsairs operate under rules from the government. We can only raid forces that don't have a treaty with us. We must pay ten percent to the government, in exchange for which we get to use the Arsenal to refit. We must follow certain rules, such as maintaining the captives in good condition. Nobody ransoms a dead body, and a broken body is no good as a slave. The pirates ignore the law and do as they please. Some of them are very cruel, and some are very rich. Some have allies in Zokhara who will accept their bribes. So the Dey is bolstering his power at home by suppressing those pirates who aren't under his control."

"Do you think the peace with Spain will last?"

"Does it ever? No. While they demand we suppress our pirates, they encourage their own pirates to prey upon us. We will come to blows soon enough. Not this year, we're not ready. Maybe next year. If not next, then the year after for sure. There is no possible peace between us and the infidels."

Nusrat shook her head. "I don't see why men find it necessary to fight over religion."

"Because we refuse to starve."

"Our country is fertile. We won't starve."

"Fertile enough. But so many things we want are made in Europe, and they won't sell to us! All of them—even the French!—have forbidden trade with us. Because they are Christians and opposed to Islam. They and their Crusades! They want to crush us. The English are the only ones that trade with us, but they only want certain things. It's not enough. Sugar and ostrich feathers! Do you have any idea how many ostrich feathers it takes to pay for a boatload of shoes? Fortunately, the price of ostrich feathers is high, but all the same, there are only so many ostriches in the world. Looting the infidels is how we get shoes and clocks and timber and many other things."

"Why do infidels want ostrich feathers?" she asked in bewilderment.

"For their hats. Every gentleman must have a feather in his hat. If he doesn't, he's looked down as being a commoner."

"How odd."

"They have a lot of odd fashions, like wearing wool coats in summer. This explains why they are prone to apoplexy. They overheat too easily."

Nusrat nodded.

Talking and tobacco had soothed Isam's nerves. He returned to the matter that had vexed him. "I have decided to forgive the women for peeping, but they must not do it again. Give them one rap of the cane each on the backs of their hands. And do something to keep them from peeping. Rearrange the sea chests or something."

"Very good, rais. It shall be as you say." Nusrat bowed again and rose from her place. She padded back to the women's quarters and slipped inside. She was well pleased with her promotion, and even more with the captain's confidence.

Ami had spied on the captain and female chief the whole time, so she was able to scramble away and don an innocent expression before Nusrat returned. It was not a convincing expression, but the veil covered it.

"The captain is willing to forgive you this one time, but I'm going to rap your hands to make certain you understand what the punishment will be if you don't behave yourselves. Ami, give me your hand."

The girl reached out and gritted her teeth. Nusrat took her hand to steady it, and brought the cane down with a sharp snap. It stung dreadfully. Ami bit her lip but didn't cry out. Then Nusrat took the hand of the other spy and rapped it sharply. She cried out and rubbed it vigorously.

"Go to bed," Nusrat told them. They undressed to just their long tunics, then crawled into their hammocks.

Ami's head was very full, but she was also very tired, and she slept.

CHAPTER 15 : THE DABCHICK PIRATE

Exactly where the pirates were, Isam didn't know, but there were various coves and river bays along the eastern coast of the Sallee Republic that could hold any number of pirates. The *Sea Leopard* looked into every hole and queried all the traffic she came across, but everyone they asked either didn't know or wasn't telling. Meanwhile, the crew received a great deal of practice in rowing in and out of tight spaces, of tacking and shortening sail, beating to quarters, and in the evening when they were alone on the water, target practice. They were gaining in skill, and in Ami's case, improving in wind. She could now run up two flights of ladders without gasping for air. Everyone settled into the rhythm of life on board. Nusrat had to smack several sailors before they learned to respect her authority, but after that, they kept their distance.

After five days of no luck, the *Sea Leopard* flagged down a one-masted felucca. She hove to and waited for them to approach. As they drew abreast, Isam and his quarterdeck crew could look down into her.

Isam's eyes narrowed. "That's no fishboat."

Imrich looked too, but all he saw were some brown and black men, stripped to the waist, their heads covered with cloths. "How can you tell?"

"She doesn't stink like fish and her crew is tense."

"Anyone would be wary if hailed by a big xebec like this."

Isam leaned over the rail and hailed, "What vessel?"

The captain looked up and shaded his eyes against the glare of the burnished sky. "*Dabchick,*" he replied. "Mohammed Rais. That's me. Who are you?"

His tone was belligerent. He had a short curly beard and his head was shaved with a white scarf tied over it to shelter his pate and nape. He had a scar over his left eye and another on his right cheek. A pair of gold hoop earrings hung from his ears. Several more scars marked his arms and cut through his chest hair. While a fishing captain might have golden earrings and even acquire a scar or two, they didn't look as hard-bitten as this one did.

"Isam Rais al-Tangueli, of the *Sea Leopard*. I'm on commission from the Dey of the Sallee Republic. I'll need to inspect your vessel."

"We're honest fishermen. Why do you need to inspect us?"

Isam smiled, but it didn't reach his eyes. "Routine. We're looking for pirates. I'll need to see your papers, too." Over his shoulder, he told Yafi in a low voice, "Prepare a boarding party. Be prepared for treachery."

"Aye aye, rais," he replied and hurried away.

"We haven't got any papers. We're poor illiterate fishermen." Although they had stripped to the waist like fishermen did, their pantaloons were not so ragged or coarse as what poor men wore.

Isam smiled insincerely. "What's your home port?"

"Biya," he replied.

"Biya! You're far from home. How's the fishing?"

"Not so good. That's why we're so far from home. Who's the woman?"

All the quarterdeck crew were gathered along the rail to look down at the stranger, Ami included, her pair of leather cartridge satchels hanging over her shoulders.

Isam looked over and scowled. "To your posts!" he barked.

The crew scrambled back. The men who normally manned the two stern chasers were instead manning three small swivel guns on the port rail. Ami retreated to the far side of the deck to be out of the way of the gunners and officers.

Isam turned back to the pretended fishboat. "None of your business. My officer is coming aboard now. Gather all your men on the main deck, yourself included."

Mohammed Rais scowled, but he ambled forward. He and his men waited as Yafi and his men climbed over the rail and descended to their deck. The boarding party jumped down to the deck of the small vessel without opposition.

Isam called down, "Mohammed Rais! Order up your men from down below."

Mohammed Rais spread his hands placatingly. "We are the whole crew."

Isam barked, "Lieutenant Yafi! Pry up the hatch and throw a grenade down."

Mohammed grew alarmed. "Wait! There might be one or two still below."

Isam sneered. "I thought as much. Call them up. We're on to you."

Mohammed glared at him, then tossed the hatch aside. He barked down, "Everybody up." He continued hanging over the hatch and conversed with those below.

Isam shouted, "Yafi! Beware of an ambush! Swivels ready!"

The men came up from below in a rush. There were twenty of them, which taken with the half dozen on deck, more than doubled Yafi's boarding party. As soon as they started swarming out of the hatch, Isam shouted, "Fire!"

Ami realized that this was for real and darted down the ladder to fetch another load of cartridges. She heard the bang of the swivels like big firecrackers going off and the agonized cries of men, then she was belowdecks and could see nothing of the carnage.

At pointblank range firing into a mass of men, the swivels couldn't miss. Red blood blossomed. Bodies fell. Blood slicked the deck. The pirates shouted and drew their blades, but Yafi and his men charged the mass of pirates, for that was what they were. They pressed them around the hold so that those climbing up the ladder found their way blocked as they came over the coaming. The pirates who came out of the hold were dressed in shirts and fezzes and carried scimitars in their hands.

Another swivel gun barked, then Ami scrambled up the ladder with three smaller swivel cartridges in each of her satchels. She handed them over. Glancing down at the battle on the smaller vessel, she saw the blood, looked away, and flew down the ladder to fetch more powder.

Reloaded, another barrage of balls cut through the defenders and clattered against the wooden deck. Two more pirates fell mortally wounded. The clash of blade on blade rang through the brassy air. Yafi thrust and parried with his scimitar, brown eyes alight, and the tail of his turban flipped back and forth over his shoulder as he parried and reposted. Red splattered the dove grey sleeve of his jacket and the white of his pantaloons, but it wasn't his blood. The man before him gurgled and slumped to the deck. The marksmen in the *Sea Leopard's* mizzen top fired into the pirates climbing out of the hold, and a wounded pirate fell back into the darkness.

The battle was over in a matter of minutes. The pirates threw down their weapons and dropped to their knees. They held up their hands and begged for mercy; they had no taste to die and didn't believe their Muslim brothers would deal harshly with them. Mohammed Rais, wounded in three places, was sent aboard the *Sea Leopard*.

Isam descended to the weather deck and met the man. "You're accused of piracy. Do you have a letter of marque or any evidence to give in your defense?"

"We don't need a letter of marque! We prey upon the Christians as Allah commanded!" Mohammed Rais was held in position by a pair of black men-at-arms from the *Sea Leopard*.

"Which Christians?"

"All of them!"

"Spain?"

"Of course! Especially Spain, may Allah burn their fathers and grandfathers!"

"The Sallee Republic is at peace with Spain, and Spain has paid tribute for the safety of her vessels. You're an admitted pirate, and I consign you to hang. Lieutenant Khadim, rig tackle for a hanging. Lieutenant Yafi, bring your prisoners aboard and lock them in our hold."

Mohammed glared his hatred. "Allah will burn your entrails before you, you perfidious renegade! Allah hates you for what you do to your own people!"

"Allah hates pirates who cheat their own country," Isam replied. Then, "Gag him."

The guards tied Mohammed's hands behind him and used his own sash to gag him.

A messenger came to Isam with a leather case in his hands. "We found this when we searched the cabin."

Isam took it and opened it. Inside was the *Dabchick's* log and several letters and other documents. He riffled through them, then paused to read some of the entries. He held up the papers. "Proof of your robberies. I have no qualms about hanging you." He put the papers back and called, "Messenger!" Ensign Taslim appeared. "Keep hold of these until I call for them."

"Aye aye, rais."

Meanwhile, the main antenna was brought low and a rope secured to it. The noose went around Mohammed's neck. He was gagged, so he couldn't have any last words. Isam made certain that the knot was properly set below his ear, then stepped back. "Haul away."

The antenna was hauled to the upright position. Mohammed's feet left the deck and he kicked frantically for a couple of minutes, then his motions slowed. He passed out from lack of air and went limp.

"Leave him there," Isam directed. The pirate captain's corpse twisted slowly in the wind like a grisly pennant. "Lieutenant Yafi. Select a strong prize crew; I want you to be able to fight with the *Dabchick*. You're going to be our bait for the rest of the pirates. You will pretend to be a pirate, so make your men look as disreputable as possible. I will write you orders in case we get separated."

"Aye aye, rais." Yafi selected the men who had gone aboard with him and a few more. Meanwhile, Khadim supervised the transfer of prisoners into the *Sea Leopard's* hold.

Isam went below to write the necessary orders. It bothered him to hang a Muslim, but all the same, the man was a pirate. He was cheating his own country out of the taxes and fees privateers paid, and he was violating the laws of his country and the treaty with Spain. That the Dey would find a reason to break the treaty in a year or two was irrelevant. At the moment, the law and treaty stood.

Kneeling at the table with his reed pen in hand, the captain wrote out the necessary orders so that Yafi, if taken, would be able to prove he was not the pirate he was pretending to be. Theoretically, privateers were to be treated as prisoners of war while pirates could be, and often were, summarily hanged, but Isam knew that the Christian powers rarely made such distinctions where non-Europeans were concerned. It was one of the reasons he was so aggressive in battle. He would rather go down fighting than be hanged.

He shook his head to clear the gloomy thoughts, but that only brought Kateb to mind. Shakil had gone to Murad to negotiate, but no agreement was reached. On the other hand, Shakil had brought him word that the Dey was seeking a corsair to carry out a mission for him. Karliss Rais wasn't back from his own cruise yet, so Isam had set sail without resolving the matter. The only good thing was that he was properly supplied with decent food in honest measure. He didn't blame the butcher's son for failing to obtain Kateb's release; Murad Rais was as proud and stubborn as all the other corsair captains. If only Isam were in funds! He could have afforded to be magnanimous with the prize money then. The tip of the reed pen broke with a snap. He was pressing it too hard and had blotted the page as well. With a sigh, he trimmed the pen and took out a new piece of paper. He carefully copied the order and signed it with his sigil.

CHAPTER 16 : THE PIRATE BAY

Scouting the coast proved easier with the *Dabchick*. Although the xebec was able to work in close to the shore, the *Dabchick* could work in even closer. The smaller vessel had a draft of only a few feet and could skim over reefs and mudbanks where a man could have walked with his head above the water. Isam Rais was none too happy with his anti-piracy commission, but he used it as an opportunity to sound the rivers and coast and to correct his charts. That meant he was often aboard the *Dabchick* to make the soundings himself. When he did so, he wore a white shirt with cap sleeves and short white pantaloons that stopped above the knee, and sandals. A dingy white turban topped his head. In other words, he made himself look as much like an ordinary fisherman as possible. His men did the same and kept their weapons belowdecks. The *Sea Leopard* loitered in the offing.

Several days after the capture of the *Dabchick*, they found the mouth of the Biya River. Isam had timed it so they came ghosting up to it in the dawn light. Mist filled the air. This time Isam did not go aboard the *Dabchick* and he kept the *Sea Leopard* at quarters. The men ate their morning meals as they stood beside their guns. Ami, on the quarterdeck with her cartridge cases over her shoulders, had to slip her food under her veil to eat. One of the sailors, a man of about twenty, with a shaved pate and topknot, stared at her in fascination.

Isam noticed his stare, turned to see why, then boxed his ears. "Stop staring. Pretend she's your sister." As for the captain, he had perfected the art of ignoring females and turned away immediately. It helped that he had no interest in women to begin with.

Ami retreated to the far corner of the quarterdeck and turned her back to the men to finish her breakfast.

The sailor held his ears and dared to protest, "But she's a woman, rais!"

"She's a sailor, and that's all that matters. She does her duty, so you'd better do yours. Quit skylarking and look to your gun."

"The guns are fine, rais," the sailor muttered.

A thunderhead instantly loomed up in Isam's face. "You will do as you're told!"

The sailor skipped away as if the force of the roar had blown him away. "Aye aye, rais!"

Meanwhile, the smaller vessel coasted along. Her lead was going constantly. One of the master's mates from the *Sea Leopard* was aboard her to note the soundings. They found a broad mudbank lying parallel to the shore and a narrow channel through it. They had their orders; they entered the narrow mouth. Behind the mudbank they found a shallow channel betwixt sea and shore, then the river proper. The river flowed strongly and carved out a channel deep enough for the *Sea Leopard*. They raised the prearranged signal and worked up the river.

"Out oars. Silent running," Isam said.

The men went quietly to their duty and the *Sea Leopard* entered the narrow cut. The mudbank was no more than half a cable in width, but the slim length of the xebec fit. Nothing bigger could have made it. It was a good place for pirates in shallow-drafted vessels to hide from deep-breasted Spanish frigates.

"That's a strong river current," Master Imrich remarked. "It has cut right through the mudbank."

Isam replied, "Just as well. It will be easy to get out. When you're putting your head in the lion's mouth, it's better to be hard going in and easy coming out."

Imrich gave him half a smile. "Is it a lion's den?"

"Could it be otherwise? The chart shows Biya as inaccessible due to the mud, yet it turns out to have a cut deep enough to admit a xebec. I bet more than one pirate calls it home."

Inside the mudbank they discovered a dilemma, and the *Dabchick* waiting for them. The debouchment through the mudbank served not one, but two river mouths. It was an unusual feature. The river to their right came from the southwest and was broad and slow. Its western margin merged with mud and marsh grasses, but its eastern edge was a ridge of hills that divided it from the river on the left. That river had a strong flow of current. It went straight inland about a cable's length then suddenly hooked left, to the east.

With a wave of his hand and pointing finger, Isam indicated that the *Dabchick* was to explore the western river. She set her sail and cruised slowly into the slow river, all hands on the alert. She disappeared around the first bend and Isam cocked an ear, but no gunfire erupted. She had not sailed into an ambush.

"Oars, give way together. Helm, take us up river."

The *Sea Leopard* made her way inland. The bigger river had scoured out the base of the ridge to create a line of low and irregular cliffs of tan stone as it swept around the bend. That meant the deepest water was right up against the cliffs, and Master Imrich kept the *Sea Leopard* to it. The lead was going constantly and his mates recorded the soundings.

Isam scanned the heights. They were topped with greenery turning brown in the summer heat. The sun was still low in the sky, but the mist had burned off except in the shadows. The night's coolness was gone. It was pleasantly warm, very humid, and promised to swelter before long. A line of clouds was rising in the west that boded ill, but not for a few hours at least.

"Messenger! Check my thunder glass and thermometer."

Taslim touched his forehead, "Aye aye, sir." He went below.

Isam continued scanning the heights. "If I were a pirate and had any kind of discipline in my crew, I'd post a lookout on those heights, but I don't see anything."

"Maybe they're not here," the blond Dutchman replied.

They came around the bend and found . . . nothing.

Isam cocked an ear to listen. Sea birds wheeled and cried forlornly above them. The *Sea Leopard's* oars creaked in the oarlocks. The sweating men bent their backs in unison as they threw their weight on the oars and pulled them back again.

The river ran straight for a short distance, then bent again into the interior. Once again the river had carved its deepest channel under the low cliffs. The inside of the bend was shallow and a beach of sorts had formed from mud, sand, and rock. Small boats lay on the beach, and adobe houses with tile roofs dotted the hills that rose from the beach. Chickens and goats wandered unattended. As they came into sight, the boys playing on the beach stood and stared at them.

"We have found the pirate village," Isam said. "Hoist the purple ensign."

The signal midshipman quickly got out the purple flag of the Sallee Republic and raised it to the peak of the mizzen sail. "Agha of marines! Fire a musket shot."

The agha was not Kateb, but Belim, a lean, hard-bitten Arab that had been a sergeant for him in the past. Belim turned to his men, picked one out, and gave his order. A single musket shot cracked through the morning.

At the sound of the shot, the boys ran and dogs barked. Women who had been working inside their houses came out. The strange ship alarmed them, and they went running to the biggest house in the village. Pretty soon an old man dressed in white accompanied by several blacks descended the hill, got into a boat, and rowed out to the *Sea Leopard*.

While waiting for him, the *Sea Leopard* had spun in place so that she was pointed downstream. This meant the old man had to come around her bow to reach the starboard side to make a formal entrance, but Isam didn't care if he inconvenienced him. He was watching the river and wanted to get out quickly when the tide ebbed.

The old man climbed the ladder to the quarterdeck. He was at least fifty with a grey wispy beard that still had some brown in it. He wore a clean white turban, a fine white haik, and under it, a white shirt and pantaloons.

His feet were encased in rope sandals. A scimitar was thrust in his sash, and although he used a stick to support himself, he drew himself up proudly.

"Who are you?" he demanded as soon as he reached the tall corsair.

"Isam Rais Hamet al-Tangueli, captain of the *Sea Leopard*. Who are you?"

"Ali Bey Hasim, governor of Biya."

Isam was pretty sure the man had not been appointed by the Dey in Zokhara, but then, local governors rarely were. They often took the title of 'bey' whether entitled or not. As long as they paid their taxes, the caids didn't care what they called themselves. Isam had expected to find a pirate camp with doxies, slaves, and chattel, and so it seemed he had, but he had to proceed with caution, given the representative of civil authority (however dubious) before him.

"I have come to inspect your tax receipts and other records. I and my men will go ashore with you immediately." Assuming that the people of Biya were in cahoots with the pirates, the bey's papers would not be in order. That would give him the evidence he needed to take more forceful action.

Ali Bey gave him a sour smile. "I will of course be happy to receive you for lunch. You can present your credentials to me then and we will chat about what you need. I will need several days to organize my papers. I'm an old man and I'm afraid I don't see too well anymore."

"How very lucky for you. I can see very well. I'll bring my purser and his mate. They can go through the papers for you. They're very efficient."

Ali Bey's smile grew more sour still. His thin lips pinched together. "It's very gracious of you to offer help, but I assure you, I have my own affairs well in hand. If you had sent word in advance, we would have been prepared to receive you."

"I'm certain you would have been. I know my presence is a surprise to you, so I won't stand on ceremony. We will go ashore immediately to take care of the paperwork. The sooner we are done, the sooner we can move on and relieve you of the inconvenience."

Ali Bey's faced hardened. All pretense of blandishment vanished. Without the veneer of courtesy, his face had a raptorial mien. His nose was long and hooked, his eyes deep set and glittering beneath their shaggy grey brows, and his cheeks hollow beneath the beard.

"I must insist on following protocol. You will come to lunch." His voice was steely.

"If you will not cooperate, then you and your men will remain aboard as hostages while I attend my business ashore. Belim Agha! Arrest these men. Confine them in the hold."

The Arab warrior stepped forward. He signaled his guards and they surrounded the bey and his suite.

Ali Bey's face contorted in fury. "What we do here is none of your business!"

"The Dey has made it my business. He's noticed the lack of revenue from this neighborhood and has sent me to correct it."

"I pay my caid!"

"In that case you have nothing to fear. If I find the receipts you claim, I shall release you and take up the matter with the caid."

Ali Bey gnashed his teeth and glared. His voice grew cold, "I assure you, I have all the necessary papers. If you don't find them, it's because you are a fool. Or because you're corrupt and have deliberately destroyed them so that you can loot me and claim I was at fault. I know your kind. I will complain all the way to Zokhara!"

"Not if I hang you for piracy, you won't."

Ali Bey's face went grey. He had thought he was being shaken down for money as happened from time to time. He had not thought his life was in peril. "No! I'm an old man! I have no part in piracy!"

Isam smiled. "If your papers are in order, I'll release you. If not, you hang." Jerking his chin at Belim Agha, he said, "I told you to put these men in the hold."

The bey and his servants were dragged away.

"Ransom! I'll ransom myself! How much do you want?"

"All the gold in Biya," Isam replied. "Thank you, but I'll help my self!"

"You'll never find it!"

"Someone will tell. Pirates can always be bought. Get rid of him."

CHAPTER 17 : BIYA'S BOOTY

Biya was not entirely devoid of defense. A small militia of about ten men remained behind, but when Isam Rais landed fifty marines under Belim Agha, they fled. Belim sent a party of men to the heights that separated the two rivers to give warning; indeed, the militia had kept watch there, but thanks to the invader's purple flag, no alarm had been delivered. Looking down from their hiding place on the heights, they had clearly seen the Muslim crew aboard the *Sea Leopard*. The stranger was mysterious to them, but they assumed he was another pirate like themselves. Although they knew about the treaty with Spain (and ignored it to their profit), never did they think a true believer would lift his hand against his brothers in religion to please the infidels.

Isam had a small party of his own trusted sailors in addition to the marines. This included the purser and his mate. While Belim and his men swept through the village, Isam and his men took possession of the bey's home. The house was accompanied by stables, a barn, sheds, and a couple of cottages for servants and soldiers, all of them linked together with a low stone wall to form a compound where chickens scratched, a dog barked, and the goats ignored everyone. The house was larger than most of those in the village. Isam was not surprised to find it furnished with contraband and luxuries.

An elderly black man with a cap made out of a bit of coarse Tunisian lace met them at the door. His brown eyes were wary at the sight of the much taller Turkish corsair. "Ali Bey is not at home," he informed them.

"He is a hostage aboard my ship. Stand aside. I am here to search his papers."

The old man fell back. "Who are you?"

"Isam Rais al-Tangueli, captain of the *Sea Leopard*, sent by commission of the Dey of Zokhara. I am here to suppress piracy," Isam replied, striding into the orange-tiled reception room. His men crowded after.

The old man grew worried. "What will happen to his servitors?"

"Are you a slave or a free man?" Isam asked.

"A slave, effendi," the man replied. He remained wary as the stranger studied him. He was bent with age and his white garments hung loose on his frame. They were very old, mended in places, and irrevocably stained.

"Who are you?" Isam asked.

"Mustafa, head servant to the house."

"You are not very well-dressed for a head servant."

"I am better dressed than my fellow servants."

"Do you love your master?"

Mustafa hesitated, then replied, "I give him the honor his position requires. There are worse positions for an old man like me."

Isam replied, "There are a better masters for an old man like you."

The old black sighed. "If I had grown old in the service of such a master, perhaps, but an old man like me has no value in the market."

"Would you like your freedom?"

Hope flared in the brown eyes, then swiftly dimmed. Quietly he said, "No, effendi. I have no children to support me. An old free man is of even less value than an old slave. If I were free, I would have to beg in the streets. I would most likely starve. It is too late for me."

"It is not too late to earn a reward, and your freedom too. Bring me your master's papers and reveal to me the hiding places for his money and valuables, and I will give you a tenth of what I find."

Mustafa's head came up in shock. He stared at Isam in disbelief. Then he shook his head slowly. "If I do that, you must carry me away. If I remain here, they will turn on me and rob me of everything you give me, and no doubt my life as well."

"Agreed. I will carry you back to Zokhara."

Mustafa's trembled from head to foot, but he dared to say, "I had an old wife. She was fat and saucy, but I loved her. She was sent away to another village. I have never seen her since. If she lives, I want her back."

"What is her name and where is she?"

"Tomeka. She was taken to the village of Old River."

"Where is Old River?"

"On the banks of the Old River, about two miles from here."

"I will send a messenger to fetch her if she lives. If she is dead or has been taken elsewhere, I cannot do more."

Mustafa shook harder and for a moment it seemed he might swoon. He got down on his knees and bowed his head to the floor. "You are magnanimous, effendi. I will do all that you ask."

"Do the pirates keep any property in Old River?"

"Yes, noble master." The old slave bowed again.

"Very well. You must bring me your master's papers and answer all my questions. Once you do that, I will send a party of men to Old River to fetch your wife and the pirates' other property."

Mustafa rose in dread. He was afraid that Isam would not keep his word and he would be left behind, destitute, betrayed, and helpless against the pirates' revenge. Still, if he did not obey, he would no doubt be punished. Therefore he must obey and pray to Allah to make the strange corsair keep his word. He rose and said, "I will fetch the papers, noble master. You will want to question his clerk, too."

"Bring him."

Pretty soon the governor's papers were spread out on his coffee table with Isam's own clerks going through them. The governor's clerk proved to be a handsome fellow with a narrow nose and large, luminous eyes. His lips were sensuously full. He could not be more than an eighth black, but he had the nappy hair of his African ancestry.

"What is your name?" Isam began the interrogation.

"Akil, noble lord," he replied in a light voice.

"How long have you been the bey's clerk?"

"A few months, noble lord."

"What were you before that?"

"A gentleman's valet."

"To what gentleman?"

"Don Diego de Calavera, if it please you, noble lord."

"You do not need to address me as 'noble lord.' I am a corsair captain. You may address me as 'rais,' 'captain,' or 'sir.'"

Akil bowed deeply. "Yes, rais."

"Don Diego was Spanish?"

"Yes, rais."

"How long were you in his service, and how is it you speak Arabic so well?"

"I was five years in his service, sir. Before that I belonged to Selim Rais for a long time. He had me castrated and used me in his cabin. I was not sorry to be captured by Don Diego. He treated me well." The slender shoulders squared, but he was careful to keep his eyes down as a servant and slave ought.

"Do you read and write Arabic?"

"No, sir. Only Spanish. I translated Spanish documents into Arabic, and his other clerk wrote them down."

Isam's transferred his gaze to Mustafa and barked, "Where is the other clerk?"

"He ran away when you came, rais," Mustafa replied. "I cannot produce him. He has fled." He trembled.

"If he is still in Biya, Belim Agha will round him up. Very well. Tell me where Ali Bey keeps his treasure."

Mustafa pointed at Isam as he sat upon the divan. "You're sitting on it, rais. It's under the dais."

Isam jumped up and got down on the floor to have a look. The elevated portion of the room was made of wood covered in carpets, as opposed to the main portion of the floor that was covered in tile. He searched for a handle or lock or other device.

"Do you know how to open it?"

Mustafa shook in his sandals. "No, rais. I saw it open at times, but he was careful no one but he knew how to unlock it."

"Fetch me an axe," he said to the old man. "You, go with him. Don't let him escape."

The guard touched his forehead, then stepped forward to take Mustafa by the arm.

While he was gone, Isam turned his attention to the young black man. "You are a beautiful young man. How did Don Diego treat you?" He looked the eunuch up and down.

Akil was dressed in white robe that came down to his ankles, but nothing else. He stiffened as Isam examined him. "Very well, rais. He was generous and brave. He died at the hands of the pirates. He would not surrender. They abused his body in revenge." Grief etched lines on his young face.

Isam spoke more softly. "You loved him."

"He delivered me from infamy, rais. He was kind. He taught me to read Spanish. He used to like to have me sit on the side of his bed and read to him as he fell asleep. He was generous to his friends and implacable to his enemies. He was a noble man."

"How does Ali Bey compare?"

Akil's nose wrinkled. "Ali Bey does not compare," he replied flatly.

Isam rose from the divan and walked a circle around him. "You're very pretty."

Akil turned his face away. "You are not the first man to say so, rais."

"Did Ali Bey say so?"

Akil swallowed audibly, then answered, "Yes."

"Are you a Christian or a Muslim?"

"I am a Christian, rais." Akil schooled himself to blandness.

"Were you raised a Christian or a Muslim?"

"Muslim."

"You are apostate then. The law is harsh to those that turn their backs on the true faith."

Akil dared to look at Isam then. "I have only the example of mortal men to go by. Those who call themselves true believers violated my body and made a eunuch of me. Those you call infidels were kind and generous to me. Who then is the true example of God's grace?"

Isam frowned at that. "I don't concern myself with religion. That is between you and God." He paced away restlessly, paused, and turned back. "You don't like Ali Bey, so regardless of what you think of Muslims, will you help me to spite him?"

Akil's spine was stiffer than ever, but he thought it over. "Yes. What do you want from me?"

"The same thing I told Mustafa. All of Ali Bey's papers and everything of value. Plus anything Mustafa tries to conceal from me. If you do, I'll take you back to Zokhara with me and manumit you."

Akil nodded abruptly. "If you keep your word, I'll do what you ask."

Mustafa and the marine returned with the axe. Mustafa looked back and forth between the captain and the eunuch, but no one enlightened him regarding their conversation. He had become an old man by being an astute reader of others. He gave Akil a piercing look, but the young slave remained enigmatic.

Isam took the axe from Mustafa, and the others moved out of his way. He approached the dais, and swinging the axe in a great arc, sank it into the floor. Wood splintered, and Isam pulled the axe free. He swung again and again. He was filled with emotions he could not describe. He had been a comfortably self-contained man, confident in his own abilities and satisfied with his course in life, but a nameless trouble bubbled below the surface. He had taken it for granted that his side was in the right in the eternal struggle between the House of Peace that was Islam and the House of War that was Christianity. Long after the Crusades were over, Spain had carried her holy war into Africa. She held enclaves at Tanger, Sebta, Melilla, and other places along the shore. Even in times of peace, her ports were closed to Muslim merchants. All of Christianity was the same. A few nations, like the Dutch and Italians, would send their own merchants to Zokhara, but no merchant of Zokhara was welcome in Amsterdam or Leghorn. Surely he was on the side of the righteous. Yet here he was, raiding Muslim pirates. Pirates who had directed their energies against the infidel, not their brothers in religion. He had no quarrel with them. Then again, they had cheated their Muslim kin and defied their lawful ruler. The law must mean something or else it meant nothing at all. If there was no law, there could be no religion or any good thing. Man would prey on man. As these pirates had done.

Blow after blow fell. The wood shattered to reveal the hollow beneath the dais. He swung the axe in a paroxysm of passion until at last he spent himself. He set the axe down, reached into the debris, and hauled out the strongbox. It was secured with an iron lock.

"Who has the keys?"

"Ali Bey, effendi," Mustafa replied anxiously.

Isam took up the axe again. Precise blows shattered the lock. He dropped the axe, fell to his knees, and opened up the chest. The box was full of neat bags of coins. Opening one, he found it to be copper. He tied it up again, and opened another. That one was gold.

Isam rose. Addressing his purser, he said, "Have you found any letters of marque or other suitable documents?"

"No, rais. But there are ledger books with names of pirates, their vessels, and their prizes. They are paying five percent of their ill-gotten gains to Ali Bey, but he is not forwarding money to his caid or directly to Zokhara as far as I can tell."

"Collect the documents and send them to the *Sea Leopard*. They will be necessary for his trial. Now count up this money for me and make a true receipt for it."

"Aye aye, captain."

Isam turned to the Akil. "Tell me the names of pirate captains who frequent this place."

Mustafa provided the paper and ink he required and wrote down the seven names Akil provided. Mohammed Rais and the *Dabchick* were on the list.

Isam handed the list to Taslim. "Take this to Belim Agha. Tell him to loot the houses belonging to these men of all their valuables. Money, slaves, livestock, saddles, anything that matters. All free people belonging to the houses, including the women and children, are to be seized. When the buildings are empty, burn them. Load everything on the *Sea Leopard*.

"Also, he is to send a party to Old River and do the same. He is to look in particular for an old black woman named Tomeka and bring her away in safety and comfort. If she is not there, he is to make inquiries about whether she is alive or dead, and what happened to her if alive. Whatever his party finds in Old River, they will take to the *Dabchick*. "

Taslim took the list and said, "Aye aye, sir."

Mustafa prostrated himself. "Allah bless you and your descendants for five generations!" he cried out.

"I keep my word," Isam replied. Turning away from the slaves, he went to stand over the purser and his mate. The mate had bound up all the papers and ledgers into an oiled sack he had brought for the task, but there was so much money the pursuer was still counting. Once he was done, he toted up the column of figures. "Six thousand, five hundred, and seventy-eight sequins."

"Give one tenth to Mustafa and make a receipt for it."

The purser made over six hundred and fifty eight sequins in mixed coinage to Mustafa. The old man fell to his knees and prostrated himself again. "Thank you, noble lord. May you live forever in the blessed garden of Paradise! May houris attend your every need and sing your praises as a righteous man!"

Isam was not interested in the houris of Paradise; his eyes went to Akil. Observing his gaze, Akil stiffened. The slender slave had been the plaything of a certain kind of man, and he recognized the look Isam gave him.

Isam asked Mustafa, "You are entitled to a tenth of the slaves and other contraband as well. Do you want this slave as part of your share?"

Mustafa and Akil looked at each other. Horror crept into Akil's expression. Mustafa's gaze turned calculating as he looked the attractive young slave up and down. "He's prettier than my wife, that's for sure," he commented.

Akil threw himself on his knees before Isam and held up his hands. "You said you would take me to Zokhara! I beg you, keep your word, rais! Don't give me to this spiteful old man! He shows a benign face to those in power, but he beats the rest of us! If I were not the bey's pet, his hand would have fallen on me as well!"

Mustafa glared at the younger black. "You deserve it! Such a spiteful, lying tongue you have!" He cuffed Akil across the top of his head.

Their animosity convinced Isam that they had not connived together to hold out on him. "Enough!" he roared. "I won't have demonstrations like this. I'll give you some other slaves."

Mustafa clutched the heavy money bag against his belly and fell to his knees. "You are noble and generous, rais. I wouldn't want a slave like that anyhow. He thinks he's better than the rest of us, even though he's a whore."

Akil's face went white then red as he turned to the old man. His fists clenched, but he held his temper. "May Allah reward you as you deserve, you old monster."

Isam smote his thigh with his hand. "Shut up, both of you, or I'll cane you both!"

The two blacks fell silent.

"You, Akil. You have appealed to my mercy. Will you work for it?"

Akil gave him a wary look, then nodded in resignation. "If it's work that an honest man may do, I'll do it." He bowed his head and stared at the floor.

"Very well then. You can organize the household servants to pack up the rugs and other valuables and take them to the *Sea Leopard*."

Akil bowed in resignation. "Yes, rais." He went out to see it done.

CHAPTER 18 : A RISING STORM

Isam Rais was suffering an embarrassment of riches. The loot was stuffed into the *Sea Leopard's* capacious hold, but he couldn't take the livestock with him. He had only permitted the looting of the pirate captains' households, so most of the people in Biya were untouched—so far. They would suffer the pirates' wrath when they returned. The pirate households didn't own much in the way of livestock, but there were still several dozen head of sheep, goats, chickens, donkeys, and a pair of camels. He decided to eat at much as he could, feed the locals, and auction the rest. Accordingly, sheep and goats were slaughtered and roasted to provide the midday meal. Chickens were more portable, so the ship's carpenter and his mates built crates for them and they were loaded on the deck of the *Sea Leopard*. The *Dabchick* and guard at the river mouth were not forgotten; crates of chickens, some sheep, and a goat were sent to them to devour as well. The auction of the remaining livestock was left in the hands of the purser's mate.

Belim Agha reported, "Fifty captive Europeans are being held in a barn. I've put my guards on it so they won't escape. In addition, I have rounded up twenty-seven slaves, and twenty-one free women, children, and old people belonging to the households of the pirates."

"Are there any single men and women among the pirate households?"

"A few youths."

"Separate out the unmarried girls and boys twelve and older. They'll be sold in Zokhara. The rest put up for ransom. Take anything of value in exchange, money or chattels, but no livestock."

The relatives of the pirates' children and wives bought them back with a combination of cash, jewelry, slaves, rugs, and other valuables, but begged in vain for the return of the young people. There was much weeping and begging, but when Belim was unmoved, they appealed to Isam. Since everyone in the village was related to everyone else, the whole village came to beseech him.

He climbed up on a crate full of chickens and shouted for their attention. They fell silent. "Listen to me! You have all profited from piracy! Now you must suffer for it. You have cheated your own country and invited disaster upon yourself. You're lucky I didn't loot the entire village, enslave you all, and burn it to the ground. That's what the Spanish would have done! If you continue your piratical ways, that's what they will do! Think on it. Why should the Dey protect you when you defy him and cheat him?

If you want to turn corsair, you must go to Zokhara and get a letter of marque. If you pay your fee to the Dey and respect his laws, you will have loot from lawful prey, and the Dey's protection against your enemies. Look at my ship! Did you ever see such a large and fine vessel? She's brand new, built and paid for with the lawful proceeds of privateering. I have my letter of marque, so I receive a much higher price for my booty than you ever will. The agents here in Biya are corrupt!"

All the vessels operating out of Biya were small like the *Dabchick*. The *Sea Leopard* was the biggest vessel they had ever seen, and they were a little awed by her.

"What you suffer now, you have brought upon yourselves. I have been judicious and taken only the property of the pirate captains. I have even allowed you to ransom the married women, children and old people, but your youth I will not return to you. They are the children of pirates. They will become pirates, or marry pirates, and will continue the trade they have learned from their fathers. I am doing you a favor to remove them. If they continue the pirate trade, they will bring a worse vengeance upon you."

Mothers wept, but the tall Turk was unmoved. "Do not plague me further, or I'll have you caned for every word that comes out of your mouths!"

The morose feast continued. Everyone was fed on the slaughtered livestock. Isam and his crew ate in shifts while Akil and other slaves served out food to the captives. When they were done eating, the boys were put into the hold with the rest of the captives. Baskets of food were sent to the captives who ate without knowing it was their own livestock that fed them. Meanwhile, the three girls were separated and given into the charge of Nusrat. They were kept prisoner in the room in which the female crew had been living, which meant the space was entirely too crowded. Still, they could not be put with the rest of the crew, either, so more canvas was hung to enlarge the women's share of the captain's cabin. The canvas extended all the way to the larboard gun.

Nusrat proved to be clever. A number of carpets had been seized as booty. Rolled up in the hold they took up a great deal of space. At her suggestion, they were brought up and laid on the floor of the women's berth one on top of another. They formed a stack twenty inches high. The worst carpets were put on the top and bottom to protect the rest. The *Sea Leopard* had been built with a high deckhead to accommodate Isam in his boots and turban, so all the women but Ami could stand up right even though the floor was raised.

Stowing the captives proved problematic. The European captives, the slaves, and the pirates were at odds with one another and could not be kept together. The *Sea Leopard* was divided into watertight compartments belowdecks, so there were three secure spaces, but they were not equal.

The powder magazine was in the lowest part of the ship in the stern, and Isam had no intention of putting captives in with it. He put the European captives into the middle hold. There was room enough for them, but the forward hold would be severely cramped with twenty-five slaves. Having put the Europeans below, he addressed the slaves that had formerly belonged to the pirates.

"You are slaves without hope of redemption. Those of you who are European know that your families have not been able to raise your ransom. You can hope that your church or government will raise money to free you, but that will take years. Are any of you Spanish?"

The slaves shuffled uncertainly and looked at each other. Two men tentatively raised their hands. They were greasy and scrawny and dressed in ragged clothes.

"A peace treaty has been signed between Spain and the Sallee Republic. Negotiations are in progress for the redemption of captives. Accordingly, I make you an offer. Work for me as crew, and you will be well treated, then turned over to the Spanish consul in Zokhara. I'll accept your labor as your ransom." Given that there were only two of them and they were people of no import, he was willing to take the loss in exchange for having more hands to work for him.

The two men brightened noticeably. They looked at each other and nodded. The first one said, "We'd much rather be free on deck than in the hold. If you swear by whatever you hold holy that you'll give us over to the consul, we'll work for you." They spoke Arabic on account of their long captivity.

The second one said, "But we won't raise our hand against any Christian. We'll do whatever work you assign us, but not that."

"Agreed. Are you sailors?"

"Yes, rais," they replied.

"Excellent. You'll join the main mast crew. That is your chief over there. Go to him."

They scampered over.

Two down. Twenty-three to go. He needed crewmen and was willing to do whatever it took to obtain them. He wanted the women off his ship.

He addressed the remaining slaves. "The rest of you have no hope of ransom. I am willing to offer a chance to work for your own redemption, if you join my crew. You will be given the same work and rations as free men. You will not be paid, but a credit equal to half a share will be entered in the books. When your price has been made up, you will be freed. Working as a common sailor, it will take you several years to earn your freedom. If you attempt to escape, all your earnings will be stricken from the books, and you must start over from scratch. Meanwhile, you may be ransomed, or you may not. If you are ransomed, your earnings will be turned over to you in cash. I need at least six men. Who will take the deal?"

More than dozen black, brown, and white men raised their hands; Akil among them.

"Which of you are sailors? Step forward."

Two blacks, a Moor, and two whites took one step towards him. "Excellent. Go to the boatswain. He will assign you berths."

Eight men of various colors watched anxiously as the chosen men were taken away. Isam then asked, "Who has a skill that might be useful aboard ship? Carpenter, cooper, blacksmith, surgeon, cook, tailor?"

Four men raised their hands, and Akil was one of them.

Isam looked at Akil. "What are your skills?"

"I was a gentleman's servant aboard ship. I know how to do laundry, to cook, and everything else that an officer needs done aboard."

"Very well. You will be the steward for the women. Go to the boatswain."

The others were a mason, cook, and caulker. "I have no use for a mason. Step back. The rest of you are hired. Go to the boatswain."

"The rest of you, listen to me. Some of you are pirates, and some of you are slaves. You have good reason to despise each other. If I had a way to separate you, I would. However, I don't, so you must get along. I make you responsible for each other's welfare. If any pirate is hurt, all the slaves will be flogged. If any slave is hurt, all the pirates will be flogged. If you cause a ruckus that I can't sort out, all of you will be flogged and put on half rations until you're starved into submission. If that doesn't settle you, you'll be put in irons."

Isam spoke to Urve, who was back on duty and walking with a crutch. With Yafi away in the prize, Isam was short a lieutenant. "Put these men in the forward hold. It will be cramped, but it's the best we can do."

One of the captives spoke up. "Excuse me, rais, but we're sailors." He indicated himself and two other men. "We'd like to work for our freedom."

Hearing that, the rest of the pirates clamored, "Me too!"

Isam scowled at them. "No. You're pirates and I don't trust any of you. You're liars, thieves, and murderers. I won't have you as crew."

They murmured in resentment and their faces turned ugly. He drew his scimitar. "You will submit, or you will be executed."

"What are you going to do with us?"

"Turn you over to the Dey. What he does is not my concern." Still on his chicken crate, he loomed over them with his sword in his left hand. The hens in the box didn't understand anything, but they were anxious at the confinement and clucked. Feeling the clucking undermined his authority, he scowled extra hard to intimidate the pirates.

The pirates shifted restlessly and Belim Agha called to his marines, "Present arms!" The marines set their muskets against their shoulders and the pirates found themselves gazing into the muzzles of a dozen muskets.

"Go quietly, or die on the spot," Isam warned them.

With malevolent glares that boded ill, they allowed the marines to herd them onto the ship and lock them in the forward hold.

When the officers regained the *Sea Leopard's* quarterdeck, Urve spoke lowly to Isam. "I'm worried by having so many slaves and captives."

"So am I, but we need the hands. I don't think the Spaniards will give us any trouble. We'll give two slaves to the *Dabchick*, and parcel the rest out among different watches and duties so they won't be able to congregate together. Work them hard. Keep them too busy and tired to revolt. I'm going to head straight to Zokhara. We'll have to beat up the coast, but barring bad weather, we'll be there in a week." He looked up at the sky where the clouds were piling up into ominous accumulations.

"Aye aye, sir. I don't like this business, but it's come off well enough. We made a good haul."

"Indeed we did. The Dey should be happy. He has actual pirates to prove his good faith to the Spanish for a while longer, and we have loot."

A sudden burst of female sobbing drifted up through the skylight from below. What had served to bring on the outburst, he didn't know. He closed his eyes and rubbed them with his hand. "Messenger. Tell Chief Nusrat to keep the captives quiet. As long as you're going below, check my thunder glass."

Allah willing, he would be quit of the women within the week. Not only that, but he had loot enough he could afford to accede to Murad Rais' demands and retrieve Kateb. He was already planning the offhand way he would flaunt his success, needle Murad, and bed the agha. A few more awkward days, and the unpleasantness would be behind him. The ordeal was almost over.

CHAPTER 19 : AMBUSH

The *Sea Leopard* did not put to sea with a storm looming. She sent a messenger to the *Dabchick* to join her and the two vessels sheltered under the lee of the cliffs at the mouth of the twin rivers. Isam retreated to his cabin to do his paperwork—and there was a great deal of paperwork in the wake of the raid. This confronted him with the alterations to his own cabin, which annoyed him. He could hear feminine voices and giggles and it raised his hackles. He suspected he was the subject of their discussion.

Raising his voice to drown them out, he said sternly, "If you're peeping at me, you should be ashamed of yourselves!"

"We're not peeping, rais," came Nusrat's voice through the canvas. "By the way, thank you for the rugs. They are very comfortable. We like them better for sleeping than the hammocks."

A chorus of females voices offered their affirmation.

Isam snapped, "Be quiet! I have paperwork to do."

A gust of wind rocked the ship. A woman gave a little shriek. Isam pulled his beard in distraction, then rose and went over to the canvas. Speaking to them through it, he tried to placate them—for his own peace of mind, not theirs. "A storm is coming. You must not worry about it. We are in a protected anchorage. From time to time, the ship will rock when the wind comes over the cliff, but it is nothing. However, the movements will be irregular, and since you are not seasoned yet, you may get sick. You'd better provide yourself with a couple of buckets. Nusrat, make certain the captive women understand how to live aboard a ship. Considering the situation, you women may use my roundhouse." The last thing he wanted was a seasick woman falling overboard in a storm.

At the announcement, a woman immediately darted through the canvas door, ran into the roundhouse, slammed the door shut, and set the hook. The sound of vomiting came clearly through the door. Previously, the women had been using the first lieutenant's private privy in the wardroom, given that the lieutenant was away in the prize. The common sailors used the heads, but women could not hang their bums off the bow of the ship.

The *Sea Leopard* rocked again and her timbers creaked. It was the natural sound of the ship, but one of the women began to cry. Zokhara was only a short cruise away, but Isam was sure he would be driven mad before they arrived. He pulled the center of his beard in exasperation.

"By Allah! You've been through a battle already! Why are you afraid of a little wind?" A greater wailing burst out in response.

The sound of crying was annoying enough, but he heard some of the women murmuring reassurance, and cocking an ear, heard himself described as "cold" and "cruel." He'd had enough. He put away his papers, dressed in foul weather gear, and went on deck.

Rain came pouring down. Ever practical, the boatswain had rigged canvas collectors to funnel the fresh clean water into barrels. With so many souls aboard, they would drink up their water rapidly. Isam took a turn around the deck. Men in oiled burnooses came to attention. "As you were." They relaxed. "Keep a sharp lookout. We're in hostile territory."

"Do you think they'd try anything in this weather?" one of the men asked.

"If it was me, I would. For precisely that reason."

"Most men aren't you, rais."

"That's true. But stay alert anyhow. The weather may bring us unwelcome surprises."

The late afternoon had already turned to dusk. The heavy clouds drenched the countryside. There was little lightning. It was a nice gale of rain, that was all. The *Sea Leopard* could have faced it easily at sea, but not the *Dabchick*. It was a good anchorage to ride it out. As Isam mounted his quarterdeck, the sun slipped below the level of the clouds and sent rays of golden light across the watery scene. The cliff blocked him from a direct view of the sun, but the brilliant rays streaked beneath the clouds and lit up their bottoms with amber light. It was beautiful and eerie.

It was also a blessing from Allah. In the improved light, the lookout in the mizzen top sang out, "A sail! Three sail! On course for the cut!"

"Beat to quarters quietly. I don't want them to know we're here. Extinguish all lights. Make the signal for three enemy sail." The ensign on duty opened the flag locker and selected the necessary pennants and ran them up the signal hoist. Leaning over tafferel, Isam waved to get the attention of the *Dabchick*. The smaller vessel was anchored upstream from them. When someone waved back, he pointed to the signal pennants fluttering in the gust. He pointed to the sea and held up three fingers. The lanterns on the *Sea Leopard* were winking out one by one. The *Dabchick* understood well enough. Isam had already given instructions to Yafi what to do in case the pirates returned.

The new arrival was no fishboat. She was a low slung *brigantin* with small lateen storm sails set. As she approached, she furled her sails and put out her oars and rowed. She was in the cut before she saw the *Sea Leopard* sheltering in the shadow under the heights. With her great lateen antennas down on the deck and her bow pointed at the sea, the xebec's superior size was not immediately apparent. She was larger than the local fishboats, of that there was no doubt, but nobody but a pirate or pirate's friend would take shelter in that location, so at first the *brigantin* was not alarmed.

As the stranger approached, Isam left his customary place on the quarterdeck and strode to the bow on long legs. He hailed the new arrival. "What ship?"

"*Sumbalet,*" replied the stranger. "Malik Rais. You?"

"The *Sea Leopard,* Isam Rais," Isam replied. "Did you have good hunting?"

"We did! We have two prizes our wake!"

"Will you join me for dinner? Your prize captains too!"

"With pleasure!"

"You can raft alongside us."

Malik Rais considered his options, then said, "If you don't mind, I'll accept."

"I don't mind at all!" Turning back to his own crew, he said, "Help the *Sumbalet* tie up."

He left the bow, called to Belim and Khadim, and spoke in low voices to them. They nodded their understanding, then went to make the necessary arrangements while the crew caught lines from the *Sumbalet.* She was a half-size version of the xebec, but her quarterdeck was small and her captain's cabin cramped. Her deck was lower than the *Sea Leopard's* so the big xebec's men looked down into her. She carried twelve guns on her weather deck and was rowed by thirty-two men, two men at each oar. They were all wearing foul weather gear consisting oiled or tarred burnooses or jackets as the rain came down in buckets. They had to get their antennas down; so much weight aloft in bad weather was dangerous for such a low, sleek vessel.

Isam met Malik Rais as he climbed up the accommodation ladder and swung his leg over the railing. He was a small, active man dressed in brown and red.

"Peace be upon you and all within this vessel!" Malik Rais greeted him. "I'm delighted to meet the celebrated Isam Rais."

"And also upon you. Welcome aboard. I'm looking forward to getting to know you better. Is Biya your home port?"

"No, it's not, but any port in a storm. I'm surprised to see you here. You're so large you can barely turn around in this river!"

"True enough, but as you said, any port in a storm. I've had a good cruise myself and there's no point in taking an unnecessary risk."

"That's very true. Allow me to introduce my first lieutenant, Ibrihim, and my favorite ensign, my son, Muwafaq."

They greeted him and Isam replied, "I'm delighted to make your acquaintance. This is Belim Agha, commander of my marines, and Lieutenant Khadim, my first lieutenant." He stepped away from the side, luring the men further aboard the xebec and away from their own vessel. His own men moved behind them to cut them off.

"Have you had any luck?" Malik Rais inquired.

"I have. Tell me, whose letter of marque are you sailing under?" Isam's baritone was warm and friendly. He kept smiling. The rain drummed down.

"No marque. It's a fool's peace to treat with the Spanish. They are the enemy now and forever." Malik's face darkened as he said it.

"I regret to inform you that you are under arrest. I am the Dey's man, and I have been sent to round up pirates."

Belim and his men leveled their pikes and pistols at the visitors. Stunned, Malik whirled around. He cursed, "May your father burn in Hell, and you with him!"

"I require the surrender of your vessel."

"I will not surrender." Raising his voice, he shouted, "TO ARMS! It's treachery!"

Isam punched him in the face, silencing his next words. "Run out the guns!" he roared.

Below him the deck of the *Sumbalet* was in confusion as the gun ports of the *Sea Leopard* flew open and the muzzles of the guns ran against their gunwale. The *Sea Leopard's* guns were depressed as far as possible, but still she couldn't aim directly down into the deck. It didn't matter. At point-blank range, the muzzle blast alone would kill or cripple anyone within a few yards of it. The *Sumbalet's* crew hesitated.

Isam walked up a cannon and from thence to the railing. He shouted, "Stand down! You are taken! Resist, and we blow you all to Hell! We have your captain and his son as hostage!"

Behind him, Belim's men forced Malik and his companions to the deck.

"Resist!" Malik shouted. "Save the ship!"

Still the *Sumbalet's* crew hesitated. The prospect of escaping the *Sea Leopard* was slim. They would have to get free of the grapples, then row backwards out to sea, which was impossible because the first of her prizes was entering the cut and blocking the way. The *Sumbalet's* crew threw down their weapons.

"Lieutenant Khadim! Take a prize crew and secure her. Lock her crew in the hold. Throw Malik Rais and his party into the *Sea Leopard's* forward hold. I'll deal with them later."

Malik's first prize was a handsome little schooner. Isam was busy securing the *brigantin*, so he let her approach unmolested. With her petite guns and minimal prize crew, she was no threat to the *Sea Leopard*. However, she realized something was wrong. She had only four sweeps to maneuver in tight spaces, but she pivoted in place and tried to flee.

"Fire a warning shot," Isam snapped. He strode along the deck to the bow of the *Sea Leopard*.

At the sound of the gun, the schooner let her sheets and tacks fly. Isam swore, but it was too late. The other prize was coming up, but when she saw the schooner's sails flapping in the universal signal for an enemy sighted, she sheered off. The schooner tried to save herself by putting out her sweeps and turning into the channel between the shore and the mudbank, but the water was too shallow. With a shudder that shook her entire framework, she lurched against the mudbank and stuck fast.

"Acting Lieutenant Hamza! The schooner is your prize. Take a boat and crew and secure her."

"Aye aye, captain!" they responded.

Isam felt the *Sea Leopard's* ability to hold so many prisoners stretch thin, but like a cat that has hooked her claws into her prey, he wouldn't let go. The *Sumbalet* was a very good prize; he would have no trouble selling her. She was small enough to be nimble and affordable, strong enough to snap up most merchantmen, and fast enough to run from warships. She was the ideal privateer. Or pirate. He was well-pleased with the day's profit.

CHAPTER 20 : MUTINY

The weary hands turned in. It had been a long, busy, successful day, and everyone was tired. The new watch came on deck. The rain continued to pour down, but the howling of the wind barely touched them in their sheltered place. Isam Rais made a tour of inspection, and with a word to the watchmen to be alert, retired to his cabin.

Akil roused at the sound of the door opening. He had been sleeping on the floor of the great cabin in order to be at hand when the women wanted him. It was dark in the room. "Captain?" he said.

Isam recognized the voice. "My steward has already gone to bed. I don't want to disturb anyone unnecessarily. Will you fetch me a light?"

"Yes, captain." The slender slave stepped out into the coach and used a taper to bring a light to the hanging lamp in the cabin. The soft yellow glow lit the room.

"And a bath. You were a body servant to a sailor, so you know how, yes?"

"Yes." He found the necessary items in the roundhouse, drew up a bucket of water from the river, and brought it in. While he did that Isam rolled a rug out of the way, then stripped off his clothes and hung them on the clothesline. Wet clothes were a recurring issue for sailors, so he had a clothesline permanently strung in his sleeping area in receive them.

Although they moved quietly, the light leaking through the canvas and the low male voices roused some of the women, Ami among them. She crept to the canvas wall, and peeping through one of several holes the women had poked in the old canvas, spied shamelessly on the captain. She had learned her lesson, all right: don't get caught. When she realized the captain was undressing, she blushed and fell back, but temptation pulled her back. She again put her eye to the seam.

The Turk was a very tall man, that she knew, but without his clothes, the rangy muscular build was revealed to her. He had broad shoulders, big biceps, and a deep chest like all sailors. His torso tapered down to narrow hips and lean flanks. His long legs were muscular, although not as muscular as his magnificent upper body. Black hair covered his chest, forearms, and legs. He knelt over the bucket of fresh water and washed his face first.

Akil, who had been a gentleman's valet, washed his back with skilled hands. Isam was not used to such ministrations, but he was tired so he didn't protest. The crew was stretched thin and worn out; every able-bodied man had been put to work. Even the captain. Akil lathered his hair and massaged his scalp. The headache he didn't even know he had eased away.

"That feels good," he said out loud.

"Doesn't your body servant do this for you?" Akil asked.

"I don't have a body servant. My steward washes my clothes and cleans the cabin and serves my food."

The captain's short hair was quickly done. He shook off further ministrations, rose, and washed his body himself. Ami was still peeking, and turned bright red to observe the corsair was properly shaved below the waist like a clean and godly Muslim should be. The gold rings that pierced his scrotum were visible on either side of the large flaccid organ. That sight sent her scrambling back into bed. The men of her household were modest in dress, so she had never had sight of a fully developed male organ before. She had helped take care of little boys, but the body of a small child was as unlike a man as the body of a lamb was to a ram.

Akil waited tensely. "Do you require anything else of me, captain?"

Isam shook his head wearily. "Go to bed."

"Which bed?" the slave asked with studied blandness. He tried to pretend the answer would mean nothing to him.

"Your own. Where else would you go?" The tired captain used a coarse white towel to dry himself.

"You don't require me this evening?"

Isam paused with the towel in hand. "Oh. That. No. I'm too damned tired."

Akil kept his bland face. "In the morning?"

"Not in the morning, either. I hired you to attend the women. Nusrat will tell you what they want. You report to her, not me. I don't need to be bothered with it."

Akil eyed him warily. Then his eyes flicked to the canvas behind which the women were sleeping. "I see. You have made other arrangements."

Isam laughed shortly. "No, I haven't. They're sailors and nothing more. Nusrat is in charge of making certain of that. You too. I won't have amorous congress between men and women aboard my ship. It will only cause trouble." He hung the towel over the clothesline.

Akil was puzzled. "What do you do for yourself?"

Isam sighed. "I have a lover, if you must know. But he was kidnapped. So what I do now is to try and earn enough money to ransom him."

"He must be a beautiful boy if his ransom is so high."

"He's a soldier," Isam replied shortly. "I won't brook any criticism about it, either. I am the captain and you are not. Who sleeps in my bed is none of your business."

Akil bowed. "As you command, rais." He picked up the bucket, took it to the roundhouse, and dumped it down the toilet.

"I am not like other men!" Isam told the roundhouse door. "I own my own ship and I am captain of my own destiny. The sooner you learn that, the better!"

Akil returned from the roundhouse. He kept his eyes down as he knelt to collect the bath things and put them in the bucket. "Yes, rais."

"I'm going to bed. Blow out the light when you're done." Isam disappeared into his sleeping chamber. Akil hung the bucket on the hook in the roundhouse where he'd found it, opened the lamp, and blew out the light. Then he rolled up in his blanket next to the canvas.

Ami, having received an education highly improper for an unmarried woman, stared at the ceiling in the darkness. Finally, unable to sleep, she got up, dressed herself, and went on the deck.

The rain was still coming down. Several men huddled in the coach. A single red lantern illuminated the space with ghostly light. The midshipman of the watch murmured, "Peace be upon you." He was watching the sandglasses. It was his job to strike the triangle every half hour to announce the time.

"And also upon you," she replied.

Ami climbed to the quarterdeck and uncovered her face. Isam was safely in his bed, so she didn't fear recognition. None of these men knew who she was. On a dark and miserable night, one burnoose clad figure was indistinguishable from another. The cold damp air blowing against her face felt good and she was glad to be free of the stifling veil. The watchmen on duty kept their heads down, periodically lifting them to scan the sea, the sky, and the deck, before returning to the lee of the mast or whatever shelter they had found. At least the cliffs protected them from the wind that still roared overhead. The *Sea Leopard* rocked as the airy tumult caught the upper masts and give her a tweak.

She looked upstream to where the *Sumbalet* was anchored. As she watched, the darkness moved. She stared at it in puzzlement. The dark bulk slipped silently through the waters of the river and its spars were fine lines that were barely discernible in the night. The white splash of oars swept the water of the anchorage. The ship angled to come abreast of the *Sea Leopard* on the windward side. At this close range she could see the gun ports as dim grey squares pierced by round black things. Above the rail she could see the ghostly figures of hooded men with the shimmer of scimitars in their hands. The enemy was so silent she thought for a moment that she was imagining them. Then her sense of self-preservation awoke. They were under attack! She screamed.

The high-pitched shriek pierced every ear and made every heart jump. The sound was massively loud and unnatural; it was a sound never before heard aboard the *Sea Leopard*. It drowned out the howling of the wind and the snoring of the sleepers. It woke every defender, and later some men swore that they saw the ghosts of the dead rise up in answer.

There was no longer any need for the attackers to keep silent. They raised their own keening battle cry and it drowned out her screams. The *Sumbalet* came alongside with a wooden thump that rocked the xebec on her anchors. Grapples grabbed onto her gunwale. Mutineers scrambled up onto the *Sea Leopard's* deck. The defenders drew their daggers—they had no time to rush to the arms lockers in search of pikes and cutlasses. Once she was over the initial shock, training took over. Ami was a powder monkey and the swivels would be needed. She flung herself down the ladder to the main deck. A pistol fired at Ami at pointblank range but missed fire. The powder was damp. The triangle clattered out the alarm.

Some one roared, "Repel boarders!"

Ami dodged into the coach and nearly collided with Isam running out. He was dressed in his nightshirt, bare foot and bare headed, his scimitar in his hand. He and she dodged each other. "Battle stations!" he roared at her. "By Allah I'll gut you for a coward!" In the darkness she was just a crewman in a burnoose to him.

Ami hastily pulled the veil up over her face. Battle stations. Yes. They had drilled for this. She must not fail him. "I'm a powder monkey, rais!" she croaked out.

Discovering that a woman had been out fraternizing with the crew in the middle of the night was a problem Isam didn't have time to deal with. He ignored her as she darted for the companionway.

She couldn't get below: a swarm of men was boiling up from the berth deck. They were dressed in their drawers and shirts—whatever they had worn to sleep in. They had pikes in their hands and snarls on their faces. The *Sumbalet's* boarders rushed the coach, but they met the stream of defenders erupting out, and the battle clogged the space at the foot of the quarterdeck ladders. Dead and wounded men fell under foot.

Isam was the captain; he did not participate in hand to hand combat. He tapped one of the men in the coach. "You. You're a gun captain. Go into my cabin and turn one of the guns around." He saw her veil. "You, woman. Go with him. You'll find a little ammunition in the shot locker." He tapped other men. "Into the great cabin."

Ami ran into the great cabin where all was confusion. The women in their nightdresses were crying and frightened. They couldn't get to their posts and assumed the worst. "We'll be raped!" one of the women wailed.

Akil shooed them into their room. "Get out of the way! We're going to work the gun!"

Ami had no idea what or where the shot locker was. The great cabin was normally cleared for action. She ran into the sleeping chamber, attempted to tear open the sea chest she found, but it was locked. She shook it, but it didn't sound or feel like it had shot in it. The men heaved the divan out from between the two guns and shoved it into the sleeping cabin in two pieces, nearly running her over. She tore the cushions and kilims off, and found that the divan had been made from a pair of chests. Yanking the lid off the first one, she found rope and other things. Putting the lid back, she crawled on top of it so she could reach the other chest. Pulling the next lid off, she found a quantity of six pound cannonballs and several cartridges.

"I need a light!" she called, but was ignored.

Maybe they hadn't heard her in the tumult. The heavy rumble of the gun trucks made the deck vibrate as the men slewed the gun around. They heaved it into the center of the room to command the doorway. Akil scampered out of the way and heaved a rug past her into the sleeping area. Normally the furnishings would go to the hold, but tonight was not a normal night.

Raising her voice to a piercing level, she screeched, "Nusrat! I need a light and two powder monkeys!"

The high-pitched shout drilled through the noise and confusion. Nusrat tapped three women who had not entirely dissolved in terror and sent them to her.

Akil heard the cry for a light. He knew Isam kept his tinderbox in his desk, so he ransacked its drawers until he found it. He opened up the tin, grabbed one of the women, and said, "Bring me that wall sconce."

She groping blindly, found it by touch, then held it for him as he struck flint and steel into the tinder in the small metal box. It lit, and he lifted a burning twig to light the sconce.

"Bring it here!" Ami shouted. She and one of the women unwrapped a pair of cartridges by the light of the sconce. "Be careful! Keep the fire away from the shot locker!"

If a spark ignited the powder, the shot locker would explode in her face. The quantity of gunpowder stored in it was small; it would probably not do the xebec much hurt, but it would tear apart the locker and the women hunched over it. She was simultaneously terrified and resolute. She had become a gunner; she must handle the demon powder safely, get it to the gun, and ensure the safety of herself and her crew. Fear gnawed her stomach, but her hand was steady. Her eyes were bulging from her head, but they didn't blink. The safety of the ship depended entirely upon her. Without powder, the gun couldn't fire, and this was the only gun that could fire because it was the only one equipped with its own private store of ammunition. Without the gun, the defenders were trapped in the coach and must be whittled down by the pirate onslaught. All these thoughts registered in an instant; she had no time for thought. She knew them as if by instinct.

She tossed aside the oilskin wrapping and handed the canvas cartridge into the outstretched hands of a pale-faced woman. Tears of fear tracked the woman's face, but she did her duty. She ran to the gun and handed over the precious cartridge to the gun captain.

Taking the cartridge in his left hand, the gun captain shoved it down the barrel. "Rammer!" he barked.

He had his improvised crew sorted out and assigned to their duties. The rammer jammed the tool down the barrel of the gun. Ami lifted up a six pound cannonball and handed it to the other woman. She was so charged with excitement that it weighed nothing to her.

Wad, shot, and wad were rammed home in the gun. The gun captain shouted, *"Sea Leopard,* stand aside! Ware the gun!"

Isam dove to the larboard—right into the women's cabin. Female screams erupted as he plunged through the canvas curtain, tripped over the rugs, and fell. The girls he had captured at Biya had no training, knew nothing, and could do nothing except scream, and scream they did.

With the retreat of the defenders, the mutineers surged forward right into the gun's line of fire. The men in front saw the cannon and attempted to retreat, but they were shoved forward by the mass of men behind them. An ululating battle cry arose as the attackers in the rear sensed victory and jammed into the space.

"Fire!" shouted the gun captain.

He touched his linstock to the gun, and a second later, the gun bellowed. An eight foot long tongue of flame shot into the passageway, scorching all the attackers who crowded the small space. The cannonball tore through the attackers at torso height, passing through the bodies of five men who cried out suddenly, then fell silent and still upon the deck.

"Sea Leopard, charge!" bellowed Isam.

He leaped out of the women's room and led the attack in person. His scimitar flew and his nightshirt lashed around his hairy legs as he cut through the mutineers. His men ran after him and the wounded tried to scramble out of their way. They trod on the smoking corpses of the dead— there was no room for anything else. They pursued the retreating mutineers all the way to the *Sumbalet.*

"Beat to quarters!" Isam roared.

Belowdecks came the rattle of the snare drum. The drummer boy had not been able to get on deck, but he could hear his captain and beat the tattoo where he stood. The companionway now clear, the rest of the crew swarmed on deck and ran to the guns.

"Go to your stations!" the gun captain shouted at the women.

Ami and the other powder monkeys ran down the companionway to the powder room.

CHAPTER 21 : CAPTAIN DOWN

Isam ran up to his own quarterdeck. The greater height gave him a better view of the situation. Both vessels were encumbered by the long lateen spars that stretched fore and aft along their decks. Supported on their gallows, they were lashed securely in place to ride out the storm. The *Sea Leopard* was beamy enough her guns still had room to work, but the smaller *Sumbalet* was hampered.

Isam bellowed, "Man the guns! Canister!" The canisters were loaded with musket balls and would spew a fearsome death on the decks of the *brigantin*. "Prepare boarding party!"

Belim Agha knew his business; he gathered his men on the far side of the *Sea Leopard* where they would not be in the direct line of fire from the *Sumbalet*. The cold rain swiftly drenched them and made their drawers and shirts stick to their bodies, but there was no time to change their clothes. The fate of the vessels would be decided before any man could put on his shoes.

Ami came running up to the quarterdeck with cartridges for the swivel guns. She only glanced at Isam in his saturated nightshirt. He paid no attention to her.

"Keep the powder dry!" the gun captain snapped at her.

She bent over the leather satchel and used her body to shield the precious gunpowder from the rain. The gun captain swiftly rammed the first cartridge into the mouth of the first swivel gun, then the next, and the next. Below them, on the bow of the *Sumbalet*, the gun crews traversed their own stern chasers to aim up at the quarterdeck of the *Sea Leopard*. Ami trembled in terror, but she held her ground until the last cartridge was out of her satchel. She ran then, ran for her life, ran for the ladders and threw herself down. The *Sumbalet's* guns barked and a pair of cannonballs punched holes in the *Sea Leopard's* quarterdeck. A man howled.

The swivels from the *Sea Leopard* replied in a chorus of smaller voices. The shot peppered the quarterdeck of the *Sumbalet*. A pirate spun and fell, but the crews on each side kept working. All the guns reloaded as fast as they could.

Isam had to stand near the larboard side in order to survey the battle. He knew he was a target, but he didn't worry. If he retreated to a safe position, he wouldn't be able to see. If he couldn't see, then he couldn't win. His own marines went running up the mizzen shrouds to the top to snipe at the enemy. The smaller *brigantin* had no tops, and with her antennas on deck, no way to put marksmen aloft. He was not in much danger from snipers.

The windward position was usually desirous in battle; it had let the *Sumbalet* rush on them, but now it was making it impossible for her to claw off, even with the oarsmen throwing themselves bodily on the sweeps. The wind and current pushed the *Sumbalet* back against the *Sea Leopard*. This time her quarter struck the xebec amidships. Since she was only half the *Sea Leopard's* length, her bow was even with the xebec's bow. As the taller ship, the *Sea Leopard* had the advantage in boarding.

Isam snapped at the messenger, "Grenades. Go tell Belim Agha they're massing aft along the rail."

The midshipman shot down the ladder and nearly collided with Ami running up. They swerved around each other. Ami delivered her charges and again the swivels were loaded. She ran back down. She was panting and thought her lungs would burst as she gulped air. Her legs ached from careening up and down the ladders. The powder room was in the deepest part of the ship, so it was two flights down and two flights up every time. There should have been a second powder monkey for the quarterdeck, but no one had been assigned to that position yet. The new hands were too new to know what to do with themselves.

Tense moments went by, then Belim Agha met his grenadiers in the coach. They lit the fuses in there on account of the rain and let them burn halfway down. Then they jumped out of the coach and tossed them over the side. One burst immediately and showered attackers and defenders alike with shrapnel. A few seconds later, another one went off. One more landed on the *Sumbalet's* deck, rolled through the wet, and extinguished itself.

The pirates saw the grenades and leaped up and ran. Some of them escaped, but others were caught in the blast and thrown to the deck.

Isam gave another order. "More grenades! Disperse—" The bark of the *Sumbalet's* stern guns cut him short.

Grapeshot tore through the *Sea Leopard's* quarterdeck. One of the swivels exploded into shrapnel as it was hit by a fist-sized piece of grape. Pain ripped open Isam's right shoulder and he spun around and went down.

Ami was running up the ladder when she heard the guns. She nearly tripped over the fallen captain as she delivered the powder. At first she didn't realize who it was. Then, as she stepped over the supine body, it seemed like she had stepped off a cliff and was now floating in midair. Her legs moved through the motions and her hands opened her satchel, but she felt like she was watching a puppet show and her body was a marionette operated by somebody else. She threw herself on her knees beside the prostrate rover. He lay on his back, blank eyes staring up at the sodden sky. Rain beat on his face and he blinked, so she knew he was still alive, but his right shoulder was torn open and bloody. Blood splattered the deck around him and soaked the torn remnants of his nightshirt.

A panicked cry erupted amid the shambles. "Captain down!"

The terrible cry caused all heads to turn and look. Stunned by this sudden turn of events, nobody moved. The pirates heard it too. Trapped against the *Sea Leopard's* side as *Sumbalet* was, the shout was heard on both vessels.

"Attack!" roared the pirate lieutenant.

Much heartened, the pirates let out a fierce cry and leaped onto the rail of their own ship. From there it was easy to crawl over the *Sea Leopard's* rail. When their heads appeared above the railing, the *Sea Leopard's* crew snapped into action. The guns roared, but the pirates, being so close at hand, knew where they were and were climbing up between them. In the mizzen top, marksmen sniped at the attackers, but Belim Agha's marines charged forward and met them with pikes. The heart had gone out of them, though. The pirates pressed them back.

Master Imrich, stared down in horror at the prostrate captain. Ami shook his good shoulder. "Rais! Wake up! Rais!"

The woman's voice penetrated the stunned brain of the downed captain. He blinked and groaned and tried to move, but pain lanced through his shoulder, and lower down, where a piece of shrapnel had penetrated his leg like a bullet. His head was ringing and he felt faint, but he could tell from the noise that the battle had moved to his own vessel.

"Help me up!" he gasped.

Ami grabbed him and heaved him up. How she had the strength, she never knew. He cried out in agony and nearly fell over, but Ami pressed under his good shoulder and wrapped his arm around her, braced her legs wide, and took his weight on her own slender body.

Seeing the chaos on his own vessel, Isam roared, "God damn you slaggards! Fight them, you whoresons! Clear the deck!" He locked his knees to keep himself upright, but he needed Ami to keep him from toppling over.

At the sound of their captain cursing at them, a cry of joy went up from the *Sea Leopard's* crew. Invigorated by the sight of his tall form at the quarterdeck rail, they redoubled their efforts. The effect on the pirate crew was equally demoralizing in inverse effect.

"Bring the swivels to the forward rail!" Isam barked.

The quarterdeck gun crew leaped to obey. They lifted them up, lugged them forward, and settled their pivots into holes in the rail designed to receive them. They loaded with the powder that Ami had brought, but she could not run any more because she was holding up the captain. The gun captain snapped his head around, pointed, and said, "You! Get the powder up!" The man grabbed up the satchels and ran.

Ami was glad someone else was having a turn as powder monkey. She was gasping for breath and happy to have the easier task of supporting the captain, even if he was a hundred pounds heavier than her. Her aching legs cramped and she thought they would never unbend from their current position, but she didn't wobble. The captain was the heart and brain of his ship; the *Sea Leopard* needed him. The most important thing she could do was to keep him on his feet.

The battle on the deck of the *Sea Leopard* raged fiercely. The marksmen sniped at pirate officers. The swivels took careful aim, and waiting for their opportunity, fired into the pirates when fresh men crawled over the rail from the *Sumbalet*. Swords and pikes clattered in general melee. For a few tense moments that seemed like forever to those involved, the battle persisted. Then the tide turned. No one called a retreat, but some of the pirates leaped back onto their own vessel. Some of them fell wounded, then others threw down their weapons and surrendered. The pirate officer shouted, "Rally! There is no hope but victory!"

A marksman in the mizzen top fired on him, and he fell to the deck. With the collapse of their leader, every pirate did as he thought best. Some surrendered, some leaped into the *Sumbalet*, and some leaped into the river. Fifteen minutes later, the *Sea Leopard* had command of both vessels. Belim Agha leaped onto the *brigantin's* deck and organized his men to root out the fugitives belowdecks.

Isam turned his head and told Master Imrich in a faint voice, "You have the conn," and fainted.

Ami couldn't hold the captain's weight by herself. She went to the deck with him and cushioned his fall.

"Rais! Rais! Answer me!" She begged. No answer came.

"Put pressure on his wound. He's bleeding out," Master Imrich said urgently.

Ami whipped off her hijab and folded it up. "Don't die!" she screamed at him. She pressed on the bleeding shoulder with all her strength and weight and fear. Isam's eyes stared up glassy as the rain splattered his face.

Isam was not dead. He was faint, but above him he could see a female form limned against the lantern light. He couldn't make out her face, but he was sure it must be beautiful because all the houris of Paradise were beautiful. He was surprised to wind up there. Aside from fighting infidels, he hadn't done anything particularly noteworthy, but somehow, Allah had seen fit to extend His grace even to a stubborn corsair. Darkness covered him like a warm blanket. Dying didn't hurt. It wasn't even uncomfortable. He was grateful for Allah's mercy.

Chapter 22 : Houri in Paradise

With the *Sea Leopard* securely in the hands of her own crew, the loblolly boys started picking up the wounded and carrying them below. A stretcher came to fetch the captain and Ami accompanied him to his cabin.

"I need light and a table to work on," the surgeon said.

Akil and Ami grabbed the lockers and pulled them together in the middle of the room. The loblollies put the wounded captain on it. Akil lit the bronze Moorish lamp that hung in the middle of the cabin and it shone on the wounded man below. Isam didn't wake.

The surgeon's mate cut away the torn cloth of the nightshirt while the surgeon readied his instruments on the captain's desk. Akil brought a bucket of water, and the surgeon used it to sluice away gore. He picked shreds of fabric out of the mess with tweezers, and blood began to ooze from the wound again. Probing it, he found a piece of shrapnel and pulled it out. The captain's face was ashen under his well-tanned complexion.

"He's lost a lot of blood," the surgeon commented.

"Will he live?" Akil asked.

Ami held her breath as she waited for the answer.

"Allah willing. He has survived the immediate wound, so I am hopeful of recovery, but that will depend on how much blood he has lost and whether infection sets in."

"I'll nurse him," Ami said.

The surgeon looked askance at her. "Nursing is not suitable work for a woman."

"Carrying powder isn't suitable work for a woman either, but I've done it," she retorted.

The surgeon glanced at her again and grunted noncommittally. He knew the captain had been desperate for hands. He finished probing the captain's shoulder, then threaded silk into his needle, and stitched up the wound. The bloody arc ran from clavicle to armpit with a jagged gouge that laid open the wound to the shoulder bone. Next he moved to the wounded leg. Assuming only the lowest sort of woman would have signed on as crew, he didn't think he was offending her modesty to hike up the remains of the captain's nightshirt to expose the hairy muscular thigh. A chunk of metal from the swivel gun was embedded in the captain's thigh. Ami was a butcher's daughter and had seen living animals slaughtered, but to see a man in such a bloody condition bothered her immensely. She looked away.

After that the surgeon cut the nightshirt enough to pull it down to the captain's waist, exposing the muscular pectorals with their swirls of black hair. The surgeon's mate lifted the captain's body while the surgeon passed the bandage around his chest, under his back, and over his shoulder. Isam moaned in complaint and his eyelids fluttered, but he didn't speak. The surgeon bound up the thigh next but ignored several small cuts and scrapes.

"Put him to bed," the surgeon said. "I have other patients to attend." He and his mate left.

"I'll find a clean nightshirt," Akil said. He went to the sleeping chamber.

Ami gently removed the remnants of nightshirt from the inert body. She tried diligently not to look at the exposed loins as she tugged the fabric underneath his butt, but she couldn't help it. She needed to see what she was doing. She pitied him. He was insensible and badly wounded. She was certain that the prescriptions for modesty applied to an active and randy male, not a wounded man who needed her help.

Akil returned as she pulled the shreds of the nightshirt entirely away. He gasped, "By Allah's name, woman! What are you doing!"

Ami gave him a hard look. "He can't stay in these wet clothes. We have to get him dried off and dressed in something dry. Now bring me a towel."

Voices penetrated Isam's aching head. He groaned again and moved a little. Ami swiftly took hold of his arms. "Hold still, rais. You're wounded."

Glassy eyes rolled in her direction. He heard a female voice, but he didn't understand her words. Looking up at her, the light of the lamp directly above him combined with his own blurry vision to render her an indistinct but luminous figure. That it was a woman, he was certain, but addled by his injury, he knew nothing else.

In slurred words, he asked, "Are you a houri? It's cold for Paradise."

Akil returned with a pair of towels. He handed one to Ami and said, "Dry his hair. I'll dry his body." His voice was prim.

The towel swiftly covered the naked man, and Ami found herself relieved that he was covered. She took the other towel and gently rubbed the short black hair while Akil patted his body dry.

"Akil?" Isam asked in a weak voice. His eyes tried to follow the black man, but the lamp was too bright.

"I'm here, rais. You must rest. You're badly wounded."

"I could have sworn there was a woman here just now. I must be dreaming."

"I'm here, rais," Ami said.

Isam tried to raise his eyes to see her, but it only made his head hurt. "Let me see you."

Ami moved around to his side so that he could see her without straining himself. He lifted his left hand to shade his eyes against the glare of the lamp. The flesh around his eyes was tight with pain and the hand trembled with fatigue.

"Who are you?" he asked in confusion.

"Jamila bint Nakih. I followed you to sea."

His eyes snapped open. "Jamila! But why?"

"I ran away from home and veiled myself when I heard you were hiring women. I wanted to be with you. I had no idea what it would really be like. I have seen things that frightened me, but the worst of all was when you fell and I thought you were dead." She picked up his hand in hers and clasped it tightly.

"You wear blue. Wait, where's Ami?"

"I am Ami. I changed my name so you wouldn't know me. I was sure you would send me home if you knew I was Nakih's daughter."

"You're Ami, the tall one," he said stupidly.

"Yes, rais."

"Who ran the powder."

"Yes, rais."

"You were a good sailor. You worked hard." His baritone was so faint she barely heard him.

"Thank you, rais." She blinked back tears.

"Your family will be angry." The conversation was tiring him out. "They'll think I carried you off."

"I'll tell them the truth. They'll believe me. They love me. I know they'll be angry, but I thought I was going to come home with a dashing corsair as my husband and all would be forgiven. Now I know that won't happen. Since I've been on the ship, I've come to understand you aren't like other men. I didn't really know what that meant when you said it before, but now I do. You don't need a woman." Tears came then. They left marks in the gunsmoke on her face.

"Yes." He was too weak and tired to say anything else.

She put his hand on his chest and patted it. She rubbed her eyes and said, "We must get you dressed, rais. You're cold. We'll help you to bed and you can rest. We'll get you some hot bricks to help warm you up. You'll feel better tomorrow."

With that she became brisk and business-like. She was the daughter of a butcher; she'd seen plenty of bleeding flesh during her life. So she told herself. She and Akil put the clean white nightshirt on the captain, then heaved him up and tottered him to the sleeping chamber. They tipped him into his hanging bed, wrapped him in blankets, and put a nightcap on him to keep the damp hair warm. Akil went to the cook to get warm bricks and Ami sat on Isam's sea chest and kept watch over the sleeping man.

She began to pray, "I ask Almighty Allah, Lord of the Magnificent Throne, to make you well." She recited it seven times as prescribed, counting the iterations on her fingers to make certain she didn't lose track.

Akil arrived with heated bricks wrapped in cloth. He slipped them under the bedclothes to warm the captain.

The steward came in a little while later. He was lugging the glass panes for the stern lights. The glass turned the gun ports into windows and admitted the watery light of a grey and gloomy dawn. Akil stowed the deadlights while the steward trooped down to the hold to bring up the glass for the quarter lights. Overhead, the booming voice of Belim Agha called out, "Come to prayer! Come to success!"

"You should go to prayer," Akil said. "I'll watch him while you're gone. Pray for his recovery."

Ami nodded wearily. Now that the night was over, she was exhausted. She went to the women's berth and changed into her spare set of clothes and put a clean cloth over her hair. She no longer veiled her face; she had only done that so Isam wouldn't recognize her.

Not usually religious, the crew answered the call to prayer in mass. Many of them didn't know their prayers properly, but they followed along as best they could as Belim led them in the prostrations and recitations. They had fought a hard fight and gave thanks to Allah that they had been delivered from their enemies. The women kept to the side as far away as they could manage from the men, but within the confines of the ship, that wasn't very far.

Jamila's voice rose clear and true and confident—she knew the prayer perfectly. Her brother Shakil had made certain that everyone in their family knew their duty to Allah. When the women heard how well she recited the prayer, they deferred to her and followed half a beat behind her. Some of the men heard her too and glanced at her distractedly, but they all knew Ami was a proper young woman who wouldn't even speak to them, so her command of the prayers only served to reinforce her reputation with them.

In his bed, Isam opened his eyes. He rolled over, but he couldn't clamber over the side of the bed. "Help me up. I must go to prayer."

Akil came and spoke soothingly. "You're wounded, rais. You're exempt from prayer."

"No, a houri came to me. I must pray."

"You're not in your right mind, rais."

Isam persisted in trying to climb out of bed. He managed to get a leg over the side, and fearing he would fall, Akil helped him out. Pulling the Turk's good arm over his shoulder, he supported him on deck.

As the staggering captain appeared, Belim suddenly paused in the prayer. Everyone was silent, but the men gave way and Isam plopped into the front row next to Belim. "Continue," Isam said.

The black man had lost his place and mumbled uncertainly.

Seeing his hesitation, Jamila recited, "Allah listens to him who praises Him," in a clear and confident voice.

Belim repeated, "Allah listens to him who praises Him."

The congregation answered, "Our Lord, Thine is the praise, the praise which is bountiful, pure and blessed."

The prayer continued. Isam wasn't capable of rising by himself, but the men on either side of him lifted him up. When his legs buckled, they eased him to the deck again. When he swooned, they let him lie. When the prayer finished, they carried him back to bed.

Jamila bustled into the cabin and scolded Akil. "Why did you let him out of bed! He's too weak to come to prayer!"

"He's the captain! I have to do what he says!" he protested.

"He's a wounded man and belongs in bed! It doesn't matter that he's the captain. The surgeon sent him to bed and that's where he is going to stay until the surgeon says otherwise!" She put her hands on her hips and glared at him.

"You're not his wife!" Akil argued.

Her eyes narrowed. She snapped back, "Neither are you!"

His face colored. "No. I'm his slave. How can I argue with him? It will take me years to earn my freedom even if he keeps his word. I must do as he says."

Jamila had heard that conversation. "Because you're stubborn. He offered you a better job and a better wage."

"What sort of offer is made to a slave? It's not like I have a choice in the matter. You are free even if you are a woman, and so you're free to choose your own fate. I am not. Whatever you have done, you have done because you chose to do it. You will pay the price for it, but that price was yours to choose. I have no choice. My only choice is to please this man, this man who owns me. I made a bargain with him to escape a worse situation, but that doesn't mean I want to be here."

Only seventeen, Jamila had never been obliged to confront the complications of the real world. She didn't know how to answer Akil. He was only a few years older than her, yet he had experienced far more than she had. She turned his doubts over in her mind, then said, "He'll keep his word. I know he will. He's an honest man."

Akil shook his head and schooled himself to blandness. "He's not an honest man. He's a corsair."

"He's a warrior against the infidels and obeys the laws of his own country. You of all people should know that. There's a world of difference between him and those pirates."

Akil folded his arms over his chest and became like wood.

Jamila sighed. She didn't know what to say to him once he quit talking to her. "If he doesn't, tell me and I'll make Shakil fix it."

She had her own troubles to deal with, so she retreated to the women's quarters. She threw herself full length on the rugs and began to cry. She was only seventeen and the romantic dreams she had entertained were shattered. Her story was not going to end like one of the Arabian nights and she was not going to live happily ever after. She was immensely homesick and missed her gentle brother Shakil and the gruff but friendly Kasim. She missed her father who was always wise and kind and gentle. All around her was the scent of the sea, gunsmoke, and blood.

CHAPTER 23 : THE RELUCTANT PATIENT

The *Sea Leopard* and her train of prizes set sail for Zokhara at Isam Rais' command. They had to beat against a northwestern wind and progress was slow. The captain stayed in bed and his officers came to him to receive his orders, but they were general: stick together, avoid combat, go to Zokhara. Lieutenant Urve (barely ambulatory himself) and Master Imrich had charge of the *Sea Leopard*. Khadim was dead, slain by the mutineers when they obtained control of the *Sumbalet*. It was a gloomy victory. Fighting fellow Muslims, even if they were pirates, sat poorly with most of the crew.

After two days, Isam insisted on getting up. He refused laudanum. He wanted a clear head. He was sure the ship needed him, and he was intent on resuming his duties, even if it made him dizzy to sit up. Akil bathed him because he was in too much pain and unable to move his shoulder enough to do it himself. Akil changed his bandages, then put a pair of clean white pantaloons on him. The shirt proved impossible because Isam couldn't move his shoulder enough, so Akil wrapped him in his robe. Supporting him under his good shoulder, he helped him totter to the divan where he laid down. In spite of his ambitions, that was as much activity as the captain could manage.

Peeking through the canvas, Jamila saw he was properly dressed and came to visit him. "Good morning, rais. Are you feeling better?"

Isam did not want to admit that the minor activity of dressing and moving to the divan had tired him out. "Yes. It's a nice day. Open the windows. It's warm in here."

Akil maneuvered around the guns and swung the glasses up on their hinges and looped their lanyards over the hooks above. Jamila came to the divan, and noticing the condition of the captain's bare feet, said, "You need a pedicure."

"A what?"

"Taking care of your feet. I'll get my kit." She rose gracefully and disappeared, then reappeared a moment later with a decorative red bag. She knelt by his feet and took one in her hand. "You have warts."

He pulled his foot away. "I don't have warts!"

She pointed to a small circle. "That's what we call a 'plantar wart.' It might not bother you now, but if it gets bigger, it will. You are on your feet all day. As long as you are convalescing, we should take it off. It will be better by the time you're back on your feet."

He eyed her skeptically. "And you know how to do this?"

"My father gets them all the time. Sometimes Kasim and Shakil, too. Shadha showed me how to do it. It hurts a little, but considering your big injury, you won't even notice."

With a wince, Isam pulled his foot up to look at it. He did have several small bumps, but they were so small he had not thought anything of them. "You're sure they're warts?"

"Yes. They start like little seeds and grow."

Isam was a mighty corsair. Something as small as a wart was beneath his notice. On the other hand, she was right: he was on his feet all the time. He had injured his feet in the past and knew how it hurt. Grumpily he said, "All right then. Do it." He put his foot back down on the divan.

"I'll do it last. That way your feet can rest after I'm done."

"Do what?" he asked.

"Everything."

"Huh?"

She went to work trimming and cleaning his nails. She buffed, filed, washed, and applied lotion to his nails and feet. All the fussing made him even grumpier. He was a manly man and unused to such attention. He let her do it because she seemed to think it needed to be done and he was too tired to argue. Then she massaged his feet. His legs twitched and jerked, but she kept digging her fingers into the sensitive spots.

"Ow!"

"It'll feel better when I stop."

"Yes, it will!" he retorted.

She laughed and kept doing it.

Eventually, his feet gave up their resistance. When they did, he discovered that he had apparently been living with sore feet for years. He was so used to it he never thought about it.

"That's good!" he exclaimed. The improvement to his feet reconciled him to all the prissy effeminate stuff she was doing to him. His manly dignity found it very easy to accept feet that didn't hurt. Then she picked out a wart. "Ouch!"

It was a pinch and nothing more, but it was a pinch that tore the little wart away from the skin, leaving behind a dot of blood and a sore spot where she dug it out.

"Warn me before you do that!" he said crossly.

"Goodness. You're a big baby when it comes to warts!"

He scowled at her. "I'm not a baby."

"Then hold still while I do the next one."

He gritted his teeth and lay back on the cushions. He used his good hand to press his wounded shoulder.

Jamila noticed. "If your wound is bothering you, we'll stop."

Isam was too stubborn to admit defeat to a girl. "I'm fine," he snapped.

She removed the next wart with her tweezers. She watched him grimace and saw the weariness in his eyes. She hesitated.

"Is that all of them?"

"No, there are two more."

"What are you waiting for?" he grumbled.

Reluctantly, she plucked out the next one. Isam stared at the deckhead above. He curled his lip, but said nothing.

"One more," she said softly.

It annoyed him that it bothered him so much. He had suffered a far worse wound that made his whole body ache and was bearing it stoically, but the wart removal was an irritation that set his teeth on edge. It was much easier to suffer nobly with a heroic wound. Warts were just ugly. Once again he pressed the aching shoulder.

Jamila laved his foot with water, then applied ointment to each small wound. She wrapped his foot with a bandage, then massaged the wart-free portion to make it relax again. He was exhausted. Reluctantly he admitted to himself that Akil was right. He shouldn't have left his bed.

"Would you massage me here, near the wound? My neck aches and so does my chest."

Jamila brought her kit to the head of the divan. Feeling awkward to be so close to his face, she knelt out of his line of sight. Gently she touched the robe over the bandage and traced the outlines. He swallowed and she felt his adam's apple bobbing against her fingers and the bristles of his beard lightly scratch the back of her knuckles. The muscles of his neck were powerful and tense. She had massaged her father and brothers before, but never an unrelated man. She was keenly aware of the closeness of his barely clad body. She began to knead the tight muscles she found.

Isam let out a little sound, then closed his eyes. "That feels nice," he mumbled. "I think I'd like some brown paper and vinegar. My head hurts."

Akil spoke. "I'll get it for you."

When he returned, he folded up the brown paper to make poultice and poured white vinegar onto it. He handed it to Jamila and she pressed it against the captain's forehead. The sour smell of vinegar was strong in the air, but the cool paper soothed his aching head. His eyes closed.

Gentleness was a strange sensation for the bold corsair. He didn't know how to react. Slowly he settled beneath feminine hands. They worked down his neck, hesitated a moment, then continued the same gentle massage onto his chest. She was careful not to get too close to the wound. All of the corsair's upper torso was knotted tight. She blushed to be touching a man's chest, but as Isam gave a groan, she reminded herself that this was medical care for a wounded man. Isam saw nothing erotic in it; the idea never even crossed his mind. Gradually his pain eased, and he fell asleep.

On the fifth day, Jamila and Akil supported Isam on either side and helped him up to the quarterdeck. It was humid and close in the great cabin and the patient was glad to get out. He braced his feet and hung onto the shrouds for support. The breeze blew over him and refreshed him.

"Report, Lieutenant Urve."

Urve had improved over the last few days himself. His arm was still in a sling, but he was standing up straight. "We are off Oued Laou. Allah willing, we'll reach the mouth of Modiq Bay by evening. If the wind holds from the north, we should be able to sail all night and reach Zokhara in the morning."

"Excellent. Carry on."

He turned and looked over the tafferel and lazy board. There, trailing in his wake, were the three prizes. The *Sea Leopard* could have outsailed them all, but had deliberately checked her pace to keep together. They had been won with too much blood to take a chance of losing one. He was well pleased. The Dey had underwritten the expenses for the expedition, so the prizes were pure profit. They would set his finances to rights.

Unfortunately, arriving in Zokhara would give him another headache. He turned and looked at Jamila. Her family's honor would require him to marry her. It wasn't his fault she'd run away from home! But he was certain that they wouldn't care and would press him to make an honest woman of her. The thought filled him with dread.

"Ami," he said. "We need to talk."

Akil and the steward brought up a wooden box to serve as a seat for the captain, and Isam settled onto it gratefully. Although he felt better for the fresh air, he tired easily. He had lost blood and it would take time to rebuild it. He was short of breath and dizzy when he moved.

The rest of the quarterdeck crew kept away to give him his privacy, but Jamila came to stand close enough to speak to him.

"Your family will be angry. You've disgraced them and ruined your chance of marriage."

Jamila settled on her knees before him. She bowed her head. "It didn't turn out the way I imagined," she admitted.

"I'll speak to Shakil about it."

"What will you say to him?"

"It's not my fault you ran away!" He was positive the moralistic young man would blame him.

"I will tell him so. It was my own choice, even if I did it to be with you. I'm not sorry I did, either."

"Even though your hopes of marriage are dashed?"

She clasped her hands tightly together in her lap. She didn't answer at first. Finally she lifted her eyes and said, "I have had an adventure and I am glad of it, in spite of the thing terrible things I have witnessed. I don't wish to be a sailor any more, and I'm glad to go home. But I'm also glad that I came. I've learned a lot of things I never would have learned if I'd stayed home like a proper daughter."

"You have courage. You should marry a corsair. You will give him brave sons."

Jamila looked down at her hands and bit her lip. "Do you think one of your officers would want me?"

Isam rubbed his wounded thigh and thought it over. "I believe all the crew hold you in the highest regard. It might be possible. Still, it would be awkward, since I am the captain. I wouldn't want anyone to say—" He bit his tongue before he said what he didn't want said.

"That I am your cast off," she supplied. "A soiled woman for which you had no further use."

Isam frowned. He didn't speak. He looked up at the azure sky as clear as a virgin's heart before she knew what love was. The silence stretched out.

"It appears I must marry you myself. There is no honorable way around it."

Jamila kept her eyes downcast. "I am not trying to trap you into marriage, rais. I know what sort of man you are and I know you would be unhappy. If you marry me and are unhappy, then I will be unhappy. I don't want that for either of us."

"Who said marriage is about happiness? But I am always at sea and I live on my ship in port, except when she needs repairs. So we wouldn't see much of each other. You'd be free to spend as much time as you wish with your family. I'll give you a decent dower; you'll have what you need. Being that I am a corsair, you can reasonably expect to be a widow at a young age. You'll be free to remarry soon enough."

"I don't want to be a widow!" Jamila blurted out. "If you are my husband, I will pray always for your safety!"

Isam tugged the center of his beard when it seemed Jamila might cry. He had no idea what to do when faced with feminine tears. He wanted to run away. "I will talk to your brother about it. Now I am tired and want to go back to bed."

Akil and Jamila helped him back to his hanging bed and left him to stare at the deckhead above him. The compass mounted over the bed pointed north, towards Europe—but he was wending his way west towards Zokhara. Towards matrimony.

Marry? Him? If only he had thrown her out of his cabin when he first discovered her identity. Then she would not be his responsibility. He had been weak and let her attend his body. She had seen him naked, touched his flesh, stroked his face. All for medical reasons, but it wouldn't matter. She had lost her modesty and would always be suspect. He would have to give her a dower so that a husband would take her for the money.

He scowled. He shouldn't have let her give him a pedicure. That was his downfall. It was an effete thing and had undermined his fitness as a corsair. He was a seaman with no use for the soft luxuries of shore. Indulging himself had softened his spine. He was wounded, but getting better. He could get around on his own two feet now. He didn't need help. With that resolution, he crawled out of bed and promptly fell flat on the floor. A bolt of pain went through his shoulder, but he gritted his teeth and got up. He took a seat at his desk and opened it. He had paperwork to do. All the prizes had to be proved as pirates in a court of law. He started organizing his evidence. He needed the money so that he could ransom Kateb.

The vision of the big black filled his mind and made him smile. That was the kind of company he needed and wanted. Kateb was a strong man; it was a relationship of strength and strength. Then he worried. Would Kateb still respect him now that he was weak in body and petulant in manner? A corsair captain ruled the hardbitten men of his crew by showing himself to be an indomitable victor. He shouldn't have spent days lying in his bed like a weakling. He ought to go on deck again, but he had already done that and it tired him. The paperwork needed to be done, too, so he would do that. That he was seriously wounded was irrelevant. He had responsibilities. He buried himself in the paperwork and put his personal problems out of his mind.

CHAPTER 24 : THE PRICE OF FREEDOM

The *Sea Leopard* arrived in the well-protected harbor of Zokhara in the morning. The health inspector had taken a good look at Isam, pronounced him free of infection, and allowed them to dock. Sailors moved through his cabin to secure the stern lines to the big cleats in the floor of his cabin. The hemp lines as thick as his wrist chuckled as they rubbed through the hawse holes and the ship bobbed gently at her berth. The captives were brought up from the hold and marched off to the bagnio by his marines. Lieutenant Yafi went with them as his agent. When Yafi returned, the female captives were rounded up and taken to a separate prison. That done, the female crew were given pay tickets they would turn in to claim their share of the prize money after the matter had been adjudicated.

Jamila received her pay ticket with the rest, but she was called back and made to wait in his cabin. Akil remained with them to ensure propriety. For the sake of both their reputations he didn't care to be an object of gossip. Why it bothered him for people to think he was keeping a woman, he didn't know. He didn't care what they thought of his male paramour. Or perhaps he did, but he had long been accustomed to showing an iron face to any criticism. That being so, no one bothered to criticize him. It wouldn't do them any good and might well earn them a punch in the nose. As for the crew, what they cared about most was prize money. If they had it, they didn't care what he bedded. Corsairs were pragmatic men.

Akil and Jamila helped him transfer from his bed to the divan. He hated being so weak in the body. Standing up made him dizzy. He turned a little green and settled gingerly on the divan. Shimmering reflections of light danced across the deckhead and walls and hurt his eyes.

"Are you all right, rais?" Jamila asked.

Isam rubbed his aching head with his left hand. "Pipe," he said.

Akil went to his sleeping chamber and opened his sea chest. He mixed a bit of hashish with the tobacco in the bowl, then brought it to him. He lit the tinder, and then the pipe. Isam sat up and puffed gently on the pipestem. Slowly the hashish made itself felt. It dulled the edge of his pain and settled his nausea. The pipe had become a routine over the last few days. With it he could sit up and attend to business, or sleep in spite of the aching in his shoulder.

"It's starting to itch," he commented.

"It's healing then," Akil said.

"I know. I've been wounded before." He stretched his right leg along the divan. It was not as severely injured as the shoulder, but it was inconvenient enough.

Jamila had said little, but she spoke now. "I hate to leave when you're unwell, rais. I know your servants will take care of you, but I'll worry all the same. A corsair's life is a dangerous one. I'll pray for you."

Isam wanted to be grumpy about being called "unwell," but he was unwell. He didn't like it, but these two had tended his prostrate body, so there was no point in pretending otherwise. He sighed. "You have to go home, Ami. You can't stay here."

She bowed her head and pulled her scarf over her face for a moment.

Akil said darkly, "They'll beat her. Maybe worse. You can't send her home. You have to make some kind of arrangement to mollify her family."

Jamila lifted her head in horror. "They wouldn't!" Then she said, "Kasim might. He hits his wife." She twisted the end of the blue headscarf into a tight tail until her knuckles turned white and the silk squeaked from the strain. "My father won't hurt me. He loves me."

"All the more reason for him to beat you. You've disappointed him and ruined your prospects for marriage." Akil had a low opinion of the human race. Especially the male half.

Tears spilled out of Jamila's eyes. She unwound the scarf and pressed it up against her face. "He won't," she said through the fabric.

Isam smoked his pipe, but the hashish couldn't insulate him from the woman's tears. "Some sort of honorable arrangement has to be made. Akil, fetch her brother Shakil. He's a reasonable man. Bring him here to discuss it."

Akil's eyes lit up, then he carefully banked the fire those words had lit. Neutrally, he replied, "Yes, rais. Where will I find him?" He spoke with studied casualness.

Jamila uncovered her tear-streaked face. "It's in the meat market." She explained how to find it.

Akil listened carefully, then rose and bowed. "I'll go now, rais."

Senses dulled with the hashish, Isam nodded. He was too preoccupied with his own problems to remember Akil's.

Akil hesitated at the door, then turned to Jamila, "May Allah watch over you, brave girl." Then he stepped out. It was all he could do to force himself to walk nonchalantly. He went down the gangplank to the quay and lost himself in the busy narrow streets. No one paid any attention to yet another black man in plain white clothes.

The minutes ticked by, and then the hour. At last Taslim knocked on his door, entered, bowed, and said, "Nakih bin Nasir and his sons are here, rais."

Isam gave a groan. He didn't want to deal with the full force of male relatives. "Send Akil to me, then let them in."

Jamila's slim form drew taut like a bowstring when she heard.

"Akil isn't with them, rais."

Isam bestirred himself. "Where is he?"

"I don't know, rais. It's just Nakih and his sons."

"Find him."

Akil was nowhere to be found. Nakih and his sons hadn't seen him, either. They had come of their own accord when they heard the *Sea Leopard* was in port.

A spate of angry Turkish erupted from the captain. After a moment, he recollected that he was not alone. "Sorry for swearing," he said sulkily.

"I heard worse when I was serving the guns. It doesn't bother me." Jamila was surprised to realize it was true. The hardship of life on board had made her realize her own life was comfortably genteel, even if she was a butcher's daughter.

"Akil has run off. We'll never see him again."

Jamila was distracted from her own problems by this new development. "He wanted his freedom and he took it. I hope he gets away with it."

"Why?"

"Everyone chases what their heart desires. If he's brave enough to try for it, I hope he succeeds. Surely a corsair can understand that." Her brown eyes met his without flinching. "I chased what my heart desired. I failed to get what I wanted, but I refuse to be ashamed of trying. I won't accept an inferior husband to get rid of me respectably, either. I'd rather be a spinster."

He stared at her. She was slim and bright like a sword. She had run the powder in the midst of battle and propped him up when he was wounded and bleeding. She had been both brave and gentle, and she wasn't tainted by the blood and smoke that had swirled around her. Most people were charred by the fires of war, but some rare people were made pure. She was one of them. She was unlike any woman he'd ever known. Or any man, for that matter.

In the silence, Jamila rose gracefully to her feet, bowed with her hand to her forehead, and said, "I wish you all success and happiness, rais. May Allah watch over you and the man you love." With that she turned on her heel, picked up the small bundle of her possessions, and walked out. The guard outside his door shut it firmly.

When she disappeared, his heart leaped. He wanted her to come back, but she didn't, and her going made him frantic. He worried what would happen to her when she returned to her family. The thought that they might hurt her made him angry. He lurched to his feet, but his head spun and his legs buckled. He sat down abruptly and held his face with his one good hand until the world stopped whirling.

What was he thinking!? To care for a girl? How foolish. It was a moment of sentimentality. He liked her because she was brave. That was all. She had made her own fate and it was no worry of his. He didn't worry about his sailors when they left his ship; he shouldn't worry about her, either. He didn't worry about the other female sailors; their lives were their own once discharged from the ship. They weren't his problem. He had important things to think about. He had to ransom Kateb from Murad Rais and recuperate from his wound. He had prizes to submit to the court and debts to pay. Life went on, and it didn't include women. He was relieved to have them off his ship. He inhaled deeply. Yes. It was good that they were gone.

"Strumpet! Shameless!" the bellow of an angry man penetrated the wooden sanctuary of the captain's cabin.

The voice sent a jolt through him. He lurched to his feet, went to the quarterlight, and looked out.

An older man wrapped his arm around a younger man. They were both stout, not particularly tall, and had curly hair. They were father and son: Nakih and Kasim. Next to them was a slim figure dressed in white—Shakil.

"She's a whore! She disgraced the family!" Kasim shouted. His hand flew for his sister's face in spite of his father's grip.

Shakil threw his arm up to block the blow. "Stop it! She's your sister!"

Jamila stood straight and unmoving as the words and blows fell on her. A crowd gathered, but nobody interfered. It wasn't their business, but they would enjoy gossiping about it all the same.

Fury animated the captain and overcame his dizziness. He stormed out of the cabin. "Marines! To me! *Sea Leopard*, awake!" he roared.

The sight of the captain striding out in his slippers and shirtsleeves made his crew jump. The fox-faced man who was Kateb's replacement bellowed, "Marines, to arms!"

"A rescue!" Isam shouted. "Agha, give me six marines for a shore party!"

Half a dozen men armed with scimitars followed their captain as he strode down the gangplank. His head throbbed with every pulse of his heart, but he was upright and bearing down on Jamila and her relatives like a xebec under a full press of sail. Meanwhile, aboard the *Sea Leopard*, the remaining marines retrieved their muskets from the armory, loaded, and lined the rail.

On the quay, passersby who had stopped to gawk quickly scattered. The busy waterfront was suddenly deserted—but curious faces peeped from windows and alleys, or from behind stacks of rugs and barrels of other goods the *Sea Leopard* had been unloading. Nakih and his sons froze where they stood. Jamila turned around to see the wounded captain with his arm in a sling charging down the gangplank. The sun shone on the glossy black of his uncovered head, and the white short-sleeved shirt exposed a muscular bicep. His brown eyes flashed like scimitars.

Transfixed by the sight, she didn't notice the half dozen marines with drawn swords backing him up, but her menfolk did. They fell back. Nakih and Shakil immediately bowed to the corsair captain, but Kasim stood his ground. He bared his teeth. Isam's first act was to punch Kasim in the nose. Kasim staggered back and both Nakih and Shakil caught him and kept him from falling.

"You will not lay hands on a member of my crew!" Isam Rais roared at him. "None of you will! Jamila bint Nakih served honorably and bravely. You wrong her with your insults and you owe her an apology!"

Back on his feet, Kasim snarled, "You ruined her! You made a whore of her!"

"I did no such thing. She's virgin."

Giving the captain a hard stare, Shakil asked, "Do you swear by all that's holy?"

"I do. Ask her. Did you even bother to ask before flying off the handle?"

"She ran away from home! She compromised herself!" Kasim sputtered as blood ran from his nose.

Jamila said firmly, "The captain and crew treated me with respect. No one laid a hand on me."

Nakih kept a restraining hand on his son's arm. He looked back and forth between his sons, the captain, and his daughter.

Isam looked Shakil in the eye. "I swear it. All the women were kept separate and supervised. I didn't even know who she was until after I was wounded."

Nakih heaved a sigh and released Kasim. He held out his arms to Jamila. "Foolish daughter, I believe you."

She flung herself into her father's arms and bawled. She was safe now, safe ashore and away from the dangers of battle, safe from her brother's anger, safe from whatever would happen as long as her father loved her.

Nakih fussed over her. "Why did you run away? We were so worried! We didn't know what happened to you until Shadha gave us the note."

Kasim was not mollified. "Her reputation is ruined! She went to sea like a common whore!"

Shakil put his hand on his brother's arm. "Stop shouting! You don't have to tell the entire world. Don't make it any worse than it is!"

"Everyone knows already! How can we tolerate such wanton behavior? No one will respect us. 'Your sister is a whore,' that's what they'll say."

Shakil spoke crossly, "You like to hit people, so hit them for telling lies. The Qu'ran says no one can impugn a woman's honor unless he has four eyewitnesses."

Isam sighed and was glad he was a bachelor without family. "You might as well come aboard so we can tell you about it." To his marines he said, "Bring them all."

The surge of excitement that had carried him ashore ebbed. He swayed, stumbled, and crashed to the pavement. His eyes rolled up in his head and the blank white orbs stared unseeing at the sky. Jamila ran to him. His marines sheathed their swords and looked down uncertainly.

"What's the matter with him?" Nakih asked.

Worriedly Jamila put her hand on his throat to take his pulse—she had learned to do that while caring for him. "He was badly wounded. He lost a lot of blood. He shouldn't be out of bed."

Slowly Isam's senses returned to him. He blinked. Something blue and gold was hovering in his line of vision. Sunlight haloed a familiar face. "Ami?" he asked. "What happened?" His baritone was weak.

"You fainted. You need to go to bed," she scolded him.

The agha bent down to take a look at him. "Can you get up?"

Isam gave a groan. The sun was unbearably bright where it streamed around the girl. She was a sheltering presence that gave him comfort in his misery.

"Carry him to his bed," Jamila told the marines.

They slid their scabbarded swords under him to make a makeshift stretcher and lifted him up. Jamila cradled his head for support. Red blood seeped through the white shirt. "He's bleeding again. Somebody call the surgeon."

The marines carried the fallen captain up the gangplank and into his cabin. They settled him in his hanging bed and withdrew. Nakih and his sons followed them into the cabin. Shakil stood with hooded eyes while Nakih watched his daughter. Kasim roamed restlessly, kicking at the carpets and inspecting the cannons. He'd never been aboard a corsair vessel before.

When the surgeon was done changing the bandage, Nakih said, "I'd like to speak to the captain alone."

Shakil gathered Kasim and led him to the door.

"You too, Jamila," her father said gently.

She shook her head. "I'm going to watch over him."

Nakih spoke softly, "Go, my daughter. Go and wait."

Nakih didn't often give orders, but when he did, she knew he was serious. Reluctantly, she let Shakil pull her away. "He needs someone to take care of him," she argued.

"So he does, but you're not his wife. Go." He gave her a push and she went.

Isam had recovered his senses while the surgeon tended him. Now he looked up at the broad face of the butcher. Nakih's beard was streaked with grey, and the crows-feet were deep around his eyes, but the brown eyes were kindly.

"You need a wife."

Isam groaned. "I'm not the marrying kind."

"Every man is the marrying kind. You just don't know it yet. She loves you. She'll take good care of you."

"I'll recover."

"Yes. This time. But eventually, you'll be either old or crippled. Time weighs on us all. Marriage protects us against the ravages of fate. She'll be good for you."

Isam was too weak to argue, but he tried. "I have a lover. He was kidnapped. I have to get him back."

Nakih folded his arms. "Yes, you do, but that has nothing to do with your marriage. Your own father died when you were young, so he's not here to advise you. But think: what would he say? Get married. She suits you."

The image of Hamet Rais rose before his eyes: a tall, bold, daring, laughing man who didn't laugh much after his wife died. Then he was dying, dying on the quarterdeck of his own vessel, his guts spilled beside him, dying with his young son bending over him and crying. Isam knew what loneliness was when his father died, and all the company of his uncle's house had not blotted out that emptiness.

"I have no house. I'm in debt. I'm not a good husband."

"After this cruise, I think you'll clear all your debts. As for the house, Jamila and her brothers own one. It was their mother's property."

"You're twisting my arm," Isam complained.

"Yes. I'm doing it for your own good."

"Why on earth would you want a man like me for your son-in-law?"

Nakih was quiet for a moment. "Because you won't hit my daughter." He looked away then. "I love my sons, you understand that. But I know their imperfections, too. Shadha is a lovely woman, but she isn't happy. Kasim treats her badly. I have remonstrated with him, and for a while he improves, but always, something happens and he hits her again. He blames her for everything and never himself."

A silence fell. Each man understood what would happen to Jamila. Either she'd remain a spinster and a target of her brother's ire, or she would marry a man that would take her but not respect her.

"I am a corsair. My life is at sea," Isam said quietly.

"I know. Buy out her brothers' share of the farm and give it to her. Then she'll be supported properly. That's all I ask."

Isam thought it over. Marrying her and setting her up with her own farm was a good plan. He would have his life and she would have hers. It would even be good for business; he could buy food for the ship direct from the farm, cutting out the middlemen. Kateb would go to sea with him, and Jamila would stay on the farm and learn to be a sensible woman. It was the best possible solution to the problem.

"All right. I accept your terms."

Nakih's face lit up. "We'll set the date for a month from now. You should be well enough to ride to your wedding by then."

A month! Isam panicked. A date made it all too real.

Nakih chuckled at the look on his face. "Cold feet already? Don't worry. You'll get used to it. She'll be a good wife for you. She loves you."

"How can she love me? She barely knows me. It's an infatuation, nothing more."

"It was when she first saw you, but it's more than that now. I know my daughter. She loves you. Treat her with respect and all will be well. You'll see."

Isam rubbed his hand over his face. "I feel like I'm making the worst mistake of my life."

Nakih was silent for a while. "Then let it be a temporary marriage. One year. That will be enough to be respectable, and you will both be free afterwards."

Isam uncovered his face. "Yes. One year. That is acceptable to me. I'll buy out Kasim's share of the farm so he has no claim on her. That will settle the matter."

Nakih nodded. "A year then. It will be enough. I'll ask Shakil to draw up the marriage contract."

Isam exhaled the breath he didn't know he was holding. "Good. Send him to me tomorrow so we can talk about it."

Nakih took his hand and squeezed it. "Good luck to you, rais. May Allah watch over you."

"Thank you. And may He bless you also."

Nakih let himself out. Isam continued lying in his bed watching the sequins of sunlight reflecting across the beams overhead. Only a year. Nothing would change during the course of a year. He would settle his debts both financial and moral and be done with the matter. Yes, this was the best solution. Best for him, best for Jamila. In a year they would part and never look back. He was able to sleep then.

CHAPTER 25 : A NOT SO HAPPY REUNION

"Ahoy the ship!" a deep bass voice sang out. Looking down the gangplank, the watch saw a tall, broad, black man dressed all in white with a red fez propped on his shaven pate. A short scimitar was thrust through his red sash.

"Kateb!" the watchman cried out. "Come aboard, and welcome, habibi!"

Grinning, the big black stalked up the gangplank as his name flew from mouth to mouth. The crew dropped what they were doing or rushed up from below. The officer of the watch sent a midshipman to knock breathlessly on the captain's door.

When the muffled, "Enter!" came through the door, he flung it open, stuck his head inside, and called, "Kateb's back!"

Isam Rais's head came up, and he rose swiftly to his feet. He had to pause a moment to let the dizziness to pass. The purser, who had been at the table with him, jumped up to grab his elbow. The middy left the door open and stood aside respectfully as the captain shook off the purser's help and made his way on deck.

Blinking in the bright sun, Isam scanned the mob of men who surrounded Kateb. White, tan, brown, and black, his crew came from all the nations of the Mediterranean and even further afield than that, but the big black was taller than most, and their eyes met over the heads of lesser men. Kateb's eyes lit up when he saw his captain. He began pushing his way through the mob.

The two smiled as they met at arm's length on the aft deck. Then they kissed each other on each cheek. Isam clasped him with his good hand and Kateb gave him half an embrace to avoid hurting the arm in the sling. "I missed you," Isam said. His baritone was deep and the Turkish accent came through more strongly than usual.

Kateb thumped his good shoulder. "I'm glad to be free again."

The corner of Isam's eyes crinkled. "Come to my cabin and I'll show you how much I missed you." He pulled the other man with him.

In the great cabin, he reached up and slid the shutters closed across the skylight. "No show for you, lads," he told the crew who were peeping through the glass.

"Shakil told me you were hurt," Kateb said.

Isam nodded mutely. "Laid out. I can only stay on my feet about half an hour before I'm too tired."

"Maybe you shouldn't exert yourself then."

"I want to. But I'll let you do most of the work this time." Isam's eyes twinkled.

Kateb's eyes grew warm. "I think I can manage that. I exercised while I was a captive. I had nothing else to do." He leaned forward and kissed the taller man full on the mouth. The moment elongated. Isam slipped his good arm around Kateb's waist while the heavier man adjusted his grip to avoid the sling and embraced his captain more fully. Their mouths had a good deal to say to one another without any words.

One by one, items of clothing fell to the floor. They were in no hurry; they had missed each other and were taking the time to reacquaint themselves fully with one another. Kateb sprinkled kisses as each bit of Isam's skin came into view, which slowed down the removal of his shirt. Isam couldn't get it off by himself and had to remove the sling to get it off at all. The white bandage wrapped around his chest contrasted strongly with the swarthy skin and swirls of black chest hair.

Kateb expression turned concerned. "How bad is it?"

Isam grunted noncommittally, then admitted, "It almost killed me. It missed tearing out my throat by an inch. The whole shoulder is torn up." He splayed his hand from clavicle to armpit to show the extent of the injury.

Kateb regarded him soberly. "Good thing you're left-handed. The scar tissue is going to leave that shoulder tight."

Isam flexed it experimentally, but quickly lowered his arm before he had raised it more than a few inches. "I'll exercise it. I'll have a few weeks here in port while disposing of the prizes and resupplying. I'll be fit by the time I go out again. Especially if I have somebody to help me work out." He gave Kateb a wicked grin.

Kateb took that as an invitation and pulled him onto the divan. The injured arm required some creativity to accommodate, but a motivated man can overcome all obstacles. They enjoyed themselves very much, even if Isam was not used to letting the other man take the lead. Afterwards, they lay spooning together with Kateb's dark arm around Isam's waist, his finger lazily twirling in the hair around Isam's belly button.

"Shakil said you had news for me," Kateb eventually remarked.

Isam tensed. "He didn't tell you?"

"Tell me what?"

A long silence fell. "I'm betrothed to marry."

Kateb's amazement was palpable. "You? Marry? Who?"

The silence settled heavier. Eventually Isam replied, "Jamila bint Nakih. Shakil's sister."

All the muscles of Kateb's face tightened as he stared at the back of Isam's neck. "Why?"

"Her family requires it to restore her honor. She disguised herself and joined my crew."

Kateb was relieved to find out it was something so silly. "Send the harlot on her way and be done with it. Who cares what happens to her?"

"I do," Isam said quietly.

Kateb scowled. "You!" he said scornfully. Then after a pause. "You didn't! Not her, not a woman! Did you?"

"I didn't."

"Then what's the problem? You owe her nothing!"

Isam struggled to explain it. "She was a member of my crew and she served the ship well. She was a virgin, and she's a virgin still. I feel an obligation to her. I don't want her to suffer the fate that awaits women suspected of immodesty. She did it because she loved me."

Kateb's jaw dropped. "A virgin! You don't believe that, do you? She's probably pregnant and only Allah knows who the father is."

"She's a virgin, and I won't hear you speak ill of her." Isam set his jaw and the short black beard bristled.

"If you marry her, we can't be lovers. Adultery is punished by stoning. I won't risk it. Not for the sake of a strumpet!"

"It's nobody's business but mine! You're on the ship, she's on the shore, and I plan to stay at sea like I always do, except for the wedding."

"If you plan to cheat on her, why marry?"

"Why does it matter if I'm married? Besides, I've decided on a temporary marriage: *nikah mut'ah*. A year and it's done. She'll be respectable after that."

"If you're not even going to try to be a husband, why marry in the first place? Maybe she's not the harlot in this marriage."

Isam sat up and threw his arm off. "I won't stand for such talk!"

"Your reputation is made by your actions, not my words. If you don't like what people will say, then don't do it."

"You said you don't care what happens to her!"

"I know you're not a religious man, but I thought you were a man of your word. You're going to lie to your wife and do as you please. I can't respect that."

"I haven't lied to her! She knows how it is with me. She knows I prefer men."

"That may be so, but I won't lie with you if you're married."

"It's only for a year."

"Then look me up in a year." Kateb rose and put on his clothes. He went to the sleeping area and locked his sea chest. The clicking had the sound of finality.

Isam watched in alarm. "You don't have to go."

"Did you find someone to serve as agha while I was gone?"

"Yes. But he knows it was only until you returned."

"Did he give good service?"

"Yes."

"Then good luck to him. I bear him no grudge. I'm a soldier with a strong right arm. I won't have any trouble finding another place. Give me my ticket so I can draw my pay, and I'll be on my way."

"I'll give you your ticket, but I don't want you to go."

Kateb heaved his sea chest up on to his shoulder. "I'm a free man, thanks to you. I won't forget that. If there's ever a favor I can do for you, call me, and I'll do it. But I won't help you diminish yourself."

Isam went to his desk, opened the top, and picked out the quarter sheet of paper that was Kateb's pay cheque. "I carried your name on the muster roll this last cruise, so you'll have a share of the money when the prizes are auctioned."

Kateb took the piece of paper and smiled. "Thank you, captain. I'm sure I'll find another berth, but it may be a few weeks. This will persuade a landlord to give me credit until then." He stuffed the paper into his pocket with a crumpling noise, then put his hand on Isam's shoulder. "Live large, habibi. You're a bigger man than all these rascals. Never be content to be as small as they are, and Allah will make you prosper."

Isam caught Kateb's hand and held it where it gripped his shoulder. "Don't go. You have no idea what a relief it was for me to have someone I could talk to. Being a captain is a lonely business. I will miss that even more than sex. You were a friend to me."

"I'm a friend to you still, rais." His grip tightened. "Call me when you're divorced. It's only a year."

Isam grumbled deep in his throat. "A year then. You must look for me. I won't know where to find you."

"I'll send you word. Until then, fare well, my friend." Kateb leaned forward and kissed him on the mouth. He lingered there, and Isam closed his eyes and kissed him back. He slipped his good arm around the stocky body and hugged him close. The kiss deepened.

It was Kateb who pulled away. "You're testing my resolve, habibi," he scolded.

"That's why you're running away. You're afraid you can't live up to the rules you set for me to live by!" Isam retorted.

Kateb gave him a lopsided smile. "Maybe so. But I must do what I must do. So must you. If you marry, be a good husband. It's only a year. Remember that when you're tempted to grumble. You might even wind up with a son out of it." He winked.

The idea of what he would have to do to produce a son appalled Isam. He sulked at him. "You're still giving me advice when you should be going. If you're going, go!" He gave Kateb a shove.

Kateb grinned at him and white teeth flashed in the dark face. "I'm going! Now you make me think you want to get rid of me!"

"If you insist on leaving, then I insist on you going!" Isam replied indignantly.

Kateb laughed and swaggered to the door. Isam watched the muscular buttocks moving beneath the loose fitting white pantaloons as they walked out of his life. Kateb paused on the threshold and looked back. "Farewell, habibi. We'll meet again, Allah willing."

"Farewell, habibi," Isam replied with feeling.

Kateb hesitated a moment longer, then turned, and stepped through the door.

The sight of Kateb with his sea chest on his shoulder brought cries of dismay. The crew accosted him, but he wouldn't stay. He bid them farewell and descended the gangplank to the shore. They would miss him, but they were Sallee rovers. All of them came and went with the restlessness of waves washing a foreign beach. No piece of land could ever truly be home to men of the sea. Already Isam's heart was yearning for the turquoise waters of the Mediterranean and the grey storms of the Atlantic. Adventure lay over the horizon. No man became rich and famous by staying in port. What good was a wife to a man like that?

Isam's father had been a man like that. He had also had a wife and loved her. There was no doubt of that in Isam's mind. Hamet Rais had never remarried after Miriam died. He had taught his son to sail and dream and that boy had wanted nothing more than to grow up to be a great corsair like his father. How proud the old man must be to see the *Sea Leopard!* Hamet Rais had never had such a fine ship.

Who would inherit the *Sea Leopard* when he died? Isam had not thought that far ahead. Hamet Rais would like to have a grandson, he thought. Isam had been his only child. Who else would carry on the line if not for Isam? He felt the burden of a parent's expectations even though he was now older than his father had been when he died. A year wasn't very long. Then would come another, and another. They crowded upon him now that he was thirty in a way they never had when he was young. He had always assumed that he would die in battle and never grow old, but having had a near miss, he was glad to be alive. Troubled by thoughts he had never had before, he retired to his divan to smoke a pipe and let the hashish ease the ache that affected more than his shoulder.

CHAPTER 26 : ON PATROL

A month later, the *Sea Leopard* drifted quietly as autumn breathed its first breath upon the waters. The ebb tide carried her in silence through the misty world as the estuary that was Modiq Bay debouched into the Mediterranean Sea. Tendrils, like ghosts, rose up from the glassy waters and drifted until they merged with one another to form a pale haze that chilled exposed skin. To the north, on the port bow, gleamed the yellow light of the lighthouse and fortress that guarded the entrance. Modiq Bay was seventy-five miles of shoals, narrow channels, islands, inlets, islets, and reefs between the Mediterranean Sea and the harbor of Zokhara.

Isam Rais, clad in a navy blue wool jacket and his right arm still in a sling, said quietly, "We'll anchor here until light."

Master Imrich replied in an equally quiet voice, "Aye aye, rais."

The watch below was snoring in their hammocks. They needed their sleep; there was no telling what daylight would bring them. For that matter, Isam needed his rest as well. He had come on deck with a bounce in his step, but now, merely an hour later, his shoulders were stooping as weariness dragged him down. He was cold and his injured shoulder ached in the damp.

"Make it so," Isam replied in a crabbed voice. Usually he liked to set the anchor himself; there was no element of the ship's management that was too trivial or too routine to escape his attentive notice, but he was still weak and sore. He had not recuperated as fast as he had thought he would. Imrich was perfectly competent; there was no reason not to trust him. Isam's wound had forced him to give his subordinates more latitude and to depend on them. It fretted him to delegate the task, but it wasn't doing his wound any good to hunch miserably in the chilly damp. Still, he couldn't bring himself to leave the deck.

The anchor ran out and slipped into the water with a small splash. The *Sea Leopard* drifted leisurely until the scope ran out, then came up gently at the end of the line. Master Imrich took out his compass and studied his bearings. One, the lighthouse. He made a note with pencil in the rough log. Next . . . there were no good seamarks in the dim fog. He studied what appeared to be an outcropping of rock, decided it was sufficient, and held up his compass once again and took the second bearing. Both bearings were to the north. Looking south, east, and west, there was nothing at all to be discerned in the dark.

"When it's light enough to take another bearing, do so," Isam told Master Imrich and Lieutenant Yafi.

They murmured their acknowledgement.

Finally he gave up and said, "You have the conn, Lieutenant Yafi. I am going below. Wake me if anything unusual happens. Deliver the salute at dawn."

"Aye aye, sir. Wake you for anything unusual and salute at dawn."

Isam eased himself down the ladder to the weather deck and into the coach. Ensign Taslim was on duty to tap the triangle in indication of the hours. A messenger arrived. Isam lingered to see what was said.

The messenger told the middy, "Lieutenant Yafi says, ring the fog alarm every five minutes."

"Fog alarm every five minutes, aye," Taslim replied.

The sailor disappeared back up the ladder to the quarterdeck. Satisfied, Isam turned to his cabin door. The marine on guard opened it and held it for him. He stepped inside, removed his boots, and crawled into his hanging bed fully dressed. He covered up in the blankets that were cold after having been left for so long. He was drifting off to sleep when he heard the striker on the triangle, ting-ting-ting-ting-ting-ting-ting-ting-ting-ting. The tempo clearly distinguished it from the hours and half hours which were struck with a steady rhythm, and the general alarm that was a wild clanging. The metallic ringing penetrated the fabric of the ship. A few drowsy sailors half-roused, realized it was just the fog alarm, and went back to sleep. Ensign Taslim turned over the five minute glass. When its sand had run out, once more he rang the fog alarm. He turned over the glass again, the sands ran out, and once more the triangle rang. The ringing of the alarm became just another sound in the sleeping breath of the ship.

An instant later, or so it seemed, the triangle rattled out a wild tattoo. Someone was at his bedside saying urgently, "Rais, wake up! Rais!"

Blinking blearily, all he could make out was the dark bulk of the ensign above him. He turned his head to see the pale grey mist covering the quarterlight. "What?" he asked, not quite awake.

"A vessel in the fog!"

A single gun boomed from the xebec's bow. With the skylight shuttered and the gun ports closed, he couldn't smell the brimstone, but the ship gave the slightest of shudders. He felt it at the same moment as the noise assaulted his ears. "I'm awake," he said and sat up. "Tell them I'm coming."

He eased out of his bed and sat on his sea chest while he felt for his boots. His steward and several other men rushed into his cabin, struck down the bed, and carried it away. As he pulled on the first boot, he heard the answering signal, one gun, pause, one gun, pause, one gun. The Sallee private signal! So, it was a friend. Probably. Assuming that a corsair had not been taken captive and this year's signal book seized. Which seemed unlikely, even if the Sardinians were out in force.

He donned the other boot, plopped his fez on his head, and stuck his scimitar through his sash. Two men nearly ran into him as he came out of the cabin. They stood aside, and when he passed, ran into his cabin to pick up his writing desk and sea chest. In fifteen minutes, the contents of the captain's cabin had been removed and two gun crews with burning matches and cartridges stood by the stern chasers. The stern ports were open and the bronze guns loaded and run out.

On the quarterdeck, Isam Rais said crisply, "Report!"

Yafi replied, "The watch spotted movement in the fog. We've been sounding the fog alarm—" He paused as the tinny triangle rang once again "—but we didn't hear anything from them, so we fired the challenge. They replied with the private signal."

"Very good. Hail her," Isam replied. The yellow light of the stern lanthorn was feeble in the fog.

Yafi cupped hands to his mouth and shouted, "Ahoy the ship! What ship?" in Arabic.

"The *Renegade*, Murad Rais!" came the voice through the fog in the same language. "What ship?"

Isam smote his thigh with his one good hand. Of all the people he had to meet while on guard duty, Murad Rais was his least favorite.

Yafi shouted back, "The *Sea Leopard*, Isam Rais!"

There was a pause in which he imagined Murad Rais' reaction mirrored his own.

The masthead lookout called down, "Oar flash! Dead astern!"

In the fog it had been difficult to tell what direction the disembodied voice was coming from. Isam and all the quarterdeck crew snapped their heads aft to peer into the pale grey nothingness. Isam saw it and shouted, "Stand off! You're dead astern! Don't you see our light?"

There was no reply from the *Renegade*. Isam's heart pounded as the prow of the other xebec emerged from the fog not thirty yards away. The sky was continuing to lighten, but the mist was growing thicker. For a heart-stopping moment the *Renegade's* bow pointed straight at him, then turned to the port. She rowed past at pistol shot range, then held water as she came alongside. The *Sea Leopard* bobbed gently in the wake of her oars. At a distance of no more than ten yards, the two vessels could see one another even if they couldn't make out the paint. He recognized the stocky bulk of Murad Rais and Murad could probably recognize the tall lanky figure opposite.

Murad deigned to communicate with him. "We were chased by a Sardinian frigate. I think we lost her in the fog."

Isam replied, "They can guess you're running for Modiq Bay. How bad is your damage?"

"We're all right. We sheered off before she could get in range."

"How long ago?"

Murad Rais rubbed his beard thoughtfully. "About two hours ago."

"Were they rowing?"

"They put out their oars when they saw us, but they couldn't keep up."

A xebec was made for rowing. Although the lighter frigates rowed well enough, they were not as fast as a xebec. Still, since the Sardinians could guess where Murad was running to—they wouldn't be far behind.

"We'll see them within the hour, if not sooner!"

"Are you staying? She's a forty-eight gun ship."

"Are you running?"

"All the way to Zokhara! I don't plan to get myself shot up for nothing. If you're smart, you'll run too!"

"I'm on commission to patrol the mouth of the bay and ensure the enemy doesn't enter it."

"Good luck with that!" Murad replied.

"Stay and help! The fortress will cover us!"

Murad made a rude gesture. He turned back to his crew and gave orders. The crew leaned into the oars again, the drum beat the rhythm, and they pulled away upstream.

"A forty-eight gun ship," Yafi said nervously. "That's even bigger than the *Eleanor d'Arborea!*"

"Feh. This new captain won't be half as good. It won't matter," Isam replied with more disdain than he actually felt. Although he was sure the new frigate wouldn't be as well handled as the *Eleanora,* he felt a certain trepidation. He looked up at the fort. "They need to know."

"They can't make out any signal in this murk," Imrich replied.

Isam's brain was in a foment as he estimated the Sardinian frigate's progress. "They can't be more than four miles away. They have probably heard our challenge, so they know we're here, but they don't know what we are. As long as they can't see us, we can fool them. Give an admiral's salute."

Imrich gave him a long look. "Very well." He gave the orders.

Yafi stepped forward, "Stand by for salute! Twenty-one guns!" The crews down below looked up in surprise. "Ready," called the lieutenants on the gun deck.

"Fire one!" The number one gun belched brimstone and the boom went rolling away through the fog, echoed off the bluffs, and dissipated in slowly lightening gloom. "Fire two!" Again the sound rumbled and echoed and was lost in the fog. "Fire three!"

One by one the guns thundered in a brazen announcement. Anyone who heard it must assume that the Salletines were sending out a fleet. That should frighten off a lone frigate. The last thunder of the guns rolled away and the xebec was left wreathed in a fog of silent gunsmoke. It hung listlessly about the vessel instead of blowing clear. Men waved hands in front of their faces, and smoke eddied and twirled, but it did no good. The air was so humid that the pall of smoke was trapped.

The fortress on the hillside replied. Its bigger guns gave a throaty roar and the sound rolled across the placid sea. The guns faced the sea in three directions, so it was not until the last few shots that they were able to see the muzzle flashes of guns that covered their berth. Up on the fortress they had been surprised to discover a vessel beneath them, but obediently answered the salute they had been given. Spyglasses were trained on the xebec below and the water all around was swept for the rest of the admiral's squadron, but they couldn't discover them in the fog.

Isam cocked an ear to listen to the silence after the guns.

Nothing.

He waited two more minutes.

Still nothing.

He pulled his watch out of his seam pocket, and flicked it open. He watched the minute hand sweep around for five minutes.

Silence.

"Ahoy the masthead! Do you see anything?"

"No! Just fog!" the lookout shouted back.

Isam bit his lip and closed his watch. He listened hard and peered into the gloom. The sky lightened imperceptibly. The spars were now visible against the grey sky, but at water level, nothing could be seen except the ship, the fog, and a placid pool of water. The shore was invisible. The smell of sulphur hung in the air.

After fifteen minutes, Isam Rais said, "Call the men to prayers, one watch to pray while the other stands by the guns."

"Aye aye, rais," Lieutenant Yafi replied. He stepped to the quarterdeck rail. Tense faces looked up at him. In the fetid light, even the dark-skinned men looked greyish yellow. "Watch below, say your prayers. Watch above, stand by your guns."

The man who had the best voice stepped forward, and lifting his hands to either side of his face, called out, *"Allahu Akbar. Allahu Akbar. Allahu Akbar. Allahu Akbar. Ash-hadu alla ilaha illallah. Ash-hadu alla ilaha illallah. Ash-hadu anna Muhammadar Rasulullah. Ash-hadu anna Muhammadar Rasulullah."*

Isam turned to Yafi, "You have the conn. I'm going to pray. Master Imrich, will you join me?"

"Aye," Imrich replied. The two men descended to the main deck.

The men off duty lined up across the weather deck, fitting themselves among the cannons and hatches as best they could as the call continued, "Come to success, Come to success. Allah is great. Allah is great." Isam thought the words a good omen. *Come to success*.

In the past, Isam had not paid much attention to religion. He was too busy clawing his way up through the ranks of the corsairs to the level where he could afford to build his own vessel. He had succeeded. Now that he had achieved his goal, what next? Earn enough prize money to keep her floating. He had really not thought further than that.

The congregation replied in a masculine chorus, "Peace and blessings be on you, O Messenger of Allah."

Aching, he followed the movements of the prayer, bowing, turning, bending, and prostrating himself. With an arm in a sling it wasn't easy. His knees hit the deck and a jolt of pain lanced through his shoulder. He had to move carefully and mindfully, something he had never done before. He wondered, *why am I doing this when I'm wounded?* Then more thoughtfully, *why does anyone do it at all?* He had no answer to that, and it troubled him.

If he had asked any of the crew, they could have told him they were praying for Allah's help against the infidel frigate, but Isam had been orphaned at the age of twelve and was accustomed to shifting for himself. Although he assumed beating the infidels would please Allah, it never occurred to him to beg for divine aid in doing so. He was a man certain of his own abilities.

CHAPTER 27 : LETTERS FROM HOME

Moment by imperceptible moment, the darkness of night faded into a shimmering grey twilight of mist and pre-dawn paleness. The crew was subdued as they broke their fast in the hushed dampness. Nothing moved. No bird sang. The coast remained hidden in the sepulchrous shroud of fog. Nothing could be seen in the murk except for the ship herself and her anchor cable disappearing into the glassy water.

When he could see a cable's length away, Isam Rais mounted the quarterdeck. Massaging his bad shoulder with his left hand, he said, "Set a course to round Sunrise Point by the landward channel." Like all corsairs, he knew the shoals off Sunrise Point by heart. They contained channels deep enough for the shallow-drafting lateeners, but too shallow for the deep-bellied frigates of the European countries. That meant they could stay under the fortress' guns while taking a look, but if the enemy frigate was still out there, she would not be able to close with them.

Imrich knew his business and was privately pleased that being wounded had forced the captain to let his subordinates do their jobs without the captain constantly breathing down their necks. "Anchor stations," he told the crew below.

"Anchor stations!" the main chief and fore chief repeated.

Wooden sweeps clattered as they unbundled from where they were strapped to the inside of the gunwale. As they worked, the pink sun lifted above the horizon in a rosy aurora that gleamed through the sodden air and gave the wisps of mist sensual shapes, like dancing girls. The rising of the sun thinned the mist, but the headland to the north appeared as an island rising from the fluffy grey cloud. The southern headland two miles away was a dark lump in the sea of fog. From here it was impossible to tell there was a great lagoon to the right, a small mountain to the left, or the Mediterranean Sea in front.

The sun broke above the mist and her golden rays fell upon the deck and warmed them with her brilliance. The yellow light made everything luminous: the beads of mist clinging to the sails, the shiny silver shimmers of salt on the railing, the glistening sweat on the faces of the men. A faint breeze puffed across them as cat's paws trod the placid waters of the nearby lagoon. A silver fish broke from the surface of the river then disappeared with a splash as it swam into the turgid waters of the Mediterranean. In the beauty of the moment, everybody aboard the vessel was well-pleased that he had decided to go to sea again. Even Gümüsh came out on deck.

The anchor came up and the fore chief cried, "That's well!" The great iron anchor dangled from its cathead.

"Well done," said Isam Rais.

"Thank you, captain," replied Master Imrich.

Light twinkled on the ramparts of the Sunrise Fortress. "Mirror code, rais," the signal midshipman reported to him.

Isam had been watching the anchor detail and had missed it. "What message?"

"One enemy sail on a course due north, five miles from Sunrise Point, sir."

Qaadir had replaced a casualty from Isam's last voyage. He was a coffee-colored man of about twenty or twenty-one. He wore a short grey wool jacket and a white turban. He stood respectfully at attention.

Isam was pleased. He said to Imrich, "We've scared him off with our ruse. He's running to report the Salletine fleet is coming out. He'll get his ears boxed for not staying long enough to find out what force. It's well for us that he's not made of the same stuff as Captain Vargiu."

"That might bring the Sardinian fleet down on us."

"Possibly," Isam replied. "They may have been planning to invade Modiq Bay anyhow." He tilted back his head and called up, "Ahoy the masthead! Do you see the frigate?"

"No! Too hazy!"

"What visibility?"

"About a mile!" the lookout shouted back.

With its greater height the fortress had spotted the topmasts of the frigate poking up from the mist. The discovery had caused them some alarm since they had seen nothing in the darkness. They were also surprised to discover a lone xebec sheltering under their guns when they had expected a fleet, but there was nothing they could do about it except flash their mirror code to report. One by one the beacons along the coast passed the message up the peninsula to Tettiwan and Zokhara.

"All right then. Things seem quiet enough. Continue to the vicinity of Sunrise Point and see what there is to be seen. Lieutenant Urve, you have the conn. I'm going below. Call me if anything changes or if there's any sign of the enemy."

"Aye aye, rais. I have the conn," Urve replied.

Isam went to his cabin, smoked a little hashish because his shoulder hurt, and crawled into bed. The next hour should be uneventful. Unless the Sardinian fleet was just out of his range in the mist. Still, if they were, the fortress should have seen them. They hadn't, so he imagined he had a hour, maybe two, before meeting the Sardinians. If they were out there. It seemed likely the frigate was running to inform the fleet shelling Tettiwan that the Salletines were coming out in force.

He was deep in an erotic dream about Kateb when the bark of the *Sea Leopard's* bow chaser jerked him awake. He lay blinking stupidly for a moment as the dream clogged his brain. The softer bark of a smaller, more distant gun informed him that the *Sea Leopard* was accosting somebody. He crawled out of bed and found that he had been sweating and it wasn't just the dream. Sunlight streamed through the skylight. All the glasses in the great cabin were shut and the room was hot and stuffy. Summer was refusing to surrender to autumn's first advance.

He stripped off his sticky clothes and went to the roundhouse. A tin ewer of water hung from a hook above the matching basin. It sat on the washstand with its bottom fitted into the hole in the stand to keep it from sliding off. He washed in tepid sea water, attended the demands of nature, and walked naked into his cabin. As he did so, he heard the sounds of a small boat hooking on the chains. That seemed like it would require his attention, so he fetched clean clothes from his sea chest. He was pulling on fresh drawers when a knock came on his door.

"Enter!" he called, pulling up the underwear. He tied the drawstring, then stepped into a pair of loose blue pantaloons.

Ensign Taslim entered the cabin. "Mail for you, sir." He had an oiled canvas satchel in his hands. It wasn't the sort sailors carried; they usually wanted something more certain to be waterproof, like tarpaulin or leather. Taslim took a surreptitious look at the captain's exposed upper body to judge for himself how the man was recovering. The captain was the brains of the operation; their success or failure depended on how well he performed. The captain's hairy chest was muscular and his swarthiness contrasted starkly with the bandage that wrapped around his chest and over and under his shoulder. Yet he was steady on his feet, and something like the old vigor was in his voice and expression. Taslim was cautiously optimistic.

Isam took the satchel and opened it, asking, "What ship? And what time is it?"

"The *Full Moon*. A pearl diver. She's on her way to sea and is dropping off mail for us. It's rising ten of the clock, sir."

The time surprised Isam. "Damn, I slept. Why did no one wake me?"

"There was nothing to report, sir. We reached Sunrise Point, stood out far enough to see a sail very far to the west that we couldn't identify, and nothing else but the usual traffic. There's no other mail, just your package."

"All right then. Pass the word for my steward."

"Aye aye, sir. Pass the word for the steward. Anything else?"

"No, thank you."

The steward arrived promptly. He swung the sternlights up on their hinges and hooked their toggles into the loops above for support. The quarterlights were opened the same way, but Isam said, "Take the glass out of the quarterlights. I want some air in here. Don't open the skylights. In fact, close the shutters. It's too bright."

"Aye aye, captain," the man replied. He moved efficiently about the cabin as Isam settled on the divan.

Isam didn't recognize the handwriting on the tag attached to the satchel. It seemed rather young, as if a boy had written it. His curiosity piqued, he opened up the satchel.

Inside he found blue cloth. He pulled it out and it turned out to be a rolled up nightshirt in light blue fabric. A folded letter tumbled out of the cloth. He set the nightshirt down and opened the letter.

Dear Husband-to-Be,

I hope you will find the nightshirt useful. I know blue is your favorite color, so I made it blue instead of white. I did the embroidery myself. I hope you like it. If there is anything else that would be useful to you, please let me know. I can make shirts and pants and Shadha is teaching me to knit socks.

I hope your patrol is going well. They say the Sardinians are shelling Tettiwan, but they doubt it will last. Shakil says they are demanding the return of Captain Vargiu. Apparently he is married to a niece of the King of Sardinia. There is a letter from Shakil about that in the satchel. I hope the matter will be settled soon. This isn't the first time the Christians have shelled Tettiwan, but it is the first time I've known somebody that might be involved. May Allah watch over you and bring you home safe.

Jamila bint Nakih

Isam was an orphan. He had never had a letter from home, no, not since he had shaken the dust of Tanguel off his feet ten years before. When he had been a young sailor with his uncle's galley, he had sometimes received letters from his female cousins and had upon occasion been compelled by his uncle to write a letter home, but in the years since he had never received a personal letter. It felt odd to have one now. It opened a strange hollow in him that he couldn't identify. He was saved from introspection by the arrival of the surgeon. He stuffed the shirt and letter back in the satchel, discovered a bag of pipe tobacco and a letter from Shakil in the bottom, and put the whole thing aside so the surgeon could work on him.

The removal of the bandage revealed a massive jagged scab that reached from armpit to clavicle. The shrapnel had cut deep and ripped the flesh from his upper arm and chest. The surgeon lifted the arm and flexed it and Isam grimaced as the motions pulled at the wound. "I think it's time for you to exercise it lightly, just enough to work out the stiffness."

The *Sea Leopard's* surgeon was a balding Arab with thin lips. His long nose with flared nostrils made him look disdainful even though he was an easygoing fellow. He was thirty-something, bearded, and dressed in a moderately clean tan tunic and pantaloons.

Under his direction Isam circled his arm, lifted it as high as he could, and worked it back and forth like a chicken wing. His lip curled in pain, but he didn't complain. The exercises done, the surgeon inspected his scabs. One was not firmly attached, so the surgeon used his tweezers to lift it, then ripped it off with a sudden jerk.

"Ow! Warn me when you're going to do that!" Isam complained.

"It's better if you don't know it's coming," the surgeon said placidly.

Blood oozed from the wound. He inspected it carefully, sniffing, daubing his finger in it and tasting it, and ruminating over the texture, taste, and smell. "No putrescence. That's why you're having such a long recovery. It's necessary for the putrescence to rupture and drain out. I think we should lift your scabs and lance the wound. It must drain."

Isam inspected the injury. It was healing cleanly with only a small amount of redness next to the scabs. He pressed his hand over the scabs, but they were only a little warmer than his flesh. "They seem to be healing well," he said cautiously.

"I know pus seems bad in a wound, but it's a natural part of healing. If you don't have it, that means you're not healing properly." The surgeon opened his case wider and took out a small forceps and scalpel. "Sit still, please."

Isam scooted away from the doctor. "I don't see any need to do that," he replied.

"Come, come. I'm the surgeon. I know what's best for you."

"I don't think it's infected," Isam said more forcefully.

"I'm telling you, that's a problem. You're not healing properly. I will lance it and we will see what's going on below the surface."

Isam's black brows knit together. "No. I'm the captain and I say you won't."

"Rais, don't be stubborn. I am an expert in medicine and you are not. My patients usually live."

"I feel very much alive, so I don't see the need to take a chance on becoming otherwise!" Isam retorted.

"You want to recover more quickly, don't you?"

Isam chewed his lip. "I don't see how sticking a knife into my wound will speed things up."

"By stimulating the generation and release of pus. You're a corsair. You've seen wounded men before. Do they not always develop pus, and do they not improve when it is drained? The pus draws the evil humors from the body and enables healing."

"They seem to recover better when there is no pus," Isam replied crossly. He folded his arms across his chest. The wounded shoulder complained, so he cradled his right arm with his left.

The surgeon's good humor was starting to fray. "You haven't attended as many wounded men as I have, so your opinion doesn't count."

"I am the captain of this vessel, so mine is the only opinion that does count!" Isam roared at him. "OUT!"

The surgeon put away his instruments and closed up the case. "You'll regret it, captain. I say that with all due respect."

The marine held the door for him as he left and pulled it shut. The surgeon would have slammed it.

In exasperation, Isam said, "Abdul, dress my wound, please. And don't take any orders from the surgeon about me unless I approve them first."

Approaching warily, the smaller man said, "As you command, rais." The fresh bandages had gone with the surgeon, so Abdul had to go and beg one from him. It was given with ill grace, but it was given. The servant returned and wrapped the shoulder. Since he was the one that usually changed the captain's dressings, he made a neat job of it.

Isam sent Abdul for fruit and coffee to tide him over until the midday meal. While he was gone, he sat down on the cushion before his low desk and wrote a left-handed letter to Jamila. She had offered to do anything she could, so he began with some pleasantries, thanked her for the nightshirt, and asked,

If you could consult a surgeon at the hospital about my shoulder, I would appreciate it. There is very little redness and no pus, and no fever. The imbecile of a surgeon aboard my vessel wants to stick a knife in it and make it ooze. He says it can't heal properly until it does. I feel that it is healing well enough without the pus. Will you ask a learned doctor if pus is truly necessary for the healing of the wound?

He tapped the end of the reed pen against his chin for a bit, then added,

Please buy yourself something suitable for your trousseau with my money, too. I know it is customary for husbands to give their brides jewelry for the wedding, but I don't have any jewelry to give you. Tell Shakil to use my credit to pay.

Letters of credit were passed around from one merchant to another, so he wouldn't have to pay it immediately. He signed off with rote wishes for her health and set it aside to await his seal.

He opened the letter from Shakil and instantly saw red.

The Dey has asserted his primacy and laid claim to Captain Matteo Vargiu.

He threw it down and thumped his fist against his thigh before he could school his temper enough to read on.

He is taking Vargiu as his ten percent from your raid on Biya.

He stopped and did the calculation in his head, then grunted in satisfaction. Vargiu's ransom was about the right amount for the Dey's share of Biya's loot, with the added benefit that he would not have to part with any cash or wait for Vargiu to be ransomed. He was quit of the recalcitrant captive. It pleased him beyond all reason that it also meant Murad Rais was cheated of his claim to half of Vargiu's ransom. But he still owed Murad. Kateb's release had been obtained with the promise of future payment. He took out paper, reed pen, and India ink. He wrote in a strong angular hand,

Please inform His Excellency the Dey that I am happy to accommodate him in the matter of Captain Vargiu. I have also reflected upon your advice to appease Murad Rais' claim about the Eleanora d'Arborea, and I have decided to graciously sign over the remaining captives to him in satisfaction of that debt.

That left him free and clear of the *Eleanora,* her bothersome captain, and Murad's claim. He had retrieved Kateb, didn't have to wait for the ransom of the *Eleanora's* captives, and consolidated his loot from the Biya raid, a raid to which Murad had no claim at all. There would be no complication about settling those prizes.

He cackled to think what a nuisance it would be for Murad to collect the petty ransoms of the ordinary sailors over the next ten years. "Serves him right," he muttered. He drank his coffee, then finished the letter with directions about Jamila's dower.

If Kasim will not sell his share of the farm at a reasonable price, then you shall spend the money for your sister on whatever she needs instead. Once Kasim realizes he might not get anything, then perhaps he will be reasonable. If he settles for less than three thousand sequins, Jamila is to have the difference.

There. He was one up on both Murad and Kasim, the two men in the world who annoyed him most. It had been a difficult season so far, but it was finally going well. He was pleased.

CHAPTER 28 : THE DEY'S REVENGE

A pair of dispatch boats were berthed in a cove below the fortress. As the officer on patrol, Isam Rais had the right to use them. He wrote up his dispatches to report the unexciting events so far and to send his mail to Shakil and Jamila. The Dey would hand over Vargiu. The Sardinians would go home with their pride satisfied. Tettiwan would patch the holes in its roofs. The *Sea Leopard* would lie in wait behind Sunrise Point and pounce on their rear and pick off a couple of small vessels from their convey, then retreat under the protection of the guns of the fortress. They would come after him, of course, but they wouldn't be able to reach him in the shallow waters. They'd have to fire on him at long range with little chance of hitting him while the much heavier guns of the fortress would have at least a fifty-fifty chance of hitting them.

Several days of patrolling the approach to Modiq Bay passed by uneventfully. On the fourth day, a dispatch vessel arrived and handed over a mailbag.

Opening it in the privacy of his cabin, Isam was astounded by what he read. He swiftly laid out his charts and plotted points on them. Satisfied, he went to the door and told the marine, "Pass the word. All officers to meet me in my cabin immediately. Midshipmen too." He needed to make certain his middies understood how to fill in in case of further casualties among the officers.

The crew of the dispatch boat knew what the news was and the whole crew was in a state of suppressed excitement while they waited for the captain's decision. The officers and midshipmen arrived as soon as they were called; they had been hovering near the coach in anticipation of his summons.

Isam Rais was no longer wearing a sling. Having decided to ignore the surgeon's advice, he was using his arm as much as he could and felt his mobility increasing daily. He also felt the pain of overexerting it, so tucked his hand into his sash for support when not using it.

As they gathered around the coffee table, he sat up straight on the divan. "The Dey of Zokhara has rejected the Sardinian demands. He strapped Captain Vargiu to the mouth of a forty pound mortar and blew him to pieces in front of the Sardinian consul. Spain professes to be shocked, shocked! at the barbarity displayed, and has declared war against us in support of the Sardinians. We are going to nip out and grab those three Spanish schooners we saw yesterday before they make it to Oran. They won't know that war has been declared, so they won't fear us or have any reason to hide. We are going to cruise and cruise hard to snatch as many prizes as we can before the Spanish are on a war-footing. With a little luck, they won't make a serious effort this fall and winter will close their season without any action. The Spanish don't like to sail in winter."

Nobody liked to sail in winter, but corsairs sometimes did so because they were effectively unopposed during cold weather. Winter was an especially good time for looting coastal towns since bad weather made it difficult for messages and reinforcements to arrive over mud-choked roads.

"When we send in prizes, the prize crew will drop an agent in Jallone to recruit crew. When we come in for supplies, we'll pick up the recruits so we have enough crew for our prizes. Any questions?" The Modiq Bay was a fertile zone with numerous small towns and villages.

"But rais, how will we patrol if we are chasing prizes?" Lieutenant Urve asked.

"If we leave immediately, we should be able to overhaul them by evening and return by dawn," Isam replied. He had been so caught up in the opportunity for prizes that he had forgotten he was on commission from the Dey.

"Prizes will be good," Lieutenant Hamza replied.

Isam was reminded that two of his three lieutenants were inexperienced in their positions. "Aim well and victory is ours," he told them. "But the schooners won't put up any fight. They can't outrun us or outfight us, and they know it. If there are no further questions, hoist the Man in the Crescent Moon, and weigh anchor. I want all possible speed."

The purple ensign that was the sign of Salletine government service was hauled down, the red flag of the Sallee rovers rose in its place. The silk flag fluttered out as the breeze caught it. The *Sea Leopard* had been cruising far enough off shore to catch the western breeze, and now she turned before it, seized a bone in her teeth, and went leaping eastwards like the leopard for which she was named. The dun colored coast of Africa's late summer sped past. All hands were alert—for prizes, for Spaniards and Sardinians, for corsairs that could give them the latest news.

As they tore past a fishboat, they shouted, "Spain has declared war!"

The corsairs were jubilant, but the fishermen were not. They weren't afraid of the Sardinians who never bothered them, but they were very much afraid of the Spanish who would raid the coast of Africa in revenge for the rovers' raids upon their own commerce. The red warning was nailed to the mast, and the fishboat ran out to carry the news to another vessel in the offing.

Remembering that he had a commission to fulfill, Isam directed Imrich, "Make a note in the log. 'Stood off the coast to warn the fishboats about Spain.'" Yes. He was supposed to be protecting them. Giving the warning was part of his job. Yet pretty soon the *Sea Leopard* had ranged too far to even pretend it was part of her defensive patrol.

In the middle of the afternoon, the masthead lookout called out, "Ahoy the deck! Sail north-northeast, range five miles!"

Isam Rais and Master Imrich raised their spyglasses. They could see a pyramid of white in the distance. Isam lowered his glass thoughtfully. "Hoist the Spanish colors. She's probably Dutch." Remembering his decision to teach his midshipmen something, he said to them, "Because the Dutch are a trading nation and one of the most common sorts of vessels encountered in the Mediterranean. The Spanish tend to avoid our coast even during peace. They don't trust us." He flashed a wolfish grin. They didn't trust Spain anymore than Spain trusted them.

Isam said, "Helm, touch left." The *Sea Leopard* subtly altered her heading to bring her course closer to the stranger without sailing straight at her. From a distance it would not be apparent that she had shifted to come closer to them.

In the next twenty minutes, the distance shrank from five miles to one mile. The stranger, a lofty fully-rigged ship, crossed their hawse. As she did so, she boomed a challenge to them. It was too far to make out the stranger's ensign, but it was yellow and red in the spyglass. Isam's heart sank. The Spaniard was even bigger than the *Eleanora d'Arborea*.

He had no idea what the signal code was for the Spanish navy. "Acknowledge with one gun."

The command was passed. Isam's brain worked feverishly. She was coming from the direction of Italy and Sardinia; she probably had not heard the news about Spain declaring war. She was certain to have a crew of hundreds; he only had a crew of a hundred and fifty. Even if he could get under her guns with his false flag, they were too badly outnumbered. There was no way he could take her.

The Spaniard tacked north, hove to presenting her broadside, and sent up signals. Now, at a distance of half a mile, he counted six gun ports.

"She's a merchantman," he said in relief. Her crew would certainly be fewer than his, although the male passengers would probably fight.

He had not checked the *Sea Leopard's* impetuous speed. Lights flashed on the quarterdeck of the stranger as they turned their spyglasses toward the xebec with the Spanish flag. The *Sea Leopard* had a yellow hull, not red like a Spanish warship. The game was up; they were recognized. The stranger ran out her guns.

Suddenly, he knew his gambit. "Haul down the Spanish colors. Hoist the Silver Crescent. Fire a live shot across their bows."

The false flag came down and the purple and white flag of the Sallee Republic went up. The white crescent and star rippled on the purple silk. The strangers were staring at the eleven guns of a Sallee rover's broadside.

"What are you going to do?" Imrich asked him.

"Board her and impound her. They don't know we're at war yet."

"But—" Imrich said.

"If I don't come back, sink them."

He ordered his gig. While it was being lowered into the water, he went to his cabin, fetched the dispatch satchel, and came on deck again. He climbed down into the sternsheets, and the triangular sail bellied out and carried him swiftly over to the Spaniard.

He was greeted by men-at-arms who stood to attention as he came aboard. It tickled him; he had never been saluted by a Spaniard before. The captain of the vessel was there to meet him and with a worried look. Isam looked him up and down, but he didn't speak much Spanish. He called for his translator.

"Tell him I am Isam Rais al-Tangueli, commander of the Sallee squadron stationed at Sunrise Point. He is in Sallee waters. I require his papers."

The Spanish captain listened carefully, then he got a knowing look on his face. "Of course, captain," he replied in Spanish. "I am Juan Bautista, master of the *Plenitud*. I am in route from Syracuse to Málaga. If you will join me in my cabin, I will make you comfortable and show you all that you require." He nodded meaningfully.

"That suits me very well. My marines will secure your vessel while I examine your papers."

"Of course, rais," the man replied.

Isam waited for his marines in the longboat to arrive before going below. Once the marines had control of the deck, he, Taslim, and three marines ducked under the break of the quarterdeck and arrived in Captain Bautista's commodious cabin. It was almost tall enough for Isam to stand up in. The deck was carpeted with floral rugs to create an illusion of a garden. The furniture was upholstered in black and rose, a silver and crystal chandelier hung over the mahogany dining table, and an oil portrait of a woman and two children hung on the wall. "My family," Captain Bautista said. He settled behind his mahogany desk and opened the drawer. He took out his papers, then took out a black velvet bag and spilled silver coins on the desk. He laid a paper next to them on the desk. "My passport," he said. He waited expectantly.

Isam moved a little closer to the desk. His eyes glittered as he took in several dozen silver pieces. "I can't see it from here. You'll have to make it clearer to me."

The captain had not expected his first bribe would be successful. He was prepared to haggle in the elegant Spanish way. He opened his drawer and pulled out another velvet bag and set it on the table next to the spilled coins. "Of course, so sorry. Let me help you see."

Isam folded his arms over his chest and smirked at the man. Bautista was not yet discouraged. Another bag appeared on the desk. He watched Isam's curled lip and set up another bag. When that failed to move the corsair, he spread his hands helplessly. "I'm sorry, perhaps if I loaned you my spectacles you would be able to make it out better," he said a bit testily, indicating that he had come to the end of his generosity.

"I insist you try harder. You are in Sallee waters, and you have not given me a satisfactory explanation as to why."

"The wind, *sí?* It is out of the west-northwest. We cannot sail straight to Spain, or we would. We must bear as far south as we can, then make a board to Málaga."

It was a perfectly reasonable explanation. But they both knew that was not the real question on the table.

Isam glanced around the cabin and eyed the various ornamental fixtures. He was trying to figure out where the captain hid his cashbox—it was certainly not the pittance he kept in the desk. The two hundred or so *reales* was bait so that a thief would think he had found the treasure and not look further. That Bautista revealed that much money told him the man must have much, much more. Or if not cash, then something so valuable that two hundred pieces of silver was a fair fee to protect it.

Bautista mistook his look. He gestured. "Allow me to make you a small gift. A token of my esteem."

Isam grinned at him. He was enjoying the game. "That is very generous of you. I am about to be married, so I am looking for a suitable gift for my bride."

Bautista nodded wisely. "My wife advised me on all the furnishings. They will please any lady. Please, allow me to give your lovely wife something."

Glancing down at the floral rug, Isam said, "The rug. She likes flowers." At least, he supposed she did. All women liked flowers, didn't they? He really had no idea. Bautista paled. Retaining his poise, he spoke carelessly. "Oh that? It is nothing, a rag. I have a better one in the hold I will give you."

"I'm not greedy. This one will suit me fine," Isam replied, not missing the captain's reaction.

Bautista spread his hands. "You are too modest. Let me give you the good rug, and a pair of chairs as well." He kept a well practiced smile on his face.

Isam turned to his marines. "You two, roll up the rug."

Bautista rose to his feet in alarm as the two Salletines started moving furniture while the third menaced Bautista to prevent his interference. Less cunning than their captain, they thought the rug was simply a piece of loot. The Spaniard came out from behind the desk and trod upon the rug.

Planting his weight firmly up on it, he grasped Isam's hand and lifted it. For a moment the corsair thought he was going to kiss it, but he didn't. Instead the captain drew a diamond ring off his hand and slid it onto Isam's finger.

"Jewelry for a lady, *sí?* That is even better than a rug. You can have the gems reset if you don't like the ring." He held his breath as Isam studied the ring shining on his finger.

"It sparkles. I like it."

He gripped Bautista by the arm and led him over to the sofa and pushed him on to it. Standing over him he said, "I like the jewelry very much. I accept." To the two marines who had been obliged to stop rolling the rug when Bautista stood on it, he said, "Carry on."

The rug rolled up. There in the floor was a trapdoor.

"What's this?" Isam asked in mock surprise. He wagged his finger at the man. "You have been holding out on me." To his marines, "Break it open."

They had to go out to find axes, but when they returned, they hacked into the planks with a will. The wood splintered and crunched, and the metal box within was revealed. They laid aside the axes and heaved it out. It thumped heavily upon the deck.

"There's another one!" exclaimed one of the marines. He reached in, caught it by the handle in the end, and pulled it out. Feeling around under the planks, they found a total of three metal boxes. They were so heavy the two men struggled to lift them out.

"Robbery!" Bautista seethed. "Outright, thieving, robbery."

"Not robbery, war," Isam replied. He reached into his satchel, pulled out a wooden ruler with a wavy irregular edge, and said, "This is the new passport ruler that was just issued. Let's see if yours matches."

He walked over to the desk and laid it on the paper passport. The curves at the bottom edge of the paper did not match the curves of the ruler. He held them up to show Bautista.

"You are my prisoner. This ship is a prize of the Sallee Republic. You have your own country to blame; Spain has declared war on us."

Bautista was sick and grey as the marines seized him and led him out.

CHAPTER 29: DISPATCHES

The *Plentitud* was not a fast sailer. It was rising midnight before they arrived in Modiq Bay. The *Plenitud* was too deep-drafted for Isam to be willing to try the shoals at night when she would go aground at the slightest miscalculation. That meant anchoring her a hundred yards outside the narrow strip of land that was the eastern edge of the lagoon—she was too big to bring under the guns of the fortress. Isam spent a sleepless night. Having seized the most magnificent prize of his career without firing a shot, he was terrified of losing her. Just as he had acted quickly to take advantage of Spanish ignorance to surprise his prize, somebody in Spain might have done the same and could even now be rounding Sunrise Point. His only consolation was that they probably wouldn't try the shoals by night, but even so, if they swung far enough east, they would find deep water that would let them get up close to the *Plenitud*.

The crew and male passengers over the age of twelve were all locked in the hold, and the ladies and children were locked in the chief mate's cabin so they could use his roundhouse. There would be no excuse to let them out. There were only two women: the lady and her maid, and her two young children. Her husband had been undersecretary to the ambassador to the Kingdom of Sicily. He and his clerk were stuffed in the hold with the common sailors. Isam and Imrich were sharing Captain Bautista's fancy cabin because none of his lieutenants knew enough about square rigs to serve as prizemaster for her. He appointed Imrich to be the *Plenitud's* master. Hamza proved to have served in square-rigged prizes, so he had come over as the one and only lieutenant. Taslim was brought over because he was the oldest and most experienced of the midshipmen. In addition, there were twenty Muslim hands who had worked square-rigs before— brigs and snows and ships were common prizes for the rovers, albeit not one as big as this. Twenty crew was just barely enough for them to work the ship. Still, all they had to do was get her up to Zokhara. It would be enough. He brought over plenty of marines and some gunners. The *Sea Leopard's* crew was significantly depleted.

Isam wished more than anything Kateb was there to sooth his nerves and help him sleep. All he could do was tend himself and imagine what he would be doing if Kateb were there to do it with him. It helped, and at last he dropped off into a fitful sleep.

A tremendous clatter right outside his cabin woke him. He leaped out of bed and snatched up his scimitar and drew it, convinced that the prisoners had mutinied and somehow found a way out of the hold. Pale sunlight lit the room and he blinked at the unfamiliar surroundings before he had his bearings. The wooden latch slid to the side and the door eased open. He held his scimitar high and prepared to bring it down on the head of the man invading his cabin.

Abdul screeched and dropped the silver tray he was carrying. The coffee pot crashed to the floor and a flood of scalding brown liquid flowed out. Isam checked his swing. "Abdul! What are you doing!"

Abdul threw up his hands, "Mercy, effendi!"

The pair of marines stationed outside his door looked at him in astonishment. Feeling foolish, he lowered his sword, then glared at them. "Is something the matter?"

They gawked and answered, "Uh, no, rais."

He sheathed his sword with a show of nonchalance. "You shouldn't startle me when I'm sleeping. You should have knocked." He looked around, but Imrich was nowhere to be seen. He was probably on deck already.

"I did knock, rais. You didn't answer, so I banged on the door," the marine replied.

Isam felt a fool. So that was what had startled him awake. Now his breakfast was a mess on the floor. "Clean that up," he said gruffly to his steward.

Seeing that Isam had put away his sword, Abdul got to his knees and started picking up spilled sugar cubes and using the napkin to soak up spilled cream.

"It needs a mop," Isam said. He shut the door and retreated into his cabin. He had been about twelve inches from killing his own servant. His heart throbbed with anxiety. But, it was morning. He had made it safely through the night. He was excessively tired and his shoulder hurt and even his leg was complaining, but his prize was still firmly under his control. He opened the door to the stern gallery and stepped out into the cold. The coolness refreshed him even as it chilled his naked toes. While leaning on the railing and taking deep breaths to calm himself, he saw something that riled him all over again.

The *Renegade* was cruising down Modiq Bay. As he watched, she hove to and made signals to the *Sea Leopard*: dispatches. "He's the last person I want to see," he muttered. With a sigh, Isam dressed himself and prepared to meet his rival without benefit of coffee.

Murad Rais came aboard the *Plentitud* in person. He could not suppress his look of envy as his head turned every which way to take in the big ship. The *Plentitud* was not the biggest nor the richest prize ever taken by the Sallee rovers (that was a Spanish treasure galleon decades ago), but she was the biggest prize of the last five years, and what's more, the *Sea*

Leopard had taken her single-handedly. Murad had been part of a wolfpack of five rovers working in concert to take the previous big prize. Parceled out like that, the booty had been no greater than if they'd taken five smaller prizes, but there was considerable glory in it all the same. A glory now eclipsed by Isam's feat of derring-do.

Isam smiled contentedly as he saw the look on Murad's face. "You look like you could spit nails, my friend," he remarked.

"How did you do it?" Murad demanded.

Isam shrugged. "Bold and swift action. We surprised her."

There wasn't a mark on either of the vessels. Murad glowered as he handed over the satchel. "I have dispatches for you."

Isam accepted it. "Salaam," he said finally. He wanted to keep gloating, but they were both on the same side in a war against Spain, so he swallowed any further remarks. He couldn't help smirking though. "Will you join me in my cabin for breakfast? I was just about to break my fast."

Murad looked like he'd rather put poison in Isam's food, but he said, "You're too kind. I wouldn't want to trouble you."

"We have a lot to talk about. It will be easier with full stomachs and a pipe of tobacco."

"If you insist," Murad said gracelessly.

"Follow me." He could feel daggers in his back as Murad fumed in behind him. The pair of marines stood to attention and opened the door into the well-furnished cabin.

Murad Rais' eyes went left, right, up, down, and all around. The floral rug was back in place hiding the repaired deck planking. The boxes had been sent aboard the *Sea Leopard* for safekeeping. The *Plentitud* didn't have cushions or stools for sitting on, so they had to perch awkwardly on the Spanish chairs. The heavy dark furniture had a medieval look to it: the dining chairs were throne-like with high backs and painted scenes. The light of the silver and crystal chandelier added a much needed brightness to the space that was paneled and ceiled with dark wood. The rose colored upholstery with its floral pattern did little to soften the heaviness of the furniture.

"It's amazing how much money the Spanish spend on ugly things," Murad said.

Isam was also used to the Moorish preference for graceful curves rather than heavy blocks. He couldn't help agreeing. "In spite of all its glass, it's darker in here than the *Sea Leopard's* cabin."

Belatedly it occurred to him that Murad might have been attempting a backhanded insult, but decided it didn't matter. He pulled the heavily embroidered bell rope, then sat down at the head of the table. It was big enough to seat twelve. Murad sat to his right. Neither of them was comfortable with European furniture, but they both feigned nonchalance. Neither wanted to seem a bumpkin in the eyes of the other.

Isam opened the satchel and started reading. No wonder Murad was sullen! Isam was in the Dey's good graces; he had been appointed *Kapitan* —squadron commander—and Murad Rais placed under his command. So had several other corsairs in port at the time, but they hadn't arrived yet. With no navy of his own, the Dey had to deputize corsairs, and that required invoking a provision of the *taifa's* charter that required them to provide a certain number of vessels for the Dey's use in times of war, to be compensated at rates determined by the Dey. The full details were spelled out in the dispatch to Isam.

The steward arrived with a tray of food. One of the ship's boys had been released from the hold to help Abdul with his work—the cabin was much too large for him to keep clean all by himself and the bizarre varieties of blue and white china pieces in the vitrine bewildered him. The boy, no more than fourteen, had been a servant in the wardroom and was able to explain what all the pieces were for.

Isam waited until the plates and glasses had been put on the table and the silver plate covers removed to reveal omelettes stuffed with vegetables and cheese. The two servants stepped back against the wall to wait.

"You can go. I'll ring you when I want you," Isam told them. They shuffled out. Even the ship's boy was relieved to be out of the oppressive magnificence of the great cabin.

Isam ate his omelet with his left hand. His right shoulder was still giving him trouble with tasks that required precision. He did not want to stab himself in the face with a fork with Murad watching.

Murad ate sullenly. Finally, about half way through the omelet, he asked, "What are your orders, *kapitan?*"

"A reconnaissance around Sunrise Point to see what can be seen. Do you have a mirror man aboard the *Renegade?*"

"No, I don't."

"I have a midshipman that can read the mirror code. I'll send him with you. That way you can signal the watchtowers if you find anything."

"They can see farther at sea than I can."

"But most of the time you won't be in sight of a signal tower. If you do spot something, sail for the nearest signal tower and send the message. Don't engage with anything you find. Withdraw back to this side of the peninsula."

"As you command, *kapitan.*"

"When Yuttuy Rais gets here, I'll send him east along the coast to patrol."

Murad glowered. "You're giving me the more dangerous job."

"The more important job. Danger will come from the west."

Resentment glowed like coals in Murad's eyes. "You're trying to get rid of me. You're hoping the Spanish will do your dirty work."

Isam felt his own ire rising. "I am doing the work that needs to be done. You are here first, and we must know what the Spanish are up to. We find that out by scouting west. You will be busy with that, so when Yuttuy Rais arrives, I'll send him east. I will remain in the mouth of Modiq Bay with the *Sea Leopard*. The prize crew will take the *Plenitud* up to Zokhara."

"Why don't you patrol west if it's so damned important? You've got a faster ship than I do."

"Because I'm undermanned with so many men in the prize."

"I could tow it to Zokhara, then you could go out at full strength."

Isam would rather drive a nail through his thumb than to let Murad Rais get hold of his prize. "Thank you for the offer, but we will be fine as we are. I won't detain you any longer. I know you're eager to get started."

Murad glared at him. "You're in the Dey's favor for the moment, but it won't last. He'll use you and discard you, the same as all the others."

Isam glared at him. "Maybe the Dey and I understand one another better than you do. It is to our mutual benefit to cooperate."

"It's to your mutual benefit to play false with other corsairs, you mean."

Coldly Isam replied, "You have your orders, rais. Get moving."

Murad accidentally knocked the chair over as he jumped up. He threw his napkin on top of the food. "You haven't seen the last of me." He turned his back on the *kapitan* of the squadron and yanked the cabin door open, then slammed it shut as he disappeared.

Isam's food grew cold while he fumed. Finally he forced himself to eat it. It was perfectly good food, even if it did taste like sawdust in his mouth.

CHAPTER 30 : ENEMY SIGHTED

After breakfast, the tide was slack and the breeze was too weak to move the *Plentitud*. The massive cargo ship was a leviathan of the deep, and in deep water she remained. Although the lateen fishboats skimmed out of the lagoon at a leisurely pace, and even the larger *Sea Leopard* was able to begin a slow amble, the fat-bottomed merchantman simply sat. Isam Rais set her topsails and topgallants and raised the anchor, after which it was only by intently staring at the headland that he was able to discern any motion at all.

Isam muttered, "At this rate, a dung beetle will reach Zokhara sooner than we will."

"If we wait for the rising tide, it will take us up river. That's the way we did it in Holland," Master Imrich replied.

"High tide isn't until afternoon. I don't want to wait that long. We have to tow."

"Our crew isn't big enough. We barely have enough to work the ship as it is."

"The *Sea Leopard* can tow us."

"But she is supposed to be on patrol at the mouth of the bay," Imrich pointed out.

Isam shrugged. "Murad Rais is here. That's good enough. Besides, once the wind comes up, we can drop the tow. I want to get the *Plentitud* far enough up the bay that she won't be seen by nosy infidels. If they don't know she's here, they won't try to rescue her. Besides, it will only be a few miles. The *Sea Leopard* will be back in her place by noon."

Imrich nodded to that. "The *Plentitud* isn't late to her port of call yet, so no one will be looking for her. But it is better to move her around the bend where she can't be seen."

Isam had been up and working since dawn, and he was tired and sore. "You can supervise the tow. I'm going below for a rest. You have the conn."

"Very good, rais I have the conn."

Isam went below. His cabin was cold, so he took a chair into the gallery. The stern gallery was a marvelous thing. Five windows—actual windows, not gun ports—lined the back of the vessel with a shallow but wide gallery made of carved and painted wood. Long beams of early morning light warmed it. The scant breeze was from the northeast, so he settled his chair in the corner where he was protected by the protrusion of the roundhouse. The corner was warm except when the breeze grew strong enough to push around the roundhouse and flit across him. The upholstered chair was too small to sit cross-legged on, but it had a back to lean against, so it was good enough.

He tamped a little hashish into his pipe and smoked leisurely. Gently the herb worked on him and eased the aching of his shoulder. He was comfortable and happy, so he decided that he ought to give thanks to Allah. He was much too comfortable to rise and perform the prescribed motions, but he said, "Allah, you know everything, so you know I am wounded and exempt from daily prayer. You also know I not much for praying, but all the same, I am grateful for Your generosity in granting me an easy victory over this great prize. It will solve all my financial problems. Therefore I will be generous to the first charity I encounter when I return to Zokhara."

He blew out a cloud of grey smoke and smiled at the way it eddied in the light. Then his eye moved past the smoke to a shape moving in the distant mist. He dragged the spyglass out of his pocket and put it to his eye. The glass showed him the *Renegade* had turned around and was running back towards him. Wondering, he scanned the misty offing. Was that a another shape moving through the mist? He watched intently for several minutes, then the mist thinned briefly and showed him the topsails and topgallants of a distant square-rigger.

He clenched his teeth tight on the pipestem and it broke. The pipe tumbled down, scattered its burning embers on the deck. Without thinking, he stomped the sparks with a booted foot, then he gave the broken pipe a mighty kick and sent it hurtling into the *Plentitud's* placid wake. The *Renegade* fired a gun and the hollow report boomed across the waters. A few seconds later a second gun sounded.

He heard Imrich shouting above him, "Signal the *Sea Leopard,* 'Enemy sighted! Drop the tow!"

Isam rushed into the great cabin, grabbed his scimitar, and thrust it through his sash. The messenger was rapping at his door. He opened it with a jerk.

The messenger boy reported, "The enemy is sighted, sir!"

"I know," Isam replied. He brushed past him and strode to the ladder.

Arriving on the quarterdeck, one of the men cried out, "Captain on deck!" They stood to attention.

"As you were," he told them. To his officers he barked, "Report."

Imrich replied, "Enemy sighted, sir. We don't know how many or where, but the *Renegade* warned us."

With the *Renegade* running for the mouth of the bay, her signal flags were masked by her sails. She ran slowly given the faintness of the air, but as Isam held up his thumbnail to check her, she grew steadily larger by comparison.

Light twinkled on the fortress' watchtower. The signal midshipmen reported, "Mirror signal, sir. The fortress is reporting one enemy sail north-northeast, seven miles."

Isam muttered, "They were sleeping up there. They should have seen her before Murad did."

"They have fog north of here. The enemy may have been hiding in it," Imrich replied.

Isam gazed in frustration at the concealing mist. The wind being scant, the stranger would make slow progress. At this rate, it would take her three or four hours to come up on them. It didn't matter; the wind would rise with the sun. In an hour or so there would be a good breeze. Good enough to move both square-riggers. The stranger wouldn't have closed by then. Unfortunately, the *Plentitud's* round bottom was built for cargo, not speed. She would not have gone far.

The stranger was most likely a Sardinian frigate. Possibly a Spanish frigate. Either way, twice as fast as the *Plentitud*. Not only that, the merchantman was constrained by draft. Modiq Bay was wide but the channel was narrow. To the right lay the shoals under the fortress, to the left lay the shallow green waters of the lagoon. Worse, even if the stranger hadn't spotted her yet, she soon would if she kept chasing Murad. The *Plentitud's* half dozen six pounders were no match for the frigate's battery. Even if she were a very small frigate she would have at least thirty-six guns. A frigate of any size was too big a ship for the *Sea Leopard* to take on by herself. He'd learned that lesson the hard way.

He eyed the fortress. The stranger would have to come within range of its guns. That cheered him a little. If the stranger was afraid of the fort, the corsairs would make their escape up river. Still, if she was brave enough to try it, she might succeed in cutting out the *Plentitud*. Thank Allah it was daylight. Had it been night the strangers certainly would have tried it. He would have.

"What are your orders, rais?" Master Imrich asked him.

Isam rubbed a hand over his face, then made his decision. "Continue upstream. The *Sea Leopard* to cover us. The frigate will have to brave the fortress to get close enough to do any damage. She'll have to sound her way to find the channel and that will slow her down. She'll be pounded. I'm going to transfer to the *Sea Leopard*. There's nothing the *Plentitud* can do but creep upstream. If the infidels get past the *Sea Leopard* and the *Renegade*, abandon ship. Save yourselves and let them have the *Plentitud*." They all knew what their fate would be if captured: summary execution, or if they were lucky, a lifetime chained to the oar of a Spanish galley. Best not to dwell on such things. "Rendezvous at the dispatch station if we must abandon ship," he finished.

Imrich gave him a look. After a moment, he nodded. "Very well, rais."

The *Plentitud's* gig carried him back to the *Sea Leopard*. He took several hands from the merchantman as well: the *Plentitud* was too unwieldy to fight. The hands were more use to him aboard the *Sea Leopard* where he would have to sail, row, and fire the guns. He climbed up the side of the *Sea Leopard* and sighed in relief to be back aboard his own vessel. He knew her. She was low, fast, and agile. Like the cat for which she was named, she was a predator. His previous adventures had taught him her capabilities. He had her measure now.

First Lieutenant Urve was relieved beyond words that the captain had returned to fight the *Sea Leopard* himself. "What shall we do?"

"Take to the shoals and stay under the guns of the fortress. The enemy will have to come within range of the fortress to fire on us. We must aggressively tease the enemy to lure her in."

Urve boggled at him. "You want her to come after us?"

"I don't want her to go after the *Plentitud*," Isam replied crisply. "Or would you rather hand over a fortune to the enemy?"

"No, rais. Of course not." He gulped. The captain worried him; he had a tendency to bite off more than he could chew. At the same time, he had seized victory yesterday when circumstances seemed impossible. Allah favored him. The junior officer stewed in his own sweat and hoped the captain was right this time.

Isam stood at the railing and looked down at the men. They looked up at him. Some were stolid, some alert, some eager, but most were worried. He had to put heart into them to make them fight and fight hard. If they gave up, the battle was already lost. He forced himself to smile at them. His baritone rang out as resonant as a drum.

"We had an easy victory yesterday! We embarrassed the enemy! Now he's come to strut and pretend that he fought! That frigate was supposed to be protecting the *Plentitud,* but she did a piss poor job of it, didn't she?" Isam had no idea if the frigate and *Plentitud* had even seen each other, but it didn't matter. Protecting Christian shipping was part of her job.

The men on deck murmured and nodded in agreement.

"We fought the most powerful frigate in the Sardinian navy, and she blew herself up because she was afraid of us!"

"Murad was there too," one of the men dared to point out.

"And there he is again, running as fast as his heels will fly," Isam replied scornfully. Suddenly Isam knew exactly what to do. "He will be our bait."

He gave orders and the men listened carefully. When he was sure they understood, he dismissed them to their work.

CHAPTER 31 : THE FAILED TRAP

The sun rose higher in the sky and the morning warmed. The fog burned off and the wind rose, but sheltered under the headland where the fortress stood, the breeze was blocked from them. It didn't matter; Isam didn't plan on going anywhere. Screened from sight, he dropped anchors and mounted springs upon them so that he could crank the *Sea Leopard* around to fire another broadside in short order. His signal midshipman kept an eye on the fortress' watchtower. While they were making preparations, the *Renegade* turned into the channel and passed them as she ran upstream.

"Coward!" Isam shook his fist at the fleeing corsair. "Signal the *Renegade*, 'Stand and fight!'"

The *Renegade* did not acknowledge. She kept skimming away and passed the *Plentitud*. The big ship had managed to creep less than a mile up the river. The *Renegade* disappeared around the bend.

Isam feigned insouciance to hearten the crew. "It doesn't matter any way. He was only the bait."

The *Sea Leopard* finished her preparations. The tubs of sand with their slow matches stood at the ready. Smoke curled upward from each bit of match while the smell of brimstone wafted across the deck. They were downwind from their target, so the unnatural aroma would not give them away. Even if it had, the fortress on the hill above gave ample explanation for the scent. With all preparations completed, there was nothing to do but wait.

The minutes ticked by. Maybe the stranger had given up? After all, there was no point risking a frigate under the guns of the fortress. More minutes passed. The men sat on the guns or leaned against the rails and waited.

The fortress boomed out a single shot. No answer was given. A couple of minutes later and the fortress tried another shot. From this they could deduce that the unseen vessel was at very long range. The fortress wasn't wasting shot while it tried the distance. The stranger didn't fire in return; there was no point. Her smaller guns couldn't do any damage at that range even with a lucky shot. At last the vessel herself came into view. At two miles away, neither she nor the *Sea Leopard* could do each other any damage. Spotting the lurking corsair, the frigate promptly wore ship and headed back north, disappearing behind the headland again. Several more desultory shots rang out from the fortress with no greater effect than before.

"That's that then. Unrig the springs and haul up the anchors," Isam said. He leaned his butt against the railing and massaged his aching leg and shoulder. He was very tired—he had spent more hours on his feet today than any day so far. He was continuing to improve, but he wasn't well yet. "Pass the word for Abdul. Tell him to bring me a hammock chair."

That more than anything relieved the tension on the ship. If the captain was lounging at his ease, there was nothing to be worried about. The men chattered as they went about their work.

"Now is as good a time as any for you to take some practice," Isam told Lieutenant Urve. "Once the anchors are up, get the oars out. Bring us to a position in the middle of the shoals over there. What do you need to do to accomplish that?"

Urve's nerves were frayed from the fruitless waiting. To be the sudden target of the captain's instruction made them snap taut again. "Uh, I'll have the master . . . I mean, the master's mate supervise the raising of the anchors." Master Imrich was away on the *Plenitud*.

"Then what?"

"Um, I'll tell the crew to out oars. We'll row over that way."

"What bearings?"

Urve looked around helplessly. "I don't know."

"You know how to steer, don't you?"

Urve flushed and paled. "Yes, sir."

"So. What marks will you use to set your course?"

Urve understood what was expected now. He looked around, then said, "If I keep that sandbar about two points off the starboard bow, it should bring me into the middle of the shoals. And I'll order the lead out to take soundings." He gave Isam a questioning look.

Isam nodded. "That will do. Carry on."

The master's mates had been well-trained by Imrich; without much ado the senior mate ordered up the anchors. The bower was left hanging from the cathead as was usual in shallow water. That done, Urve felt surer of himself, and called out clearly, "Oars, out oars!"

The men moved briskly as they unlashed the oars from where they were stowed against the inside of the gunwales. Wood clattered as the big sweeps were hauled into place up and down the deck and fitted into the oar ports.

"Oars, give way together!" Urve's tenor rang out with more surety. The drummer set the beat and the oars began to leisurely pull together. At first the blades of the oars stirred the waters into swirls, then the vessel gained way and glided forward.

Urve looked around, made note of his seamarks, and said, "Helm, touch right."

"Touch right, aye," the older man at the helm replied. He turned the tiller a little to the left and the xebec curved slightly to the right.

"That's well. Steady up," Urve told him.

Isam smiled to see the young man standing erect as he unconsciously drew himself up in the attitude of command. Urve wanted to do well; what young officer didn't? Up until recently, Isam had himself been that young man. Now he was the master of his own vessel. He didn't have to prove himself to anyone anymore. He was his own man.

He smiled. "Well done, Lieutenant."

Urve's face lit up as he turned to face him. "Thank you, rais." Tension flooded out of him and heaved a sigh of relief. He had earned the captain's approval! He grinned happily as he kept watch over the quarterdeck crew and the sea.

Isam said, "Lieutenant Urve, give the men some rowing practice. Stay under the guns of the fortress and maneuver around. Execute turns, back up, rotate in place, and so forth. Set an easy pace. We want to exercise them, not wear them out."

"Aye aye, captain. Rowing practice it is." Urve turned away. Isam closed his eyes and let himself doze.

An hour later, the signal midshipman stepped up to Urve and reported, "Mirror signal, sir. Sunrise Point signal station reports, 'Fleet of five sail northwest, range ten miles, course southeast.'"

Isam's eyes popped open. "Bloody hell. Somebody is feeling feisty," he complained.

The mirrors twinkled and passed the word from post to post along the hills. The message would reach Zokhara within the hour. The squadron, whether Sardinian or Spanish, was heading for the mouth of Modiq Bay. There was no other plausible target; all the towns and villages on the east side of the gulf were of no particular import, but Modiq Bay was the gateway to Zokhara and the Sallee Republic. Isam felt uncomfortably alone with five enemy vessels out there, but he schooled himself to blandness. He didn't want to spook Urve.

"What shall we do?" Urve asked.

"Carry on. I'm thinking."

"Carry on with the rowing drill?" Urve asked stupidly.

"Yes, carry on what you were doing. There's no reason to spook the men. You must pretend to be calm for their sake, even if you don't feel calm. They'll take their cue from you. Act nonchalant."

Urve tried to act casual, but the strain showed in his face. The men who could read the mirror signals told the rest, so everybody knew why Lieutenant Urve was looking pale.

Isam heaved himself to his feet and sauntered to the rail to have a look at them. They fell silent and stared up at him as they pulled the oars. One xebec was no good against a squadron of enemies, even with the fortress for support. His original plan would not work.

"Take us up river, Lieutenant Urve," he told the junior officer.

"Up river, aye," he repeated with blatant relief. Then, "Port oars, back water." With the sweeps on opposite sides going opposite directions, the vessel rotated in place. When she was pointed south, he said, "Oars, pull together!" His voice cracked, much to his embarrassment. He brooded as the *Sea Leopard* swept south at a casual pace. Isam did not relieve him, so when they cleared the headland, he gave the commands that turned the *Sea Leopard* into the mouth of the bay and carried her upstream. The tide was turning, and the current aided their labors.

"Make sail," Isam told the lieutenant.

"Oars, boat oars! Stand by to make sail!" Urve sang out. The oars were stowed. The rowers were sweaty, but the workout had tired them pleasantly while expending their nervous energy. Their mood was good as they went to the water butt and drank. After that, the watch changed. The men below came up from their meal and relieved the crew on deck. Urve was replaced by Lieutenant Cabral, and Urve went below, pleased to have survived a training exercise under his captain's scrutiny.

Isam told Cabral, "Take us upriver. Send word if anything changes, or there's a message from the mirror station. I'm going below."

"Upriver, aye," Cabral replied. He was Khadim's replacement. He was about thirty, sturdy, well-tanned, and placid in demeanor. He was almost as old as the captain and was hoping for a command of his own soon.

"On deck!" came the cry from the masthead. Isam paused on the ladder and listened to the report.

"On deck aye!" replied Cabral.

"There's a square-rigger on the other side of the bend! She's not moving!"

Isam swore in Turkish, then returned to the quarterdeck.

"There's a square—"

"I heard," Isam cut him off. "I have the conn."

"Aye, rais. You have the conn." Cabral stepped aside.

"Is it the *Plenitud?*"

"Not sure! I can only see the main topgallant, but I think so!"

"Out twelve sweeps," Isam ordered.

The channel curved its serpentine way westward with hills on the right bank screening it from the sea and mountains to the left screening it from the winds that blew up from the Sahara desert so far away. Air blowing over the seaward hills twisted as it met the line of hills south of the estuary and created eddies, sudden spots of dead air, and unpredictable gusts as the wind found its way over and between the elevations.

Suddenly the great lateens shook and thundered. The mainsail had its reefs in, but was momentarily taken aback and made leeway toward the south shore.

"Port your helm, out sweeps! Sweeps give way together," Isam ordered. The *Sea Leopard* crawled back into the channel. The wind steadied, and he called, "Boat oars!"

The sweeps were drawn partway in, but kept ready. The wind pushed them further up the bay as they approached the first sweeping bend. Watching the surface of the water, Isam could see the mischief brewing, and called, "Out oars! Oars, give way together."

The *Sea Leopard* swept closer with majestic slowness. "Mainsail! Let sheets fly!"

The immense triangle of canvas hung limp and swung lightly without its sheets to control it. The xebec eased around the bend and found the *Plentitud*. She was aground on the sloping mudbank of the curve. Just then a sudden gust whirled across the *Sea Leopard* and the mainsail flapped and blew to the port side of the vessel. The helm knew his job and kept her bow pointed northwest by west so that the grunting efforts of the rowers kept her to the channel in spite of the pushiness of the errant wind. The much loftier *Plentitud* offered far more surface to the knavish wind and no sweeps to resist it. She had driven south and gently run onto the mud.

As the xebec came further around the treacherous corner, the prize's boats came into view as they strained to tow her off. Unfortunately, with a small crew and a contrary wind, their efforts were in vain. They sweated and strained at the oars, but it was no use. Master Imrich put a speaking trumpet to his face and shouted to the *Sea Leopard*, "Tow, please!"

CHAPTER 32 : THE THUNDER OF DISTANT GUNNERY

"Mirror signal, sir. Five enemy frigates, east of Sunrise Point, range five miles," the signal midshipmen reported.

"Thank you, midshipman." Isam Rais grew pensive.

When he didn't speak, Lieutenant Cabral said, "They're coming up fast. At that rate, they could reach us within an hour."

Isam stared at his beautiful prize, the best prize of his career, the prize taken with the least hurt to himself, his men, and his vessel, the one that would cover him in glory back in Zokhara. The one that he was going to lose to the damned infidels, if they pressed into Modiq Bay. Would they? Their scout would have reported his presence. At that range, they couldn't know it was the *Sea Leopard*, so they weren't coming after him in particular. They were after any and all corsairs, damn their black hearts.

"I think it'll take them longer than that, even if the way was clear. They must reduce the fortress before venturing up the bay. Therefore we will have time to tow the *Plentitud* off the mud. She's not stuck hard. Send our boats to help tow her off."

"Aye aye, captain. Anything else?"

"After the boats are launched, the *Sea Leopard* will hide in that creek over there and cover them, just in case." He pointed to where a cove indented the eastern hills.

"Aye aye, rais." Lieutenant Cabral cupped his mouth with his hands, "Auguste! Hands into the boats to tow!" And to the signal midshipman, "Signal the *Plentitud*. 'Prepare for tow.'"

The colored pennants rose and the grounded vessel acknowledged. A rousing cheer went up from the prize. The sound was tattered by the wind, but scraps of it reached them anyhow.

"Give them an answer, lads," Cabral said.

The crew of the *Sea Leopard* ululated and the sound swelled their hearts and stiffened their spines. They were corsairs, they were in their home waters, and they would defend their country and their prize (especially their prize) from the infidels. How, they didn't know. That was the captain's job to figure out. But hadn't he fought a frigate and won? The shallow waters of the bay meant that the five strangers would not be free to maneuver. The mudbanks and swirling winds were loyal allies to the Salletines.

Lieutenant Cabral sent most of his marines but kept his sharpshooters aboard the *Sea Leopard*. If the enemy boarded them, they'd be in a bad way, but if the enemy was close enough to board, they were lost anyhow.

Isam said, "You have the conn, Lieutenant Cabral. Wake me if anything changes." Isam scrunched down in the hammock chair, closed his eyes, and tried to nap. He wanted more than anything to go to bed and rest his weary body, but with the enemy expected within the hour, he didn't dare.

The *Plentitud* was listing to port in the mud on the inside of the curve. A contrary gust had sent her sliding sideways, and she had fetched up on the soft, sloping bottom. The *Sea Leopard's* boats gathered under her bow and received the tow lines. They were made fast to the sternposts, and then the two boats rowed out until the lines came taut. Master Imrich superintended the operation from the *Plentitud's* lofty foredeck. His great shaggy muttonchops made him stand out amongst the rest of the crew of mixed renegades, Moors, and Turks.

Shouting in accented Arabic, he called, "Haul away!"

The cockswains in the boats gave their orders. "Oars, make way together."

Scores of backs bent, and the blades dipped and pulled. At first they did nothing but send eddies of brown water swirling aft.

"Put your backs into it!" Imrich roared from the ship.

The oars dipped deeper as they pulled harder. The cables straightened and tightened. Water squirted from the cuntlines.

"ROW!" Imrich bellowed. He wanted off that mudbank more than he wanted anything else in the world. If a djinn had offered him pearls and wine right at that moment, he would have turned them down in favor having his ship free. Minutes ticked by and sweat trickled down the rowers' bodies.

Gradually the *Plentitud* righted. The movement was imperceptible at first, and it was only by careful observation of her position against the background that any progress was seen. When the oars slacked or missed a stroke, the progress was lost.

"Oars, take a rest!" Imrich needed them all to pull together in a long, hard sustained pull. The men at the oars took advantage of the break to pass around waterskins. The sun passed its zenith. The mist was completely gone and the autumn morning had become a hot, hazy afternoon.

Imrich cried out, "Oars! Out oars!" The waterskins were corked and tossed into the bottom of the boats. The rowers took up their wooden implements again. "Oars, give way together! Pull hard! Pull for all you're worth! Keep pulling! Keep pulling!"

The rowers flexed and strained. Their sinews cracked as they threw all their weight and strength into it. Turbaned heads and fezzes bowed as they bent to the oars with a will. The crew at the rails shouted encouragement and waved their hats. All eyes were intent upon the boats.

Suddenly, a great sucking sound was heard and the water roiled and frothed. The *Plentitud's* motion became perceptible as she came upright.

"She's floating on her own bottom!" Imrich shouted happily. A cheer went up.

Slowly, very slowly, the brown coast with its faded grasses and summer-blighted scrub slipped past.

Isam's eyes opened. He had been listening to the shouting, and now when it seemed the tow had been successful, he rose to check the situation. He was not surprised; the *Plentitud* had not stuck hard and the rising tide was helping. While everyone's attention was on the prize, he turned his attention east. He cocked an ear. "Do you hear it?"

Lieutenant Cabral had been intent upon the towing and turned around. "Hear what?"

Isam cocked his head. Everyone on the quarterdeck stood still and strained their ears. "That!" Isam exclaimed.

Now that they were listening, they heard it too. It was the rumble of distant gunnery.

"The fortress has opened fire. The enemy is attempting to force the mouth of Modiq Bay." Isam's face was grim. "Make a signal, 'Enemy guns.' Recall the boats. The *Plentitud* must sail or sink by her own merits. Battle stations."

The triangle rang out and the chiefs bellowed the order, "Battle stations!" The word was passed below, and the cook snuffed out the galley fires. Smoke ceased to rise from the stovepipe. Those men who were below stuffed the rest of their meal into their faces and came running up. Urve scrambled up to the starboard battery and Hamza to the larboard battery. Gun captains checked their matches and sparked the dead ones back to life. The boats cast off the cables and the *Sea Leopard's* boats rowed into the cove.

Isam hailed the masthead lookout. "Ahoy the mainmast! What do you see?"

"Nothing! There are hills between me and the mirror station. I can't see a damn thing except what's in this bend!"

Isam clasped his hands behind his back. "Lieutenant Cabral, send Midshipman Taslim ashore with a mirror and one man to help him. He's to hike to wherever he can get a view downstream and still be able to signal us. If we are overwhelmed, he is to hike to the mirror station west of here to give the alarm."

"Aye aye, sir. Taslim, you heard him. Pick a man. As soon as one of the boats comes alongside, go into it and have them deliver you ashore. Get yourself some food and water and go immediately."

"Aye aye, sir." Taslim ran down from the quarterdeck.

The distant rumble grew louder.

"Both sides now engaged, sir," Cabral reported.

Isam was listening with his head cocked. "I hear it."

Thereafter there was nothing to do but wait. It was midday when the signal midshipman reported, "Mirror signal, sir. Taslim is in position. No sight of the enemy."

Lieutenant Cabral said, "Thank you. Acknowledge." The middy stepped away. Cabral turned to Isam. "Captain."

"I heard." Isam clasped his hands behind his back to keep from fidgeting. "Ahoy the masthead! Can you see the *Plentitud*?"

"Aye, sir! She's heading upstream under sail!" the lookout shouted back.

"Tell me when she's out of sight! But mind you watch the eastern road too!"

"Aye aye, sir!"

"Lieutenant Cabral, edge us a little closer to the mouth of the cove."

That was done.

Isam hailed the masthead again. "Can you see any better?"

"No, sir!"

Isam muttered, "I hate not knowing what is happening." The faint rumble continued in the east.

Lieutenant Cabral dared to venture an opinion. "I think they're assaulting the fortress. If they plan an attack on Zokhara, they need to take it."

"I know, Cabral. I know. Signalman, query Taslim."

"Aye aye, sir. Querying Taslim." The mirror winked and flashed in his hand. A moment later and a twinkle of light amid the scrub at the crown of the highest hill to the east answered him. "Taslim reports the sound of guns to the east and no change."

Isam brooded at the tafferel. "The longest part of battle is the waiting."

Cabral asked, "Do you mean to give battle, sir? There are five of them and only one of us. We ought to withdraw. There's nothing we can do."

"We will need to carry intelligence with us. We need to know if they are entering Modiq Bay, or are taking time to regroup and resupply. When I know that, we will move."

"Very good, sir."

The time stretched. The wind blew more strongly from the northeast. Clouds accumulated. The temperature dropped as the sun slid down the western sky.

"I'm going below to have a look at the thunder glass. You have the conn."

"I have the conn," Cabral replied automatically. He hunched his chin down into his collar against the chilly breeze.

Isam was stiff and hurting. He cast a longing look at his sleeping chamber, where the wooden walls held the heat of the afternoon even as the temperature dropped. He went to the thunder glass and studied it, then nodded to himself. Stepping into the coach, he made a note of the falling glass in the log, then continued up to the quarterdeck.

"The thunder glass is rising and the temperature is falling. We're going to have a blow." All the seasoned sailors had figured that out on their own. "Recall the mirror men. After we've picked them up, you may make sail upstream. Keep a good watch, but send the hands to dinner at the usual time. The cook may light fires. I'm going below. Call me if anything changes."

"Very good, sir."

Isam returned to his cabin and called for his servant. "A hot water bottle for my shoulder and some hot tea for me. I'm going to take a nap."

Abdul bowed and made his way out. With the cook fires lit, he was able to get the hot water and hot drink for the captain. With the cabin stowed for action, there was no bed. Isam made pallet from his foul weather gear and lay down on that. He was asleep when his servant returned. Abdul carefully wedged the water battle against his shoulder. Isam woke.

"Your water bottle, rais."

"Thank you. That does feel better."

"I have your tea too."

Isam propped on his elbow so that he could drink it. The hot liquid glowed inside him and spread the heat through his body. He warmed up, except for his nose and toes. "Let me sleep as long as possible until dinner. I'm tired. I'm fully dressed except for my boots, so I can roll out of bed and be ready in a moment."

"As you wish, rais."

"Tell the clerk to join me after dinner. I have dispatches to write. I'll need my portable desk."

"The clerk to join you after dinner for dispatches with the portable desk," Abdul parroted. The repetition insured that orders were correctly understood even in a noisy environment. At the moment it was quiet with only the sound of water whooshing along the hull and the creak of timbers, but a habit was a habit.

"That will be all."

Isam wished fervently that he was cruising in search of prey. It wore on his nerves to do nothing, to wait to find out what others were doing, and to have no constructive role except to make certain the messages were passed. That the Dey was paying him for this was scant consolation.

It was tempting to think that action—any action—was preferable to this tedium, but that would get him blown to bits. He schooled himself to patience. Unfortunately, he was also wide awake. He employed his brain in imagining various scenarios. The most likely was that the enemy would attempt to reduce the fortress. They would either succeed or fail. If they failed, they would leave. If they succeeded, they would proceed up the bay, taking out the mirror stations as they went. One by one they would put out the eyes that gave Zokhara vital intelligence. They would not reveal their full strength; that would come along behind the small force that was reconnoitering and ruining the Salletine intelligence system.

That raised a larger question: what was the Spanish goal and strategy? Conquest of Zokhara, it seemed. If it was merely punitive, they would have settled for shelling Tettiwan and other exposed locations. If they drove up Modiq Bay, they meant business. If they came with sufficient force, that meant he and the other corsairs were trapped. If the Spanish had sufficient force, they would pound their way up the long bay, seizing or sinking every vessel they came across and burning towns and villages. The corsairs and everyone else would retreat into the harbor of Zokhara. He didn't think the enemy could force the harbor, but they could do a lot of damage. It would be a hungry winter with so many people and not enough food.

The Spanish must have been planning it all through the long truce. For two years they had plotted and prepared, and when the Dey executed Captain Vargiu, they had the excuse they needed to put their plan into action. This was not going to be the usual desultory war. They meant business this time.

Did the Dey and his ministers see it? For that matter, did the *taifa* and the Kapitan Pasha see it? The Dey was enlarging and strengthening the fortress at the mouth of Zokhara's harbor, so maybe he did. Why did he court the Spanish attack by executing Vargiu? Nobody expected Spain to campaign this late in the season. He had miscalculated. Most of the corsairs were out and would be cruising until October when they would come in for the winter. They wouldn't be able to return home if Spain controlled the mouth of the bay. No other Salletine port on the Mediterranean was as defensible as Zokhara, and none was so well equipped with supplies and artisans for the service of ships. That meant Spain could batter the coast through the winter and wreck the corsairs in their poorly defended alternative ports. That would shift the balance of power in Spain's favor and deprive the Sallee Republic of an important source of income.

"Zokhara is not the target," he said aloud as he sat up. "Spain is planning a winter campaign to eradicate the corsairs." But what could he do about it? He was only one vessel.

CHAPTER 33 : SKULKING IN THE DARK

Rain blackened the night. A few flashes of lightning promised worse than was delivered, but it was a cold and miserable night all the same. Isam knew Modiq Bay as well as he knew his own hands, but with only fifty yards of visibility illuminated by the watch lamps, there wasn't much he could do. The great lanthorn at the stern lit a proportionally larger area, but all that could be seen was the slanting streaks of a bone-chilling rain, and the black, rain-spackled wake. The *Sea Leopard's* big antennas were down on their gallows with the large lateens furled tight. A single small storm sail spread to the wind. Only occasionally did a gust power over the line of hills that separated the bay from the ocean to grab the mast and rock them like a handle on a cradle.

The carpenter's mates were busy in the chains. Their mournful cries of, "Mark three, sandy bottom!" and "Mark four, muddy bottom!" carried through the melancholy air. The members of the watch who were not on lookout duty huddled in the coach. They extended cold hands in fingerless gloves to the log lamp to try and warm them. An infidel would have laughed to see them so cold at a temperature the northerners regarded as bracing, but the corsairs were men of the south and accustomed to the ravages of African heat, not the lugubrious drowning of a European rainstorm.

The rain thickened and the men became more demoralized. The *Sea Leopard* was creeping along at one knot. Isam sighed within his tarpaulin hood. "The infidels won't risk the bay in weather like this. Drop anchor and put out the anchor light."

Lieutenant Urve nodded. "Prepare to drop anchor!"

At that the men heartened. Once they were at anchor, only an anchor watch would be needed. They had hopes that some of them at least would be allowed to go below to dry out and warm up. They moved briskly in their oilskin haiks and burnooses as they went to furl the storm sail and lay out the anchor's scope. Water coursed across the deck and drained through the gratings into the scuppers below.

Isam's wounds ached abominably in the cold and damp. He had heard old men say they could tell the weather from the ache in their joints; now he knew it was true. He let Urve supervise the preparations for the anchor and went down into the coach. The men gathered in the cave-like space under the break of the quarterdeck cleared out of his way.

"Salaam, rais. It's awful weather tonight, isn't it?"

"It's worse for the infidel. He is on the open sea with the full brunt of it hitting him where he's anchored. His waterways will be running in torrents and his deck will be leaking on those below." He forced a false heartiness into his voice. His efforts received a few weak smiles.

Isam took a borrowed pipe out of his pocket, and with the coach to shelter him, was able to pack his tobacco. A sailor opened the lantern hanging at the log station, and held it for him as he took a bit of tinder from his box and lit his pipe. The lantern hung in a small niche to illuminate what was little more than a shelf below, but the log, ink, and reed pens were kept there in brackets. The log book was wrapped in an oilskin cover to keep it safe from the damp. He warmed his hands around the bowl of his pipe, inhaled deeply to bring the heated smoke into his lungs, coughed once, then puffed normally. Feeling a bit more alive, he shook the ink, then opened the log book, dipped the reed, and made note of the time, listing, "Rain worse, visibility 20 yards. Dropped anchor." It was the master's job to keep the log, but Imrich was away in the prize. Strong, angular strokes of the pen scratched across the page. A wreath of smoke encircled his head.

A faint rumble of thunder came to them, but no lightning. Huddled in the coach, there was little they could see other than the rain slick weather deck, the great antennas wrapped in sodden sails resting on their gallows, and the glow of the foredeck lantern. With the Spanish in the gulf, there would be no running out for one last cruise before winter set in. The rest of his season would be spent in steadily worsening weather on station in Modiq Bay. He must think of something to keep morale up, but what? He was too tired and hurting to have any good ideas. He privately thought this was the worst duty he had ever had since going to sea at the age of seven, but he kept the thought to himself. The men would take their cue from him, so he forced himself to smile.

"Think of the prize money the *Plenitud* will bring. A little rain is a small price to pay for bringing in the richest prize of the last five years!"

It was true, and they smiled at the thought. They nodded in response. "Aye, captain. We're looking forward to spending it this winter!"

"A week or two on station, and then you'll have months in which to debauch yourselves. Spend it all! Enjoy yourselves." Because when you're broke, you'll want to go to sea to replace it, and you'll gladly sign on with me, he added in his own mind. The curse of the previous summer was broken. Next year he would have no trouble recruiting crew. Men could forgive anything, if it would make them rich.

He clapped a hearty hand on the nearest shoulder, and said, "Buck up, lads. The rain is keeping the Spanish at bay. We'll have a peaceful night."

Again they nodded. Isam thought he had done as much as he could to improve their mood, so he went back to the quarterdeck. Isam supposed he ought to try and hearten the quarterdeck crew as well, so he said as he rubbed his shoulder, "I'll have a reliable predictor of foul weather from now on. You'll be glad of that. I know I am."

Urve gave him a crooked smile. "I suppose so, rais."

"Carry on."

The scope ran out as the *Sea Leopard* drifted, then caught up with a tug. They peered through the gloom, but could not discern any landmarks.

"I wish it would storm. Lightning would let me get my bearings," Urve said.

Isam nodded. "Make certain you keep your lanterns lit. While I doubt anyone will be coming downriver in this weather, it's a good habit and shouldn't be neglected."

"Aye, sir."

Again the faint rumble of thunder was brought to them by the breeze. Isam cocked his ear and looked thoughtfully to the sky. "No lightning again," he murmured. The handful of men on the quarterdeck looked up at the sky thoughtfully.

"I don't think that's thunder, rais," Urve replied respectfully.

"I don't think so either."

They all gazed to the northeast, but the blackness of the night told them nothing. Again the wind gusted and brought them the faint sound of gunnery.

"The fort will have to fend for itself. There's nothing we can do about it," Isam said. "I'm going below. Call me if anything changes."

"Aye aye, rais." Urve touched his forehead respectfully.

Nothing changed. The rain rained. The wind blew. The night remained black. The sound of distant gunnery came to them periodically. Water gurgled past the hull. Isam smoked a little hashish to ease his pain, changed into dry clothes, and crawled into his bed fully dressed with an extra blanket on top. Anticipating a quiet night, he had had his servant rig his bed for him. The watch below was likewise snug in their hammocks.

The thunder of a cannonade close at hand woke him out of a sound sleep. He leaped out of bed before he was even awake, crashed to the deck, winced as his shoulder complained, groped, found his boots exactly where he left them, and swiftly pulled them on. He rose, reached out and found his scimitar hanging where he left it. He thrust it into the sash, then jammed his fez onto his head without benefit of turban. He always kept everything in exactly the same place so at moments like this he could find them. Somebody hammered on his door, then it opened and an excited messenger rushed in.

"Rais! We are under attack!"

"I'm coming! What is it?" he demanded as he grabbed his burnoose and pulled the damp thing around him. The clamminess enshrouding his body felt like a grave. He shook his head to clear it of morbid thoughts.

That the enemy had been intrepid enough to dare the bay in such weather worried him: he had underestimated them. Now that he thought about it, he saw how it could be done: a pair of boats with lanterns and leadlines sounding the way while the mother vessel crept along. If men were daring enough to do it, it could be done, and they had.

"I don't know, sir. We can't see anything. Lieutenant Urve ordered the lights put out, but we can't see their lanterns."

"They're running dark, the bastards. May their fathers burn in Hell."

He strode out. "Battle stations" had already been called and men were racing up the companionways. They gave way as he barreled through and raced up the ladder to the dark quarterdeck.

Cabral and the other men were invisible in the murk. "Report!" Isam snapped as he arrived.

"No damage or casualties, sir. The enemy doesn't have our range. I ordered lights out and was about to order the anchor brought up." Cabral loomed out of the darkness right in front of him. He couldn't make out anything except a somewhat denser piece of darkness where he stood.

"Put two boats with small crews and bull's-eye lanterns out. Put a lead in each boat. They will sound the way for us. They will advance one hundred yards, then signal the ship. They will keep their lanterns shuttered at all other times. Double the bow watch. When they get the signal, they are to take the bearing, and we will row forward with six sweeps. When we arrive, the boats will advance another hundred yards."

"Aye aye, sir." Cabral stepped to the rail with his hands out before him to feel his way.

"Cockswains! Two boats! Carpenter's mates into the boat with leadlines."

Isam waited for his eyes to adjust. When he could see vague shapes in the night, he said, "I have the conn."

Again the Spanish broadside roared out. They saw the orange muzzle flashes about a hundred yards away. She had turned broadside to them, and although he couldn't count the flashes, by the length of the line he assumed there were at least a dozen. The cannonballs tore high through the air and passed harmlessly over their rigging. With the big lateens down and only the storm sails up and furled, there was a great deal of air above decks and very few spars. Nonetheless, the Spaniard had their range, and life would start getting interesting with the next broadside.

Isam tried to put some heart into his sodden crew. "Good news. She doesn't have more than fourteen guns in broadside." The *Sea Leopard* was outgunned, but not by much.

"Deck ho! Enemy boats in the water!" the masthead lookout sang out.

Isam swore. "What range?" he shouted back.

"Thirty yards and closing! One on either quarter!"

Isam swore again. "Prepare to repel boarders! Messenger! Tell the stern guns to fire when they have a target. There's a boat coming up on either quarter." Then he bellowed up at the mizzen top, "Marines! Fire at will! Make it count!"

"Fire at will!" the sergeant of marines cried out. The crack of a single musket was immediately heard, along with a fizzle, a pop, and a curse. "Our powder's wet, captain! We've only got one musket firing!"

Isam swore again. The rain drummed onto his shoulders and head, ran down his face in cold streaks, and dribbled into the neck of his burnoose. He pulled the hood up over his fez to prevent further neck drips.

"Let slip the anchor! Oars, out all oars as soon as the boats are clear!"

The crack of Spanish muskets punctuated his orders. Something whined past his head and thunked into the mizzen antenna. Two more shots went whizzing past in the general vicinity of the quarterdeck, but no more. "Ha! His powder is damp, too!"

The larboard swivel gun didn't wait for his command. With a sudden crack, it barked fire. A splash was heard close at hand, then the yells of Spanish battle cries practically under their transom. The starboard swivel gun barked and they heard a cry of anguish a few yards away in the darkness.

"Hit something!" one of the gunners crowed.

The gun crews in the great cabin could not traverse far enough to bear on the boats. They had rowed up into the blind spots on the *Sea Leopard's* quarters. There was a clatter of boathooks and oaths as they hooked onto the stern. They attempted to board via the gun ports in the great cabin, which was no easy thing with the guns run out. Pikes thrust in through the ports to clear the way, then a skinny fellow tried to haul himself through, but he was kicked in the face and sent toppling back into the boat below. Isam didn't know exactly what was happening beneath his feet, but he could hear it and guess well enough.

"Heads up! They'll come over the lazyboard!"

Sure enough, somebody in the boat threw a grapple over the grating that extended past the tafferel. With the rope in place, agile seamen swarmed up.

Midshipman Taslim marshaled the swivel guns. At point blank range, they couldn't miss. The lurid flash showed the shower of blood as the first man had a hole the size of a plum blown in him. He wasn't the only one to try, and as the quarterdeck crew frantically reloaded, more men swarmed up and gained footing on the grating. A musket in the mizzen cracked and the flash showed them several Spaniards lead by a young man in a broad brimmed hat. He pointed his pistol at Isam and fired. His pistol produced a fizzle and a faint acrid scent. The ball thumped Isam in the middle of his chest and he staggered back, lost his balance, and fell.

The Spaniards let out a bloodcurdling cry when they saw him fall. Desperate, Midshipman Taslim pulled his own pistol from beneath his burnoose and fired. His powder was dry, and the Spaniard in the broad-brimmed hat cried out in anguish. He stumbled, put his foot through the open space of the grating, and fell. Taslim threw down his pistol, and ululating like a madman, drew his scimitar and rushed the tafferel. A Spanish sailor met him with a cutlass and metal clashed on metal.

"Fight, you whoresons!" Isam roared as he scrambled to his feet. He was short of breath. The misfired ball had not had sufficient power to kill him, but it had felt like a mule kick all the same. For one split second he thought, "Allah saved my life," then he was too busy to worry about religion.

CHAPTER 34 : REPEL BOARDERS!

Belim Agha didn't wait for orders. He bellowed, "Sergeant Antonio! Marines to the quarterdeck to repel boarders!"

Antonio, a mulatto Italian renegade, shouted, "To the quarterdeck!" He led his men storming up both ladders. They nearly ran over Isam as he was picking himself off the deck. Nobody paused to say "sorry." He didn't care. They were backing up his quarterdeck crew in the fight against the boarders.

Another grapple hook flew up unseen in the dark, but Isam heard the unmistakeable ka-thunk of metal biting wood. He drew his scimitar and swung his head in that direction. The sole working musket in the mizzen top cracked and the momentary flash let him spot the dark metal of the grapnel hooked on the starboard rail forward of the shrouds. His blade came down with a flash and severed the line. He had a brief glimpse of a pale upturned face before a musket in the boat barked. The orange light dazzled his eyes and sent him staggering back. He blinked frantically, but he couldn't see a thing.

He heard a scuffle in the chains. Fear stitched through him. If he couldn't see, he couldn't defend himself or the ship. "Allah, defend me! If You save us, I will never neglect my prayers again!" Whether he spoke aloud or silently, he didn't know. The clatter of combat surrounded him on three sides. He put his free hand behind himself and waved it until he found the mizzen mast. He put his back to it and held his scimitar upright before him.

"Cabral! You're in command! I can't see! Tell us what to do!"

Cabral fell back in astonishment. He had been fencing violently with the men attempting to come over the tafferel. There was a crowd of marines in burnooses there as a knot of Spaniards tried to break through. The occasional bark of a musket punctuated the clamor. The rain mixed with blood and slimy gore spread across the quarterdeck.

Cabral looked around, saw the captain blindly waving his sword in front of him in the flash of musket fire, and the battle in the chains on each side. The swivels were unmanned as the crews resisted the boarders. Now that the marines were here, he could use the crews for their intended purpose!

"Man the swivels! Blast them out of the rigging!" he shouted.

The gun crews extracted themselves one by one from the fight. The starboard gun manned up first. Hand to hand combat raged to either side of the shrouds. One Sallee rover lifted the small gun from its post and brought it away. It was no use trying to load it when blades were flashing back and forth above it.

On the main deck, hands were not idle. The main deck swivels had swerved aft and were firing down into the Spanish boats. At the same time, the *Sea Leopard* was rowing forward. That dragged the Spanish boats along with them since they had latched on, but the oar wake made the boats bob and inconvenienced the boarders. The assault slowed as men had to take time to judge their leap. The marines managed to clear both rails.

"Bring the gun!"

Isam blinked and saw dark shapes moving in front of him. He recognized the Arabic voices and didn't strike. He cocked his ear to try and make out what was happening. Men were still battling at the tafferel and the sound helped him deduce where the stern was. With that for a bearing, he turned his head left and right. "Report!"

Cabral panted, "We're fighting for the lazyboard! The quarters have been cleared! But the boats are still attached."

"Are they still afloat?"

"I don't know. Just a moment." Cabral dared to stick his head over the side, and was shot at by a musket. He staggered back. "I'm hit."

"They aren't sunk then," Isam replied. "Can you stand?"

"Ye-es."

"I need your eyes."

"Aye, captain."

Cabral pressed his hand to his bleeding chest. "Still afloat larboard, sir. Check—"

Crack! The starboard swivel crew had set up their gun and pointed it straight down into the boat. A man cried out in agony, but that was not what concerned the Spanish. Somebody pulled off his cap and stuffed it in the hole in the bottom where water gurgled up.

Cabral didn't stick his head out this time. "Starboard gun, report!" He was gasping for breath.

"We holed them, but they plugged, sir."

"Do it again."

The larboard swivel was now in operation and another shot cracked out. Almost at the same time, a pair of swivels on the main deck fired.

A desperate command was shouted from the lazyboard.

"They're making their final rush! Beware!" Isam shouted.

He was drowned out by the mad cries of the Spanish who threw themselves forward with renewed energy. They had no choice. They had to take the quarterdeck or die. Enough shots from the swivel guns would sink them. They had only a few minutes left in which to take the target or be sunk in the cold embrace of the black bay.

Spanish muskets barked and men swarmed up the grapples on the lazyboard. The men on the grating hammered at the defenders. Cabral staggered to the rail, and in a hoarse voice called, "Marines to the quarterdeck!" His voice barely carried, but someone below heard it and shouted out strongly, "Marines to the quarterdeck!"

"Go below, Cabral. You've done what you can," Isam told the lieutenant.

"No, sir, as long as I can stand my post, I'll stay," Cabral whispered back.

"Are you dying, Lieutenant?" Isam asked.

After a pause, Cabral replied, "I think so, sir."

"I'm sorry, Cabral. You did well."

"Thank you, sir." He sank down on the deck and leaned against the railing.

Isam's vision was improving. He was able to make out the shapes of the marines storming up the ladder, and although he couldn't quite track details enough to fight, he was able to see enough to command. "I have the conn," he shouted so the men would know to listen to his voice even if they were too busy to look around.

The larboard swivel barked again, then a Spaniard flung himself through the line of defenders at the tafferel. He landed on a pike wielded by one of the new marines. The body thumped to the deck. He wasn't dead yet and lay moaning. He curled up in a ball and the defenders tripped over him as they tried to reinforce the tafferel. He whimpered as he was stepped on. When the marines cleared him, Isam stabbed him and put him out of his misery. He felt nothing in particular about it. The man was an enemy, and even in his wounded condition he was able to help his comrades by hampering the defenders. He had to go.

Isam wiped blood off his scimitar and sheathed it. He glanced around the deck, and seeing he had a moment, lifted the body. The man groaned again. He wasn't dead, but he soon would be. Isam threw him overboard. He crashed down into the Spanish boat below. The boat rocked wildly, shipped water over the gunwale, and the Spanish shoved their comrade overboard. He disappeared into the inky darkness of the sea and was never seen again.

A nine pound shot tore through the larboard rigging and severed one of the shrouds. The rest held. They were in multiples for good reason. He replayed the scene in his memory: the shot had come from abreast the larboard quarter. The enemy was pulling alongside. "Masthead! Report!"

The lookout had been fascinated by the battle going on below. He looked around quickly and gave his report, "Two vessels, one at short range on the larboard quarter! Another coming up on the starboard quarter!"

Isam swore. "They mean to double us." He would be caught in the crossfire of two broadsides, each of which was superior to his own. "Row, damn you! Dash speed! Don't let them double us! Cabral! Keep us ahead of the Spanish vessels! Don't wait for my orders! Fire as she bears! Boatswain! We have no tiller! Steer with the oars!"

Too late. The Spanish vessel on his larboard quarter had traversed her guns and doubleshotted them. More than two dozen nine pound balls smashed into them at short range. The *Sea Leopard* was made of African teak that was even harder than Asian teak, but still, at this short range, the balls punched holes in her. She made few splinters due to the hardness of her wood, but the ones that she made were as sharp as spears. Cries of anguish came from the gunners on the main deck. The wounded were shoved out of the way as the gun crews used their tools and heaved the guns as far as they could angle them. The first gun and the second bellowed and tongues of flame eight feet long jumped from their brazen mouths. Several more guns fired. Each blast thundered before the echoes had time to ring back from the hills. There was a pause of two seconds, then two more guns roared out, then another, another, and another. Again there was a slight pause, followed by cursing as one of the guns hung fire. He wasn't sure, but he thought ten of his twelve guns had fired. That was a pretty good show, considering the rain.

The swivels on either side barked again. The splash of a falling body followed it. He checked his lazyboard: the last of the Spanish were driven into the sea as his marines jumped up on the platform. Being marines, they weren't accustomed to the grating with its foot wide gaps and advanced cautiously. The last Spaniard threw himself overboard rather than surrender.

"We have command of the quarterdeck, sir," Taslim reported to him.

Isam breathed. He was free to look around. He rubbed at his eyes. They ached, but he was able to see more or less. He hoped it was merely the dark rain that blurred everything. "Damage report."

Taslim looked down, "Cabral is dead, sir. I'm your new acting-lieutenant."

"He was a brave man. We'll bury him tomorrow. Now, damage report."

Taslim touched his forehead with a bloody hand. "Damage report, aye." He turned to the rail and shouted, "Damage report!"

What Isam wanted to know more than anything was if they were taking water. With no sails set, she wasn't listing, so he thought not. But if he was holed at the waterline, he needed to know. Around him the marines were clearing the carnage. When they picked up Cabral's body, he said hastily, "Take him to the cockpit. Don't throw any of our men overboard if you can avoid it."

"Aye aye, sir. D'ya think he's alive?"

Isam said, "Maybe." He didn't think so, but he couldn't see well enough to know. It occurred to him to wonder if he'd been shot in the head, considering he'd been looking right into the muzzle blast. He felt his hood, then put his hands into his hair. They came away clean. He heaved a sigh of relief. "Allah has been kind to us tonight." The marines gave him a doubtful look. "We survived their sneak attack, didn't we?"

"That we did," a marine replied.

"They nearly had us. But we are alive and in—"

Another Spanish broadside roared out and drowned his words in noise and brimstone. The acrid scent drifted over the battle, only to be slowly washed from the air by the rain. He strode to the starboard side and checked the position of the other Spanish vessel. She had fallen a little behind, but he could see from the white foam that she was rowing hard and fast, even if the ship herself was only a lowslung, vague shape.

"Xebecs," he breathed. The Spanish had been planning this attack long in advance for sure. They had sent exactly the sort of vessels that could meet the corsairs on their own ground. It was no good running up a shallow creek: the enemy could come up right behind him. He had to run for Zokhara and hope he could outdistance them. He was undermanned and they were not. His crew would be exhausted before the Spanish.

"On the fore! Set the storms'l!"

Some of the men had to leave the oars to make sail. Where were his boats? He stuck his head out and found them tied onto the accommodation ladders. They had returned to the *Sea Leopard* when the fighting started. He was sailing blind into the night with two determined and intelligent enemies on his flanks. If he went aground, they would have him. He ground his teeth. Sweat began to stink inside his damp clothes. He was afraid. It was sheer good luck that he had survived so far. Now he was like a leopard with a pack of dogs clinging to his flanks. "Damn Murad for being a coward. I could use his help right now!"

Cupping his hands around his mouth, he shouted, "Adalet to the bow with a lantern! Pass the word for Adalet! I need a pilot!"

It would be death to send the carpenter's mates into the chains where they were exposed to enemy fire, but it would be death to them all to run aground.

"Carpenter's mates to the chains with leads! Make sure your replacement knows who he is!"

Men were going to die. That's the way it always was. He was a corsair. He took men into danger, and some of them died. They came of their own free will; they thought the risk was worth it. Some of them might be right, but some of them were certainly wrong. There would be a mass funeral tomorrow. If they survived that long. He pushed the forlorn thought from his mind.

CHAPTER 35 : A RUNNING FIGHT

How much time had elapsed? Probably less than half an hour. When in battle, it seemed to last forever, but in reality, the action was swift and sharp. He looked over the sides to his two evil companions. The larboard xebec had not gained enough on him to bring her broadside to bear. He consulted the map in his head. Another bend was coming up. The river curved to the right, meaning the shallower water was on the left side. He needed information.

"Carpenter's mates! Get the lead out! I need those soundings!"

The broadsides had broken up. Each individual gun on each vessel was loading and firing as swiftly as possible. Since only one broadside was engaged, all the gun crews were working on the active side to speed the loading. His crew was not seasoned; his old hands knew what they were doing, but the new hands he had picked up for this cruise had not had enough practice. He pulled out his watch and timed them. He sighed. There was no way to make them any faster. He couldn't time the Spaniard, but he thought they were a little faster on the reload. That meant in the same interval of time, they would fire more shots. Plus they had more active guns. He wished them damp powder, but this was a wish Allah did not grant. He had had two personal favors from Allah already. He was pushing his luck to ask for more. He consoled himself that his twelve pounders were stronger. Doing the arithmetic in his head, he determined that he was throwing a hundred and twenty pounds of shot for their hundred and twenty-six. That was an equal match. As long as the second xebec didn't gain on him.

The men who had scrambled up the fore antenna to loose the gaskets were back on deck. The foresail bellied out above their heads and Isam felt the ship answer.

"Main chief, make all storms'l!" he shouted.

More men left the sweeps and swarmed up the slippery wet antenna by feel. They wrapped their legs around it like they were shinnying up a date palm, grabbed onto the wooldings, and pulled themselves up. The much shorter antennas and smaller sails required fewer hands. The main storm sail opened up and the triangle filled with wind. He felt the xebec take the bone in her teeth.

"Oars, stow oars!" He stuck his head over the starboard side and peered at his wake. From that he judged he was making four knots.

"Mark four, and a muddy bottom!" sang out a leadsman.

The *Sea Leopard* was in the channel and charging ahead blindly. If she struck, she'd run hard aground. Isam peered into the gloom. There! Was that Alif Hill?

"Toss the log!" he barked.

That was Taslim's job, but he was now an acting-lieutenant, so the youth snapped, "Mohammed, toss the log!" Mohammed was the master's mate.

Isam nodded approval to Taslim. It was right for him to delegate his old job so that he could do his new job.

"You have the conn. I'm going forward to see what I can see."

"I have the conn." The youth paled a little, but his voice was steady.

Isam stepped over dead bodies without a look as he hiked to the foredeck. Adalet was there with a lantern held high. He was a thin, small black man with a white haik and a red fez on his head. The black tassel hung down to his shoulder. He was peering into the darkness, head swiveling to observe all details revealed in the lantern light. Adalet glanced at him, then turned and shouted, "Helm! Touch left!"

"Touch left, aye!" the tillerman shouted back. The xebec curved a little.

"This is what I want you to do," Isam told him." Adalet listened, but his eyes kept probing the darkness ahead. "Can you do it?"

"Aye, as long as I have good soundings, which I won't, because we're going too fast, but I'll take what I can get. I know this section of the bay very well."

"Excellent. I make that hump of darkness to be Alif Hill. Am I right?"

"You are, rais. There's a good deep channel there, and it shoals rapidly in the curve. It will work for what you want."

"Good."

He bent under the rembate, felt the ache in the center of his chest, and caught his breath. "Boatswain! Send a bucket of water around to the men. Keep them at their posts. Rowers to be ready to row at a moment's notice. If we go aground, you are to back us off immediately without waiting for orders."

"Aye aye, ready to row off immediately," the boatswain replied.

Isam returned to the quarterdeck in time for a cannonball to smash into the side a few feet away from the ladder. The hull shuddered. He heard something in the chartroom below shatter, but all the important items were safely stowed below the waterline.

Taslim spoke crisply. "I have a damage report, rais. We have taken fourteen shot above the waterline. One gun too damaged to fire; it took a hit and the mouth is warped. One misfire has been cleared. You have eleven working guns in your larboard battery. We are not taking water. The only significant damage to the rigging is the larboard mizzen shroud."

"Very good. Rig preventers and debris netting."

"Preventers and debris netting, aye." Taslim went to the rail and called down, "Main chief, fore chief! Rig preventers and debris netting."

A man opened up one of the quarterdeck lockers and took out the heavy netting. The crew tied it to the boomkin, then tied its corners to the shrouds. Isam had to duck under it, but now they had protection from falling spars, should the enemy strike their rigging. Which, now that they were sailing, would no doubt be attempted. Take their sails and they would be forced to row again, and the Spaniard would have the advantage. She was a bigger vessel with a bigger crew; she could afford to swap rowers to keep her speed up. He could not. Even if they didn't know the *Sea Leopard* was undermanned, they knew based on the relative sizes of the vessels that they had the bigger crew.

Once under sail, the *Sea Leopard* headreached on both of her pursuers. The enemy fired a bow chaser periodically, but could not traverse far enough to bring the broadside guns to bear. They didn't dare charge recklessly through the murk in an unfamiliar bay.

"Mark three, sand and mud!" the lead sang out.

"Steady as she goes!" the pilot shouted.

Isam steadied his nerve. A few minutes would tell if his trick worked, or he had doomed himself.

A minute later, "Helm half right!"

"Half right!" the tillerman shouted back.

"Three fathoms, sand and mud!" the other leadsman sang out.

A small "thunk" answered him as a musket ball buried itself in the bulwark about two feet away from him.

"Ahoy the mizzen top!" Isam shouted.

"Deck ho!" the mizzen replied.

"Ten sequins if you can shoot me a captain, and five for a lieutenant!"

Ten sequins was about as much as an honest laborer could earn in a fortnight. It was enough of a prize to spark a competitive spirit in the marksmen. A quarrel broke out. With only one powder horn of dry powder, they agreed to take turns trying for the Spanish captain. Hit him or not, it would keep things interesting on the Spanish quarterdeck. Hopefully the distraction would be enough for them to fail to realize the *Sea Leopard* was leading them astray.

"Two and a half fathoms! Sandy mud!"

He gritted his teeth, but didn't give any orders of his own. He must trust the pilot, even if his own frazzled nerves were shouting, "Turn, turn, you're going to strike bottom!" He could no longer make out the bulk of Alif Hill to his right. They were far left in the channel. He stared at the Spaniard as she was lit up by single muzzle flash. "Follow me," he willed her. It made sense. She would assume he would not risk going aground, and being a xebec, she could travel wherever he did. Did she have her leads out?

He felt a soft thump beneath the keel. The *Sea Leopard* shuddered, but continued on her way. He clenched the forward rail to give himself something to do. He locked his jaw shut. The pilot knew what he was doing. It was just a sandbar, nothing more. They were not yet on the sloping shoulder of the curve. He hoped. His chest ached where the bullet had thumped him. He rubbed it. Turn! he shouted in his mind. He wouldn't say the word.

The pilot sang out, "Helm! Hard left! Now!"

The helm threw the tiller all the way over and leaned on it. "Hard left, aye!" he shouted back.

"Mark three, sandy mud!"

Isam let out a sharp breath as the xebec headed back into deeper water. A minute glided by in their wake.

The lookout shouted, "Deck ho! She's stuck! The Spaniard's aground!"

Isam whirled around and went to the tafferel. All the quarterdeck crew were straining their eyes. The rain had let up some; but only the sharpest eyes among them could make out the uneven blotch in the darkness that was the Spanish vessel. He rubbed his eyes. Ordinarily, he was one of the eagle-eyed men who could see such things, but not tonight. "Is it so?" he demanded.

Taslim replied, "I think it is."

"Praise Allah. We have lost one of our hounds." He swiftly turned to look for the other Spanish xebec, but she was invisible to him. "Taslim. Look and see if you can see the other Spaniard."

Taslim peered into the gloom. He strained his eyes, but the other xebec was too far away. "I can't make her out. I'm positive she's at least a half cable away from us, wherever she is."

A half cable length was ideal for gunnery, if she could breast them. She didn't fire, so he supposed that meant that she couldn't see him either, or was far enough behind she couldn't traverse her guns. He looked all around to make certain his ship was dark. There was the lantern glow at the bow where Adalet swung the bull's-eye back and forth to study the seamarks and water.

"Damn. They will be able to follow us. They must be able to see that, but without it, I can't find my way."

"What if you hung the lantern under the bow sprit so the vessel blocked the light?"

"Adalet has to be able to move it to see. Keep an eye on that grounded Spaniard. She'll be off soon enough. We have bought only a little time."

He wished he could do away with the bow lantern and disappear in the darkness, but as long as he was running, he needed the light.

"Deck ho! I see a light!"

"Where away?"

"Upstream!"

"Are you sure?"

"Yes, I've been watching it move! I'm sure it's a vessel!"

"Taslim! Fire a warning signal!"

"Warning signal, aye," Taslim replied. He leaned over the rail, cupped his hands to his mouth, and shouted, "Main deck! Make a signal!"

"Signal, aye," Urve replied. He had fully loaded guns. "Number two, fire." A pause, "Number four, fire." Another pause. "Number six, fire."

Anything coming down from Zokhara was a friend. If a merchant, she needed to know the danger. If a warship, he needed her help.

After the signal finished, another gun boomed upstream from them. They all listened, then broke out with a cheer as the proper answering signal was made. They had an ally! Isam grew sour. "It's probably Murad Rais." He was less enthusiastic now. He muttered. "Now, when I don't actually need any help, he shows up."

"Ahoy the deck, the Spaniard is reversing!"

Isam swore in Turkish. "She got off awfully quick." He hated her for that. Hated her big crew, hated her competent captain, hated the wily Spanish who had planned this for so long, then leaped at the chance to put it into action when the Dey miscalculated. "He shouldn't have killed Vargiu." Still, the Spanish would have seized on some other excuse.

"Lookout! Do you see the other Spaniard?"

"No, sir!"

He wondered if she'd managed to go aground too. It seemed improbable. She was off his starboard and therefore in the channel.

"Helm, touch right," sang out the pilot.

"Touch right, aye!" the tillerman replied.

The *Sea Leopard* heeled as she came around the other side of Alif Hill and caught a gust of wind blowing hard between the hills. A wet thump struck her amidships and she shuddered, jolted, and knocked everyone off their feet as she struck mud.

"Out oars!" the boatswain shouted before he even regained his feet.

The men scrambled into position. The sweeps shot out with a wooden clatter.

"Oars, back water! Pull together! Row for your lives, damn you!"

The drum beat, and the stroke oar bent. The others followed suit. The water churned around the hull with no discernible motion. Isam watched them row for several strokes, but there was still no sense of movement. He gritted his teeth and looked over both shoulders, but he couldn't see the Spaniard. He got a cold raindrop in the eye for his trouble. The rowers bent and their muscles strained, but she was still aground.

CHAPTER 36 : A DESPERATE BATTLE

"Let fly sheets and tacks!" Isam shouted. As long as the sails were full of wind, they would press the *Sea Leopard* onto the mudbank. The main and fore deck crews leaped to loose the lines and the sodden sails swung uselessly in the wind.

The boatswain shouted, "Put your backs into it! Double time!"

The drum suddenly accelerated, and the stroke oar moved quickly to catch up. There was a clatter of crossed oars because not everyone was as swift.

"Pull together! Stroke! Stroke! Stroke!" he shouted in time with the drum. It didn't help; they could hear the drum perfectly well. Isam imagined that the Spanish could hear their drum too. Then again, they had not heard the Spanish drum when the Spaniard had gone aground, so maybe they couldn't hear him. If they knew he was aground, they would surely pounce.

"Lieutenant Urve! Give me a broadside!" The shock of the larboard guns recoiling against their tackle might break any suction between the mudbank and the hull.

"Gunners! On my command!" Urve shouted.

The rowers were standing between the guns and were leaning over them as they swept the oars through the water. With the guns loaded, all that was needed was for the gun captains to fire them. It was reloading that required multiple men. Nobody was going to come up on Isam's larboard side if he couldn't get her off the mudbank, so he wasn't worried about preserving his larboard battery. His starboard battery was still loaded and primed with the leather seals in place to keep the rain from running into the touch holes. Each gun likewise had what appeared to be ornamental rings running around the barrel to either side of the touch hole, but the real purpose was to keep the water from running into the primer.

The gun captains had to wriggle their way between the rowers. It was an awkward, unfeasible way to fire a gun, but Isam was desperate.

"Ready?" Urve ordered.

"Ready!" came a chorus of male voices.

"FIRE!"

The leather seals were slid aside and linstocks touched primer. A second later, and a roar of thunder sent the guns hurtling across the deck to be brought up short by a violent yank on the tackle. Two guns hung fire and remained with their muzzles poking impotently through the ports. Swearing erupted. Isam held his breath. The oars swept and swept again.

"She's moving!" Urve shouted.

Isam closed his eyes for a moment. He felt the deck beneath his feet shifting, and smiled.

The bow pulled slowly away from the mudbank, but their stern was still stuck. The oars kept pulling. The water churned around them and her bow eased out a little further, but he felt the heavy way her larboard quarter stuck to the mud.

"Sir, the tiller is stuck. I think we've jammed the rudder in the mud."

"It'll peel away when she comes off the mud. Do the best you can until then."

"Ahoy the deck! Enemy on the starboard quarter!"

Isam looked. The Spanish xebec was a dark ghost barely visible in the rain. White flashes of oar foam swirled around her hull. She had heard and was coming to pounce on him while he was helpless.

"Starboard oars, boat your oars! Gunners, prepare to fire on my command!"

The oars ran in. The gun captains blew on their linstocks. All waited tensely. The ghostly Spanish xebec loomed larger and closer.

The *Sea Leopard* pulled off the mudbank. "Tiller is free!" the helm reported.

With only the larboard oars pulling, they were bending to the right. The current helped wedge them away from the mudbank. "Fore chief! Make sail!"

The lookout sang out, "Deck ho! Collision danger!"

The two vessels were on converging courses and only yards apart. The Spaniard didn't change course, and Isam had no room to change. The two would strike—and that suited the Spaniard.

"Marines! Stand by to repel boarders! Brace for collision! On the deck, everyone!"

She was right alongside them, not ten yards away. They saw her clearly now, a black monster with a row of hungry mouths. He flattened himself along with his crew. Only the helm and pilot remained standing.

The Spanish broadside tore into them at deck level. Splinters flew. Number seven gun spun around and a man screamed as it ran over his leg. The carriage came to a stop with his severed leg beneath it and the full weight of the gun on his mangled limb. He shrieked in agony.

Isam leaped up. "FIRE!"

The starboard broadside blazed out as the Spanish hull touched the mouths of the forward guns. They shot back against their tackle, and shrieks of agony split the night. The Spanish marines fell back as the *Sea Leopard's* broadside mowed them down, but that didn't staunch the assault.

They recovered and leaped over the gunwales and onto the deck of the *Sea Leopard*. Spanish marksmen fired down onto the quarterdeck and a bullet went through Isam's right forearm.

"Mizzen top! Clear those snipers!"

They didn't need to be told what to do. As the two ships swung together so that half of the Spanish larboard overlapped the quarterdeck and midships, the distance between the two mizzen masts reduced to pointblank range. The first grenade was lobbed by a strong arm and exploded right in the Spanish mizzen top. Isam was too busy to notice. The orange flash and roar was just one more detail in a lurid night. The prow of the Spanish vessel ran over his foredeck and the weight of the larger vessel pressed him toward the mudbank again. The *Sea Leopard* heeled slowly to the left, which caused her starboard guns to lift their barrels from the Spaniard's side to her railing, then higher still, to point up into her rigging. That didn't do him a bit of good, but it didn't matter because they'd lost the starboard railing. Defenders retreated fore and aft. Isam's quarterdeck crew lifted all the swivels and set them in the forward rail and fired down into the mass of Spaniards below. This close, he could make out that they had grey uniforms. They rushed both ladders and he drew his scimitar and stood back. With only one working musket in the mizzen top, he had little support. The crew in the coach did what they could to impede access to the quarterdeck ladders, but they were outnumbered. A Spanish marine reached the quarterdeck. Isam stabbed him and the man staggered aside. Another attacker pushed up beside him. The swivels on the forward rail fired again, then retreated to the sides so that they could command the ladders. They reloaded as fast as they could, but the defenders had to slow the advancing Spanish long enough for them to do that.

Isam was at the larboard ladder when he heard a warning cry from above. He smelled burning match, glanced up, saw a small cherry glow, and averted his eyes. The Salletine marine held the grenade to the last second, then lobbed it among the knot of Spaniards crowding the starboard ladder. The grenade exploded in a rain of shrapnel and agony. A man died and others were wounded, but although grenades were good at breaking up formations, the mass of Spaniards swiftly filled in. The good news was that the starboard ladder was blown half away, slowing the advance up that side.

Another grenade launched, passed over the heads of the Spanish, and landed behind them. It exploded and sent shattered bits of iron into the legs of the Spanish swarming the foot of the larboard ladder. In the next moment, the larboard swivel barked, and a plum-sized ball tore a hole through the stomach of the man at the top of the ladder. Bodies toppled, fell down the ladder, knocked into those who were attempting to come up behind, and sent them to the deck in a snarl of limbs and blood. The rain continued to beat down and mixed with the blood to create extra-slippery footing. A flicker of distant lightning gave a brief view of the entire hellish scene.

The quarterdeck had a slight breather as the attackers regrouped. Another grenade dropped among them and more destruction was done. They recoiled and went to the mainmast to escape the grenades while they pulled themselves together.

Isam wiped his eyes with his left sleeve. The swivels returned to the forward rail. In the momentary pause, he could hear the Spanish officers exhorting their men. What they said, he didn't know, but he could guess well enough. His fore deck crew were fewer in number and isolated.

He shouted into the coach, "Get the guns from the cabin! Turn them around!"

Some of the men in the coach went to the cabin and proceeded to do just that. They rolled one of the six pounders into the narrow passageway just as the Spanish rushed the quarterdeck again. The rovers shouted a warning and the men in the coach squeezed to either side. The gun shot forward. The Spanish leaped to get out of its path. By sheer brute strength, a dozen men slewed the gun to angle to the right. The linstock was brought to the touch hole, and the gun bellowed, leaped back to crash into and through the bulkhead into the chartroom. The ball plowed through the *Sea Leopard's* bulwark and into the second wave of Spaniards massing at the rail. Shouts and cries rose up, but the Spaniards already aboard the *Sea Leopard* rushed the gun. The defenders didn't have time to reload. They were swiftly engaged in bitter hand to hand fighting. Over their heads the swivels barked to mow down grey uniforms and turn them a gory shade of black, but the defenders were outnumbered. Another Salletine went down beneath the pikes of the Spanish boarders.

Once again Isam defended the larboard ladder as assailants surged up. His arm was getting tired as he hacked and hacked. The end was inevitable; they were being whittled down. Once they were few enough, the attackers would rush them and overwhelm them. A marine spun and sprawled at his feet as a Spanish marksman brought him down. A ball plunked into the mast beside him. He moved to keep the mast between him and the other xebec. It was all the cover he had. He didn't feel selfish; he was the captain. If he was killed, his men would surrender and the battle would be lost. As long as he was alive, they would fight. He shouted exhortations. He could remember only a few verses from the Qu'ran, but they were verses suited to fighting men.

"It is the enemy who is without issue!" he roared. He had a good set of lungs and it carried.

They all knew what fate awaited them: to be chained to a Spanish oar for the rest of their short lives. They would be treated with great cruelty by the Spanish. The Spanish would torture them to make them convert, and then, vexed by the possibility their conversion might not have been sincere, punish the prisoners for any perceived lapse of their new faith. The men of the coach started to ululate. It was a desperate cry, the cry of men who knew they were going to die and who were determined to take as many of the enemy with them as possible.

Another grenade dropped into the crowd of Spaniards, then immediately after that, a second one. Some of the Spaniards broke and tried to run back to their own ship, but their comrades struck them and screamed in their faces. One more grenade fell into the mass of attackers. More men were sent sprawling with torn limbs. They writhed in anguish. The Spanish reached down, picked them up, and heaved them overboard. They needed a clear deck more than they needed to tend wounded men. It was one of the ordinary cruelties of war.

The grenades were used up. The one working musket cracked, and the Spanish lieutenant leading the boarding action fell. For a moment the Spanish milled about uncertainly. The ordinary mass of men followed the momentum of the attack. Without it, they didn't know if they were winning or losing. Just then, a Spanish midshipman shouted in Spanish. He exhorted them and they listened. Picking up the fallen lieutenant's sword, he pointed at Isam. All eyes turned to him.

"Shit." There was really nothing else to say as the Spanish began to shout in anger and surged toward the quarterdeck in one great mass. Isam prayed, "Father, I am about to join you. I will die on my quarterdeck as you died on yours." Then there was no time, because an angry mass of Spaniards led by a boy of no more than sixteen was clawing their way up both ladders.

CHAPTER 37 : A WELCOME FRIEND

The *Sea Leopard* heeled harder to larboard. Her guns in their tackles ran themselves in and slammed into the Spanish. They found themselves under a new assault from an unexpected quarter. Several were injured. The youth leading the assault on the quarterdeck never looked back. There was only one route to victory, and that route was over Isam's dead body. For a moment they locked eyes. They each knew their meeting would determine the victory. The youth was a few men below on the bottom rung of the ladder. Isam was at the head, thrusting and stabbing the men coming up. The swivel tore through the attackers again, but there was too much momentum. They were prepared, caught the body that fell down the ladder, and tipped it over the side.

Another defender fell. Now it was Isam and one man defending the ladders while the swivel guns reloaded one last time. Their ammunition chest lay open and empty; there was no more shot for the small guns. The great mass of grey uniforms was pressing the fore deck, the coach, and the quarterdeck. Death was near, but Isam wouldn't surrender. He would lose the *Sea Leopard* and die—if he was lucky. If he survived, the Spanish would hang him as a pirate. He could only die once. He might as well die like a man. He would leave behind the wailing of Spanish widows. That would be his legacy. He had taken the biggest prize in recent history and gone down fighting. He would be a legend. It was cold comfort, but it was all he had.

Step by step the young Spaniard climbed the ladder. His eyes were alight; they blazed like black diamonds with the fervor of his courage. Isam admired him. He had been such a youth himself. Plenty of Spaniards had fallen beneath his blade as he blazed a trail of victory that led from his orphaned childhood to the quarterdeck of the *Sea Leopard*. Other men would follow after him, and they too would fight and win and die. It was the nature of the business. A man did not go to sea because he expected a long and comfortable life.

Isam's blade was getting heavier. His old wounds were a blaze of pain, and his new wound was filling his hand with blood. It wouldn't be long now. He was breathing hard and his chest was hurting—not only where the ball had kicked him but in each corner of his lungs where he was straining for air as sweat rolled down inside his collar and soaked his shirt from the inside. He felt every fiber of it sticking to him with the preternatural alertness of a man who was about to die. It seemed as if everything was happening in a slow moving but inevitable dream. He had heard that when you die in a dream, you die for real. Now he knew it was true.

The youth gained the quarterdeck. He was fresh and eager and he lunged at Isam. The captain parried, but the force of the young man's blow drove his tired arm back almost to his shoulder. That opened him up, and the youth darted to take advantage of it. He lunged sideways; the younger man's sword pierced through his sleeve and tore it out. He felt nothing. Had he been wounded? He couldn't tell. He was in an exalted state in which pain had become a part of his ordinary sensations. He made no sound except for the harsh breathing and clatter of the blades. The youth pressed him hard; the boy could see that he was tired. He'd fought a long hard fight. He would have fared better if he had had a little rest before this fight, but Allah had not granted it. A glance at the mass of Spanish on the deck below said it didn't matter. He were too badly outnumbered. If he hadn't run aground, this wouldn't be happening. It had been a calculated risk and it had almost worked.

He lunged in sudden counterattack as the youth blinked sweat from his eyes. A piercing cry erupted from the young man's throat as Isam's blade took him through the lung. He fell back with a gurgle of blood on his lips. His face turned white, and Isam saw the terror as the boy realized he was dying. To have come so close! He had almost had the notorious corsair, the captain of the big new xebec, the one that had tormented them with his victories. Isam grinned. He felt a renewed surge of energy. He was victorious! There was not a jot of pity in him. The youth had come within inches of killing him. It was kill or be killed. The youth would not have pitied him.

The Spanish soldiers shouted, then passed the wounded youth down the ladder. They loved him and they wouldn't let Isam kill him. He respected them for that. The boy deserved to be loved. If he survived his wound, they might meet again. If he survived. Both of their futures were bleak. Isam bared his teeth in a feral grin at the man at the top of the ladder. As the man turned to face the corsair, he received a scimitar in the gut. Isam used his foot to shove the man off his blade and back into the arms of the men climbing up. The dead marine toppled down and landed on the wounded youth, and the men on the shattered ladder fell with them. Isam howled like a wild animal then. He brandished his bloody sword in his left hand and shouted in Turkish, "I dare you! Let any man who wants to die set foot on my quarterdeck!"

Nobody understood him, but they knew a challenge when they heard one. "VENGANZA!" *Revenge* they shouted in Spanish.

Suddenly, a mighty broadside roared out. The ululating cry of true believers rose from the other side of the Spanish vessel. All eyes turned in consternation toward the noise. There, drawing alongside the Spaniard, was another xebec, a xebec with the purple flag of the Sallee Republic flying from its sternpost. Salletine oars jerked inward in perfect unison as the two hulls clashed lightly and the newcomer slid along the Spaniard's side. Grapples were thrown and turbanned men leaped over the gunwales onto the nearly deserted Spanish deck. They charged for the quarterdeck. The Spaniard had thrown everything at the *Sea Leopard* and was able to mount only a brief defense before their quarterdeck was overwhelmed. The ululations rose in pitch and volume as the new arrivals exulted in their victory. Dismayed Spaniards suddenly abandoned the *Sea Leopard* to race back to their own vessel. Returning proved more difficult. The slant of the *Sea Leopard's* deck meant they had to fight their way up a slope slippery with gore. Some of them fell and went sliding down the deck to fetch up against the lower gunwale.

Isam glanced over and realized a new danger: the open gun ports. If the *Sea Leopard* continued listing, water would pour in through the gun ports. Worse, her scuppers were already under water. The main deck of a Salletine xebec was made in two layers: the flat weather deck to permit easy footing for working the guns and rowing, and the true deck, which was the convex deck that curved in an arch beneath the weather deck to provide structural support. The narrow space between them was the waterway that drained the weather deck. Water was already coming in through the scuppers to flood the waterway. The added weight encouraged the list. He had to get her upright and quick.

When he had thought he was going to die, he had felt no sense of urgency to do anything. Who wants to hasten his own death? Now that he was alive, he wanted very much to remain alive. No one was trying to attack the quarterdeck anymore, so he wiped his blade and said, "We must right her and quickly!"

The exhausted survivors looked at him uncomprehendingly. The sudden change of subject left them confused, but when they looked around, they saw what he saw. Despairing faces turned to him. "What can we do?"

"Grapple to the Spaniard with a Spanish windlass in the line and cinch her upright." He grinned at them. "It seems only fair the Spaniard should save us, don't you think?"

They were not in a mood to appreciate his grim humor, but they understood what was wanted. They cut loose a brayle, and working together, tied it to the Spanish chains. They secured the other end to the mizzen mast with a belaying pin in the middle of it. Then they cranked the belaying pin and took up the slack. They cranked harder and harder, the rope twisting around itself, shortening the line, and pulling the two vessels together. At first the Spanish xebec drifted closer to them by inches, then pressed her midships firmly against their quarter. It became extremely difficult to crank the line then. Two on each side of the belaying pin jammed their hands on and tried to crank it tighter to no avail.

"Avast. We need more lines for this. Go to the main deck and rig anywhere you can," Isam said.

While the additional lines were being secured, he looked down to see that an old friend, Achmed Rais, was leading his men to attack the Spanish at the rail. About half the Spanish had made it back to be killed or captured. The rest threw down their weapons and put up their hands.

Isam grinned in delight and waved a hand at Achmed Rais. "I am delighted to see you! Come on over and make yourself at home. Take as many prisoners as you want for your own prize!" He was in a mood to be generous. He clambered down to the deck and grabbing hold of gun tackle, hauled himself to the high side.

Achmed Rais met him at the rail. He was a man a few years older than Isam with curly hair and beard. He wore a green coat to mark him as a descendant of the Prophet. "You're in a spot, all right. Pass a line and we'll pull you upright." Over his shoulder he said, "Boatswain! We're going to give the *Sea Leopard* a hand! Put those prisoners to work!"

The defeated Spanish might have been crying, but they were so soaked with rain, sweat, and blood, nobody could tell. Inch by inch the *Sea Leopard* rolled upright. Water poured from her scuppers in a flood. Isam heaved a sigh of relief.

"We're stuck on the mud. We can't get off with the Spaniard leaning on us."

"We'll tow you off," Achmed replied.

Achmed gave orders to his own crew and his vessel released her grapples. She put out her oars and started to push away.

Isam remembered something important and shouted, "Achmed! There's another Spanish vessel out there!"

"We saw her! She turned tail and ran."

"She might be going for reinforcements! There was a squadron of at least five vessels in the gulf. They were attacking the fortress, but I don't know if they took it."

Achmed smiled. "Yuttuy Rais has gone after her."

"She's bigger than he is."

Achmed shrugged. "It's not the size of the man in the fight, it's the size of the fight in the man. The Spaniard ran. She won't fight."

"I hope so. This one fought like a Tartar!"

"I can see that. How bad are your casualties?"

"Bad. I have been a little busy. I don't have a report yet."

Achmed nodded sympathetically. "We'll soon have you off."

A cable was run between the *San Toribio de Astorga,* as she turned out to be named, and the *Sea Leopard.* The prisoners were put to the oars and suffered the humiliation of pulling the corsair off the mudbank where they had put her in the first place. Relief flooded through Isam as the *Sea Leopard* floated free.

"A foot of water in the well, rais," the boatswain's mate reported. "She's leaking, but not bad. Some of her planks are sprung. It's ugly, but we can keep ahead of it. None of the planks broke."

Isam nodded. "Thank you. You may use prisoners to pump."

Achmed had declined to take more than his fair share of the prisoners, but since the *Sea Leopard* was in such difficult straits, part of them had been transferred to the *Seven Stars*, and some put into the hold of the *San Toribio*. Those working on deck were kept under close guard by rovers with itchy fingers and sharp scimitars. Thoroughly demoralized by their loss, the Spaniards blamed their companion for running away. If she had supported them, they would have been in possession of the *Sea Leopard* and could have faced off the *Seven Stars* and the *Sword of Righteousness*. Or so they told themselves.

After the *Sea Leopard* was safely afloat and repairs underway, Achmed invited Isam to join him in the Spanish captain's cabin for a midnight supper. Isam discovered he was ravenously hungry, so he accepted. He gave permission to light the galley fires and ordered a meal to be served up to the men when it was ready. They were tired, wet, cold, thirsty, and hungry. A sharp lookout was kept for the enemy, but Yuttuy Rais returned empty-handed. He joined Achmed and Isam over a leg of mutton.

"They turned to fight. She's a big xebec, about twenty-eight or thirty guns. I've only got eighteen guns. Prudence dictated I not engage." He was a freckle-faced man with a rangy build, although not so tall as Isam. He spoke with the nasal accent of a man from the interior.

Isam was too busy eating to reply. He merely nodded. Achmed and Yuttuy had both had plenty of food and rest on their way down the bay. They were in a chatty mood. Isam gulped down his meat and asked, "How did you happen to show up so timely?"

"We met Murad Rais running away up the bay. He told us there was a big Spanish fleet. We hurried down to see what was happening. We were afraid we'd find you in the custody of the enemy. We were right to worry!"

"I was worried too!" Isam replied.

They laughed at that. Crinkles appeared at the corner of Achmed's eyes. "I bet you were! What was your plan?"

"My first plan was to trick the Spanish into going aground. That succeeded, but they managed to pull off. Then we caught a gust of wind and were blown onto the mud ourselves, and the Spaniard came up before we could escape. We had managed to get off the bank, but he rammed us on purpose and drove us onto the bank again. You know the rest."

"You're lucky to be alive."

"All credit is due to Allah. He saved my life three times tonight!" He proceeded to tell the story. They insisted on seeing his chest. When he opened his shirt, a perfectly round bruise was revealed smack in the middle of his breastbone.

"Allah was watching over you, for sure!" Achmed said.

"I know. I have promised to be regular in my prayers after this. I was never much given to religion before, but I have changed my mind."

Achmed nodded soberly. "That's well then. Perhaps Allah let you get into a scrape so you would learn to appreciate His magnanimity."

Yuttuy said, "Maybe it was just luck. If Allah wanted to teach him a lesson, there are less drastic ways."

Achmed clucked. "Spoken like a man with no children. Sometimes we have to let our children hurt themselves to learn a lesson. You can tell them fire is hot a dozen times, but they don't believe it until they burn their hand."

Isam was the sort of person who had a collection of scars to show for lessons learned. He made a face. "This time, I have taken the lesson to heart." Brown eyes glared a warning at Achmed.

His point having been made, Achmed didn't press the matter. He lifted his cup of tea. "To victory. May our enemies never have one."

"I'll drink to that," Yuttuy said.

They lifted the black and white china cups looted from the Spanish captain's possessions. "To victory. May it always be ours," Isam agreed.

That night, he fell into bed, thought briefly about Kateb, Jamila, and an assortment of scattered images. Before he could form any coherent thoughts, he was asleep. He ached from his old wounds and new injuries, but not even that could keep him from a deep and dreamless sleep.

CHAPTER 38 : THE WEDDING FEAST

As the day of his wedding neared, Isam Rais discovered that the population of Zokhara had apparently doubled. Previously he had never noticed the female half of the human species, but with the *Sea Leopard* safely in the Arsenal to repair her sprung planks and other damage, he was obliged to think about something other than his ship, the sea, and his ambition. As the reality of his impending marriage sank in on him, he found himself scanning all the females he met as if they each carried a secret known only to women, a secret which his orphaned and bachelor state barred him from knowing, but which he would be expected to understand once the rite of holy matrimony was completed and he was brought to bed with a wife.

The women he saw were mostly working women: thin and haggard from their labors and lack of food, but they wore a sort of vest or bodice, often red in color, over their long-sleeved tunics to bolster their breasts and make them look plump. The same women had henna on their hands as they tried to make themselves attractive before poverty robbed them of their looks and the chance of marriage. Women who didn't wear such vests were nearly flat beneath their loose white clothes and their eyes were pinched, tired, weary, angry, unhappy, bitter, or resigned. These were the wives, daughters, and servants of men with little money. What money their men made, they spent first on themselves and the rest on the women and children. No one questioned it. Obviously, a man must eat. If he was fainting from hunger, he couldn't work. If he couldn't work, he wouldn't bring home any money and they would all starve.

Now Isam understood why men liked plump women. Plump women were well-fed women. They had lazy, sensuous gazes, and they walked with a swaying of round hips that was hypnotic. When women in precious silk or cotton clothes swayed past with bundles balanced on their heads, they were approached by men who begged to carry their burdens for them. They never let them, but they certainly didn't mind being told, "You're too beautiful to carry such a burden." If a servant or daughter was plump, it meant her house had money, and money was as much of an aphrodisiac as the curves of her body.

Prosperous women only left their homes to go to the mosque or baths, so were rarely seen. Sometimes they were glimpsed in their sedan chairs as their slaves carried them along, or, if they were of the wealthiest caste, rolled past in carriages pulled by four horses. Fat women were rich women.

They lavished themselves with cosmetics, perfumes, jewelry, and sweets. Their silks were brilliant, and so was the livery of their slaves and horses. It was forbidden for them to show themselves to strangers, but they were not adverse to letting one henna-painted hand with long, colored nails, burdened with rings of gold and ruby, to rest upon the window sill of their carriage. That soft, uncallused hand, perfumed and adorned, was worth more than an entire year's worth of labor from the hands of a working woman.

Isam tried to remember his mother. She had been pretty, he thought, with her dark eyes and olive skin. She had smiled at him, he remembered that. She sang him lullabies when she tucked him in at night. His perceptions of his mother were colored by his love for her: she was the woman who had tickled him and slipped him dates after she told him to wait for supper.

He wasn't marrying his mother. He was marrying a young woman, who, as far he could tell, was merely adequate in figure by the common reckoning. That was fine with him. He preferred Ami the sailor over a sloe-eyed bellydancer. She was 'too tall' for a woman to boot, but he preferred that as well. He was a tall man and her head came up to his chin. That made it easier to talk to her without having to stoop and give himself a crick in the neck. His right shoulder had become cantankerous about such things.

For the first time he wondered: would they have a child? He had no idea how long it took to conceive. How often would he be expected to lie with his wife? He must consummate the marriage on the wedding night; would that be enough to produce a son? Or a daughter? His own father had taught him to read the stars. If he had a son, he could teach him too. To raise a son all he had to do was to teach him to be a sailor. That shouldn't be difficult. But a daughter? Again he watched thin women trudging past with urns of water balanced upon their heads. He tried to imagine what it would be like to spend his youth walking back and forth between the public well and the family home with a fifty pound burden upon his head. Marriage would be an escape from that, but then there would be . . . he wasn't sure. Housekeeping, he supposed. How hard could it be to sweep a house? They weren't as big as ships.

On the day arranged, Shakil came to him with a white horse richly caparisoned with a blue saddlecloth and bells on its bridle. Not having any brother to make these arrangements for him, Shakil had become his agent in this most personal of matters. It was Shakil who told him what sort of coat he should buy, what sort of gifts were expected, who ordered the wedding feast and musicians, and took his money to pay for it. The Dey had bought *San Toribio* outright, so he had plenty of money even though the much larger *Plenitud* and its cargo was taking longer to sell.

He felt like he was floating. A month ashore in a soft warm bed, good food and plenty of it, and a reliable agent in Shakil relieved him a great deal of worry. He only ached when it rained, and the bruise in the middle of his chest faded away. His sight was clear, his beard neatly trimmed, his turban new and large, and the horse restive. He disliked riding.

"Do I really have to ride a horse? Couldn't I just walk to the farm?" he asked Shakil.

The younger man was at his horse's head with a hand on the bridle—as if he were secretly worried the bridegroom might bolt. Shakil was dressed all in white with a long blue vest over his clothes. He smiled at the corsair.

"If you hadn't captured the *Plenitud*, yes. But you are the greatest corsair of the season, so you must look the part." He gestured to the people lining the street to watch the musicians and acrobats and the horde of seaman and marines in their best finery who accompanied him.

"It's a spectacle," Isam complained.

Shakil bent down and made a stirrup of his hands to help the bridegroom into the saddle. When Isam mounted, he rose and said, "It's supposed to be. The Spanish are besieging Tettiwan and blockading the mouth of Modiq Bay. You hearten them with your display. You are proof that the Spanish do not have the upper hand, even if we feel hemmed in and thwarted right now. The greater the spectacle, the more courage they will have."

More softly, he added, "It isn't just for you, you know. So many of us are depending on you. We wish you well, and we hope for your success because it will bring success to all of us. Not just the sailors and marines and their families, but the farmers who furnish you with food, the carpenters and armorers and sailmakers and gunpowder mills and ropewalks and all the other crafts. Not to mention, their families, and beyond that, the schools and mosques that depend on them for donations. Speaking of which, I know you've given to the seamen's benevolent fund, but you should consider a grander, public gesture." Isam merely grunted.

The cavalcade moved out at a walk with Shakil walking sedately alongside the groom's white horse. The musicians rang and blew and beat their instruments, the jugglers juggled and the acrobats sprang along doing cartwheels and handsprings. The populace paused their daily activities to watch the parade go by and cheer the hero of the moment.

Isam's eyes went to the young women with the water jars on their heads who had to stand aside and wait for him to pass. "If I must, then dig a well somewhere convenient to where those poor women live."

Shakil's expression softened. He glanced over to the cluster of women, then looked up him and nodded. "I will make the arrangements. It's a generous gift. They will bless your name for generations to come."

"I don't need blessings," Isam grumped.

Shakil smiled good-humoredly at him. "You should not eschew the good wishes of strangers. Some day you may find yourself dependent on their kindness."

"I really don't see how a poor woman will be in a position to do me any favors."

"That makes your gift more noble: you don't see any benefit in it for yourself."

'Noble' was not a word that Isam was accustomed to hearing attached to his name. "Eh, I'm a corsair. There's nothing noble about me."

Shakil smiled broadly. "I think you resent a compliment as much as most men resent an insult."

Isam scowled at him. "Am I supposed to be offended by that?"

Shakil almost laughed. "If you wish."

"Now you're making sport of me!"

Shakil shook his head. "No. I am starting to hope you might be a good husband for my sister. Be kind to her and all will be well."

"I'm not planning on being cruel!"

Shakil sobered. "I don't think any man plans on being cruel to his wife, and yet, some are."

He turned around and Isam had his stiff back to make faces at. "I'm not like other men," the corsair muttered.

The piercing wail of the reedy clarinets and the throbbing of the drums gave him a headache. His new boots pinched. The gold rings he was not accustomed to wearing made him fidget. He couldn't imagine why a wedding was thought to be a joyous occasion for the groom. He was enjoying it about as much as a long march to the gallows.

The parade wended through the city, out the eastern gate, and down the dusty road to the farm where his bride awaited him. When he spotted the masts of the local small boats in the creek in front of the farm, he cheered up. At least he would not be entirely landlocked while staying at the farm. Then he saw the state of the dock.

"Shakil! Why hasn't that dock been repaired? I plan to come by boat next time. It looks like it'll collapse if anyone steps on it."

Shakil glanced at the dock. "I'll see that it's taken care of, rais."

The house was directly opposite the dock. It was a single story Greek style farmhouse with rustic pillars to create a shaded porch level with the yard. It had a fresh coat of whitewash and the yard around it mowed. It was a large, unpretentious dwelling suited to a yeoman farmer.

Arriving in the front yard, Isam dismounted. Shakil brushed him off and the blue appeared from beneath the tan road dust. The various musicians, guests, and hangers-on went to refresh themselves from the tables set up in the yard. Nakih came out. He was dressed in new brown and blue clothes. Kasim, looking like a much younger copy of his father, was with him. Isam had finally paid him his asking price, but neither was happy with the exchange. When the *Plenitud* came in, Kasim was sorry he hadn't asked for more while Isam thought he had paid too much. Shakil had shuttled between the two to persuade them that it was better to settle and be done with it.

Nakih came forward with a glass of fresh cool mint water in his hands and offered it to him. "Salaam. Welcome to Bessilama House. Refresh yourself and be at home."

Isam being the son-in-law, bowed to the older man. "Salaam. Peace be upon you and all within this house." He accepted the tumbler and drank it down in great gulps. The coolness refreshed him. Shakil swatted the skirts of his coat and little puffs of dust floated away.

The facade of Bessilama House did not improve as he approached it. It was fronted by a broad porch lined with simple columns that did not belong to any of the classic Greek orders. The pavement of the porch was broken in several places, but the weeds had been pulled. The broad double doors made of heavy wood were handsome with their geometric carving, but dry as a desert. They had lost any paint or varnish they had formerly held, but they were clean and in good repair.

The doors opened and a tall slender black majordomo stood aside to allow the guests to enter. Isam glanced at him, then did a double take. "Akil! What are you doing here?"

"I work for Mistress Jamila now," the man replied.

He turned to Shakil for an explanation, but Shakil took his arm and dragged him into the house. "Later, rais. Come inside."

Shakil led him into the reception room. More guests were there: friends and relatives of Nakih and his sons. There were no women, of course. They were all in the weaving room making the bride ready. The interior of the house had been swept and cleaned and freshly whitewashed. The reception room had a raised half, and kilims had been thrown over the ancient divans. He forced a smile and received the compliments of Nakih's kin.

Farmers, herders, butchers, fishermen, servants, and a few other trades were represented. Isam could not help thinking he had made a serious mistake. He should walk out. What could a miscellaneous pack of tradesmen and laborers do to him? He was a great corsair. They told him so repeatedly, told him how glad they were to have him as their kin, told him that they would be happy to sell their land to him. Well, some of them did. They wanted to negotiate right on the spot, but he shook his head.

After interminable conversation in which he forced himself to smile and to nod agreeably to whatever was said, the feast was served. Rugs had been spread over the cracked tiles of the courtyard. The fountain had no water in it but was clean. So this is what three thousand sequins had bought him. Or more precisely, his wife. Kasim was little better than a robber. He forced himself to smile. One year. He had to bear it for one year, then he would be free.

Isam ate heartily and so did the guests. The food was good and plentiful. Being a sailor, he was not particular about his food as long as it was edible, so the homey fare satisfied him. The rumble of conversation was stifled by the amount of food served. Couscous, lamb, soup, fruit, and vegetables, were served from brass trays or wooden bowls. He watched the scores of guests eating his money and forced himself to smile. The women were nowhere to be seen: they were dining in private. If Jamila had behaved properly, he wouldn't even know what she looked like. The guests ate and drank and listened to music and watched the juggler and the acrobat. In short, everyone but the groom thought it was a fine affair.

CHAPTER 39 : THE RELUCTANT BRIDEGROOM

After the dessert was served, Isam rose and slipped out back to the outhouse. Plenty of food and mint tea (it couldn't possibly be nerves, the mighty corsair told himself) had the inevitable effect on him. As he started back from the outhouse, he paused and stared at the building. The bridal party and friends were inside. Those guests who were too numerous and those not close enough to have an inside seat were eating on the front lawn. If only he had come by boat, he could walk right past them, board it, and flee. He shouldn't have come by horse. If he did flee, where would he go? The *Sea Leopard* was laid up in the Arsenal. He had been living in an inn for the past month. The weather was cool and bright; maybe he could walk down the highway and find an caravanserai to hide in.

He tucked his hands into the long bell-shaped linen sleeves that were part of the Turkish style formal dress. The short-sleeved blue velvet coat was deliberately cut to display the shirt sleeves. He didn't like it. His usual clothing was practical and suited for life on a ship. He twisted the tail of the sleeve in his hands until it squeaked.

"I don't want to marry." There, he said it. He meant it. "It's not my fault she ran away to sea. Why should I have to be the one to fix it?"

Black hens pecked the dirt around him. They were content to scratch the dirt and peck at bugs, so they reminded him of landlubbers. How could anyone be content with being tied to one place? How could anyone be happy with the everlasting sameness of the scenery? He was yearning already for turquoise waters and swordfishing, or even a grey gale shredding spindrift as far as the eye could see.

Achmed Rais stepped out of the house. He watched the younger captain roving back and forth as his steps unconsciously traced out the length of his quarterdeck while he was lost in thought. Achmed said nothing for a few moments, then walked over to the taller man.

Isam paused his pacing and looked up. Achmed smiled. "It's time to sign the marriage contract," he said. His voice was friendly.

"Should I do it?" Isam asked.

Achmed turned serious. "Do you have objections to the bride or her family?"

"No."

"Then what is the matter?"

"I don't want to marry. You know me. Did you ever think I would marry?"

Achmed studied him. "Yes."

Isam jerked around to look at him. "Why?" he demanded. "You know about Kateb."

"Kateb can't give you an heir. All men must marry, if they have any sort of property."

"So I've been told."

"If you had been a nobody, you wouldn't need to marry."

Isam gave him a rueful look. "I had no idea what price I would have to pay for my ambition."

Achmed smiled faintly. "Then you were short-sighted."

Isam snorted. "Did they send you out to drag me in and make me do it?"

"No. But I noticed Shakil is fidgeting and Nakih is looking worried. Are you going to run away?" There was no judgment in his voice. It was a simple question.

Isam flinched. "No. I said I'd do it. Everyone is here for that, aren't they? I've already spent a lot of money on my bride and her rotten brother, Kasim."

"If you're going to do it, you should make the best of it. If you're not willing to be gracious about it, don't do it. There's no point in being miserable."

"I'm nervous about the wedding night, to be honest. I have never been with a woman. What should I do?"

"Start with compliments. I've never seen her, but even if she's hideous, you can always compliment her eyes, or her hair, or her complexion. I'm sure she is hennaed up for you, so take her hand in yours and look at it. Henna can be quite intricate. She'll be flattered if you notice."

Isam was listening. He nodded as he stored these suggestions in his memory. "I guess I am afraid of making a fool of myself. I am not used to failure, and I'm afraid I won't be able to fulfill the husband's part."

"If that's so, then think about something that arouses you and don't think about her."

Isam immediately had a vision of the black and muscular Kateb. Jamila was nothing like. "It's easier with men. They understand the world. Women don't."

Achmed gave him an amused look. "Suddenly you've become an expert on women!"

Isam scowled at him.

"Women are like men. Some are idiots. Some are wise. Find something to like about your wife and focus on that. I'm sure there's something your wife can do for you that Kateb didn't."

"She removed my warts."

Achmed had to suppress a laugh. "How very romantic of her. Still, it's not a bad thing to have somebody looking after your well-being. It's only a year. You'll survive."

Isam reviewed the advice he'd received. Compliment her eyes. Look at her henna. Find something useful she can do. Now that he had a plan, he squared his shoulders. "All right then. I'm coming."

The two friends walked into the house side by side. Shakil looked relieved as he saw them return. Nakih kept a smile fixed on his face and gave no sign that he had doubted, but beneath the affable expression, brown eyes followed the captain as he crossed the courtyard.

"Shall we sign the marriage contract?" Isam asked with forced heartiness.

Shakil came to him at once. "Yes. It's in the office. Come this way."

Akil went to fetch the bride. Jamila was hovering anxiously just inside the weaving room door wishing Isam would hurry up and decide if he was going to run away or get married. The suspense made her bite her nails, so her sister-in-law scolded her. When Akil called her, she stepped out into the courtyard.

All heads turned, even Isam's. The bride was dressed in azure from head to foot with a long veil over her hair held in place by a cap of gold coins. The gossamer veil could not conceal the cascade of auburn curls that fell down her back in thick waves to the level of her knees. It was the most extraordinary hair that any of them had ever seen. It almost made them overlook that she was tall and slender, not short and plump like an ideal bride. The blue caftan gown was split open over a yellow underskirt and bodice that in turn covered blue pantaloons. Gold braid trimmed the edges of the caftan, its hem, and the opening of its bell-shaped sleeves. A silk veil covered her face so that only her kohled eyes appeared. Isam glanced at her hands and noticed the tell-tale redness of henna. She approached and courtesied to the men without speaking.

Nakih beamed proudly at her. "You look lovely, my dear." He took her hand in his and tucked it into his elbow. "Let's go in now. We don't want to keep your groom waiting."

The signing of the contract was a mere formality; they all knew what was in it. Isam felt light-headed crammed into the small office with half a dozen witnesses: three for his side, three for hers, plus her male relatives. He made his sigil left-handed with a bold, angular flourish, then laid down the reed pen. Jamila knelt beside him and took up the pen. She held her sleeve back with one hennaed hand and wrote her name carefully. Her handwriting was neat, but not so elegant as his. With her right beside him he became aware of a faint herbal scent wafting from her clothes. It was pleasant and calmed him. She had not doused herself in perfume or cosmetics. He was grateful that she was a sensible woman, not a simmering minx that thought tarting herself up was the way to win a man's attention. He was marrying Ami the sailor, a brave and dependable woman.

She laid down the pen and rose and he rose with her. They stood together and he slipped his hand in hers and gave it a squeeze, more to reassure himself than her. She was real and solid, not a fantasy. He remembered her running up and down the two flights of ladders to bring the powder up. Her hand tightened on his. She dared to steal a glance at him. Feeling a faint motion, he turned to look at her. Brown eyes gazed up at him from within the veil. She had ringed them with a line of kohl that emphasized their shape and luster, but it was the only makeup she wore. Gazing into her eyes, he felt something he couldn't explain. Leaning down, he whispered to her curls, "We are going to have an adventure."

She squeezed his hand hard. "I will go anywhere my captain commands."

She said it with the trust born of experience. She had served aboard his ship and knew what dangers he faced. She had seen his skill in handling his vessel and his courage and commitment under fire. More than most women, she had a very good idea as to the character and qualities of the man she was marrying.

My captain. She said the words with a simple grace that warmed him. He smiled at her. He lifted her hennaed hand to his lips and kissed it softly. "I couldn't marry any other woman. A woman who has never been to sea could never suit me."

She trembled and said, "I will worry about you all the time you're gone."

"You won't have to worry any time soon. It's the end of the season and the *Sea Leopard* is being hauled out and repaired. It will be spring before I go anywhere."

The witnesses signed the paper with Shakil supervising. Nakih kept a discreet eye on the newlyweds. He was pleased to watch the two of them together. His brown eyes twinkled. "It's time," he said.

The witnesses and a number of the guests trooped along the cloister with the bridal party. Kasim opened the door to the bedroom with a lascivious grin. The guests hooted and shouted at them in ribald humor. Jamila blushed and stepped through the door. Isam stepped in behind her. He saw Kasim lean forward to make a salacious remark so he shut the door swiftly. He wasn't sorry when he felt it thump his brother-in-law in the face. He shot the latch and put the latchpin in the door so nobody could open it from the outside. He didn't trust the guests to refrain from playing a prank on them.

Jamila stood in the middle of the room and Isam stared awkwardly at her. She was a figure the color of the sea, fresh and fair by the light of the lamps. As he watched, she inhaled deeply, reached up, and unpinned her veil. The gossamer cloth shimmied down her front to land in a heap on the floor. Her features were fine, her nose long, straight, and Greek like her grandmother. Her cheeks were smooth and unblemished, her jaw firm but refined, and her complexion a healthy caramel color. Her eyes were large, brown, and lustrous. She was slim and taller than the average woman, neither fat nor thin, with the firmness of good health. The yellow bodice lifted her bust and a golden chain with a red amulet rested on top of the blue fabric. She bore no resemblance to any of the women he had observed in the streets and he was glad.

"You're beautiful!" he said. He didn't care what other men thought a woman should look like. He was pleased with this one.

Jamila smiled and lowered her eyes at the unexpected compliment. "You're very handsome today. Is your shoulder better?"

"Yes, I'm much better," he replied. He stepped forward. "I can do what we're supposed to do. How shall we begin?"

She blushed and took a step towards him. "I'm told it usually begins with a kiss."

Isam was relieved. He knew how to kiss. He nerved himself up, bent down, and kissed her on the cheek.

She smiled up at him. "We're married now. You can kiss me on the mouth." She turned her face to his.

Feeling like a bumpkin, he flushed hotly, but nodded and put an arm around her. His other hand cupped her cheek and he brought her face up as he bent down. The kiss began slowly, but it went on for a very long time. When it finally ended, both of them were feeling rather warm. Not trusting himself to speak, he unbuttoned the top button of his coat. Jamila's eyelashes fluttered, then she reached up and undid the next button. After that, things progressed from one button to the next, and from there to her buttons, and so on for a long time.

For such a very long time indeed, that not only did they consummate the wedding, but they remained happily married for the rest of their lives. In the end, it was she who left him when she passed away in her sleep at the age of eighty-two. After she died, he laid himself down and stopped living. He was ninety-six. They were buried side by side. They had seven children, six of whom lived to adulthood. Three of the children became captains in their own right, including the eldest, his favorite, their daughter Tahirah.

But that is another story.

Publications by Keibooks

M. Kei's Novels
in print and ebook

Pirates of the Narrow Seas 1 : The Sallee Rovers
Pirates of the Narrow Seas 2 : Men of Honor
Pirates of the Narrow Seas 3 : Iron Men
Pirates of the Narrow Seas 4 : Heart of Oak

Man in the Crescent Moon : A Pirates of the Narrow Seas Adventure
The Sea Leopard : A Pirates of the Narrow Seas Adventure

Fire Dragon—Asian-themed sci-fi/fantasy

Poetry Journal

Atlas Poetica : A Journal of Poetry of Place in Contemporary Tanka

Poetry Anthologies

Bright Stars, An Organic Tanka Anthology (Vol. 1–5)
Fire Pearls : Short Masterpieces of the Human Heart (Vol. 2)
Take Five : Best Contemporary Tanka (Vol. 4)

M. Kei's Poetry Collections

January, A Tanka Diary
Slow Motion : The Log of a Chesapeake Bay Skipjack
Heron Sea : Short Poems of the Chesapeake Bay